The Rules for Lying

Big Easy Shaman Book 1

L. A. KELLEY

Dedication

For all the little liars out there. Keep up the good work.

Table of Contents

Chapter 1: Wising up to the Rules...7
Chapter 2: The Dark Man...25
Chapter 3: Death in the Carriage House...45
Chapter 4: A Desperate Escape...69
Chapter 5: Where Did You Find the Crazy Children?...88
Chapter 6: Flight to Terrebonne Parish...113
Chapter 7: Reading the Bones...144
Chapter 8: Feu De L'enfer...162
Chapter 9: The Frog King...184
Chapter 10: Nothing Instills More Confidence Than Watching the Blind Lead the Insane...208
Chapter 11: The New Rules...224
Chapter 12: An Alarming Letter...251
Chapter 13: Pike's Army...275
Chapter 14: The Lower Worlds...298
Chapter 15: The Last Lie...325
Chapter 16: The Afterlife...338
A Note from the Author...352
Lagniappe...354

Acknowledgement

Nobody does it alone. My thanks to family and friends for their continued support with a special shoutout to Lara, the guru of grammar.

The Rules for Lying

Big Easy Shaman Book 1
By L. A. Kelley

Chapter 1
Wising up to the Rules

Flick-flick-flick.

There it was again. Like an itch I couldn't scratch, that curious indescribable feeling demanded my attention. It prodded my brain with a ghostly finger, the message clear.

Listen to me. Someone is lying.

I cocked my head and concentrated on nearby voices. *I found you.* No need to look farther than Chauncey Edwards at the next lunch table. He was as useless as a sack of pig turds, but lucky enough to be the son of Police Chief Percival Edwards. Girls fussed over him because he had money. Boys followed him because he had push. Mess with

Chauncey and you mess with the chief. Mess with the chief and you might as well blow town.

Chauncey pleaded with a girl. "Come on; let me copy your homework. Trust me. This is the last time I'll ask."

Lie.

"Maybe." She smiled coyly. "If you dance with me at the party on Saturday. You're the best dancer in school."

Lie.

"And you're the prettiest girl."

Lie.

The girl giggled and handed over her notebook. They bought each other's lies and practically begged for more.

Chauncey caught my gaze and sneered. "What are you looking at, Whistler?"

A big fat sack of pig turds. I turned my head away. No need to draw attention, especially from other students at school. No one knew my secret, and I wasn't about to share with Chauncey.

I can always spot a lie. No boast, flat truth.

The gift came early. Even during my rechristening on the hospital steps, I bawled up a storm. You have to reckon when a baby senses something fishy, the talent must be inborn.

My rightful name disappeared among the dead in the Spanish Flu epidemic of 1918. The illness started in the Army camps and then raced like an Oklahoma cyclone across the rest of the country. Millions perished before the virus finally burned out, including a nameless woman who collapsed on the steps of Saint Peter's Hospital in New Brunswick,

New Jersey. Clutching me tight, she breathed her last without uttering a word. The doctor figured I was a goner, too, but to his surprise I coughed out a whistling squeak. Needing something to write on the patient chart, he scribbled the first name to pop into his head.

You can imagine my reaction. Mrs. Hart said I still hollered up a storm when she came to fetch me. Well, of course I did. I wanted to let everyone know that wasn't my name and he was a dirty dog liar, but the fuss did no good. I became Peter Whistler on the spot and forever after. All in all, the doctor could have done worse. Most folks back then weren't given to coddling an orphan. If he called me Squeaky MacFlu no one, except Mrs. Hart, would have clucked disapproval. Orphans weren't supposed to have any feelings.

Mrs. Lucinda Hart owned the Little Angels Home for Orphan Boys. Mr. Hart wasn't in the picture. By the time I arrived at Little Angels, he was gone from her life, whether by death or two legs I didn't know as he was a forbidden topic of discussion. I spent the next fifteen years at Little Angels, but never did earn a halo.

Mrs. Hart received a modest sum from each couple with a baby's adoption. Her other income was a small monthly stipend from the county to feed, clothe, and house the orphans. By necessity, she became an expert in the bottom line as babies came and went through the doors of Little Angels.

Except for me.

For some reason, I never appealed to couples. Mrs. Murphy, the neighbor next door, believed her civic duty included a constant tally of my flaws in case I didn't notice them myself. "His face is simply wrong," she tsked to Mrs. Hart on my first day of school. "The nose is too sharp, the ears too long, and the placement of the eyes better suited for an aquatic reptile. No wonder you can't get rid of him."

I hurled the worst insult a six year-old brain can fashion. "Stinky fatty fat-fat." Immediately, Mrs. Hart ordered an apology.

"Sorry," I spit out under my breath. "Fat old bat stinks worse than a dead rat."

"He has a disagreeable personality, too," Mrs. Murphy screeched as she stomped home.

"Peter," Mrs. Hart admonished, "that's no way to address your elders."

"She said I was ugly." I wallowed in a good solid pout, but Mrs. Hart didn't tolerate self-pity.

"You shouldn't care what Mrs. Murphy thinks. She's a foolish woman who will never be more than she is today. You have an excellent brain, Peter, but lack self-control. Success only comes when you learn to master yourself. Only then will you guide your fate as well." Her shoulders stiffened. "I learned that lesson the hard way."

I kicked at the carpet. "Brains don't get you adopted."

"You won't be here forever."

An undefined emotion swept across her face. Was it pain? Sorrow? Exasperation with my bad manners? I quit pondering and headed to school, excited at the thought of making friends, but as soon as kids discovered I lived at Little Angels, they shied away as if being an orphan was a contagious disease.

New Brunswick back then was a hard place if you were small, poor, or different. I checked the box in all three categories.

The only kid who had an immediate interest was Chauncey Edwards. He took special delight in tormenting anybody he judged powerless to fight back. "Whistler has the cootie touch," he sang every time I walked by. His voice followed me down the hall, into the lunchroom, the gym, recess, and back to class again. "Whistler has the cootie touch."

I knew he lied. Chauncey wasn't even good at it, and the insult didn't stick. It flew from his mouth and bounced off me, drifting away like so much lint in the breeze. After all, once you spot a lie, the power is gone. Soon his words became background noise, day after day the same old thing. "Whistler has the cootie touch."

To break the boredom, I started to count. "That's only seven. Can't you do better than that? Boy, you're slow. You missed me back there." I soon grew tired of that too, and decided to beat Chauncey to the punch. Every time I spotted him, I yelled, "Cootie touch. Ha! I win, I said it first." Chauncey was big and easy to peg in the hallway. I was short and skinny and could slip behind him unnoticed. I enjoyed watching him jump. I even got him in the boys' bathroom when I stood on the toilet seat, popped my head over the adjoining stall, and caught him with his pants down. "Cootie touch. Ha! I win."

I enjoyed the game, especially since I was winning, but it had the unforeseen effect of driving Chauncey batty. After a week, he followed me home from school. I didn't know he was behind me until I set foot in the front yard and got a rough shove into the grass. "Think you're funny, Whistler. Who's laughing now?" He dropped to his knees and pinned my arms to the ground. "I'm gonna squash you like a bug."

He yelped as a hand grabbed his ear and yanked him off.

Mrs. Hart's jaw tightened. "I think not."

Chauncey rubbed his ear and howled, "You hurt me. I'm gonna tell my dad. Do you know who I am?"

"Chauncey Edwards, Chief Edwards' son. Do you know who I am?"

He regarded her with smug contempt. "No. Think you're some big deal?"

"My name is Lucinda Hart."

Chauncey's sullenness disappeared. He licked his lips and glanced right and left as if plotting the best escape route. "S-so what?"

Mrs. Hart's voice dropped to a whisper, "Do you know what I did?"

The color drained from Chauncey's face.

Mrs. Hart took one step forward and he stumbled back. "Do you know what I'm prepared to do if you ever touch Peter again?"

Chauncey's eyes widened. "I-I-I…"

"From now on, you'll ignore Peter. He'll go about his business and you go about yours or we'll have another word. This time in private." Her eyes narrowed. "Just the two of us. Am I clear?"

Chauncey nodded then turned tail and bolted down the street. Mrs. Hart watched him go, a smile twitching the corner of her lips. "Whoever would suspect a baby hippo can sprint?" She helped me to my feet and brushed dirt off my pants. "Are you all right, Peter?"

"Yes." I watched Chauncey run around the corner. "I don't get it. Chauncey was scared. He's not even afraid of the teachers at school. All he does is push his weight around. What did he think you'd do?"

"Nothing to concern you. Weak-minded people believe everything they hear. Chauncey won't bother you again."

A lump rose in my throat and I swallowed it down. "I hate it here. Nobody likes me. Nobody wants me."

Her voice softened. "I like you. I'm sorry I can't offer a better life than this, but I swear you'll have a home with me as long as you want." A moment of indecision flitted across her face and then her expression set. She rested a gentle hand on my shoulder. "I'll tell you something nice that will happen in the future. The day you turn eighteen, you'll receive five hundred dollars. A special gift to start your adult life. I promise."

Her words were straight-up true, and I brightened instantly. In hindsight, I should have asked questions, but all that mattered to me was the money. "I can leave New Brunswick and never look back?"

"Yes, Peter." Her voice held a wistful tone. "Leave and never look back. Now come inside and I'll make cocoa. You can drink it in your room. I have a set of parents coming to discuss an adoption."

I took my cocoa upstairs. The doorbell rang. The couple had arrived. I sat on the bed, sipping my drink

13

and wondering what lies Mrs. Hart told in the parlor. A good lie was part of her foolproof system to place an orphan. Skilled at reading people, Mrs. Hart tossed out a few innocent questions to potential parents, zeroed in on likes and dislikes, and crafted a lie accordingly. The deal always closed. Once, I eavesdropped outside the parlor and heard Mrs. Hart swear to a preacher and his wife their potential son had been found floating down the Hudson River in a basket. They didn't doubt her straight-face for a second and weren't about to reject their own personal Moses.

Whatever lies Mrs. Hart told about me obviously never worked, so I figured I was an especially hard sell. Even a well-polished fib couldn't get me a home.

I was dead wrong, of course.

The real reason stayed hidden until years later, but for the moment, I drained the last cocoa from my mug, content in the knowledge someday I'd have enough money to kick Chauncey Edwards in the pants and then skedaddle out of New Brunswick before his father tossed me in the clink.

Life continued swell enough at Little Angels. Chauncey ignored me at school. So did everyone else for that matter, but I had three square meals a day and a roof over my head. After a while, I got used to being alone. Mrs. Hart wasn't one of those silly, hovering women afraid to let a kid climb a tree for fear of skinning an elbow. My time was my own once the chores finished. Instead of friends, I explored the streets and back alleys of New Brunswick until I could draw a mental map to every place in the city with my eyes closed.

As soon as I discovered a route through the woods to the train station, I spent my spare time perched on the knoll above the track. I watched boxcars streak by and daydreamed about the five hundred bucks. Years passed and I never once asked where the dough would come from, assuming a government program for orphans to use the money to scram from New Jersey and leave decent folks alone.

Watching the trains was my favorite pastime until age twelve when I finally learned the real power of a good solid lie. One rainy day, I piled up empty crates, commandeered an old mattress, and built a secret hiding place in the basement. I hunkered down happily to read a comic book swiped from Grimaldi's Market.

Nico and Carlotta Grimaldi were a couple of high-hatters with plenty of scratch who donated heavily to Police Chief Percival Edwards' election campaigns. In return, he encouraged the public to spend at Grimaldi's Market and hinted those who didn't would find the police slow to respond in emergencies. Big surprise—their store raked in cash from the get-go.

The Grimaldis kissed the feet of the rich and boondoggled everyone else. Chauncey bragged how they slipped him chocolate bars and then padded other customers' bills for the cost, and that was no lie. On principle, I stole a comic book or penny candy from the counter display every time Mrs. Hart sent me to Grimaldi's Market.

I popped another caramel in my mouth and froze at the sound of voices overhead. Every syllable from the conversation in the upstairs parlor rang clear through the duct from the heating grate. Mrs. Hart discussed an adoption. She shifted to a lie, as expected, but something was different. The little pointy finger jab in my brain was more persistent.

Pay attention, it seemed to say. *This is important.*

For the first time, I listened not only to the words, but also her tone. Mrs. Hart sounded completely legit. The reason suddenly became clear why no one questioned the sketchy stories on the orphans' backgrounds. A stammer or sudden shift in pitch was a dead giveaway. Mrs. Hart never missed a beat.

I sucked in a breath. "So that's how she does it."

Catching a person in a lie was a snap, but telling one was tough. My early success rate was spotty. Like most kids, some worked, some didn't. The reason hit me like a bolt of lightning. Lying had rules. I instinctively knew I stumbled on an important truth. From then on, I eavesdropped when Mrs. Hart met with potential parents. The first two rules came easy.

Rule One: A lie on the fly will surely die.

The more important the lie, the more practice needed. A guilty expression was a dead giveaway.

Rule Two: A lie prevails with few details.

Simple lies are best. If caught standing over a dead body with a smoking gun, tell the coppers, "I didn't know it was loaded." After that, keep your mouth shut and demand a lawyer.

I itched to run a test. My chance came with the delivery of twins to Little Angels. Mrs. Hart ran out of condensed milk. Short of funds, she sent me to Grimaldi's Market with instructions to put three cans on her account. No one had credit cards in those days. Grocers wrote the date and amount of purchase in an account ledger by the cash register—bills settled on the first of the month. Usually, I hated going to the Grimaldis. Neither Nico nor Carlotta liked kids, orphans, or anyone who didn't flash cash. That was me to the letter. Now, I gleefully practiced all the way downtown until the lie flowed from my lips like storm water through a gutter pipe.

Mr. and Mrs. Grimaldi were with a customer. Both paused long enough to regard me as if I was an unexpected spot of dog crap on the sole of a shoe. Once they turned away, I snitched a piece of bubble gum from a jar on the display case and jammed it in my pocket.

Esther Roth perched on a stool behind the front counter. Esther was six years old and Carlotta's distant cousin. She lost her eyesight to a measles epidemic as a baby, and then recently her folks died in a car accident. As her only relatives, the Grimaldis grudgingly took her in. They boarded Esther at a school for the blind, with rare visits to New Brunswick. I would have felt sorry for her, but she was also a real pill. Fortunately, our paths didn't cross often.

Esther ran her fingers delicately over the page of a Braille book. I stood dead-still, but her ears were as sharp as a sack of ten-penny nails. I swore that girl could hear a hummingbird's heartbeat. Her hand froze. She cocked her head in my direction. "Who's there?"

"Me."

"Peter Whistler, what are you doing here?"

"None of your bees wax."

"Is so."

"Is not."

"Is so."

"Is not."

"Shut your yaps," Mr. Grimaldi bellowed, storming to the counter. "What do you want, Whistler?"

Esther's empty eyes bored into me. I hadn't planned on an audience, but was too pigheaded to retreat. I calmly asked for three cans of condensed milk, and without a pause or shift in tone added, "And a chocolate bar. Please put everything on the account."

Mr. Grimaldi didn't buy the lie for a second.

Rule Three: If your reputation is iffy, the lie flops in a jiffy.

Appearance counts. Mr. Grimaldi was naturally suspicious of kids and also knew Mrs. Hart watched every penny, so candy bars were rare in our household. At once, he telephoned Mrs. Hart to squeal, and then gleefully assured me a severe beating waited at Little Angels for telling lies. I thought for sure Esther would say something smart, but she kept her mouth shut. Those ghostly eyes even held a hint of sympathy.

I didn't fear a beating. Mrs. Hart never laid hands on me. Instead, she assigned a week of weeding the rose garden, but my actions upset her more than the usual mischief. As she handed over the spade, I squirmed under her piercing gaze.

"Life is hard, Peter. A nickel isn't worth much." Disapproval colored her expression. "At least to people like the Grimaldis. However, your choices affect this household. Please consider in the future a nickel for a candy bar means a nickel less milk for the babies."

I stabbed the spade viciously in the soil, done up tight by her words. The babies weren't my responsibility. They were strangers, briefly crossing my path. I wasn't responsible for a soul. I planned to live the rest of my life the same way as soon as I turned eighteen and got my five hundred bucks.

With nothing to gain, I decided at that moment not to involve Mrs. Hart in my new pursuit of the rules for lying. She already knew everything about me, so lies were obvious. Besides, even I couldn't argue her punishments were severe or undeserved. Everybody else, though, was fair game.

I failed miserably at the Grimaldis, so must have missed rules. I eavesdropped on Mrs. Hart and discovered others.

Rule Four: Lies from a stranger don't signal danger.

The less known about a person, the quicker folks fall for a well-delivered line.

Rule Five: Hone your tone.

Keep a steady voice. A stammer or slight upturn in pitch is a dead giveaway.

Rule Six: Don't squirm like a worm. Be firm.

Bad liars fidget as if the truth inside fights to come out, but tell a good story with a straight face, look 'em square in the eye, and folks fall for anything.

The new rules meant another test. This time I went to a bakery on the outskirts of town where no one knew me (Rule Four.) Through the window, I spied an open account ledger near the cash register. I pressed flat against the wall, working up the courage to enter. Lying here was more dangerous than at the Grimaldis. The baker didn't know Mrs. Hart. If caught, I'd land in juvenile hall. That dump made Little Angels seem like Buckingham Palace.

When the baker entered the back room, I darted to the ledger and scanned the entries. Clara Fergus' tab was over three dollars, high in those days. She was a good customer. He'd want to keep her happy.

The baker returned wiping floury hands on an apron. "What can I do for you, young man?"

My heart hammered so loud I wondered why he didn't hear the thump. With a swallow, I forced my voice steady (Rule Five.) "I'm Wally, Mrs. Fergus' cousin from Cincinnati. She asked me to fetch a loaf of white bread. Please put it on the account."

He raised an eyebrow. "Why, I saw Mrs. Fergus a few days ago. She didn't mention relatives coming to town."

I fought the urge to bolt for the door. (Rule Six: Make eye contact. Rule Two: Make the lie real.)

"My sister has the measles," I meekly replied. "Cousin Clara took me in until she gets better."

The raised eyebrow lowered. His facial features softened. The lie made perfect sense. Measles was no joke—ask Esther Roth. Doctors only had aspirin for the fever. If someone got sick, the family hung a big red MEASLES QUARANTINE sign on the front door to warn visitors, and shipped healthy kids to relatives until the infection passed.

The baker packaged the bread, and I thanked him politely. Once outside, I raced to my hiding place at Little Angels. I pressed flat against the wall, half expecting the wail of a siren out front, followed by Chief Edwards pounding on the door. The only sound in the basement was my heavy labored breathing.

With trembling fingers, I tore open the bag. The loaf squashed under my arm, and now sported a dent in the middle. I didn't care. I ripped off a chunk and stuffed my mouth. I ate until my flat stomach puffed up like a marshmallow. No bread ever tasted better. Soon nothing remained but crumbs. I proudly contemplated the crumpled paper sack. With the promise of five hundred bucks and a knack for lying, my future loomed aces high.

Over the next months, I approached eight different stores with equal success, but as I couldn't go to the same place twice, the lie soon ran the course. Buoyed with confidence, I lied one last time at a bakery that made fancy lemon meringue pies. My excitement was hard to contain when the owner complied without as much as a howdy-do.

I strolled through the park to Little Angels, envisioning a gluttonous feast in the basement. The pleasant daydream ripped apart when I rounded a clump of bushes and came face to face with Chauncey Edwards.

A recent growth spurt pumped up his meanness. At school, Chauncey graduated from insults to rousting kids for their lunch money while his mindless flunkies cackled with glee. He still kept his distance from me, but here we were in the park. Chauncey wasn't much for deep thinking, but gave me the once-over, and I practically heard the rusty gears grinding in his head. *We're alone. No witnesses.*

"Well, well, well, if it ain't the world's ugliest orphan. Where's your bodyguard now? I'm gonna take you apart, Whistler, piece by piece."

I could run. His fat legs would never catch me, or…I hefted the pie. It was wrong. Mrs. Hart definitely wouldn't approve, but what a noble end for a common pastry.

Chauncey looked into my eyes. He must have glimpsed the future and concluded his wasn't going to be pretty.

"Don't you dare," he hissed.

I nailed him right in the kisser, and he fell backward into a mud puddle. I leaned over and ground the pie into his mug forcing globs of merengue up his nose.

"I'm telling," he howled with a spluttering cough. "My dad will throw you in jail. He'll shut Little Angels. Mrs. Hart will end up on the street."

My temper snapped. I hadn't considered how my actions affected Mrs. Hart and wasn't about to lose the only home I ever knew because of a moon-faced puke like Chauncey. "No you won't, mama's boy, or else."

Chauncey snorted out a gob of meringue. "Oh, yeah," he snarled. "Make me."

The itch I couldn't scratch.

Shifting, turbulent energies inside me aligned with a *click* as if tumblers in a lock slid into place. My pulse raced with a sensation of untapped power. The very air shimmered.

"Rat me out," I shouted, "and I'll hunt you down like a mad dog and not with a pie. Believe me more than anything in your sorry life!"

My words slammed into Chauncey. Blood drained from his face until skin tone matched the white merengue. "I-I believe. I'll never tell." He scrambled to his feet and raced away like a bloated jackrabbit.

The mysterious sense of power vanished as quickly as it came. I thumbed my nose at Chauncey and hurried from the park. By the time Grimaldi's Market was in sight, my head pounded. Both legs were weak and shaky as if I ran a marathon instead of a block. I detoured to the alley behind the store to take a shortcut to Little Angels.

"Chauncey had it coming."

Startled, I pulled up short. Esther was home on a rare break from school. She sat under a tree with a Braille book in her lap and a white cane by her side. Her head cocked in my direction. She put the book aside. "Chauncey is a big fat jerk. He comes in the store and sticks my cane on a shelf I can't reach. He pulls my hair and makes fun of me. I told Cousin Carlotta. She doesn't care."

An uneasy feeling churned in the pit of my stomach. "I-I don't know what you're talking about."

Esther shook her head with obvious regret. "You wasted good pie, though."

My jaw dropped open. At that moment, Mr. Grimaldi's black roadster pulled into the alley. I didn't need a cross-examination from him, so scrammed.

By the time I reached Little Angels, my nerves held a raw edge. What had I done? Nobody messed with any of the Edwards and walked away clean. If news of Chauncey and the pie already reached Esther, Mrs. Hart surely heard. To my surprise, she said nothing. No one did, including Mrs. Murphy who sucked in gossip like a vacuum cleaner.

Even stranger, Chauncey continued to avoid me at school except for snide comments in the lunchroom and an occasional wary look my way. Esther returned to boarding school before we spoke again. Eventually, I forgot the funny clicking noise and put Esther's curious comments out of mind, accepting whatever happened had been a lucky break for me.

I had the rules now, but kept my gift secret; ready to unleash the moment I fled New Brunswick. I didn't need to snoop on Mrs. Hart's private conversations anymore, but I did. Adults never tell kids the good stuff, and if I hadn't eavesdropped, I'd have never learned Police Chief Edwards and the Grimaldis were in cahoots with the mob.

Chapter 2
The Dark Man

In the 1920s, the government banned the purchase of alcohol. Prohibition was supposed to control crime caused by liquor sales, but the opposite happened. While the supply of booze dried up and saloons shut down, those willing to bend the law saw a spectacular business opportunity and rejoiced. Alcohol sales went underground and found a new outlet in speakeasies, secret nightclubs hidden behind closed doors—some run by gangsters, some by enterprising individuals.

The key to success was secrecy and people willing to look the other way for a price. Bootleg hooch flooded areas like New Brunswick with easy access to New York City and Philadelphia. Lots of people were involved and, brother, heaps of money was made.

One night in the winter of 1929, someone knocked on the front door. The Grimaldis and Chief Edwards stood under the porch light. Mrs. Grimaldi glanced around in a shifty fashion as if she didn't want the neighbors to see their arrival. I anxiously rifled through my mental filing cabinet in a desperate search for a forgotten felony. Fortunately, they didn't come for me.

Mrs. Hart ushered them into the parlor. Naturally, I scampered to the cellar to eavesdrop. Anxious feet shuffling and throat clearing came from overhead. It struck me none of the guests wanted to speak first.

Mrs. Hart broke the silence. "It's late for a social call."

"Actually," said Mrs. Grimaldi, "we want to cut you in on a business opportunity."

Her husband coughed. "Grimaldi's Market has a large delivery truck. Lately, we branched out to moving other, shall we say, liquid assets."

"You mean smuggling bootleg liquor," said Mrs. Hart.

Her blunt honesty must have been unnerving. The chair creaked as Mr. Grimaldi's weight shifted from side to side. "Um, yes. In truth, business is booming. We need a quiet out-of-the way place to stash bottles until shipments can be arranged."

"You want to use the carriage house."

At the rear of the property sat an old carriage house from the horse-and-buggy days. Rich people converted them to garages, but Mrs. Hart couldn't afford a car so the building was empty.

"The carriage house is perfect," declared Mrs. Grimaldi whole-heartedly. "It's surrounded by woods and vegetation, shielded from neighbors, and invisible to the street. We'll pay cash to rent it. I know you can always use extra money."

"How very thoughtful," Mrs. Hart murmured. My skin tingled as the lie drifted down.

"You needn't worry about police interference," assured Chief Edwards. I imagined his sly wink. "If you know what I mean."

"We wouldn't present this opportunity to just anyone," insisted Mrs. Grimaldi.

I glared at the ceiling. No, just folks with no push, easy to keep under their thumbs. If the Feds ever came snooping around, the Grimaldis and Chief Edwards would waste no time fingering Mrs. Hart to save their own skins.

"The answer is no," said Mrs. Hart. "We don't have a lot of extras at Little Angels, but enough to get by." I relaxed. She understood the truth.

"I'm not accustomed to having my wishes ignored." Mrs. Grimaldi's voice rose in pitch. "Think again before you refuse."

"I won't be involved in illegal liquor sales." Mrs. Hart answered with rock-hard certainty.

Chief Edwards cleared his throat. "I trust you'll be discreet concerning our little talk."

"I couldn't care less about your sideline. I'll show you out." Footsteps shuffled across the floor once again and then the parlor door slammed shut.

While relieved Mrs. Hart gave them the old heave-ho, I regretted the loss of extra cash. The Grimaldis obviously scored big. They bought the lot behind their store and built a fancy house. Pricey rings dripped from Mrs. Grimaldi's fingers. The Edwards didn't suffer, either. Their new car was worth more than most folk's homes and Chauncey always had a pocketful of dough.

The country was flush with money. People partied like the booze and their livers would never give out—they didn't call those years the Roaring Twenties for nothing. What no one saw coming was the good times wouldn't last.

The end came with the stock market crash in October 1929. I never understood what happened. It had something to do with stocks and too much easy credit. In other words, people bought with money they didn't have. When the stock market tumbled, the rest of the money supply went, too. People panicked. They ran to empty savings accounts to find banks already gone bust. Businesses folded. Jobs disappeared. No money came in, but creditors still demanded payment. People lost everything including belief in the future. Choking poverty gripped the country. Historians later called it the Great Depression, but to those of us who lived the times, it was really the Great Despair.

For a while, life continued as usual for Mrs. Hart and me. She had the steady income from Little Angels, but when the county's own investments dwindled, payments were cut by three-quarters. No more orphans came through the door. Women didn't have babies, unwanted or not. The adoption fees evaporated.

By late spring of 1933, when I was fifteen, a change occurred in the atmosphere of the house. Mrs. Hart grew anxious around the first of the month when bills came due. In her forties now, she looked older than her years.

One afternoon, Mrs. Grimaldi arrived at the door. Although word on the street was the Feds had cracked down on local bootlegging, rumors spread the couple's gangster connections forwarded other illegal business. Mrs. Hart was pale and tense as she showed Mrs. Grimaldi into the parlor.

I raced to the cellar in time to hear Mrs. Grimaldi say, "Nico and I have been very generous. We carried your account for several months."

"I appreciate the assistance."

"You're in the red not merely at our store, but all around town, and will lose the house after another missed payment on the mortgage."

My heart sank. Lose the house? Were things that bad?

Mrs. Hart's voice was tight and angry. "My business is not your concern."

"Yes, it is. If you're thrown in the street, I'll never collect money due me."

"I need more time. I have jewelry to sell—" The lie vibrated with an anxious tremble.

"You have nothing of value left." Mrs. Grimaldi sniffed with disdain. "People talk. Everything of worth has been sold. You're cleaned out, but…" Her voice dropped to a conspiratorial whisper. "I can help."

"How?" Mrs. Hart's tone was naturally suspicious. Acts of kindness went against Mrs. Grimaldi's nature.

"A doctor named Pike needs a secluded building. The carriage house is perfect. He's willing to cover your debts plus a little extra as a rental fee."

"What does he want it for?"

"I didn't ask," Mrs. Grimaldi snapped. "Dr. Pike is an eye doctor with a reputable practice in New York. Perhaps, he plans to open an office in New Brunswick, too. When he mentioned need of a place,

I immediately thought of the carriage house. You should be grateful."

"Very kind, I'm sure." Her voice was cold, the words clipped.

"You have no other options. Either take Dr. Pike's money or end up on the street. Whistler will go to the state orphanage."

I drew in a sharp breath. The state orphanage was for those who weren't in privately run homes like Little Angels. I passed by once. Each window was barred. The kids in the yard had empty, dead expressions. Not one of them smiled. I had the sick feeling none of them could.

"All right." Mrs. Hart's voice was so low I barely heard her.

"Dr. Pike will be by tonight to discuss the details—nine o'clock sharp."

I spent the rest of the day stewing over the reason a rich doctor wanted the carriage house. He had to be rich. Nobody else had money to spare. Mrs. Hart said nothing to me and, naturally, I couldn't admit to eavesdropping in the cellar.

We barely spoke during dinner. The picture of the state orphanage stuck in my mind. I had confidence Mrs. Hart wouldn't send me voluntarily, but if she lost the house, Chief Edwards would gleefully hogtie me to the front door himself.

I pushed away from the table and announced homework to finish. Mrs. Hart was so deep in thought she barely acknowledged with a nod. I dashed upstairs and fretted by the window as I watched for the mysterious Dr. Pike.

Bang on the dot of nine, Mr. Grimaldi's black car parked at the curb. I swallowed hard. Had the doctor changed his mind? Was Mrs. Hart penniless? No way would I go to the state orphanage. I had three years before collecting five hundred bucks from the state, but now debated whether to cut my losses and scram.

The car door opened. The slim, fit driver wasn't tubby Mr. Grimaldi. Keeping to the shadows, I snuck down the back stairway to the unlit kitchen and spied into the hallway. A man stood under the porch light. He wore a long duster coat and a black fedora hat pushed low over his eyes.

Mrs. Hart presented her hand in greeting. "Dr. Pike, before we proceed, I must know your intentions about the carriage house. I won't have illegal—"

"I am a friend," he crooned. "You are in no danger."

Mrs. Hart's hand dropped limply to her side.

My muscles instantly relaxed; cares drifted away. Peace descended on the house, no sound except two words beating in time to my heartbeat.

A friend…a friend…a friend.

They washed over me, filling my head, stealing my thoughts. Worry melted like an ice cube on a hot plate. I'm a dope to hide in the dark. Everything is Jake. I'll just step out and welcome Dr. Pike, too…

Liar!

The brilliant light of truth ripped through the haze poisoning my mind. I halted mid-step and gasped for breath. What was I doing?

The doctor murmured, "You are my servant, Mrs. Hart."

"I am your servant," she echoed.

The windows were shut tight, but an icy wind skittered up my spine. I hugged my arms to my chest and shivered.

"Show me the carriage house," said Dr. Pike.

She led him to the kitchen. I ducked into the pantry until the rear door slammed and then crept to the window. A light flickered, barely illuminating the path of the dark man and Mrs. Hart. He must have carried a flashlight, but the beam was sickly yellow as if the batteries were dying.

Burning with curiosity, I stole down the steps and dove into the bushes separating our yard from Mrs. Murphy's. Through the leaves issued a snuffle, followed by a soft whine. Honey Bun, Mrs. Murphy's little terrier, had been left ignored in the backyard again. Anxious for company, Honey Bun once dug a hole under Mrs. Hart's rosebushes onto our property and I made the mistake of tossing her a bone. Now she constantly dug tunnels and my responsibility was to fill them in. You might say Honey Bun and I had a complicated relationship. She doted on my attention. I did my best to ignore her.

"Shhh, Honey Bun. Go home. I don't have bones." The whining cut off with a disappointed yip.

Mrs. Hart opened the carriage house door. As she stepped aside for Pike to enter, the eerie yellow light played across her face. Mrs. Hart dropped her gaze as if she couldn't bear to look at him. The dark man stood in the doorway, taking in the space in one sweeping glance. He nodded in satisfaction. The glow from the flashlight followed every move of his head.

Without warning, Honey Bun darted from the rose bushes. She planted her paws by the doctor, lips pulled back in a vicious snarl. Pike turned around. Through the leaves of the bushes, I caught a glimpse of his face and then bit my lip to keep from screaming.

He had no flashlight. A yellow glow came directly from his eyes.

The light played across Honey Bun. Tail between her legs, she backed away with a whine and disappeared into the foliage. The glow vanished, plunging the yard into gloom. Pike led Mrs. Hart to the house. I cringed in the bushes as they passed.

"Do you have infants on the property now?" he demanded.

Mrs. Hart hesitated, and I held my breath, but she answered no without elaborating on the one constantly rejected orphan-in-residence at Little Angels.

"Don't speak of me to anyone. I was never here."

The lie whipped out, captured Mrs. Hart, and drew her in. "You were never here."

They separated; Pike to the street while Mrs. Hart entered the house.

I leaned against a tree, heart thudding hard against my ribs, thoughts tumbling through my head. What's going on? Was the devil in New Brunswick? Pike sure didn't resemble pictures; no cloven hoofs or horns. If the devil could go anywhere he wants, why settle for New Jersey?

From the street came the sound of a car engine turning over. I stood up straight. Hang on a sec. Pike drove Mr. Grimaldi's car. Can't the devil just *poof* appear in a cloud of smoke? Why the heck did he need a Chevy?

I went inside to find Mrs. Hart. She was always sensible and must have an explanation. The first floor was dark. Upstairs, no light shone past the jamb.

I rapped softly. "Are you awake?"

She didn't answer. With a steadying breath, I eased open the door. Mrs. Hart was in bed. Her head turned to me and lifted from the pillow. Her eyes opened, but they were glazed and unfocused. For a moment, her expression cleared. "Help me."

I swallowed hard. "A-are you okay?"

Whatever horrible nightmare ensnared Mrs. Hart overpowered her once more. She sunk into the pillow. Her eyes closed again.

I ran to my room and shut the door, adrenaline rushing through my veins. *This isn't your problem. Get out of here now.* I ran a shaky hand through my hair. Where to go was the question. Life on the road was tough for a fifteen year old that didn't have two nickels to rub together.

The answer came in a rush. I didn't need money to hop a freight train. Once free of New Brunswick, lying was my way to fame and fortune. *Grab that freedom. Don't look back. Every man for himself.*

I stuffed my meager belongings in a pillowcase and slung the bundle over my shoulder. My fingers grasped the door handle.

Help me.

Mrs. Hart's desperate plea rang through my mind. What was I doing? My hand dropped to the side. "Hang on a sec," I muttered. "Something is definitely hinky." I slapped myself upside the head. "What a dope. Glowing eyes are impossible."

Sensible explanations came in a rush. I was across the yard and didn't get a clear view of the weird light through the brush. Pike must have had a flashlight stowed in his sleeve, and the fear of being sent to the state orphanage caused my hallucinations.

That was it! They were hallucinations. Also, the Grimaldis knew lots of criminals, so the doctor had to be a gangster. Mrs. Hart felt trapped and scared because she needed money.

My temper flared. Some rich guy comes to the door expecting us poor folk to dance to his fiddle and what did I do? Left Mrs. Hart, the only person to ever care about me, to fend for herself and then practically ran down the street bawling like a baby. I caught a glimpse of myself in the dresser mirror and my lips curled in contempt. "Since when did you become such a pushover?" I chucked the pillowcase on the floor. People who have nothing in the world got to stand their ground or the world runs right over them.

The Grimaldis knew the truth about Pike. He drove their car, so they must be involved in his scheme. A little snooping to discover the truth, and then Mrs. Hart could get on the horn to the Feds. I imagined a squad of G-men storming Grimaldi's Market and then Nico and Carlotta's faces peering morosely out the back of a paddy wagon as it drove through town. Maybe I could even convince the coppers to stop for Chauncey.

The unlit streets were deserted as I made my way to the Grimaldi's house. The black roadster was parked outside the garage. A light shone in a downstairs window, so I snuck across the lawn and peeked in.

Pike sat at the kitchen table; fingers clasped placidly in front, not a glowing eyeball in sight. I gave myself a mental kick in the pants for being such a dope.

The Grimaldis huddled over a piece of paper. Mr. Grimaldi looked up and cleared his throat. "Everything is in order. The carriage house suited you?"

Pike slid an envelope stuffed with cash across the tabletop. "Yes. It was private and exactly as described. We have a deal."

Mrs. Grimaldi snatched at the bills with undisguised greed. "We wouldn't do this, you understand, but the Feds raided the local speakeasies. Our best clients shut down. Times are tough."

Mr. Grimaldi scrawled a signature on the paper and handed the pen to his wife. She added hers, and then Pike tucked the paper in his pocket. "You needn't e concerned about the girl."

My ears pricked up. Girl? What girl? If Pike meant Mrs. Hart, the doctor needed to get his own eyes checked.

Mr. Grimaldi shifted in his seat, a flush tinting his fat cheeks. "People might get the wrong impression if the arrangement is discovered. You understand—they don't realize our actions are for her own good."

I sucked in my breath. Mr. Grimaldi lied big time.

"Don't worry. No one will ever find out." Pike's voice was as cold as midwinter ice.

A teensy doubt jabbed at my mind that this had to do with gangsters, but I brushed it roughly away. Pike and the Grimaldis rose from the table. I darted from the window and ducked behind a tree right before the kitchen door opened.

Mrs. Grimaldi beamed at Pike. "If you need anything else, don't hesitate to stop by."

The dark man set the fedora on his head and snapped the brim over his eyes. "I'm quite satisfied. You won't see me again."

True.

For some reason, the truth shook me more than a lie. Mr. Grimaldi closed the door, but Pike remained on the stoop. The kitchen went dark and then a light switched on in an upstairs bedroom window.

I peered from behind the tree. Why did Pike wait? To rob the joint after they fell asleep? If so, I had no plan to stop him. I had half a mind to help.

The bedroom light flicked off and the yard went pitch black. One second…two seconds…three seconds…

A yellow beam danced across the door, and my throat nearly closed in terror. That was no flashlight.

The ray from Pike's eyes narrowed and focused pencil-thin. The smell of burning wood drifted across the lawn as he etched a smoldering hieroglyphic of a flame in the middle of the door. The outline of glowing embers flared and then snuffed out. Pike stepped back from the stoop. He paused for a moment as if to admire his handiwork and then sprinted down the alley.

Heart thumping, I darted to the door. My fingers stroked the spot where I last saw the little flame. The wood was still warm.

I snatched back my hand. The wood now blazed hot, more scorching by the second. The glowing outline flared to life again. A spark shot out, soared overhead, and landed near the chimney. Patches of shingles exploded in flames.

A long thin spark slithered from the symbol, a fiery snake writhing toward the keyhole. Without thinking, I reached to sweep it away only to jerk my fingers from the scalding heat. The spark slid into the opening. With a roar, a curtain of fire engulfed the downstairs windows.

In a panic, I banged on the door. "Wake up! The house is on fire!"

A thick choking cloud of smoke billowed under the doorframe, and I staggered back in a coughing fit. In a blink, the first floor was an inferno. How did the fire spread so fast? Mrs. Grimaldi's terrified screams cut through the crackling fusillade of flames.

Blistering heat drove me across the yard. The panic-stricken face of Nico Grimaldi appeared at the bedroom window struggling to open the sash.

Crrrack.

The wooden supports inside the house splintered and gave way. Mr. Grimaldi vanished in a thunderous crash as the second floor collapsed on the first. His wife's screams cut off.

Multiple sirens wailed in the distance. I stumbled down the alley as hot cinders rained from above. Embers lit on my clothing, and I slapped them away. The Grimaldi house was now a nightmare of hellfire. I flinched as the outside walls caved in with a deafening roar.

The first of the fire trucks screeched around the corner. Cops would surely follow asking questions I couldn't answer. As I ran across the street, the glare of a headlight caught me for an instant.

Tires squealed, and a man yelled, "You there, stop!"

I bolted, not daring even a glance back, afraid to see a pair of glowing yellow eyes dogging my steps. Once safely inside Little Angels, I went directly to the bathroom, stripped off my sooty clothes, and filled the tub. Red sores peppered my arms and legs where embers burned through the cloth, but sliding beneath the cool water eased my stinging skin. Again and again, I rinsed my mouth to flush the gritty burnt taste. Somewhere between the first scrub and the twentieth, the water washed the smell off my body, but nothing erased the memory of the Grimaldis' petrified screams.

Cold and numb, I forced myself from the tub. At least, my shoes were in good shape. I only owned one pair and would never be able to explain fire damage. I wasn't sure how much the cops saw of me, so I buried the ruined pants and shirt in Mrs. Hart's rose garden. Even from Little Angels' backyard, I heard the sirens and smelled smoke. Every flatfoot was on the alert, not to mention curious gawkers. No one slipped unnoticed out of town now.

I stumbled into bed and closed my eyes. Yes, sir, just a few hours rest and I'd be on my way.

* * * *

I see you.

I jerked awake, covered in sweat. Sunlight streamed through the window. The nightmare faded away. I was back at Little Angels; no flaming eyes searched for me in the dark. I stumbled out of bed and threw on my clothes. The long shirt hid the red marks on my skin from the embers, covering evidence I was at the fire.

Mrs. Hart sat at the kitchen table huddled over a newspaper. The headline blared PROMINENT FAMILY PERISHES IN FLAMES. I adopted my most innocent manner as I took a seat and scooped scrambled eggs on my plate. "Who died?"

"The Grimaldis. How strange," Mrs. Hart murmured. "I was talking to someone about them. Who was it now?"

"The man from last night?" I suggested with offhanded ease.

She looked up from the paper. "No one was here last night."

I blinked. Her voice held no sense of a lie. "I thought I saw a guy outside in a dark coat and fedora."

Mrs. Hart raised an eyebrow. "Honestly, Peter. Why on earth would I open the door to a strange man in the middle of the night?"

No good reason. I changed the subject. "Do they know how the fire started?"

"No, but the police say the deaths were murder."

I paused in mid bite, thankful to be an expert at the straight face. "On the level?"

"The fire started in too many places and spread too fast. The house was gone by the time the fire engines arrived. The authorities are searching for a suspect running from the scene. When they catch him, the courts aren't likely to show mercy. The Grimaldis had too much influence."

Breakfast jelled into a cold hard lump in my stomach.

The doorbell rang. "Mrs. Hart," came the unmistakable bellow of Chief Edwards, "open up."

My heart skipped a beat and I followed her to the foyer. Chief Edwards and two officers stood on the porch. "There's no need to shout," said Mrs. Hart. "My hearing is excellent."

With a nod at me, the chief said, "I got a report Whistler owns clothes matching the arsonist." My heartbeat ratcheted up.

Mrs. Hart regarded him with an icy glare. "I read the description in the paper. White cotton shirt and brown pants—every boy in town owns the same outfit, including your son."

The chief shoved a foot past the jamb. "I have the information on good authority—"

"Whose?" She stepped on his toe and he jumped back.

Chauncey skulked across the street. "I see you," I yelled.

"I told you to stay home," roared his father. Chauncey took off as if someone lit a firecracker in his pants.

Mrs. Hart raised an eyebrow. "Chauncey is your good authority?"

His face reddened. "No need to get in a twist. With such a heinous crime, I'm duty bound to follow every tip."

"You must have others."

"Plenty," he sputtered.

Liar. You don't have a single one. It took all my control not to laugh in his face.

"Be reasonable," said the chief. "The whole town is out for blood. I've got men stationed at every road from New Brunswick along with the train and bus station, but can't afford to ignore a single lead."

Mrs. Hart sniffed. "Of course not. This is an election year and your biggest campaign contributors were just incinerated."

He squared his shoulders. "The election has nothing to do with my duty to the citizenry."

Hah. Another lie.

"I'll only take a quick look-see around…"

Mrs. Hart didn't budge an inch. "Certainly not. I'm no criminal and don't harbor any under my roof. I won't have police rummaging through the house and become the topic of neighborhood gossip."

He retreated with a snarl. "I'm watching you, boy. The town has a curfew tonight. Everyone off the streets by dark. You hear me?"

Mrs. Hart slammed the door. "Curfew…absurd…complete waste of time. The man is long gone."

"What man?"

Her brow wrinkled in confusion. "Of course, the murderer was a man," she stammered. "Certainly not a woman or child, no matter what Chief Edwards believes. Yes, a strange man who doesn't belong here. I don't…" Her voice trailed away. She shook her head as if to clear the cobwebs.

"Like a strange man wearing a fedora?" I prompted.

"A fedora?" The bewilderment vanished. She regarded me sharply. "Aren't you late for school?"

Chauncey must have arrived early to spread rumors about my new murderous nature. Anxious whispers and carefully averted eyes followed me all day, even from the teachers. Not that I cared. I enjoyed the attention, rising from total obscurity to Public Enemy Number One overnight. For once, I was tough and powerful instead of forgotten and shoved in a corner.

I swaggered through half the day, all easy smiles and puffed out chest. On the way to the lunchroom, I stood behind one of the younger boys smaller than me. I passed him now and then in the hall. We ignored each other and went about our business. I didn't even know his name. He turned around. As our eyes met, he shrank back and beckoned me ahead.

Faces turned my way; watching, waiting, wondering. Students circled like a wolf pack around me and the terrified boy. I had a fearful reputation now. If I shoved him against a locker and stole his lunch money, no one would interfere.

Chauncey elbowed through the crowd. "Do it," he whispered in my ear. His eyes held a feral gleam.

I had a flash of Chauncey's life. No thought for others' feelings. Take instead of earn. Fear in place of respect. I only had to pick on a smaller kid who never caused me any harm and that power was mine. I already tasted it.

The feeling ebbed away. Nothing remained inside but a sickening hollow. I shouldered past Chauncey to the nearest exit, and then lit across town. Unconsciously, my feet detoured to Grimaldi's Market.

A *Closed* sign hung in the store window. I crept around the side of the building and stared into the yard. As horrific as the fire had been in the dark, the scorched smoking earth was more terrible in daylight. Nothing remained of the house except an ashy pile of debris and a nauseating reek. The store suffered no damage; neither did the detached garage, the Grimaldi's car, nor the nearby homes. The whole scene was uncanny. How could something burn so quickly and so hot in one place?

The door to the market swung open. Out walked a little girl about nine years old in a black dress and clutching a white cane. I hadn't seen Esther Roth in years. Although hardly friends, I experienced an unexpected outpouring of relief. For once, the Grimaldis' neglect served her well. She must have been at school during the fire.

Esther descended the stairs with practiced ease. The door opened again and Chief Edwards appeared. I hunkered down, so he wouldn't catch me spying. If he decided to haul me off to jail for the heck of it, no one would stop him. Esther would probably enjoy herself. The chief held open the screen door and ushered someone ahead.

Dr. Pike stepped outside and adjusted his fedora.

Chapter 3
Death in the Carriage House

"Will you be staying long, Doctor?" asked the chief.

"Merely long enough to attend the funeral. Business requires me to leave tomorrow night."

"It's a good thing you happened to be in town. We didn't know Esther had other family."

Esther piped up, "Me neither."

Pike ignored her. "I travel a great deal. Years ago, Nico and Carlotta made arrangements to assign guardianship to me if unable to care for the child." He patted papers in his breast pocket. "They were always mindful of her best interest."

The lie was smooth and coldly competent. Chief Edwards didn't have a clue, but Esther did.

"Nuh-uh," she insisted. "They didn't like me."

"Nonsense," sputtered the chief. "Otherwise, they never would have prepared for an emergency. You're a very lucky young lady. Without Dr. Pike, you'd be at the state orphanage by now."

I scowled. The Grimaldis sat at the kitchen table signing paperwork last night. Pike's words floated back. *The girl will never know.* Nico and Carlotta sold Esther for an envelope stuffed with cash. I eyed the pile of ashes. Fat lot of good it did them.

Pike reached into his pocket and took out a set of car keys. "Time for us to go, my dear." His hand rested lightly on her shoulder and she flinched. He escorted her to the Grimaldi's Chevy. Esther felt her way inside and sat placidly in the backseat.

I pressed flat against the building. As the car passed me, Esther turned her head. Blind eyes stared directly into mine. Her lips mouthed, *Help me.*

My legs took off directly to the basement of Little Angels, certain the one place I always felt safe and in control would comfort me now.

It didn't. Esther couldn't possibly have known I was at the store. Her pleading look must have been my imagination.

Like I imagined the fire and Pike's glowing eyes?

Esther's life wasn't my business. She was better off with a rich doctor.

Rich isn't everything.

I kicked at the wall in frustration. I was nobody...nothing. I was worse than nothing. I didn't have a real name. No one would believe me. What help could a penniless orphan give? The most sensible thing to do was leave Esther to her fate.

My fingers balled into tight fists. Not yet. I could at least warn Esther her new guardian was dangerous. Pike mentioned attending the funeral and that was true. With Esther at his side, he'd play the perfect dutiful relative. Somehow, I'd get a word with her alone, but that's all Peter Nobody Whistler could do.

First, I had to convince Mrs. Hart to let me attend the funeral. I found her in the parlor, sitting with an enigmatic expression on her face. The thought popped into my head that she waited for me.

I cleared my throat. "I'd like to come with you to the Grimaldi's funeral tomorrow to pay my respects."

"Would you?" Her voice didn't hold a drop of emotion, but I got a funny feeling in the pit of my stomach.

"Yeah, sure. I mean, it's the right thing to do."

She jumped to her feet, face flushed with anger. "How would you know the right thing to do?" A finger pointed to the fireplace. My clothing from the night before sat in a spoiled heap on the hearth. "Mrs. Murphy brought me a cutting from her new rose bush. Imagine my surprise when I went to dig and found those buried in the yard." Her eyes held a mixture of anger and pain. "I thought I knew you, Peter. I really did."

Blood rushed from my head. I was in deep water now. "I didn't do anything, I swear. Pike started the fire to murder the Grimaldis. I was there. I saw him. I tried to help, but the flames spread too fast."

"Oh, come," she scoffed. "Blaming the fire on an imaginary man. Do you think I'm a fool?"

Mrs. Hart would tell the cops. I'd be hunted like an animal. In panic, I grabbed her wrist. "You have to believe me. A man was here last night. His name was Dr. Pike. You showed him the carriage house."

"Liar." She struggled to get free. "I never...I wouldn't..."

"Listen to me." I grabbed her other wrist and held tight. My hands shook as if charged with an electric current. A shudder ran though Mrs. Hart. A force deep inside me reached out and slammed into an invisible barrier around her. With every ounce of belief I could muster, I shouted, "Pike is a liar!"

Our gazes locked and the charge exploded.

Click.

Once more, I experienced those strange energies that came to me years ago in the park with Chauncey. This time they shifted into place as if I was a jigsaw puzzle and just found my missing piece. I dropped her hands and stared in shock at my stinging palms.

Mrs. Hart collapsed in the chair, weak and confused. "A man…in a fedora."

I jumped at the words. "You remember him now."

She stared blankly at the hearth. "Yes…no…I-I'm not sure."

"He's evil, Mrs. Hart. He wants Esther. The Grimaldis signed her guardianship over to him for money, and then he killed them."

"Enough, Peter."

"I have to go the funeral and warn Esther."

"I said, enough." She struck a match from a box on the end table and tossed it into the hearth. The clothing caught fire. "We have no need to discuss this again. I-I believe you had nothing to do with the Grimaldis' deaths."

"And the funeral?"

She ran a shaky hand through her hair. "We'll go. To pay respects is the proper thing to do, of course. Now, leave me."

"Dr. Pike—"

"Go."

I knew the tone. The discussion was closed. At the threshold, I glanced back. Mrs. Hart sat frozen in the chair by the hearth, staring into the crackling flames.

Cradling my throbbing hands, I stumbled into the kitchen, jerked open the icebox, and pressed my palms flat against a block of ice. The pain dwindled, but a heavy weight settled on my shoulders. I was bone-weary as if pounding a sledgehammer all day long. My appetite disappeared with the burned clothes, so I shuffled to my room. The parlor was empty. Mrs. Hart must have gone upstairs, too. My head hit the pillow, and the next thing I heard was a rap on the door.

"Peter, hurry or we'll be late for the funeral."

I'd slept through the night. After throwing on a clean long sleeve shirt and pants, I shrugged into a jacket, and ran a comb through my hair. Mrs. Hart was already at the front door. She gave me the once over, smoothed a wanton lock off my forehead, and then nodded to herself. "You'll do."

Mrs. Murphy waited for Mrs. Hart on the stoop. I lagged behind the two women, burning with impatience. How did I get a word alone with Mrs. Hart now? I had to discover what she remembered. Pike didn't know I lived at Little Angels. Would Mrs. Hart squeal? The thought of those yellow eyes searching for me over the coffins of his victims gave me the jumps.

Despite the name, the Eternal Slumber Mortuary was wide-awake and hopping. Doesn't matter whether the dead were saints or sinners, nothing brought people out like a funeral. Pike stood in a receiving line graciously accepting condolences from the townsfolk. Esther stood next to him, pale skin even more colorless in a little black dress. She turned blind eyes in my direction.

"Esther," I whispered, although I knew she couldn't hear me. "You're in danger."

She shifted on her feet as if marking my warning. Pike immediately laid a firm hand on her shoulder. To other eyes, a comforting fatherly gesture, but my skin crawled.

Mrs. Hart approached Pike and extended her hand. The doctor bent his head and murmured something in her ear. I'd have given all my paltry possessions to know what passed between them.

Esther announced, "I have to go to the bathroom."

Mrs. Hart volunteered as escort. Pike's eyes narrowed as she guided Esther through the crowd. He obviously didn't like the idea of the girl leaving his side.

I shot from the reception area and down the hall. My hand paused on the doorknob of the ladies room. More than any place on the planet, inside was no man's land. Not only was I bound to get a stern reproof from Mrs. Hart, but I was also fair game for other women inside. For the moment, the corridor was clear. With a nervous swallow, I entered and quickly shut the door.

Mrs. Hart wasn't happy. "Peter Whistler, get out at once."

"But—"

"I said go."

"No." Esther's small voice cut through the argument. Arms flailing, she made contact with Mrs. Hart's dress and clenched the material in a balled fist. "Please, help. Don't let Dr. Pike have me."

Startled, Mrs. Hart patted her on the head. "Esther, it's all right."

"No, it isn't," she wailed. "Something is bad about him. I don't want to see his eyes."

"You can't see anyone's eyes," I snapped, momentarily irritated by her dumb statement. "You're blind."

"Enough, Peter." Mrs. Hart attempted to loosen Esther's grip, but the girl clung like a hungry tick. "Esther," she grunted, tugging hard. "He's your guardian. I know change is difficult, but the Grimaldis wished—"

"Esther?" Pike knocked at the door.

My chance for a long talk disappeared. "The Grimaldis sold her to Pike the night of the fire," I blurted in a rush. "I watched everything from the window. After they signed over the guardianship papers, he gave them a big wad of cash and then burned the house down."

Violent emotions flitted across Mrs. Hart's face as she pried Esther loose.

"Please," Esther begged, and then turned her blind eyes toward me. "Please, Peter."

Pike's patience reached the limit. "Esther, we need to greet the mourners." The handle turned.

I flattened against the wall as the door swung open. *Run...*I silently willed. Esther couldn't, of course. Escape was impossible. A blind girl was at the mercy of the people around her. Through the crack, I watched Pike take her hand in a firm grip.

My stomach knotted. The shepherd turned the lamb over to the slaughterhouse. Whatever the doctor planned was beyond my power to stop.

I'm sorry, Esther. I tried.

"Are you leaving today, Dr. Pike?" inquired Mrs. Hart in a congenial tone.

"Yes, directly after the burial. Business calls me immediately to New York." His words burned like an open sore. I wanted to scream every syllable from his mouth was a dirty, stinking lie.

"Meeting you has been such a pleasure. Do have a safe trip."

I blinked. Mrs. Hart lied.

She cradled Esther's hand between hers. "Don't worry, my dear. Everything will be fine."

Pike led Esther away, and Mrs. Hart closed the door. The mask of goodwill on her face disappeared and her skin paled. "I apologize, Peter. You're right. That man is a liar."

I gaped at her. "You remember."

She shook her head as if to clear a fog. "He inquired about the carriage house. His eyes…something is strange about his eyes."

"They had yellow flames inside."

Mrs. Hart shuddered. "Once you see them your mind goes blank. He told me to forget about him. I did." She fixed me with a searching look. "You made me remember. What did you do?"

"I-I'm not sure," I stammered. "I knew every word was a lie. He lied now about leaving."

"Yes. He said in the receiving line he needed the carriage house tonight."

"What do we do?"

"Do?" She slumped against the wall. "Peter, what can either of us possibly do against a man with such powers?"

I had no answer.

The door flew open. Augusta Edwards, Chauncey's mother, shoved past Mrs. Hart. "You're in my way—" She caught sight of me and glowered. "You filthy little beast, what are you doing in here?" Her claw-like fingers gripped my wrist around the worst burn. I winced and yanked back my arm. She wouldn't let go and ripped the thin worn cuff half off.

Mrs. Hart stepped between us. "I'll handle him, Mrs. Edwards."

"You're entirely too lenient with the little mongrel." Her double chin wobbled in indignation. "You should hear what my Chauncey has to say. Mark my words." She wagged her fat finger. "That boy is an abomination, already halfway along the road to eternal damnation."

"I sure Chauncey tries his best," Mrs. Hart murmured, straight-faced.

"I didn't mean Chauncey," Mrs. Edwards sputtered and pointed at me. "I meant him."

"Of course, a natural error. Nevertheless, he's my responsibility. Come along, Peter." Mrs. Hart quickly ushered me out the door.

"You sure told off the old cow," I said with a grin.

Her eyes twinkled. "You have no need to insult respectable farm animals, Peter."

"Those are burns."

Chauncey gawked at the blisters on my wrist exposed by the torn cuff. "I'm going to tell my father!" The little weasel pushed through the crowd shouting, "Peter Whistler has burns on his arm. He was at the fire."

Curious faces swung my way as Mrs. Hart steered me briskly down the hall. The exit led to the driveway where the hearses waited for the coffins. Angry voices came through the open window of the funeral parlor.

"I'm in a jam now," I yelped. "The chief needs to pin the blame on someone. He'll never believe me about Pike."

"Hide," she hissed. I slid under a hearse. A moment later, the door flung open. I hugged the ground, eyeing their shoes as a group of men crowded around Mrs. Hart.

"Where's Whistler?" demanded Chief Edwards.

"He took off," said Mrs. Hart, "so I followed him outside—there he goes!" Feet shuffled back and forth while voices muttered in confusion. "Don't you see him?" she demanded. "He's getting away...Don't stand there bleating like a herd of goats. Honestly, Chief, must I do your job for you? He went that way."

The chief barked, "Follow me, men." Feet took off at a run chasing The Invisible Boy.

Others exited the funeral parlor, no doubt curious about the commotion. Mrs. Hart bent over pretending to tie her shoe. "The carriage house," she whispered. "Midnight." She straightened and ordered the gawkers inside using her best no-

54

nonsense tone. Few had the moxie to argue with Mrs. Hart.

Too late to make a break for it. Chief Edwards was still nearby shouting at his men and spreading the alarm about the dangerous criminal lurking in the area. Everyone would be on the lookout.

The hearse parked right next to a small basement window. I tested the pane, and breathed a sigh of relief as it swung freely. The one place cops won't search was the funeral parlor where I'd already been. Squeezing past the sash, I dropped lightly to the floor. Jars of formaldehyde lined the walls, giving the room a funny chemical smell. With plenty of time to kill, I sat down to wait.

From above, reverberated the soft buzz of many voices. Half the town came through to pay respects. How come folks never noticed the one place where lying was completely acceptable was at a funeral? Nobody ever spoke ill of the dead, even if they were lousy human beings. People heaped tons of praise on the Grimaldis.

Rumrunners?

Nonsense.

Liars and chiselers?

Absurd.

Sold a little girl to a monster with flaming eyes?

Tut, tut.

The murmur upstairs finally died as townsfolk headed home. Footsteps crunched on the gravel outside the window. "No," grunted Chief Edwards, "we haven't caught Whistler, yet, but we will. The boy has no money, no connections, and nowhere to run. I've got men searching the roads, including those leading out of town."

I rose up on my toes. My pulse raced at the glimpse of the bottom of a black duster.

"I appreciate what you've done," said Pike.

"Yup, once we catch him, he'll talk. Don't worry. Whistler will spill everything he knows about the fire."

"I'm sure he will." Pike's voice dropped low. "Catching Whistler alive is a waste of time. The boy is obviously guilty."

The lie hit hard and fast. "Whistler is guilty," echoed the chief.

"The guilty should be punished."

"Should be punished."

A flash of yellow light danced across the windowpane. "You don't need to hear Whistler's story," murmured Pike. "He's dangerous. Your men must shoot to kill."

"Shoot to kill..." The yellow light vanished. "I'm sorry to say, Dr. Pike, the situation is desperate." Chief Edwards' voice lost its mindless tone. "I don't need Whistler's statement. The boy is obviously deranged. My men will shoot to kill. I can't chance he'll murder again."

"You made a wise decision, Chief. The citizenry must be protected."

Behind them, the funeral director walked down the steps holding Esther's hand. "We are ready to transport the dearly departed to the cemetery for burial."

From my position, I just made out Esther. She glanced once in my direction as if she knew I was there. More men arrived and after a brief shuffle of footsteps and several loud thuds, the caskets were loaded. Doors slammed and the hearses drove off.

I leaned against the cool stone wall. The building above was quiet. The only sound in the dark cellar was the wild thumping of my heart. I was in dutch now; fingered as a killer and condemned to be shot on sight.

The day crept by. I kept track of time by marking the town clock chime the hour. At six p.m., the hearses returned. The funeral parlor staff meandered upstairs for a bit before the building fell silent again. When the clock finally tolled eleven, I hoisted myself out the window.

Chief Edwards earned his paycheck. Squad cars prowled the roads while groups of armed men with flashlights combed the alleys, but nobody knew every shortcut and hidden byway in New Brunswick better than me. I made my way to Little Angels and hid behind a tree across the street. The windows were dark, the curtains drawn. The temptation to slip through the front door was great, but the parlor light shone inside Mrs. Murphy's. The old biddy perched at the front window, a perfect vantage point to keep watch all night.

If Mrs. Murphy intended to waste her time spying in the front, then the safest way to the carriage house was through her backyard. I skirted the house, eased past the rose bushes, and then froze at a suspicious growl.

"Honey Bun, shh. It's me." The little terrier yipped with recognition. "Shush," I ordered. "Keep quiet." She shivered in the chilly air and nudged my hand for food. I gave her a sympathetic scratch. "Did old lady Murphy give you guard duty to protect her from the killer arsonist? Sorry, the killer arsonist has nothing to eat. By the way, I was framed." Honey Bun snorted as if in disbelief and then turned tail and trotted away. Geez, even a dog didn't buy my innocence.

The town clock chimed twelve times. As I slipped inside the carriage house, the kitchen door of Little Angels creaked open. The light briefly illuminated silhouettes of three figures; Pike, Esther, and Mrs. Hart were on the way.

I needed a hiding place fast, but other than some old wooden orange crates tossed in a corner, the building was empty. I eyeballed the shadowy rafters. The ceiling wasn't too high. I stacked the crates and climbed onto a crossbeam. With a grunt, I hauled my feet to the top, but a toe caught the edge of a slat and the shaky pile toppled over. Now trapped, I pressed flat to the support beam.

The door opened. Pike strode to the center of the room near my position. Mrs. Hart followed holding Esther by the hand. I didn't dare a breath as the horrific yellow gleam from Pike's eyes played around the gloomy interior.

"As you can see," she assured him, "the carriage house is empty."

Esther shivered. "I'm cold."

Mrs. Hart drew her close. "I'm taking the child to the house."

Pike held out a hand. "Give her to me."

Mrs. Hart pushed Esther behind her and spoke without a quaver. "No. Do whatever you wish in here, but Esther and I are leaving."

Even with flaming eyes distorting his face, the shock was evident. "Disobedience is not possible. You are mine to command."

"I most certainly am not," Mrs. Hart retorted. Insult trumped fear every time with her. "How dare you speak to me like a dog."

Flames shot from his eyes. They encircled Mrs. Hart and Esther, trapping them inside a fiery prison. "How did you break free?" he roared. Mrs. Hart stood defiant, lips pressed shut in a stubborn line.

Honey Bun darted into the carriage house, snapping at Pike's ankles. A twisted smile embellished the doctor's features. With one quick movement, he snatched the terrier by the scruff. She squirmed in his grip, baring sharp teeth. "You're quite right, Mrs. Hart. You certainly aren't a dog. Although, I see similarities."

Desperate situation or not, no one spoke to Mrs. Hart that way. "Monster! You'll get nothing from me."

Pike looked fixedly at Honey Bun. Amber flames reflected in the dog's eyes. Without warning, Pike turned his head and a blast of yellow light struck Mrs. Hart in the face. She screamed and collapsed to the floor. Honey Bun went limp.

"Mrs. Hart!" Esther knelt next to the fallen woman and threw both arms around her. "She's dead."

Hands shaking I clutched the beam; a mixture of rage and horror swirled inside me, a pit of cold, helpless dread stole the breath from my lungs.

Pike walked through the fiery circle. The flames left no mark on his body or clothing. He tossed Honey Bun dismissively next to the lifeless Mrs. Hart. "I taught her a lesson, child. When I command, I expect obedience. Do you understand?" Esther's tear-stained face nodded. "Good. Obey me, or worse will happen to you."

With a soft whimper, Honey Bun stirred. The little terrier staggered to her feet, disoriented and confused. Then she shook her head and planted shaky legs protectively in front of Esther. Her upper lip curled and she uttered a low, throaty growl.

"So, you have fight left." Pike sounded amused. "See the girl remains calm while I prepare. Maybe I will be pleased enough to keep you alive."

Esther pulled Honey Bun close and whispered in her ear. The little dog bobbed her head as if in agreement. They both turned their faces toward me and for a brief moment, before they looked away, I caught and held the gazes of a blind girl and a nondescript terrier. I received a distinct impression neither was anxious to reveal my position to Pike.

The yellow light flared again. Four sparks jumped from Pike's eyes. "I summon the door."

The sparks hovered in the air and burst into flames. I grimaced as waves of heat billowed from below to lick at my hazardous perch.

Esther clung tight to Honey Bun. "What's happening?"

"You're very special, Esther," Pike crooned. "The Grimaldis had no inkling of your potential, but you passed every test."

She stiffened. "You killed them."

"Yes. I've killed others. I'm prepared to kill many more."

For once, the dark man didn't lie. Pike's heartless manner frightened me more than the flames.

"What do you want with me?" said Esther.

"You will open a door to a special place and then go inside and retrieve something important."

Esther's voice dropped to a frightened whisper. "I don't want to."

"Child," he murmured, "you have no choice."

Pike faced the four suspended flames and chanted mumbled words in a sing-song tone. The hair rose on the back of my neck. The heat made the air hard to breathe, and I covered my mouth to stifle a cough.

Sweat beaded Pike's forehead. His face twisted with intense concentration. The flaming orbs collided together in a brilliant flash. They stretched and flattened. Squared-off corners appeared. Before my eyes, the rectangles joined to make a four-paneled door.

The very air around me crackled and hummed with an electric current, the whole scene beautiful and terrifying at the same time. Pike muttered a few incoherent words. Another spark flew from his eyes. This one danced around to etch a tiny flame on each panel, identical to the figure imprinted on the

61

Grimaldi's house. A section of the door rippled and stretched into a handle.

Triumph oozed from Pike. "It is time."

Esther stood up, clasping Honey Bun tight in her arms. She stamped her foot. "No, I won't."

My lips twitched in an involuntary smile. Despite the danger, Esther was still a pill. Honey Bun bared her teeth in a vicious snarl. I never saw the placid dog so threatening.

Pike shoved Esther toward the portal. "Once inside, start walking. Those on the other side will lead you to—"

"I won't! I won't!"

Esther squirmed, but he grasped her shoulders, fingers digging tight into her dress. "Touch the handle!"

His voice rolled through my body like a peal of thunder. Honey Bun whined and peered overhead at me. "Do something," the dog's eyes seemed to plead.

What? I frantically scanned the inside of the carriage house for a weapon and saw nothing.

Esther's face set with stone-hard determination. "You can't make me."

Pike tensed. "You're correct." The truth hit me, then. For some reason, the door only opened under Esther's willing hand. Pike's eyes blazed, a flame lapped at her dress. "I'm out of patience, child. Obey me now or feel the flesh seared off your bones."

"Peter," she screamed.

Honey Bun leaped from Esther's arms, growling and snapping at Pike's ankles. Startled, the doctor stepped close under my position.

Fury exploded inside me. He killed Mrs. Hart without a thought, without a twinge of guilt. I rolled off the rafter and hit Pike a glancing blow on the shoulder. We both landed with a sickening thud. For an instant, I lay stunned, the breath knocked out and then scrambled to my feet, swatting at the tiny flame eating at the hem of Esther's dress.

Pike pushed himself to his knees, howling with the rage of a wolf gone mad. He turned his flaming eyes in my direction. I grabbed a handful of dirt from the floor and flung hard at his face. He fell back with a roar. Then I ripped off my jacket, and covered Esther's head and mine.

"Hold your breath," I yelled.

"No," Pike shrieked, blinking hard to clear his eyes. "Don't break the circle!"

I yanked Esther with me through the flames. The heat flared around us and the fire disappeared. The spectral door wavered and vanished. Pike blindly lunged, his hands snatched at my pants leg. A furry blur raced past and Honey Bun sunk her teeth into his wrist. Pike let go, trying to shake off the furious dog. I grabbed Esther's cane and clobbered him on the head. With a grunt, Pike dropped to the floor.

I pushed Esther past the door with Honey Bun right on my heels. Pike raised his head and white-hot lightning shot from his eyes. The fire bolts missed us and blasted into the wall of the carriage house. Sheets of flame raced to the roof.

"Shake a leg, Esther," I shouted.

The intense heat blew out half the wall. When we reached Little Angels, Honey Bun gave an urgent bark. I turned my head to see a dark figure stagger from the inferno. Pike was alive and miraculously unharmed. In blind panic, I steered Esther to the street.

Mrs. Murphy threw open the front window. "I see you, Peter Whistler," she bellowed. "Murderer! I've called the police. Come back here with Esther."

Now, I was in a mess. Good thing Mrs. Murphy was too fat to run me down. Esther stumbled over the curb. "Sorry." I handed her the cane.

"S'okay. Where are we headed?"

Flames ripped through the air behind Little Angels. Mrs. Murphy would tell the cops she saw me running from the scene. We had one option.

"Train station—we need to scram out of town fast."

"Honey Bun, come back," Mrs. Murphy yelled.

I glanced behind. The little terrier tailed us, but I couldn't stop to chase her home now.

"Dognapper," Mrs. Murphy screeched.

"Sure…great…why not?" I spit out, puffing along. "What's one more crime added to the list of the other things I haven't done?" Honey Bun darted to my side and took a gander at me with a big doggy grin. "Think it's funny?" I snarled.

"Nope," said Esther. "She's proud of you."

I rolled my eyes. "Keep moving, Esther."

Running with a blind kid wasn't easy, but after a block, we had a rhythm. "One-two, one-two…don't stop, Esther."

"How much farther?" she panted.

"The station is dead ahead."

I angled off into the woods and up a small hill to my favorite spot for watching the trains. If Chief

Edwards had assigned cops to the station, they wouldn't see us from here. A shrill whistle echoed down the tracks. We were in luck. A locomotive passed by any minute. I crossed my fingers wishing for a freight train. Passenger cars had staff with stewards and a conductor, near impossible to sneak aboard.

Pushing through the shrubbery, I led Esther over a low embankment. Nothing was scheduled to stop this time of night. The station didn't even have a depot master on duty, but ahead the line took a sharp turn. Every locomotive had to slow in order not to derail. The low rumble of the wheels on the metal tracks vibrated through my shoes as the train's headlight appeared in the distance.

"Esther, we have to hop on. Do you think you can?"

Her head bobbed. "I'll do it, Peter, if you help me." Amber light played around the rails in front of the deserted station. Honey Bun yipped.

"Pike is coming," Esther cried. "He sees us."

I had no time to ask how the blind girl knew. The whistle shrieked again. Brakes screeched. The yellow beam skewed toward us and crossed the tracks. Pike closed in.

"Run, Esther!"

The question now was whether the locomotive or Pike reached us first. The engine roared by with an explosion of wind and I suppressed a cheer. The string of boxcars rumbling behind meant freight. I pulled Esther along as fast as her legs would go. Trains sure seemed to move a lot slower from the hilltop.

Boxcar after boxcar clanked past, but the sliding side doors were shut. Suddenly, Honey Bun yipped twice and raced along the track, keeping pace with the last boxcar. I nearly cried out in relief at the sight of an open door.

"I'm going to put your hand on the car," I yelled at Esther. "You have to keep pace. I'll jump and pull you in after me." Amber brilliance raked across our faces. "Don't stop no matter what."

The open boxcar drew alongside. I positioned Esther's hand on the train and then grabbed her cane and flung it in. With a running leap, I snagged the edge. Fingernails tore as I pulled myself through the open door. Leaning over, I snatched Esther's wrist.

"Jump," I ordered.

Esther took a stumbling leap and I nearly lost my grip. She screamed as her other arm flailed about wildly. If Esther fell now, she'd be crushed underneath. Straining, I hung over the side, and caught her other hand. I yanked hard and she fell on top of me. Immediately, Esther was on her knees feeling for the opening.

"Where is she?"

"Who—"

A frantic barking erupted over the noise of the train. The little terrier's legs pumped like pistons, trying desperately to keep pace with the boxcar.

"Esther, we can't—"

"You have to get her," she wailed.

"You're nuts. She'll go home. She'll be all right."

"No, she won't." Hot tears spilled down her cheeks. "She bit Pike. He'll kill her dead, for sure. Please, Peter. Pleeeeese."

"Okay," I snapped. "Quit hollering."

The train rounded the bend and began to accelerate. I jumped down and nearly fumbled over my own feet. The ray locked onto my position. I scooped up Honey Bun and threw her inside. She landed with a yelp. (I hoped on her head.) The train lurched forward. A burning stitch tore through my side as I forced my legs faster. Gasping for breath, I watched in despair as the boxcar pulled ahead.

"Peter, hurry!"

A crackling hiss came from behind. A flame shot from the dark, slicing through the air. The fire missed my head by inches, searing a ragged scar across the side of the boxcar.

Funny how pure unvarnished terror could make an Olympic sprinter out of a skinny orphan with no athletic training. I shot ahead. With a bounding leap, my fingers snagged the edge of the boxcar. Small hands seized one wrist and sharp little teeth clamped on the other to haul me in. I landed with a thud and then scrambled up to peer outside. Far down the track, the amber light winked out. I struggled to pull the heavy door closed before collapsing with a grunt, too exhausted to move.

"He's…gone," I wheezed.

Honey Bun barked. "She said, 'Thank you'," announced Esther primly, "but you sure took your sweet time getting her onboard."

I gulped in a deep lungful of air. "Honey Bun…is dang lucky…I dragged her mangy butt…in at all."

"She's not Honey Bun, silly," said Esther. "She's Mrs. Hart."

Chapter 4
A Desperate Escape

In the past twenty-four hours, I had been accused of arson, dognapping, murder, and excessive rudeness. I was nearly burnt to toast by a man with flaming eyeballs. I was sore over every inch of my body, hadn't eaten since yesterday, and now trapped in a freight train with a yippy little dog and an obviously crazy girl. My limit was reached.

I raised myself on an elbow and bellowed, "You are out of your cotton-pickin' mind, Esther Roth. Of all the lame-brained, screwball, bat nut ideas—"

Esther wrinkled her face in a scowl. "I'm on the square, Peter Whistler."

"Mrs. Hart is dead."

"No, she isn't. She's sitting right here. Pike put Mrs. Hart inside of Honey Bun. Go ahead. Ask her yourself."

As soon as the train slowed again, I'd jump and head out on my own. We were far from Pike now. Someone would find Esther and escort her to the nearest loony bin. Honey Bun could go back to Mrs. Murphy. I was done.

"Go on," prodded Esther, "ask her to do something."

I sneered at Honey Bun. "Bark three times and sit." She barked three times, sat, and then rolled her eyes in evident exasperation.

Mouth agape, I sat up straight. "It must be a trick. Dogs can do tons of tricks. Roll over." She rolled over. "Shake." She wiggled her left front paw. I demanded she wag her tail, run in a circle, nod her head, and scratch her left ear. She did everything. After I asked her to bark the answer to 27-16, she barked eleven times and then bit me on the ankle. She pushed her little muzzle close to my face and snorted in disgust.

"Mrs. Hart lost patience with you," Esther announced with complete conviction.

I drew in a long deep breath and exhaled slowly. "I must be dreaming. It's impossible."

"And men with flaming eyeballs are on every street corner in town?" Esther turned up her nose. "Boy, you sure are slow."

"Well, excuse me for not recognizing a person put inside a dog. Hey…" I gaped at her. "How do you know what happened to Mrs. Hart?"

"I hear her. I got powerful good hearing. Then I found her eyes and saw she was in Honey Bun."

I scratched my head. "You don't make any kind of sense, Esther."

She stamped her foot in irritation. "I didn't say I made sense, Peter Whistler. I'm trying to explain what I can do. If I know someone and I concentrate, I can find my way to their eyes and see what they see. That's how I knew about the day in the park when you beaned Chauncey with the pie. I was in your eyes." Mrs. Hart barked and Esther giggled. "He deserved it, for sure." Esther must have sensed I didn't buy her nutty story because she blurted, "I've seen your hiding place in the cellar at Little Angels. It has an old mattress and comic books you swiped from the store."

"That place was private," I shouted in indignation. "You had no right to spy."

She stuck out her lower lip in a pout. "What's the big deal? I only peeked a few times when I was with the Grimaldis. They never talked to me except to yell or send me to my room."

"It just is, Esther," I sputtered. "You can't go around spying on people."

"Why not?" Clearly, Esther had a moral code even looser than mine.

"Cause you can't. Spying is not…" I fumbled for an argument. "Polite." Without thinking, I turned to Mrs. Hart. "Isn't that right?" Good God. I just requested moral support from a dog.

Mrs. Hart yipped and patted Esther with her paw. Her opinion must have mattered way more than mine because Esther said, "Okay. I won't unless you or Mrs. Hart says so."

With our ethical dilemma settled, I burned with curiosity. "Is that how you knew I hid in the bushes when Pike came to the store?"

"Uh-huh. I felt your eyes near."

"Felt them?"

"I've been to your eyes a bunch of times, so they're easy to find."

71

"You said a few," I squawked. "What else did you see?"

Esther crossed her heart. "I swear, nothing much. I was hardly home. The Grimaldis didn't like me, so I stayed at school, except when they had to get me for holidays." She scowled. "Being alone at school was better than their house. They said I was useless, and complained when they had to spend so much as a penny on me. They were chiselers, too, and cheated their customers. Not Mrs. Hart, though. They couldn't pull a fast one on her."

"She's too smart for that," I said. Was it my imagination or did the little terrier's eyes shine with thanks. "How did Pike get tangled with them?"

"They met at a speakeasy. He said maybe he could fix the blindness and offered to examine me for free. They figured if I wasn't blind, they could put me to work in the store, so said okay."

"Does he know you can see out of other eyes?"

"Nope. Only my parents knew. They said never to tell or people would take me away and sell me to a freak show. Cousin Nico sure would of. All Pike did was run a bunch of dumb tests. Afterward, he told them I was for sure blind. We didn't meet again until after the fire."

"What kind of tests?"

She scrunched her face. "Funny kinds. He made me walk through a room full of furniture to see how long it took me to figure where everything was. Pike got real excited when he found out I can memorize a path after one trip. Then he played tricks like spinning me around and pointing me to a staircase to see if I fell, but once I've been somewhere, I never

72

get lost. He tried to get me mixed up, but couldn't. I told the Grimaldis, but they didn't believe me. They never listened to a thing I said." Her voice dropped. "Pike scares me."

I scowled. "He's a dirty liar."

"He didn't fool you, though."

"I know a lie when I hear one."

Esther cocked her head as the little dog yipped. "Mrs. Hart says you freed her when she was trapped in a lie. How did you do it?"

"I-I'm not sure," I admitted uneasily. "I told her Pike was a liar, and then she believed me."

"Good thing." Esther shuddered. "I was so scared in the carriage house. I didn't know what Pike planned, so I peeked through Mrs. Hart's eyes. First, she was tall and then everything went black. When Mrs. Hart opened her eyes again, she was short and fuzzy. I heard her inside Honey Bun. She was real worried about you."

Her admission caught me short. "She was?"

Esther nodded. "She's sorry she brought you to the carriage house. She should have told you to run. She feels bad about that."

Mrs. Hart and I made momentary eye contact before we each turned away. Neither of us was ever comfortable handling emotions, so I changed the subject. "Esther, did you ever go inside Pike's eyes?"

"No." Her voice was so low I strained to hear. "H-he doesn't feel right like other people."

The train increased speed, swaying along the tracks with a mesmerizing beat. The rhythm soaked into my bones and dragged the tension away.

Esther yawned. Her thin shoulders drooped. "I'm tired, Peter."

"Yeah. Me, too. We better get some sleep."

At one end of the boxcar were the tattered remains of an old beat-up tarp. Esther and I lay down and I covered us up.

Esther pulled at my shirtsleeve. "Honey Bun's collar bothers Mrs. Hart. It's too small."

I released the buckle. The skin was red underneath. I pitched the leather strap in the corner. Mrs. Hart heaved a little doggie sigh of relief and curled next to Esther. I settled in on the other side. We were soon fast asleep.

A shrill whistle jerked me awake and I blinked. Where was I? After a blurry moment, memories rushed in. I was on a train with Esther and Mrs. Hart who was now a dog. I shook my head to clear the remnants of the sleep fog. I must have taken it on the lam from Little Angels last night and had a crazy dream. I lifted the tarp. Esther had one arm wrapped around Mrs. Hart.

Holy crud. Not a dream.

Mrs. Hart stretched. Esther opened a sleepy eye. "Peter, are you awake? Is it morning?"

I got to my feet and pushed open the sliding door a foot.

"More like afternoon. We must have traveled over half a day.

Esther felt her way to me. I steadied her against the rocking of the train and she inhaled deeply. "It smells different." The train rolled past piney woods. Warm air held none of the late spring chill of New Brunswick.

I squinted at the sun. "We hopped a southbound freight last night and must have kept heading that way."

Esther tugged on my sleeve. "I'm hungry and Mrs. Hart says she'd kill for a cup of coffee."

At the mention of food, my stomach rumbled. "Me, too." Beyond the door, the landscape barreled past. Getting off would be tricky. "Esther, once the train slows we have to jump."

"Okie dokie."

I eyed her askance. "Aren't you scared?"

"Nope. Mrs. Hart said you'll catch us both."

"Mrs. Hart has a lot of confidence in me."

"She sure does."

I gaped at Mrs. Hart in surprise, but as I didn't have expertise in reading dog faces, couldn't tell if she lied. We rode along for another hour or so and then Mrs. Hart's ears pricked up.

"She said the train sounds different," said Esther. "The engine is slowing."

The swaying rhythm took a downturn. Outside, the forested embankments gave way to roads and industrial buildings. The train approached a city.

"We're headed for the railyard," I said. "Get ready."

Exiting a train in broad daylight was a lot harder than sneaking on in the middle of the night. Bulls patrolled the yards, private security guards hired by the railroad to keep off hitchhikers. The men carried shotguns and billy clubs. If caught, a person faced outright death or being beaten senseless and thrown in jail. Alone, I wouldn't think twice about hopping aboard a moving boxcar, but toting along a blind girl and a small dog was no picnic.

The train lurched. The brakes squealed under applied pressure. Mrs. Hart pushed her nose outside and sniffed.

"Ears up, Mrs. Hart," I warned. "The bulls are everywhere." She tensed and uttered a low growl.

The brakes let loose a violent hiss of steam as the boxcar jerked to a halt. I cautiously rolled back the door. We were in the middle of a noisy yard surrounded by other trains. Voices shouted outside. Mrs. Hart cocked her head.

"She hears men coming this way," whispered Esther.

I dropped to a crouch and peered beneath the train. Several sets of feet were on the other side of the rails. One man stopped to tie his shoe and placed a shotgun on the ground, a security badge pinned to the lapel of his jacket.

I helped down Esther and Mrs. Hart. "Bulls—we have to hurry."

Without discussion, Mrs. Hart took point. I didn't think twice about her judgment. Mrs. Hart was always sensible and being a dog, she had a better chance of seeing, hearing, or smelling a threat first. We edged across the yard, freezing now and then when Mrs. Hart issued a growly warning.

A flurry of shouts erupted behind us. I didn't need Mrs. Hart to know we had to move. Taking Esther by the elbow, I dashed around the corner of a building and collided with a disheveled young man toting a rucksack. "Watch it," I yelled.

"Run," cried the hobo. "The bulls are right behind me."

I grabbed Esther and we bolted after the stranger. He turned right, but Mrs. Hart skewed left and Esther and I followed. Behind us came an order to halt. The hobo ran right into a bull toting a shotgun. Although, he raised his hands in surrender, the bull hit him with the rifle butt. The hobo dropped to his knees.

Mrs. Hart snarled and took off. I ordered Esther to stay put and ran after her. Mrs. Hart tore into the bull and chomped hard on his ankle. He bellowed a howling curse and lifted the rifle stock to bash Mrs. Hart on the head. I tackled his knees, and he hit the ground hard.

"This way," I shouted to the hobo.

He didn't need encouragement. With Mrs. Hart in the lead, we raced to Esther. The little dog darted around a building to a hole in a chain link fence. Mrs. Hart wiggled through. I followed and pulled Esther after me. The hobo came next.

"*Merci*, doggy." His voice carried a soft lilt. He reached to pat Mrs. Hart, but she growled and he snatched his hand away.

"She's not a dog," Esther tartly informed him. "She's Mrs. Hart." I shushed her, but she cheerfully rambled on. "Pike's glowing eyes put her inside Honey Bun. She doesn't like being touched unless you have her permission, 'cause she's a lady."

The young man must have been used to running into the mentally unbalanced on the road. His bright green eyes twinkled in amusement and he doffed his hat with a flourish. "I meant no disrespect. My apologies to Mrs. Hart—and thanks again." He shouldered his rucksack and sprinted off.

We skirted the fenced area and left the yard behind. Fifteen minutes of walking brought us to a business district. As we passed a newsstand, I spied the local paper. "Hey, we're in Atlanta."

"Where's that?"

"Georgia—the South."

"Oh. Where are we going, Peter?"

"To find something to eat."

I first thought to use my lying routine in one of the markets, but soon realized we needed more than a loaf of bread. Unless I scrounged traveling funds, the three of us were stuck here. I got an idea how to score a few bucks from the locals. I explained the plan to Esther and Mrs. Hart to gauge their reaction. Esther was enthusiastic. She seemed downright anxious to play fast and loose with the law. Mrs. Hart didn't bite my ankle, so I took that as approval.

A well-dressed older woman waited at a bus stop. I sauntered up escorting Esther by the elbow, and we pretended to wait for the bus. The woman noticed Esther's cane and flashed an oh-you-poor-child smile.

"Good afternoon, ma'am," I said politely.

"Good afternoon to you."

Esther tugged at my sleeve. "I want to show the lady my trick."

"Now, sister," I scolded, "the nice lady doesn't want to be bothered by your tricks."

"Please, please, please," she begged. "She'll like it. I'm sure positive. She'll like it so much she'll give me a quarter."

I pretended shock. "Sister, you can't ask people for money."

"I'm not asking. The quarter will be a gift."

By this time, the woman was amused. "What is your trick, young lady?"

Esther's blind eyes stared straight in front of her. "I can tell you how many fingers you hold up."

The woman shot me a piteous look, "Dear boy, she can't possibly…"

"Go on," Esther insisted. "Please, please, please."

Badgered into compliance by Esther's ceaseless nagging, the woman raised one finger.

"One."

"Good guess," she admitted, a little surprised.

"Do more," Esther ordered.

The woman raised four.

"Four," Esther stated with assurance.

The woman next raised three, five, two, and then in continued amazement used two hands to raise seven, ten and finally eight fingers. Esther nailed the correct answer every time. No surprise since she had a front row view through my eyes.

The woman gasped. "How does she do that?"

"Honestly," I admitted with absolute truth, "I have no idea."

"She liked my trick," said Esther with glee. She held out her hand. "Twenty-five cents, please."

I acted embarrassed when the woman good-naturedly placed a quarter in Esther's palm. I ordered her to say thank you, which she did ever so sweetly. The woman patted Esther on the head. "Very well done, my dear. You two are not from around here. The accents...?"

The lie dropped effortlessly off my tongue. "We're from Chicago, visiting Aunt Minnie. Come along, sister. You can buy yourself an ice cream." I took Esther's hand and led her away before the woman grilled us on the non-existent Minnie.

Over the next two hours we cleared $8.00, a fortune for two starving souls with an equally hungry dog. Esther would have kept going, but I couldn't stand the hollow feeling in my stomach a second longer. A man with a pushcart sold hot dogs and soda pop for a nickel apiece. We sat under a tree and I devoured seven hot dogs without slowing. Esther managed four. Mrs. Hart's smaller dog stomach, three.

I leaned against the trunk and sipped my soda pop. I'm not much given to deep philosophical thoughts, but pondered how everything took a turn for the better on a full stomach. Yesterday, I ran for my life. Today, Pike was far behind me. The sun shone bright and I filled with new optimism, now free to make my own rules and live life as I saw fit.

Next to me came a sigh of contentment, followed by a burp. Mrs. Hart nudged Esther's leg. For her, even being chased by an unthinkable evil was no reason for bad manners.

"Excuse me," Esther said.

"You're excused."

"That was a good trick, Peter."

"Thanks. You're a natural."

"I know." She giggled and then grew serious. "What do we do now?"

My optimism nose-dived into the ground. Alone, I had options. I could ride the rails and disappear into America. Plenty of teenagers did the same in these tough times, but what about Esther? I couldn't dump her in Atlanta, but life on the road was hard enough. Dragging a little blind girl around was downright impossible. Only by some miracle we made it this far. And Mrs. Hart? I discretely studied the little terrier stretched out in the shade. The reality of her situation hit me at once. The woman who took care of me all my life was a dog.

Mrs. Hart tilted her head as if she had complete understanding of my dilemma. I reckoned she did. Next to me, she was the best person I ever met at reading people.

Esther confirmed my suspicions. "Mrs. Hart says she's fine for the moment. She's not in pain. Actually, she feels better than before. Lotsa energy, no more aches and pains, probably on account of Honey Bun being a young dog."

"I'm glad because honestly, Esther, I've no idea how to change her back." I peered at Mrs. Hart, overcome with guilt. "I'm sorry. Maybe I should have tried to force Pike—" Mrs. Hart barked.

"She says no. We couldn't fight him. Running was our only choice. Anyhow, she doesn't mind. Being a dog is her punishment."

"For what?" Mrs. Hart nipped at my ankle. "Hey!"

Esther snickered. "She doesn't want to talk about it, so you better hush. She thinks we should keep moving and put more miles between us and Pike."

I jingled the coins in my pocket. "I've been thinking the same thing. Hopping a train again is risky. We have enough money now to catch a bus from Atlanta. I can check the schedule at the depot, but…"

"But what?"

I shifted in my seat. "They won't let a dog on the bus."

Esther tilted her head toward Mrs. Hart. She was silent for several seconds and then said, "Okay, if you're sure you don't mind." These one-sided conversations were mighty peculiar. "Mrs. Hart has an idea. We passed an Army-Navy store where you can buy an old rucksack. She's small and will hide inside so we can all get on the bus." The plan was sound. I left Esther and Mrs. Hart in the park to rest.

The Army-Navy store sold second-hand military equipment. I spotted an old canvas rucksack for fifty cents, big enough to hold Mrs. Hart comfortably. At the counter, my eyes zeroed in on a box of used penknives for ten cents apiece. My fingers itched with desire. I always wanted one and told myself since we were now on the run, a weapon was an absolute necessity. Never mind the blade was two inches long and couldn't cut cheese. I paid the shopkeeper and jammed the penknife in my pocket. Instantly, my shoulders squared. Peter Whistler, hard-boiled tough guy, armed and dangerous.

The storeowner pointed me in the direction of the bus depot. Once there, I studied the fares posted outside on a board. We had enough money for tickets to either Chattanooga or Birmingham. We'd pick one and then stay long enough in town to pull our little act again for more traveling funds. Then on to the next stop and then the next, eventually, reaching California. Even Pike couldn't track us that far.

The bus to Birmingham left at six that night, the one to Chattanooga an hour later. Before settling on a destination, I decided to talk the plan over with Esther and Mrs. Hart. My excitement grew with each step forward. We ran scared last night, but with Pike behind us, full stomachs, and the glimmering of a plan, the future brightened.

With one hand in my pocket, I ambled toward the park, happily fingering the penknife. Every now and then, I whipped it out to practice my quick draw. I was pretty good. I only dropped it twice.

Nearing the park, I passed a man leaning against a building reading a newspaper. He glanced up, stared intently in my direction, and then his gaze returned quickly to the newspaper. An uneasy feeling gripped me, so I upped the pace. Mrs. Hart and Esther were right where I left them. We sat in the shade of the tree to discuss our options, but I couldn't get the strange behavior of the man out of my head.

Esther tugged at my sleeve. "Mrs. Hart wants to know what's bothering you."

"Just the jitters," I said. "Maybe we should take the earliest bus." Mrs. Hart jumped to her feet.

"She says trust your instincts."

We headed for the depot. The departure time wasn't for several hours, but the need to get off the street without delay grew stronger with each passing second. I hurried them along.

"What is it, Peter?"

"It's nothing. Keep moving." No one seemed to pay attention to us, but the sensation of being followed stuck with me. I steered clear of the main roads and cut back and forth, running a zigzag path designed to bring us to the rear of the bus depot. From there, I planned to scout the area before boarding.

Approaching an alleyway, the squeal of an air brake shattered the quiet. I gulped. We had gone in the wrong direction and landed at the other end of the train yards. Before I turned us around, a police siren wailed down the block.

Across the street someone called, "Wait!"

I yanked Esther into the alley. My stomach lurched. I made another awful mistake. The alley dead-ended into a brick wall. As the siren closed in, I pushed Esther behind several empty cardboard boxes. Mrs. Hart huddled at our feet. Seconds later, footsteps approached and stopped in front of our hiding place. I slipped my hand into my pocket and clutched the pitifully small blade.

A man hoisted one of the empty boxes to his shoulder and retreated down the alley. Ever exchange puzzled glances with a dog? Mrs. Hart and I must have had the same thought. No way could he have missed us.

"You there."

A squad car pulled next to the man and an officer leaned his head out the window. "I'm hunting for two kids—a boy about fifteen with a little blind girl. Have you seen them?"

"What did they do? Skip school?"

His voice rang familiar. I fumbled to open the penknife, but to my horror, the blade snapped in half. I jammed the broken pieces in my pocket.

"The boy's a murderer who kidnapped the girl for ransom," said the cop. "Someone contacted the girl's guardian with a tip they were spotted in Atlanta. He's on his way here now."

I blanched. A few hours of freedom and we were already made. Next to me, Esther trembled.

"What is this world coming to?" responded the man carrying the carton. "Although now I recollect, a boy and a girl boarded the bus to Macon." To the untrained ear, his tone was shocked and earnest, but the lie screamed at me. As the squad car peeled away, the man shouted, "I hope you catch the little criminal." He pitched the box aside and strode directly to our hiding place. "Y'all are safe now. They're gone."

Before I stopped her, Esther stood. "I know your voice," she announced smartly. "You're the hobo from the railyard."

I recognized him now. He flashed a pearly white grin. "*C'est bon, mademoiselle.* My name's René Marchand, Renny to my friends, and folks who save my bacon from railyard bulls are definitely friends. We best get moving before the police catch up with the bus to Macon and realize Renny played them a good trick." He motioned to me. "I'll give you a boost first over the wall, then lift the girl and dog—" He bowed with a cheeky grin. "I mean, Mrs. Hart, to the other side. You help them over."

"Wait a minute." I gave him the eye. "Why should we trust you?"

"Is he lying, Peter?" said Esther. I had to admit he wasn't.

Renny reached into his jacket and retrieved a newspaper. He opened to an article on an inside page, and I sucked in my breath. We were made.

"What is it, Peter?"

"You may as well look, Esther."

I didn't feel a thing, but knew she now saw the same news story. Renny scratched his head as I held the paper so Mrs. Hart could read, too. The article concerned the hunt for a boy murderer. The story came complete with photographs of me, Esther, and Honey Bun, including a detailed description of our clothing. My photo was a class picture Chief Edwards must have gotten at the school. Mrs. Hart slicked my hair down that day despite my squawks that I looked like a sissy boy. In spite, I scowled at the camera. The photo made me out to be an undersized lunatic gangster, exactly the sort of person who torched buildings and kidnapped little girls. What chilled my blood, though, was the last sentence. Pike posted a ten thousand dollar reward for the capture of Peter Whistler dead or alive and the safe return of his ward, Esther Roth. Apparently, he didn't give a hoot about Mrs. Hart.

Renny crammed the paper in his pocket. "I overheard a police officer questioning people downtown about two kids and a dog. I've been searching for you ever since."

"We were headed to the bus depot," said Esther, "but Peter got lost."

"Dry up, Esther," I sputtered.

"The police are surely there by now," said Renny. The shrill toot of a train whistle cut through the air. "I'm hopping the express. Y'all are welcome to tag along."

I narrowed my eyes. "How do I know you won't lead us into a trap for the ten thousand dollar reward?"

"Don't be insulting. Marchands never betray friends."

The truth…I relaxed. "We'll go," I told the others. "He's not lying."

With a quizzical grin, Renny boosted me over the wall. After the four of us got to the other side, I insisted Mrs. Hart take point. Simply because Renny wasn't lying, didn't mean I trusted him completely. Her keen senses kept an eye out for both the bulls and our new companion. Renny must have been here before because he led us directly through a fence to the railyard assuring us bulls were few and trains slowed enough to board safely. We hid in the bushes to wait.

A rumbling roar signaled an approaching freight. Renny yelled, "It's the express."

We scurried from our hiding place and kept a jogging pace with an open boxcar. I had a momentary worry about getting Esther on board again, but Renny easily hoisted her into the opening. I passed off Mrs. Hart next and then Renny and I vaulted inside.

Chapter 5
Where Did You Find the Crazy Children?

Renny slid the door shut. Stacked against the rear of the car were several hay bales. I laid them flat to give Esther a place to sit.

"Well, isn't that nice, boy," said Renny. "You built a little fort for the young lady."

I gritted my teeth. Who did he think he was talking to? He wasn't much older than me—early twenties, maybe. He had no cause to come off so superior. I was a dognapping arsonist gangster and he was simply a hobo. "I don't need your approval. I'm not a kid, you know."

"I know." Renny casually examined his fingernails. "You're a dangerous wanted fugitive."

I put on my best tough guy face. "Well, I am."

No reaction.

"I'm armed." I whipped out the broken penknife.

Renny yawned. "Don't cut yourself."

"Hey—"

Esther jumped in. "Mrs. Hart says thank you for your help, Mr. Marchand."

"Renny," he corrected with a twinkle in his eye. "Traveling companions should always be on a first name basis."

"Okay. My name is Esther Roth. He's Peter Whistler."

"Who says you're a companion?" I scoffed. "We don't know you."

"Maybe I'm a fugitive, too."

"Mrs. Hart doesn't think so," said Esther, "and she's a mighty good judge of character. She wants to know your story. After that, if Mrs. Hart thinks you're a proper traveling companion, she'll let you stay. If not, you have to go as soon as the train slows enough to jump. Best believe, Peter can always spot a lie, so be truthful or Mrs. Hart will bite."

Renny shook his head. "You three are the damnedest group of hobos I've ever met."

Mrs. Hart growled. "No cussing," warned Esther. "Mrs. Hart is a lady and doesn't approve. We aren't hobos, either. We're…" She paused to tilt her head toward Mrs. Hart and then her expression lit up. "Oh, I like that. She says we're adventurers."

I folded my arms and scowled at him. "You better begin before Mrs. Hart loses her patience."

Renny threw up his hands in surrender. "Fine, but I have a feeling your story is a hell of a lot— *excusez moi*—much more interesting than mine. If I pass Mrs. Hart's approval, you must promise to tell me yours."

Esther nodded vigorously, but I grunted, "We'll think it over."

"All right, then." He settled comfortably against a hay bale. "I hail from New Orleans, though I haven't been home in several years."

"Run out of town?" I jeered.

"You do have a suspicious nature, *mon ami*. No, I left of my own accord."

Mrs. Hart yipped and Esther translated. "She said you had to go, not because you wanted to."

Renny gaped at her. "*Cher*, I can't wait to hear your story."

"Why did you leave?" I demanded.

Renny shifted position, obviously unsettled. "An expensive brooch belonging to my father's wife went missing and then reappeared in a shop off Canal Street. The owner said I sold it to him." Anger flared in his eyes. "I didn't."

Esther wrinkled her brow. "Your father's wife isn't your mother?"

"No." His jaw clenched. "My mother died several years ago. My father remarried. I refuse to call Delphine my stepmother."

"Why did they believe the store owner and not you?" I said.

Renny cleared his throat. "I'm not unknown to New Orleans' constabulary."

"You're a thief."

He dismissed me with a wave of a hand. "Such a tawdry word. My father had many wealthy friends who played poker badly. Occasionally, I heard a complaint when collecting the debt."

"And a card cheat."

"*Mon Dieu*. You sadly lack social graces, Peter. I'm happy to provide a few tips."

"I don't need—"

"Renny," said Esther, "Mrs. Hart would like to know why you left New Orleans instead of staying to clear your name."

"Delphine interceded with the police. The charges were dropped, but my father found out." Renny scowled. "He was furious. There's no talking to Jean-Baptiste Marchand when he's like that. We argued. He threw me out. We haven't spoken for two years, but, lately, I believe he may have a change of heart."

"Why?" she asked.

"My sister Amelie and I keep in touch. I write and tell her where I'm headed and she sends a letter to me in care of General Delivery at the post office. I found one waiting in Atlanta post-marked nearly two months ago. Amelie informed me Father had been preoccupied lately. When she asked what was on his mind, to her surprise he wondered where I was. Amelie encouraged him to write, but he refused and quickly changed the subject. However, she believed Father was softening and willing to speak to me again." Renny plucked a piece of straw from his hair and flicked it away in disgust. "I'm willing, too. You'd be surprised how quickly a carefree existence on the road loses its charm."

"You're headed home to see your family?" I asked.

"Mostly Amelie."

"And tell your father you're sorry?" My skepticism was obvious.

"If my father is willing to talk," Renny grumped, "then I'm willing to listen. He has to apologize first, though. I have nothing to be ashamed of. The man threw me out of the house on the say-so of a stranger."

Esther placed her hands on her hips. "Mrs. Hart says if you were a better son to begin with, your father would never have asked you to leave."

He narrowed his eyes. "For a cute little pooch, Mrs. Hart is rather harsh with her criticism."

"She says you have loose morals, a blatant disregard for the law, and are not as charming as you think."

"Don't be silly, of course I am."

"She also says being on the road forced you to grow up. You're not spoiled like you once were." Obviously confounded, Renny opened his mouth to say something, but Esther jumped in. "If Peter agrees you're not lying, you can stay."

Renny clasped his hands together in an imitation of prayer. "*S'il vous plaît, mon ami*. Take pity on a fellow traveler down on his luck. Save me from the harsh judgment of Mrs. Hart." He patted the newspaper in his pocket. "You of all people understand the pain of being falsely accused."

He had me there. "He's not lying."

"*Bon*. Everything is settled. I'll share your luxurious quarters for the next day. The train won't stop until we reach New Orleans. Now you must tell me your story. How did such a ruthless band of fugitives come to cross the path of Renny Marchand?"

"Tell him, Peter," Esther urged. "You're a good talker."

"He won't believe me. He might try to turn us in for the reward."

"Mrs. Hart doesn't think so and a deal is a deal."

I ceded the argument. If I didn't spill to Renny, Esther surely would. So I told him the whole story starting with Esther's remarkable sight and my gift for lying and ending with our escape from Pike.

When I finished, Renny cleared his throat. "You spun some fine tale."

I bristled. "You see, he doesn't believe us."

"We'll prove it, then," said Esther. Renny watched in amused silence as Mrs. Hart, Esther, and I argued back and forth as to the best method. Finally, Esther said Mrs. Hart suggested Renny try to lie to me. She reckoned he was good at it. He was, but he couldn't put one over. Next, Esther had Renny read a newspaper article silently. She followed along with his eyes repeating word for word. Convinced of a trick, his doubts wavered when he held the paper to Mrs. Hart. Her paw pointed to a word Esther nailed every time. They died completely after the terrier calculated a series of square roots. Renny muttered a startled curse. After a disapproving yip from Mrs. Hart, he quickly apologized for the impolite outburst.

"Y'all got a conjuror on your tail, for sure."

Esther scratched her head. "A what?"

"Conjuror, witchdoctor, traveler on the dark road—a very dangerous person."

"Why does he want me to open the door? What's inside?"

"That I cannot say, *mon petit*, other than I'm sure nothing good." He rubbed his chin. "Perhaps, I know

93

someone who can help. You need to speak with Odile, my old Cajun nurse. She's a shaman."

"What's a shaman?" I asked.

"A shaman travels the white road and knows the ways of healing magic. Odile's family goes way back to the very first shamans who found sanctuary in the bayou. Maybe she knows what's behind the door."

"A witch doctor worked for your father?"

"A shaman," he stressed. "It's no big thing. In New Orleans, all the best families hire one when a child is born. We live in a dangerous world and parents can't watch over a baby every minute of the day. Odile is one of the best."

I snorted. "She didn't keep you from becoming a thief."

Renny regarded me severely. "That was a choice—a bad one, granted, but not the result of black magic. Moreover, I'm reformed."

Esther broke in before I argued the point. "Where do we find her?"

"I'm not certain. Odile retired once my sister was school age, but my father knows how to reach her. He knows everyone. It seems I'll talk with Jean-Baptiste Marchand sooner than planned." Renny clapped me on the back. "Once I clear things with my father, I swear to help you find Odile."

Esther bubbled over with excitement. "I've always wanted to meet a shaman."

I sneered. "You never heard of one until today."

"It's not much different from wanting to meet a princess and I always wanted to meet one of those, too. So there, smarty-pants."

To my surprise, Mrs. Hart was for the plan, and then I remembered she was a dog. Perhaps, a shaman might have an idea or two on how to return her to normal. Funny how quickly Esther and I got used to Mrs. Hart being a dog. The peculiar situation didn't seem to bother Renny. Of course, considering how nonchalant he was about having a shaman nurse as part of the household staff, swapping bodies with an animal might be downright ordinary.

We settled in for the rest of the trip. Renny didn't grasp the concept of sit quietly and wallow in your own thoughts. He regaled us with stories of New Orleans, most of them involving him. Esther was enthralled. I tried not to pay attention except, every now and then, I felt compelled to interject a comment.

"That's a lie. You didn't steal a streetcar."

"Technically, no. I only borrowed it for an hour or two."

I gaped at him. "Why?"

"*Mon ami,* the streetcar was there, and Magnolia LeBlanc bet me a kiss I wouldn't."

"Mrs. Hart says a bet is a stupid reason to do anything," chirped Esther.

"Mrs. Hart is quite right, but…" He winked. "It was a very nice kiss."

We had no time to purchase food before leaving Atlanta, but once the sun set, Renny cheerfully shared what he brought with him. We dined on a can of Vienna sausages and a loaf of hard crusty bread he swore tasted like sawdust next to the baguettes available in New Orleans. I remarked the statement was a lie. He argued it was merely an exaggeration and, therefore, completely allowable under Mrs. Hart's rules.

Finally, I caught Esther stifling a yawn and insisted Renny shut his trap long enough for us to get some sleep. I wrapped my jacket around Esther and she curled next to Mrs. Hart. Renny made himself comfortable on a couple of hay bales and wished us *bonne nuit*.

"He's mighty full of himself," I noted to Mrs. Hart. "Are you sure going along with him is a good idea?"

"We have to," Esther whined. "I want to meet the princess."

"Shaman—not princess. What does Mrs. Hart think?"

"She doesn't know if Odile can help, but thinks we should try. She believes Renny is on the level, but agrees he is full of himself."

Renny propped up on one elbow. "I can hear every word. I'll have you know, I'm considered quite good company by the most cultivated ladies of New Orleans—and you can tell Mrs. Hart to mind her own business." He rolled over in a huff.

It was late morning when Renny roused us from sleep. By the sound and movement, the train had slowed considerably. "We're on the outskirts of the city," he said. "I know a safe place to jump."

I gathered our meager belongings. Renny pushed the door wide open, and a buffet of warm, moist air hit my face. Everything about New Orleans smelled different, earthy and damp with a faint undertone of decayed vegetation.

The brakes hissed. The train lurched and slowed to a crawl. Renny jumped first. I helped Esther to the edge of the boxcar and he lifted her to the ground. I tucked Mrs. Hart under my arm and followed right behind.

Renny threw back his head and breathed in a lungful of air. "Ah, I missed the smell."

Esther inhaled deeply. "I just smell train and Mrs. Hart." Always mindful of her appearance, Mrs. Hart appeared insulted.

"I'm afraid everyone can use a bath and a change of clothes, *mon petit*. Come, a streetcar stop is near. Once at my father's house, we can get cleaned up and a hot meal, including Mrs. Hart." Those words were the first out of his mouth that sounded pretty good to me.

An hour later, we stood on St. Charles Avenue across the street from the Marchand home. The white mansion was the swankiest house I'd ever seen. A wide front porch supported by massive wooden columns wrapped the entire front. The balcony off the second story mirrored the porch below. An inlaid brick walkway led to a mahogany front door flanked by shiny brass entrance lights. A meticulously landscaped garden flanked the house, enclosed by an ornate black wrought iron fence. The old carriage house was three times the size of the one at Little Angels. The building had been converted to a garage and a big black car was visible in an open bay. The driveway ran to St. Charles Avenue, and right inside the wrought iron gate was a guardhouse large enough for one man.

"Not bad," I muttered offhandedly.

Renny chuckled. "Don't let my father hear you so blasé. He is inordinately proud of the family homestead." His brow furrowed. "I see some changes; the guardhouse is new and the fence higher. I wonder why Father added them."

I eyed him askance. "Are you sure waltzing through the front door as if nothing ever happened is the way to get back into your father's good graces?"

"Humph. You're very astute. Father is not the most reasonable man. Perhaps, the best plan is to contact Amelie first, so we'll enter though the kitchen in the rear. You can wait there while I find my sister."

Renny boosted us over the fence and we dashed across the yard and through the kitchen door. A woman with her back to us bent over the stove stirring a cast iron pot. Spicy exotic odors filled the room, and my stomach growled in response.

She called out, "Well, it's about time you decided to eat, Amelie. I made your favorite. Ain't no good skipping meals. Lord knows, you need your strength for tonight."

"I'm not Amelie," said Renny.

The woman turned with a start, dropping the spoon to the floor with a clatter. She clasped her heart and I thought for a moment she'd faint. "Renny," she said in a choked voice.

He greeted her with a bear hug. "I'm sorry, Ruby. I didn't mean to frighten you."

"You gave me quite a start, boy, that's for sure." She dabbed at the corner of her eyes with her apron, clearly moved, and then examined him at arm's length. "You're a mite thin, and those rags you wear would have caused your poor mama no end of distress, bless her soul, but otherwise you'll do. After the first year, Amelie and I were afraid you'd never return. As it is…" She glanced toward a rear staircase. "Does Delphine know you're here?"

"No one knows, Ruby, except you."

"Best keep your homecoming a secret for now." Ruby's gaze went from Renny to us. "Well, I declare, who all is this? Y'all look like you were dragged behind a train."

"You're not far from the truth." Renny made introductions. Esther commented something sure smelled good. Ruby pounced on the words and hustled us to the large wooden table in the center of the room while berating Renny for letting us starve in her kitchen.

"Ruby, I must talk to Amelie."

"She's in her room. You sit first and have something to eat. I'll tell her you arrived."

"Maybe I should—"

"No, Renny." She barked at him in a no-nonsense tone with no allowance for argument. "I'll fetch her. If I take the rear staircase, no one will notice me. Life has changed here since you left."

Renny raised an eyebrow. "What do you mean?"

Ruby bit her lip. "You best talk to Amelie. Now sit. No one's going anywhere until y'all get fed." Ruby bustled about the stove, doling heaping ladles of the spicy-scented mixture into china bowls filled with fluffy white rice. Then she cut huge slabs of bread and laid them out with a brick of butter and big glasses of sweet iced tea. She offered a hambone to Mrs. Hart nearly the size of the dog's head. Not the most dignified meal, but Mrs. Hart accepted with a grateful woof.

I sniffed a spoonful of stew. It didn't look or smell like anything I'd ever eaten in New Jersey. I tried a bite. A patchwork of flavors danced in my mouth, and a salty, briny tang spread unnatural heat to the back of my throat; not exactly pain, but a wicked sort of pleasure. This couldn't be food. I must be eating a secret potion the kitchen gods wanted kept for themselves. I couldn't shovel it in fast enough.

Esther heaved a blissful sigh. "This is the most delicious thing I ever had." Between slurps, I added a heartfelt amen.

"Ruby makes the best gumbo in New Orleans," Renny bragged.

Ruby beamed. She wiped her hands on the apron, untied the strings, and hung it on a peg. "Eat hearty and I'll fetch Amelie. Renny, I may be a while. I need to wait until she's alone."

I was so busy chasing the remains of the gumbo around my bowl with a spoon, I hardly noticed she exited through the narrow back staircase. We polished off the contents of our bowls, the entire loaf of bread, and most of an apple pie Renny discovered in the pantry before soft footfalls descended the stairs. A girl my age entered the kitchen. She had piercing green eyes like Renny and long dark wavy hair that cascaded in loose curls down her back. She would have been a real dish if her expression didn't look as if she was about to spit out a mouthful of nails.

Renny didn't appear to notice. His eyes lit up and he jumped to his feet. "Amelie!"

The girl stormed over and slugged him in the jaw. Renny staggered back. I was impressed. She was at least a foot shorter than Renny and packed a roundhouse punch that would have done a middleweight boxer proud.

Renny rubbed his chin. "What was that for?"

"How dare you?" Amelie stamped her foot. "You disappear for two years and then parade in here as if nothing happened. You ran and left me alone, Renny. You should have stayed and made Father believe you. You have no idea what life has been like."

Renny's gaze softened. He opened his arms wide. "I'm sorry for everything, Amelie. Forgive me. I beg you."

The fire in her eyes dulled to an ember. She threw herself into his embrace. "I missed you."

"I missed you, too, *cher*."

"When you didn't answer my last letter, I thought…" Amelie buried her head in his shoulder. "Why did you take so long to come home? Where were you?"

Renny gently kissed the top of the head. "Here and there. I was delayed getting to Atlanta, but left for New Orleans as soon as I read your letter. I'm home now and see…" He gestured toward us. "I brought friends."

So intent on her brother, Amelie didn't acknowledge our presence until now. Her eyes played over us in a second. Apparently, she didn't like what she saw. "They're filthy."

"Yup," Esther crowed. "We left in a hurry 'cause we're on the lam from Pike's flaming eyeballs, and Mrs. Hart is a lady so she doesn't lick herself clean."

Amelie blinked. "Renny, where did you find the crazy children?"

"We're not crazy," I snarled, "and we're not children—well, Esther is, but I'm as old as you."

"Mrs. Hart isn't crazy, either," insisted Esther. "She's a lady inside a dog. The conjuror put her there." I hissed at Esther to keep quiet. She wasn't helping the we're-not-crazy argument.

Instead of scoffing, Amelie immediately demanded of Renny, "What's this about a conjuror?"

"It's a long story, *cher.* Trust me when I say they're perfectly sane. They saved me from a beating by the railway bulls in Atlanta, and I'm returning the favor."

Amelie's stern look softened. "In that case, I apologize, but I'm afraid, you couldn't have brought them at a worse time."

"But why? Even if Father won't forgive me, surely he understands the necessity to repay an honor debt. He won't turn them away—"

"Father's dead, Renny." Her voice choked.

He paled and sunk into a kitchen chair. "When?"

"Right after I sent the letter. The doctor said he suffered a heart attack."

"His heart was strong."

A dark emotion flitted across her face. "So, it appeared."

"What happened?"

"When he didn't show for breakfast, I went to wake him." She blinked away tears. "Father struggled to breathe. He tried to tell me something, but the pain made speaking difficult. I sent for the doctor, but it was too late."

"Where was Delphine?"

Amelie's jaw set in a hard line. "Conveniently away."

"I'm so sorry, Amelie. I should have been here so you didn't have to go through this alone." Grief tinged his voice, and he had a stricken look on his face. "I-I can't believe he's gone. I'll never have a chance to say I'm sorry. He must have hated me."

Amelie rested a hand on his shoulder. "Father didn't hate you, Renny. I know he was ready to grant forgiveness. He spoke of you the day before he died, wondering where you were and if you were well. Delphine also noticed. She came to me that night and wanted to know if she should prepare your room."

His voice hardened. "What did you tell our dear stepmother?"

"Stepmother." Amelie spit out the word. "I tell that hell-born serpent nothing."

Mrs. Hart yelped a warning and Renny's lips twitched in a faint smile. "Best mind your manners, young lady. Mrs. Hart doesn't approve of rough language."

"Please, Renny, no more of your jokes."

"It's no joke, *cher*." He told the story of our meeting and showed her the Atlanta newspaper. As Amelie read the article, her eyes widened. I squared my shoulders, trying my best to look like the desperate hatchet man in the picture. I expected to see a flicker of concern in her cool demeanor. At the very least, a little awe. After all, she now harbored a dangerous criminal. Instead, Amelie let out a derisive snort.

"How can the authorities be so stupid? Who is this Chauncey Edwards the reporter quotes? 'Peter Whistler had the eyes of a killer.' What nonsense. Look at the picture of the boy. Admittedly, he appears constipated, but certainly not psychotic."

"I told you," I sputtered, "I'm not a boy—and I wasn't constipated. How would you know what a psychotic killer is like? You ever meet one?"

In response, Amelie lifted the hem of her dress and pulled a razor sharp blade from a leather sheath strapped above her knee. "No, but I would certainly know what to do if I did." My penknife was a toothpick by comparison.

Renny patted her cheek. "No need for a weapon, Amelie. We're friends here. Esther, show my sister what you can do."

Amelie returned the dagger to the sheath. Esther read the paper through my eyes, and cheerfully agreed the picture made me look constipated. I grabbed the paper and stuffed it in the rucksack. Renny placed one of Ruby's cookbooks in front of Mrs. Hart and Esther read a recipe for lemon icebox pie word for word. By now, our impromptu routine was rock solid. Seriously, Esther, Mrs. Hart, and I could have developed a dynamite vaudeville stage act and hit the theater circuit.

It didn't take long to convince Amelie of the truth. She declined to personally test my ability to recognize a lie, noting if Renny couldn't lie to me that was good enough. Having her brother's support was a plus. Renny was a bit of a rogue, but brother and sister clearly respected each other's opinion.

"Pike is a conjuror, no doubt," said Amelie.

"I'm sure Odile can help. Do you know where she is?"

"She moved somewhere in Terrebonne Parish to be near her son and his family. They have no telephone lines so far into the swamp, but Father and Odile exchanged letters. The address should be in his book in the study. Getting inside is a problem. Delphine keeps the room locked."

Renny scowled. "She has no right."

"She has every right. The house is hers, now. Father left Delphine in charge of everything."

He gasped. "Please tell me that's a joke."

"Unfortunately, not. His will named her as my legal guardian. She has control of Father's assets and full charge of running the household. I don't inherit the estate until I turn eighteen."

"If any money remains," he snarled.

"There will be. As guardian, Delphine must produce a report each month to the bank trustees of her expenditures. I'm entitled to a copy. She objects, but rest assured I insist she account for every penny."

"I accept Father was angry and cut me off entirely, but how can he have been so blind as to give Delphine control of everything?"

"Renny, the original will named you as guardian, but she was here and you were not." Amelie's tone dripped contempt. "Father was besotted with her since the day they met."

"You shouldn't pay for my sins."

"Keep your voice down," she hissed. "Delphine dismissed servants loyal to Father and me, and staffed the house with her own people. They are armed. Not obviously, but I can tell. You saw the new gatehouse? Guards patrol the grounds at night. Delphine says the added security is for our protection, but from the looks of her people, they have more experience breaking into a household rather than running one. The only trustworthy person left is Ruby. Delphine isn't stupid enough to get rid of the best cook in New Orleans—not with her social aspirations."

Renny took her hand. "*Cher,* you can't stay here. I'll convince the trustees to put pressure on Delphine to send you to boarding school. You don't have to live under her thumb."

"No." The response was short, but emphatic. "I won't run. This is my house—our house, Renny. It will be again someday. The instant I turn eighteen, I'll show Delphine the door. Until that time, I intend to stay put and keep watch."

"I don't trust Delphine."

"Me neither." She patted her blade. "I can take care of myself. I've had to, you know, for some time."

Renny sighed. "You have Mother's stubbornness. Very well, but understand I won't leave New Orleans again. Even if I'm not welcome in this house, I'll always be nearby should you need assistance or a shoulder to cry on."

"That, too, I haven't done for some time." Amelie glanced at the staircase. "No one except Ruby and I know you're here. I forbid Delphine's servants near my room, and they never go in yours, so everyone can hide there. Delphine is hosting a soiree this evening." Amelie curled her lips in disdain. "Apparently, a mourning period of a few weeks is long enough to grieve the death of a husband. The guests will be preoccupied in the dining room. If you can get the door to Father's study open, and find the address book, tomorrow morning Ruby and I will help everyone leave through the kitchen before the rest of the staff wakes."

Renny nonchalantly rubbed his thumb against his fingertips. "Unlocking the door will pose no concern."

"The plan is settled then. Come upstairs. Each one of you is in desperate need of a bath. Renny has old clothing to fit the boy—"

"Quit calling me, boy. My name is Peter, and you don't smell so hot yourself."

"I'll find something for Esther—and I smell wonderfully."

She did, actually. Kind of like the lilacs in Mrs. Hart's garden, but I wasn't going to admit it. Amelie led us quietly up the staircase to the second floor where Ruby waited.

"The coast is clear," the cook whispered. "If you need me, Amelie, I'll be in the kitchen spitting in Delphine's teacup."

Amelie ushered us to the end of the hallway. Renny and I ducked into the corner room overlooking the front of the house. The girls slipped into the one next door.

The room had a big mahogany four-poster bed smack dab in the center, surrounded by fancy oriental chests and bureaus. The furniture was polished to such a high degree my face reflected in the wood. Renny motioned to a door. "The bathroom is through there. Clean up while I find something for you to wear."

He had his own bathroom? Nobody I knew had more than one bathroom in an entire house. The room had a porcelain sink sporting solid brass fixtures and a huge claw foot tub with a shower attachment. I peeled off my dirty clothes, took a hot shower, and then wrapped myself in a big fluffy towel. I tucked my dirty things into the rucksack and crammed everything under the bed.

Renny handed me the old clothes and went to shower and change. Old clothes…funny term to describe the nicest outfit I ever wore. I donned a white silk shirt and a lightweight linen suit. He even found a pair of barely used leather shoes. I fingered a tie, not quite certain what to do with it.

Renny exited the bathroom, the cut of his suit obviously tailored to him. Clean-shaven, with not a dark wavy hair out of place, no remnant of the hobo on the train remained. He scrutinized me up and down. "Well, Father was right. Clothes certainly do make the man." Renny secured the tie around my neck in what he called a Windsor knot. I felt awkward, but at the same time grownup. "You are no longer a gangster and have become a charming young man of society."

"You mean I don't look constipated."

"Don't mind Amelie. For a young lady of means, she can be sadly lacking in social graces, and has had much on her mind lately."

"Like your stepmother?"

"Exactly, I—" A car honked outside. Renny parted the drawn curtains a crack. "Well, speak of the she-devil…"

The sun had set since we arrived. A shiny Packard pulled through the gates leading a caravan of cars past the gaslights lining the driveway. A uniformed chauffeur sat in the front seat. Before she-devil Delphine became visible, the Packard drove under the balcony, blocking my view.

Renny cracked open the door. The chatter of laughing voices wafted from the foyer below. Another door closed and the house was quiet again. "They're in the parlor. The party has already started for Delphine and her guests."

His bitterness was plain. Feelings about Delphine ran deeper than mere dislike. "What bugs you so much about her?"

"Other than the fact she considers no one except herself?"

"Your father didn't think so."

"Father was a fool."

"That's a lie." The words shot from my mouth before I called them back.

Renny grinned wryly. "I forgot to whom I spoke. No, Father wasn't a fool. He was both smart and sensible, but even the most reasonable man can be deceived by a beautiful face and charming demeanor."

The door to Amelie's room opened. She peeked out and motioned us over. First, Renny grabbed a small leather case from a dresser drawer.

I raised an eyebrow. "That's not a manicure set."

He flashed a cheeky grin and tucked the lock pick kit into a pocket. "Like a good Boy Scout, Renny Marchand is always prepared."

Amelie's bedroom was the same size as Renny's, but everything about the decor from the white lace curtains to the floral wallpaper to the quilted silk coverlet on the bed screamed Girls Only—Boys Will Be Stabbed To Death On Sight With My Pointy Knife. I nervously adjusted my necktie.

Esther perched on a divan, seemingly right at home. She was scrubbed clean, her plain cotton frock swapped for a pink taffeta dress with matching shoes. A bow decorated her hair. Renny complemented her on the outfit.

"Yeah," I added, "you look swell, Esther. I never saw you so done up."

Esther jumped off the divan and gave a twirl. "Isn't it bee-yoo-ti-ful? It's the softest thing I ever wore. Amelie wanted to put a bow on Mrs. Hart, too, but Mrs. Hart said pink wasn't her color."

With a twinkle in her eye, Amelie whispered to me, "Today is the first time I ever received fashion advice from a dog."

Esther tweaked my sleeve. "The jacket feels nice, too. Mrs. Hart says you are every inch the gentleman." She cocked her head. The action conveyed to me she shared the little dog's eyes. "She's right."

I tugged at my collar. "Thanks. Wearing a tie is strange, though. I'm not used to having anything around my neck. Now I understand how Mrs. Hart felt about the dog collar."

Amelie examined me with a critical eye. "Nevertheless, your appearance is much improved. Very respectable."

Her green eyes lit with approval and my cheeks warmed. I cleared my throat. "What's the plan?"

"Once Delphine and her guests are in the dining room, Renny will slip into the study. The address book used to be on the desk, but Delphine moved everything around after Father died." She gasped. "I hope she didn't throw it away." Mrs. Hart and I exchanged worried glances.

"She didn't," Renny insisted. "Father knew many important people. Delphine will want to keep the names and addresses. You know what a social climber she is."

Mrs. Hart had been intently focused on the discussion, but with a yip, she hopped off the divan and scampered across the room. One paw scratched at the door.

Heat rose to my cheeks. "Um…does she have to…you know…go?"

Esther giggled. "No. Mrs. Hart already used the bathroom. She says she'll listen at the foot of the stairs and let us know when they move to the dining room." I quickly erased the mental image of Honey Bun squatting on the toilet and opened the door to let her outside.

"Now we wait." Amelie folded her arms and dropped onto the divan. "I hate waiting."

"I don't mind," said Esther. She sat next to Amelie and smoothed down her dress. "You hear the best things when you're waiting. People think if you're blind, you're also stupid, so they stick you in a corner and forget you're there. I overheard lots at the Grimaldis." She drew herself up proudly. "That's where I found out Mrs. Hart bumped off her husband."

Chapter 6
Flight to Terrebonne Parish

I gawked at Esther. "She did what?"

Renny perched on the bed, an eager light in his eyes. "Do tell."

Amelie shook a finger at us both. "You shouldn't encourage the child to repeat gossip."

"Nonsense," Renny insisted. "This is biography—completely different. Go on, *cher*."

Esther cleared her throat. "Mrs. Hart married real young, but her husband was a bad'un. He came home drunk and mean. He threw things at Mrs. Hart and called her awful names and such."

"Wait a minute," I blurted out. "I can't picture her stomaching such behavior." The woman I knew was a stern self-sufficient taskmaster who climbed over any mug foolish enough to utter one profane word in her presence. Why, she even stood up to Chauncey and the rest of the Edwards. "If he was so bad, why didn't she leave?"

"You know so little of a woman's lot," Amelie chided. "How would she support herself? Few positions are available for a woman with little education. One who leaves her husband, even someone as despicable as Mr. Hart, isn't treated kindly. No one would hire her. A divorce is very expensive and she had to prove abandonment or cruelty. He didn't abandon her and what is cruelty to a powerless young woman is not to an unsympathetic judge."

"Get back to the story," Renny urged.

"Mrs. Hart was going to have a baby."

My jaw dropped. "Now I know the story isn't on the square. She never had kids of her own. She didn't want them."

"Yes, she did," Esther insisted. "She's always liked kids, but didn't show her feelings on account of what happened. When she found out she was going to have a baby, she left her husband. He tried to force her to return, but she wouldn't go. They fought and he pushed her down a staircase and she lost the baby."

"How awful," gasped Amelie. I felt sick myself.

"What a monster," muttered Renny with cold ferocity. "I wish I had the opportunity to meet Mr. Hart."

"She left the hospital," continued Esther. "No one knows exactly what happened, but he disappeared and they didn't find a body. That's how come Mrs. Hart was never arrested."

"How do they know she killed him?" I demanded.

"Everyone thought so. No one ever saw him again, and Mrs. Hart never hid after that like she knew he wasn't coming back. She cleaned out his bank account and started Little Angels Home for Orphan Boys."

"That's why Chauncey seemed afraid of her," I murmured. "She said weak-minded people believe everything they hear."

"Such a sad story." Amelie's expression softened with pity and her voice dropped to a whisper. "And to have lost a child, too."

"It's very sad," Esther agreed. "Mrs. Hart didn't want to think about the past, so she decided to help other couples find children."

I startled. "That's not why. She started the orphanage to earn money."

"Nope. Mrs. Hart wanted to make happy families. She told stories about each orphan so couples would think their baby was a gift from heaven delivered special for them. She figured then the children would always be loved. They were, too. Some of the families shopped at the Grimaldi's store." She sighed deeply. "I was always jealous of the way they treated their kids."

My eyebrows shot up. "The Grimaldis didn't spill that."

"No, they figured like you. The orphanage was a way for her to make a living." Esther reached out for me and I took her hand. "Mrs. Hart and I talked a long time in the park in Atlanta. She cares about you Peter."

"She never said—"

"Mrs. Hart didn't put you for adoption because as soon as she held you at the hospital she wanted you to be hers. Single women couldn't adopt, though, and she was afraid to get close on account of her baby. She kept you at Little Angels and her plan was for you to leave New Brunswick and make something of yourself. Mrs. Hart figured if she hid how much she cared, the pain wouldn't be so bad when you left. She felt awful when the adoptions stopped and she had to spend the five hundred dollars she saved."

The truth landed with an agonizing bang. New Jersey never had a program to give orphans five hundred dollars the day they turned eighteen. The money belonged to Mrs. Hart, but when the Depression hit, she had to use her savings for us to live on. Pike offered her a way to get the money again.

She was in the carriage house because of me. She got turned into a dog because of me. Everything that happened to her was my fault.

Esther leaned her head against my shoulder. "Mrs. Hart doesn't feel bad inside Honey Bun, because getting turned into a dog is her punishment for not being nicer to you. She's sorry she never let you have a real family."

No knife could have ripped my insides worse than hearing the truth. "S-she was plenty nice," I stammered. "I-I mean, not lovey-dovey, but neither one of us is like that. Life was swell. I had three squares a day and a roof over my head. She kept me on the straight and narrow..." I swallowed back the tightness in my throat.

"Mrs. Hart knew about the cellar, Peter," said Esther. "She never told you because all kids need a safe place to call their own."

Mrs. Hart had struggled to give me that safe place and the freedom to explore and find my own way. Maybe we weren't a typical family, but life could have been a lot worse. I could have lived on the streets and become the heartless gangster I played at, or turned into spoiled, coddled, no-account Chauncey—as useless a human being as ever lived. How did I repay her? All I ever thought about was leaving New Brunswick and Little Angels behind.

I stood up and clenched my fists. "I have to help Mrs. Hart."

Renny rose to his feet and clapped me on the shoulder. Both his expression and Amelie's held nothing but stony resolve. "Don't worry, *mon ami*. We will."

Dog nails scratched on the door. "Pipe down," I whispered. "Mrs. Hart won't like us talking about her."

I opened the door and Mrs. Hart trotted to Esther. "She says they went to the dining room."

Renny patted the pocket with the lock picks. "I'll return in a flash."

He slipped from the room. Minute after minute ticked by. I jumped at a sudden crack of thunder. A storm moved in and a heavy downpour pelted the roof.

Amelie tapped her foot in irritation. "This is his idea of a flash? What's keeping Renny? He left over an hour ago."

"Maybe the lock gave him trouble," I said.

"Hah, not my brother. By the time Renny was fourteen, he had a nice side business with the coeds at Newcomb College. After curfew, the housemother locked the dorm. Any girl arriving late had to wake her to get in. As punishment, she was fined and restricted to the building at night for two weeks. Instead, they called Renny. His rates were much less than the fine and no restriction. There's not a door in New Orleans barred to him."

"Mrs. Hart is worried," piped up Esther. "She says she should help."

Amelie stood. "I'll go, too."

"Me, too. Me, too," insisted Esther.

"We'll all go." I waved off Amelie's protest. "Esther won't quit bugging us and the more searchers, the quicker we'll find the address book." With Mrs. Hart's keen eyesight and hearing in the lead, we descended the main staircase.

The party in the dining room was in full swing. Even with the door closed, the sound of raucous laughter drifted out to the hall. Amelie shot a furious glare at the door as we snuck by. Her bitterness toward her stepmother was obvious. Couldn't say I blamed her. Delphine didn't act like a widow consumed with grief.

Bookcases and file cabinets dominated the study. A large sideboard stood against one wall. Fancy crystal decanters full of brownish liquids rested on top. Renny was nowhere to be seen.

"Where is he?" Amelie whispered.

One of the long velvet curtains fluttered and Renny stepped out. "You gave me a start, *cher*. What are you doing here?"

"You're taking too long."

"It's not my fault," he protested. "I opened every locked drawer in the room. Wouldn't you know, the book was in the last one? Letters to Odile are sent in care of Purdy's General Store, Cypress Road, Houma."

"Do you know where that is?" I asked.

"Houma is in Terrebonne Parish. I've never been to Cypress Road, but am sure I can find it."

Amelie motioned to the door. "Let's go before we're discovered."

"Not yet. Look what else I found." Half-hidden by the curtain was a small decorative end table with a narrow drawer on top and a bigger one on the bottom.

"That didn't belong to Father," said Amelie.

Renny reached to the back. I heard a faint *snick* as the catch released and then the front of both drawers swung open from a hidden side hinge. The false panel concealed a safe. "Aren't you dying to know what Delphine is protecting?"

Amelie sucked in her breath. "Can you break in?"

Renny ran his fingers lightly over the dial. "If I hear the tumblers, but need special equipment."

"Mrs. Hart said she can help," Esther said. "Her ears are real sharp."

The little dog trotted over and sat waiting patiently for instructions. If Renny was taken aback by having an enchanted terrier as a partner in crime, he recovered quickly. I began to suspect nothing much fazed the Marchand siblings for long. Renny quickly cobbled together a system by which Mrs. Hart concentrated on the sound of the tumblers. When they fell into place, she rested a paw on Renny's knee.

They worked with agonizing slowness. Mrs. Hart's head cocked to one side with her paw raised. Renny's sensitive fingers slowly twisted the dial.

Tick…tick…tick…tap

Mrs. Hart patted Renny's knee. The first tumbler fell in place. I didn't realize I held my breath until the air blew out in a rush. Amelie did the same. The last number triggered the satisfying metallic clink when locking pins engaged. Renny grabbed the handle and yanked open the door.

We crowded around. The safe had two shelves. On the bottom rested boxes filled with glass vials. On the top was a small journal bound in faded leather. As Renny reached in, Mrs. Hart yipped a warning.

"Someone's coming," hissed Esther.

Renny rammed the book in his pocket. He shut the safe, twirled the knob, and closed the secret compartment. With no place to hide, we froze in the center of the room as the door opened. A laughing young woman entered leading a group of well-dressed partygoers. She halted in mid-stride. "What's going on here?"

Amelie stepped forward. "Renny is home, Delphine. Isn't that wonderful?"

Delphine? I had another vision in mind for the evil stepmother—someone with a hooked nose and beady eyes, smelling like Mrs. Hart's compost heap. Delphine was the most beautiful woman I'd ever seen, no older than Renny. Glistening golden blonde hair piled high on her head, the better to set off the silky perfection of her skin. How could someone so beautiful be bad? Amelie and Renny must be mistaken.

Delphine's face lit with pleasure. "Renny," she purred in a deep melodic voice. "Welcome home. I'm so happy to see you again."

The lie slapped me in the face. Delphine Marchand oozed a dark aura, and the last person she wanted to see was her stepson. Her voice dripped poisonous venom, the same as Pike. I bit my lip to keep from shouting a warning to her guests. *Run! A monster hides under those ruffles and lace.*

A hint of suspicion entered Delphine's eyes. "What are you doing in the study? I swear I locked the door."

Renny flashed a charming smile, not a flicker of guilt marked his expression. "Apparently not, as the door was open. I had no wish to intrude on your party and decided to wait until dinner ended to announce my arrival."

Her glistening blue eyes took us in. "Who are your friends, Amelie? I didn't hear them arrive."

Amelie hesitated. She didn't have a lie ready, but fortunately I always did. "Mr. Marchand hired us as entertainment for the party."

"Entertainment? How delightful." Her tone held an undercurrent of skepticism.

A woman who tells lies isn't easy to convince, but Renny forged ahead without concern. Once a lie started, he needed no instruction on how to keep the ball rolling. "I phoned Amelie this morning and told her I planned to arrive tonight. She mentioned your party, so I couldn't come empty-handed. That's impolite."

"You were always so thoughtful, Renny. To think, I came in here for a bottle of brandy, but now we also have entertainment to go with our drinks." Delphine chose a decanter off the sideboard, the very picture of an attentive hostess. "Shall we go to the parlor? I can't wait to see what you brought for us."

"Neither can I," whispered Amelie in my ear.

I led Esther from the study, striving to settle my nerves. If Delphine didn't buy our act, she'd demand to know our real business here. We entered the parlor, and Esther and I stood in front of the fireplace. Mrs. Hart sat attentively in an out of the way corner. I couldn't help but notice the butler beside the door ready to do Delphine's bidding. He was tall and stocky, more prizefighter than manservant. He also had a suspicious bulge under one arm in the exact position of a shoulder holster. The mug was definitely packing heat. His eyes narrowed and he scrutinized my face long enough for me to squirm.

"What sort of act do you do?" purred Delphine.

"An amazing act," I announced with a flourish. "An astounding feat of mental command never before witnessed in the Western world."

Smiles appeared on the faces of the guests. The lie clicked in and they believed, everyone except Delphine. She remained coolly unimpressed.

"I am Martin the Magnificent. I will send my thoughts through the air allowing my blind sister to read through my eyes. Ready, Agnes?" Esther wrinkled her nose. I jumped in before she protested she didn't like the name Agnes and could she please be known as something prettier like Princess Starlight Pixie Dust.

"Does anyone have any printed material?"

Enthusiastic hands shot up. I traveled the room and Esther did her act, reading business cards and serial numbers off dollar bills. Everyone was awed except Delphine. Oh, she mouthed the right words and acted impressed, but the muscles in her jaw contracted, tightening her smile. She didn't trust Renny's hospitable gesture one whit and her failure to determine our real intentions plainly drove her nuts.

Esther and I finished with an enthusiastic round of applause from the audience. If not for the dirty looks Delphine's servant shot me, I would have enjoyed myself. I even received an offer from an elderly woman to perform at her grandson's birthday party. I took her name and politely said my booking agent would be in touch.

Outside, the storm continued. In a respectful tone, Renny asked to borrow the car to drive us home and save poor Agnes a long wait in the rain for the streetcar. With her guests' eyes upon her, Delphine agreed to the splendid idea. She ordered the servant lurking in the corner to summon the chauffeur.

I stifled a cry of relief. We had an escape tonight. The sooner I put distance between me and this house, the better I'd feel.

Delphine excused herself from the guests to escort us to the porch. The Packard pulled up in front. The chauffeur got out to open the passenger door for Esther, Mrs. Hart, and me.

"A driver isn't necessary," Renny protested. "I can take them."

"Nonsense," said Delphine. "What is the point of having servants if they're not put to use?" She tugged at his arm. "Come inside to the party. I want to hear everything you've been up to."

That didn't bode well for Renny. Fortunately, he hopped inside the Packard with us, slammed the door shut, and then rolled down the window. "Won't be but a moment," he called with a jaunty wave. "I'll see them safely home."

Delphine pursed her lips in irritation. "Very well. The guard will let you out."

"Is the extra security really necessary?" he asked mildly.

"Renny, the added safety measures are for Amelie's sake, not mine." The lie screamed so loudly, I wondered why no one else noticed. "She's my responsibility, now," Delphine continued, "and I have an obligation to protect her. I know we had difficulties in the past, but trust me when I say, I'd never forgive myself if harm came to your sister."

Her tone dripped with warmth and concern, but I knew at that instant Delphine wanted nothing more than to see Amelie lying dead at her feet. A low growl issued from the seat next to me.

"Peter," whispered Esther, "Mrs. Hart doesn't trust her."

"Neither do I."

The chauffeur slid open the glass partition separating the driver and passenger compartment. "Where to?"

"Canal Street," answered Renny. "I'll give you directions once we arrive." He closed the window and drew a small curtain across to block the man's view. The engine started and the car pulled away.

"Where are we going?" I asked.

"The wharf. We can catch a ferry out of the city and make our way to Terrebonne Parish."

"We don't have any dough."

He held up a leather wallet. "Colonel Belvedere was most obliging."

"You picked a pocket?"

"Delphine's guests were entranced by your performance. Wasting a perfect opportunity is shameful."

The Packard slowed as we approached the fence, but the guard remained inside the gatehouse and waved us past. Through the heavy downpour, I noted a half dozen armed men roaming the grounds.

Esther tugged at Renny's sleeve. "Mrs. Hart says she has a bad feeling about Delphine."

I jumped in. "Me, too. Delphine lied about wanting to protect Amelie. She'd rather see your sister dead."

Renny sighed. "Amelie understands. So do I. She'll be careful. My father had her well-trained in hand-to-hand combat. One doesn't raise a girl to womanhood in New Orleans by neglecting an essential part of her education. After I see you safely away, I'll return for my pigheaded sister and convince her to leave. We'll rendezvous in Houma…Which reminds me, let's see how much money Colonel Belvedere donated for the trip." He turned on the overhead light and tossed the book to me. I spread the pages open on my lap.

"Are those recipes, Peter?" Esther asked.

"I'm not sure. Funny kind of ingredients, though. I've never heard of them—and you're not supposed to read through my eyes without permission."

"I just peeked," she said. "Why is Delphine collecting recipes? I can't see her in a kitchen cooking next to Ruby." After a demanding yip from Mrs. Hart, Esther scooted over. "She wants to see."

As Mrs. Hart settled down, a paper made of creamy vellum fell from the journal. Imprinted on top was the letterhead of a New Orleans law firm. Jean-Baptiste Marchand's signature was beneath several paragraphs of legalese. Mrs. Hart scanned the page and, little doggy-face or not, I knew something was wrong.

"What gives?"

"Mrs. Hart says the paper is a…" Esther giggled. "That's a funny word. It sounds like a fish…Okay, okay, I'll tell them…she said the paper is a codicil of a will. She wants Renny to see. She says Amelie is in more trouble than he thinks. Is a codicil bad, Peter, like rotten fish?"

"I'm not sure," I admitted, handing the sheet to Renny.

As he scanned the paper, Mrs. Hart pawed through the journal. Renny's face grew dark with anger and he spit out a curse. Renny didn't apologize and Mrs. Hart didn't chastise him. She growled, fighting mad herself.

"What did you find?" I asked.

"The codicil is an addition to my father's will signed the day before he passed away. It states if Amelie dies before her eighteenth birthday, Delphine inherits everything."

Mrs. Hart yipped and Esther's face paled. "Renny, Mrs. Hart had a large garden at home. She doesn't understand what the recipes are for, but a lot of the plants are poisonous."

The sick look on Renny's face was replaced in an instant by fierce determination. "Amelie must leave tonight. I'll drop you at the wharf and return for her."

"No," I said. "The place is crawling with Delphine's goons and you'll need help. We go together."

"I can't ask you—"

"We're not asking," butted in Esther. "We're telling. Mrs. Hart says so."

Renny's lips twitched in a smile. "I never argue with a lady, or rather, two of them."

At that moment, the driver slid open the glass door and announced through the curtain, "Canal Street is ahead. Where to next, mac?"

Renny directed him to drive past a big department store named Maison Blanche and then to a dead-end street. As soon as the driver parked the car, Renny got out. The driver opened his door.

Thump. "Oof!"

The Packard rocked back and forth as something heavy slammed against the side panel. Renny rapped on the window giving me a start. "Peter—a hand."

The chauffeur lay crumpled against the fender. "What are you going to do?" I asked.

"The guard at the gate waved Delphine's driver through without a second thought. On a night like this, when a man in the same uniform returns, he won't bother to leave the comfort of the gatehouse to check identities."

"If he does?"

Renny unbuttoned the unconscious man's jacket. The headlight caught the metallic glint of a pistol tucked into a holster. He hefted the gun. "The plan will get noisier."

We dragged the driver into a doorway and bound him with his own tie and belt. Renny donned the chauffeur's jacket and cap before sliding behind the wheel.

"When we get to the gatehouse, lie on the floor and keep quiet," he ordered.

Funny how the feel of time passing changes when headed for danger. I swore it took nearly half an hour in the storm to go from the Marchand mansion to Canal Street, but less than a minute to return. Renny waved us down. The three of us hunkered on the floor. I doffed my jacket and we scooted underneath. Renny approached the gate and slowed the car to a crawl. I held my breath and counted. Five seconds…ten…I gnawed on my lower lip. What took so long? Not being able to see was maddening. The rain splashing against the windows abruptly cut off.

"We're in the garage," said Renny. "Amelie's light is on. I counted two armed guards on the porch, two at the back door, and one at the gatehouse." He rubbed his chin. "Slipping in without raising an alarm won't be easy."

I eyeballed the grounds. "I can reach Amelie's room. I'll shimmy up the drainpipe to the second floor balcony. Do you think she can climb down?"

As soon as the words left my lips, I felt foolish for asking. A girl as comfortable with a blade as Amelie would find shimmying down a copper gutter nothing more than a minor inconvenience.

Renny assured me Amelie would have no problem. "The drain is visible to the guards stationed in front, so you need a distraction." He turned to Mrs. Hart. "Care to join me?" If a growl could sound pleased, hers certainly did.

"I want to help, too," said Esther.

I wasn't about to drag a blind girl up a downspout. "You can watch through my eyes and let Renny and Mrs. Hart know when Amelie and I are ready. We'll need another distraction then."

Renny seemed doubtful. "Can you see that far, *cher*?"

"Uh-huh. I'm used to Peter. Finding his eyes is easy now."

"All right, then. Peter, take off as soon as the guards move to the other side of the porch. Come, Mrs. Hart—the game's afoot." They slipped into the rainy night.

I crept behind a big oak tree draped with Spanish moss where I had a good view of the front. The guards lurked too close to the downspout for me to chance a dash across the lawn.

Bushes rustled near the other end of the house, drawing their attention. One of them left the porch. A moment later, a man yelped and cried, "Ow! Something bit me." The second guard jogged over and poked through the foliage with the rifle barrel.

Sprinting from behind the tree, I made for the downspout and climbed. The rain made the copper slick and difficult to grip. I shimmied as fast as I could, keeping an ear out for the guards. As I cleared the first level, they returned, cursing the rain and whatever small animal, hiding in the bushes, forced them to get wet.

I reached the second floor and leaned over for a handhold on the balcony. The shift in weight caused the downspout to wobble and bang against the house. Footsteps shuffled underneath. I seized the railing and with a grunt vaulted over the side, immediately pressing flat against the wall. A flashlight beam played along the gutter.

"See something?" a guard called.

"Nah," responded the other. "It's the wind." He uttered a curse. "I'm getting out of this mess."

I crawled on my hands and knees to Amelie's room. The drawn curtain blocked my view. I tapped gently and then pressed my ear against the glass. Not so much as a peep came from inside. She must be at the party. I was soaking wet and chilled to the bone, my hands skinned, and I suddenly realized I was hungry. The thought of Amelie warm and dry, packing away Ruby's cooking made me seethe. We came all this way to rescue her and she flounced around at a party. Sheesh…girls.

The window was unlocked. I eased open the sash and crawled inside. The room was empty. Now I had to wait.

The wait was shorter than expected. Amelie burst from the closet, knocked me flat on my rear end, and whipped her knife to my throat. She blinked in surprise.

"Peter? Why are you sneaking around my room?"

"I'm rescuing you," I managed to grunt after sucking air back in my lungs. "Get off. I can't breathe."

She rose to her feet. "What do you mean rescuing me? Where's Renny?"

"Waiting for us in the yard with Mrs. Hart."

Clearly irritated, she slid the dagger into the sheath. "I already told Renny, I won't leave."

"The situation changed." I quickly filled her in on the codicil. "You don't have a choice, Amelie. Delphine has no reason to keep you alive and every reason to want you dead so she can take over the whole estate."

"She hasn't tried—"

"Yet. Two deaths in the same family close together might be too much of a coincidence for the police. Face it, Delphine is biding her time. Do you really think she hired those guards to keep out intruders? Isn't the more likely reason to keep you in here and under her thumb?"

"I'm not afraid of the guards."

"Delphine doesn't need them for her dirty work. The journal from the safe contained recipes for poison." I regretted the words as soon as they left my mouth.

"Poison?" she raged. "Father had no heart attack." She whipped out the knife again. "I'll cut her throat."

Oh geez. I grabbed her arm. "No, you won't. We have no proof Delphine killed your father."

"I know she did. So do you."

"The police won't care. Trust me, Amelie. You don't want to end up in prison or hunted with a price on your head."

Conflict played across her face. "But to run like a coward? The act is beneath contempt." Her eyes widened in dismay. "I-I'm sorry," she stammered. "Forgive me, I didn't mean you were a coward. You're not."

I shrugged. "It's okay. We had to run. Sometimes escape is the best option."

Amelie's shoulders sagged. I saw behind the fierce warrior to a girl no older than me, fighting impossible odds. "This place is my home, Peter. The only one I've ever known. Mother, Father, Renny, and I were so happy here once. To simply hand everything to that viper…"

"We're not handing over the estate. Think of it as a tactical retreat in order to devise a new plan of attack."

Amusement flitted across her face. "Consider a career in politics. You make the most desperate situation sound no worse than a broken shoelace."

"Right now, all I want to consider is escape. "You in?"

"Yes." Amelie answered with firm resolve. "You're right. I can't do anything. I wish I had a chance to explain to Ruby, but she already left for the evening."

I promised we'd send a message once free of New Orleans. Amelie turned off the light. We crawled through the window and along the balcony to the downspout. Below, the two guards discussed the upcoming vote in California to legalize betting on horse races. One already had a bookie if the measure passed.

"What now?" she whispered.

"Esther's keeping watch. She'll signal Renny. We wait for the distraction and then make for the garage."

One of the guards yowled a startled curse. A dog snarled and then the man shouted, "That mutt stole my rifle." Two sets of footsteps thumped to the opposite end of the porch. "Nice, doggy," said one. The other hooted at his partner's misfortune.

I nudged Amelie. "You first."

She eased over the balcony. The drainpipe creaked and rattled as Amelie shimmied to the bottom. I crossed my fingers, but our luck continued to hold. Busy chasing Mrs. Hart, neither of the guards noticed her descent.

The instant Amelie's feet touched ground, I made a frantic grab for the drainpipe.

Ping.

My weight was too much for the weakened brackets and the top support tore loose.

"You hear that?" a guard said.

Ping! Ping! Ping! More supports gave way. The pipe bent in half sending my flailing legs below the roofline of the second floor balcony.

A flashlight beam illuminated my shoes. "Someone is there."

The gutter ripped from the house with a grating metallic crash, and I tumbled into the bushes.

One of the guards splashed through the puddles. He cocked the hammer of a pistol and ordered, "On your feet."

Amelie came out of nowhere. She socked the guard with a one-two punch that sent him sprawling into the grass. Across the lawn, a car engine roared to life. Headlights danced in our direction. The ruckus attracted the gunsels stationed at the rear of the house. Rifle shots cracked through the air. A bullet deflected off a nearby oak tree, splintering the bark.

Amelie and I raced across the yard. The speeding Packard jumped the curb, and sped toward us, fishtailing to a stop. Another bullet ricocheted off the fender as we tumbled inside. Renny hit the gas and tore through the garden, much to Amelie's dismay.

"Renny, you flattened the camellias!"

"Down," he barked. A bullet splintered the back windshield, spraying us with glass shards. I pushed Esther to the floor.

The guard at the front entrance frantically tried to shut the gate. Renny stomped on the accelerator. I flinched at the raspy screech of wrought iron against steel as we scraped by.

The lights in the main house were ablaze now. Attracted by the commotion, curious guests jostled each other out the door. In the lead was Delphine.

Amelie leaned out the window and shouted, "Death to the she-demon!"

I jerked her in as Renny tore onto St. Charles Avenue. An instant later, we were caught in the blaze of two headlights. "Her goons are right behind us," I cried and then ducked as another pistol shot split the air.

Renny jerked the wheel hard. With squealing brakes, he cut a zigzag path through several side streets, but the pursuer stayed right on our tail. The driver gunned the engine and slammed into our fender sending the car into a skid. Esther screamed. Renny clenched the wheel and fought for control. He steered the car down a sidewalk sending pedestrians scattering for cover. A bullet demolished a rear taillight.

"Watch out," Amelie shouted.

Renny took a hard right and jumped the tracks narrowly missing a barreling streetcar. Slowly, we put distance between our pursuers. They were good, but Renny was better—or maybe crazier. He cut through a yard slicing in half a clothesline full of women's undergarments. A large girdle caught on a windshield wiper. With one hand, Renny tugged it loose and tossed it away. He glanced in the rearview mirror. "We lost them."

Esther whooped. "That was some fun, wasn't it, Peter?"

"You have a strange idea of entertainment, Esther." I plucked a few errant pieces of window glass from her hair.

"Escapes are exciting." She burst out in a giggle. "Amelie tackled Peter in her room, Renny. They were so close, I thought Peter was gonna kiss her."

"Clam up, Esther." The idea of kissing Amelie made my face hot. I hazarded a sideways glance at Amelie, but she paid Esther no mind.

"I bet he'd kiss her like this." She puckered her lips. "*Mwah, mwah, mwah.*"

"Shut up, Esther."

"Peter's right, *cher,*" Renny said in a serious tone. "Whether Peter kisses her or not, is entirely their concern and none of our business, and I'm sure the kiss would sound more like this…" He made a slurping sound much to Esther's delight.

Amelie finally reacted, wrinkling her nose in displeasure. "If you're through being an idiot, Renny, how much longer until we reach Houma?"

"By morning. The weather will make travel slow going, and we must stay off the main roads in case Delphine alerted the police."

"Are you sure you know where you're headed?"

"Don't you trust me?"

"No."

"Very wise. Nevertheless, I'll get us there."

Once we cleared the city limits, the paved streets ended. We took a series of gravel roads each worse than the next. Although a warm night, Renny turned on the heat to fight the chill from our wet clothing. The steady drip of rain through the broken window didn't help.

Esther curled next to me and fell asleep. So did Mrs. Hart. I finally dozed off, too. Hours later, I jerked awake when the car hit a bump. Gray morning light highlighted mud spatter on the windows. The storm had passed.

"Are we there, yet?" I mumbled, stifling a yawn.

Renny pulled into a gas station. "We're on the outskirts of Houma."

Amelie yawned and stretched. "Must we stop?"

"I have no choice. The gas tank is nearly empty." He frowned. "The attendant is sure to wonder about the bullet holes. Let's hope we find Odile quickly so we can ditch the car."

Esther rubbed her eyes. "I gotta pee."

Amelie took her hand. "The facilities are around back. I see a public phone. I'll call Ruby."

I left to use the restroom, too, and then returned to the car. Amelie arrived a few minutes later. "Ruby was relieved to hear we're safe. She'll keep an eye on Delphine and send a letter in care of Purdy's General Store if she needs to contact us."

"Are you sure you should tell her where we're headed?"

Amelie drew herself up. "Ruby would never tell Delphine. She's not merely a cook, but a friend, and a friend's loyalty is never questioned."

Not having had much experience with friendship, I didn't argue. "Where's Esther?"

"Renny took her. He went to get directions to Cypress Road from the attendant." She glanced around. We need to leave. I don't like being out in the open."

Renny and Esther returned to the car. "The man asked about the bullet holes," Esther said. "I told him they weren't bullet holes, but a giant eagle swooped down and tried to peck us through the glass." She scrunched her face. "I don't think he believed me."

"Of course, he didn't believe you," I said. "That's the dumbest lie I ever heard. Renny, how could you let her say that?"

Renny started the engine. "Have you tried to keep her quiet once she gets an idea into her head?"

"I only wanted to help," said Esther. "I'm not an expert like you, Peter."

"Next time, leave the lying to me."

"I'm curious, Peter," Amelie asked. "What story would you have told?"

The lie formed right away and tumbled out. "Every Tuesday, Renny rode the streetcar downtown. He noticed a pretty girl with long brown hair on the same route to her job at Maison Blanche." As I spoke, I pictured the girl, and saw her behind the glove counter at the department store. "Renny purchased a pair of white suede gloves for his sister as an excuse to talk to her." Amelie rubbed her hands as if she felt their buttery soft texture.

"Renny asked her to dinner," I continued. "Afterwards, she invited him to her place for coffee. She lived in a yellow double-sided shotgun house with green shutters and a rose bush in the front."

"Roses were Mother's favorite," murmured Amelie.

"The girl neglected to mention she had a fiancé with a hot temper. He was short, with dark curly hair and a pencil thin mustache. He burst through the door with a gun. Renny escaped through the window and the man fired, striking the car."

"The noise was loud," said Esther.

"Yes, it was—" Amelie's mouth popped open. "How did you do that? The story was so real. I could practically see Renny's escape."

"What do you mean real?" Renny huffed. "Peter told the most obvious lie I ever heard. I never bolted through a window."

"What about the time Annabelle Beaufort's father came home early from a business trip?"

"I left through a door," he sputtered, "not a window, and I didn't run. I merely walked briskly."

"Not the way Annabelle told it."

"Really, Amelie," Renny sniped, "the notions you put into Mrs. Hart's head about me." I raised an eyebrow, surprised Renny cared what Mrs. Hart thought.

Esther tugged at my sleeve. "How come Renny knew you told a lie?"

"Because the story was about him. Renny never met any such girl, so I couldn't talk him into believing. A lie only works if the truth is hidden."

Amelie narrowed her eyes. "What other lies have you told us?"

Mrs. Hart jumped on the seat next to Amelie and placed a paw on her knee. "Mrs. Hart says Peter told you the truth," said Esther. "He doesn't lie to friends. Peter never lied to her or me, either." Esther's face set in a stubborn line as if daring Amelie to argue.

Amelie's expression softened. "You have very loyal friends, Peter."

"Uh-huh," said Esther. "You and Renny are friends now, too. He won't lie to you. Isn't that right, Peter?"

Heat filled my cheeks. Until that moment, I didn't realize I had any friends. "That's right."

"Good enough," announced Renny with cheerful good humor. "And no more tall tales to sully poor Renny's reputation. Agreed?"

Amelie's eyes gleamed. "No need. The real stories are so much better."

Brother and sister continued to argue. Amelie gleefully described aspects of Renny's colorful social life that Renny insisted were mere exaggerations. Esther, enjoying herself immensely, begged me to separate the lie from the truth. Renny stated since we were friends, his duty now was to teach me to be a gentleman and tattling was impolite. Mrs. Hart quietly took everything in. Renny shot the little dog a glance now and then as if to gauge her reaction.

We passed through Houma. Renny turned onto a dirt road lined with gnarled cypress trees. Houses were far apart, nestled among tidy gardens and clusters of ancient live oaks draped with Spanish moss. The route twisted and turned. Every now and then, I glimpsed water hiding behind the lush undergrowth.

At an intersection, a weather-beaten arrow pointing left directed motorists to Cassett's Fish Camp, three miles away. Across the road was a wooden building. The wide front porch had a couple of rocking chairs. Above the entrance, a hand-lettered sign read Purdy's General Store. Renny parked in the rear out of sight of the road. We climbed the creaking front steps and opened the door. A set of bells attached overhead jangled a cheerful greeting.

"Mornin'." A gray-haired woman behind the counter looked up with a smile. "What can I do for you folks today?"

"Good morning," replied Renny. "I'm looking for Delmar Purdy."

"Delmar's my husband." Behind the woman was a half-open door. She called over her shoulder, "Honey, folks here to see you."

A portly man came out wiping his hands on a rag. "Yes, sir?"

"I need to find Odile Benoit. I understand she receives her mail in care of the store."

"Who asks for his cousin Odile?" Mrs. Purdy demanded.

"I am René Marchand and this is my sister Amelie."

"The children of Jean-Baptiste Marchand?" said Delmar. "Why, Odile speaks of the family often. What brings you two this way?"

Amelie rushed in. "We're in trouble and must find Odile. I won't lie to you. We are innocent of wrongdoing, but the police may not see it the same. We desperately need Odile's advice. Please, can you contact her?"

Mrs. Purdy's eyes strayed to the front window. "I reckon y'all are right about the police." A squad car with two officers pulled in front of the store.

"Please…" Amelie begged.

Mr. Purdy motioned behind the counter. "Into the storeroom. Your car?"

"Hidden out of sight," said Renny.

We shut the door right before the jangle of the chimes. "Mornin'," said Mr. Purdy. "What can I do for you boys?"

A gruff voice answered. "We got an alert about a kidnapping. The perpetrators may be headed this way."

"A kidnapping," gasped Mr. Purdy. "You don't say?" The expressiveness in his realistically shocked voice was quite good.

A second policeman spoke. "A man named René Marchand and his accomplice, Martin, forced Marchand's sister into a car."

Now I was only an accomplice. For some strange reason, being demoted from falsely accused murderer to falsely accused kidnapping assistant teed me off.

"Marchand is a no-good'un cut out of the father's will," continued the officer. "The sister's guardian believes he's holding the girl for ransom. He has another little girl with him, too. He may have kidnapped her, also."

"And a dog," added the other.

"*Mon Dieu*," Mrs. Purdy exclaimed. I also imagined she clutched at her heart. "He kidnapped a dog? What a monster."

"Well, we're not right certain about the dog," the policeman admitted, "but a man matching Marchand's description was spotted at a gas station asking directions to Cypress Road. We're stopping at every house and business to see if strangers passed by."

"Why, a young man came through this morning," said Mr. Purdy.

"Describe him."

"Tall, dark hair, green eyes."

"That's Marchand. When was this?"

I tensed. Would the storekeeper rat us out?

"Less than half an hour ago," said Mr. Purdy. "He bought supplies and left."

"Did you see which way he went?"

"Toward the fish camp."

The other officer said, "The roads are blocked, Sarge. Marchand may be trying to rent a boat. Thanks for the tip, Mr. Purdy."

"My pleasure, boys," he responded sociably. "I hope y'all catch the scoundrel."

"So do I. The sister's guardian posted a reward. Every police officer in the parish will be searching. He won't get far." The bells jangled again.

Mr. Purdy opened the door to our hiding place. He studied Renny for a moment. "Odile thinks very highly of your family. I'll take you to her, but if she decides not to help, I'll turn you over to the police myself."

"Fair enough," said Renny.

"Odile lives with her son and his family on Bayou St. Gerard," said Mr. Purdy. "Chris usually comes in once a week to collect the mail, but I reckon to save him a trip. Since the police were kind enough to inform us roads are blocked, we'll take my boat through the swamp. Rochelle?"

His wife's eyes twinkled. "If anyone asks, you went hunting that dastardly criminal, René Marchand, in order to collect the reward money." Mrs. Purdy reached below the counter. She retrieved a packet of mail and kissed her husband. "Best get going before the police return. Give my regards to Odile."

Chapter 7
Reading the Bones

Renny stashed the car deep in the thicket, and then Mr. Purdy led us down a path behind the store to the water. Tied at the end of a rickety wooden pier sat a low-slung wooden boat with an outboard motor. The pier didn't look strong enough to hold all of us, including Mr. Purdy's impressive weight. Neither did the boat, but Mr. Purdy didn't act worried. Nobody ever seemed worried here. For all Mr. Purdy knew, we were desperate criminals ready to commit desperate acts of, well, desperation. Didn't bother him a bit. The biggest concern he voiced was to arrive at the Benoit's in time for supper.

The boat wobbled as everyone settled in their seats. I eyeballed the tea-colored water with no desire to discover first-hand what kind of people-eating swamp monsters lurked on the muddy bottom. Being on the dinner menu seemed the least of Mrs. Hart's concerns. She perched next to Renny in the bow, front paws resting on the edge of the boat. Her muzzle froze in a delighted doggie grin as if she was Mr. Purdy's fluffy masthead.

With a cough and a sputter, the engine hiccupped to life. Esther bubbled over with excitement. "The air smells so wild, Peter—and what funny sounds."

Mr. Purdy grabbed the tiller and steered us into the bayou. I tried to keep track of the route, but after a few minutes was hopelessly lost. How the heck did Mr. Purdy know where to go? The channels looked exactly the same to me, but the storekeeper had intimate knowledge of every lush blade of grass, every lily pad, every vine braided through every branch. He pointed to ibis on the banks and moss-draped cypress as if they were old friends.

The sun beat upon the bayou with a dazzling glare. I loosened my collar and wiped a shirtsleeve across my sweaty brow. The boat plowed through the water, serenaded by a chorus of eerie chirps and croaks. Leaves rustled as unseen creatures scurried into the brush. To a city boy, the boat ride felt like a distant planet. I gripped the sides, half-expecting giant tentacles to lash out and drag me under.

As the boat cruised along, warm moist air buffeted my face. The slap-slap-slap of ripples in the water lapped gently against the hull, rocking the boat in a calming, hypnotic rhythm. I drew in a long, slow breath. With each passing mile, the strange background noises became less scary and more soothing. The warm air melted tension from my shoulders. This was actually nice. I took off my tie and relaxed.

Then we came upon the gator.

Mr. Purdy gestured to a muddy streak along an embankment. "Gator slide. That's how they reach the water."

At the top of the slide was a moldy log. Without warning, the "log" lifted a head and glared directly at me with two beady reptilian eyes. The gator was huge, eight feet of solid muscle capped off with an evil toothy grin that seemed to say, *Lookee at dat juicy boy comin' by heah. I gotta get me some of him.* Cold, primal fear bubbled up in my throat.

"He's a big-un," Mr. Purdy noted brightly. "Could rip off a man's arm like that." He snapped his fingers.

My heart hammered wildly as he steered the boat over for a better look. The gator hissed. It pushed off with two front legs and glided silently down the slide into the bayou. The top of its head broke the surface of the water and glinting eyes tracked me as we motored past. *I'll have me dem crunchy legs first, boy. Dey be da tastiest part.* I swallowed hard.

Esther fidgeted, barely able to keep her seat. "Peter? Can I see?"

"Go ahead." My gaze glued to the gator. In truth, I couldn't tear my eyes away.

She gasped. "Oh, he's scary."

Amelie peered at us with a puzzled expression. "Esther wanted to see," I explained. "She's supposed to ask permission."

" 'Cause peeking ain't polite." Mrs. Hart arfed a comment from the bow. "Peeking *isn't* polite."

Amelie gazed at her in wonder. "Esther, how do you get to Peter's eyes?"

"Once I know someone, I sort of have a map in my head to find the right way in."

"Ah, like the way Mr. Purdy finds his way through the swamp." She leaned into Esther. "You can use my eyes, too, if you wish."

"Really?"

"Go ahead." Amelie gave Esther's shoulder an amiable squeeze. "We're friends now, aren't we? I'm curious as to how it feels."

"You don't feel anything," I said.

"Don't talk Amelie out of it, Peter. I want to." Esther's eyes stared blindly into the distance and then she smiled. "I can see now. She has real good eyesight, Peter—as good as yours."

Amelie took in the sights, giving Esther a panoramic view of the swamp. After a while, she turned to me with surprise on her face. "You're right. I don't feel a thing."

"Yeah, you don't know she's in there unless she admits it. Knowing what Esther can do was creepy at first."

"Now you don't mind?"

"Given what's happened in the last few days, her act is pretty tame."

"No, it's more than that," said Renny. "You took responsibility for Esther and Mrs. Hart's safety when you had no reason. You may be an orphan, Peter, but you are also a young man of character and courage." He leaned over and punched me in the arm, "*C'est bon.*"

"I agree," said Amelie with a warm smile.

Esther giggled. "Peter's cheeks are red. Are you gonna kiss Amelie now? Give her a big juicy *mwah.*"

"Shut up, Esther," I sputtered. "Get out of Amelie."

"I don't wanna. Now you're blushing all the way to your hair."

Renny distracted Esther by insisting she see through him. Then he sent the girl into a fit of giggles by peering down Mrs. Hart's muzzle and telling her what beautiful eyes she had. When he started pleading for a lick on the nose, Esther collapsed to the bottom of the boat, holding her stomach, laughing so hard she gasped for air. Mrs. Hart didn't appear amused.

The boat crossed an open stretch of water and entered a narrow channel. Mr. Purdy pointed ahead. "That's the Benoit place. Chris is home. I see the pirogue and the other boat."

A dock jutted into the water. At the top of the embankment sat a trim wooden house with a tin roof, large porch, and a bright blue door. Several fresh gator hides were tacked to the wall of a nearby outbuilding. Two craft moored at the dock; one the small boat Mr. Purdy called a pirogue and a larger one with fishing nets and the name Sweet Marie painted on the stern. The screen door opened. A tall muscular man stepped onto the porch followed by a passel of barefoot children. He waved an arm in greeting.

"Delmar?" he shouted. "What brings you this way?"

"Howdy, Christophe. I got visitors for Odile."

The man turned to a boy about a year older than Esther. "T. Chris, run get *Mamere*." The lad raced away at a gallop.

A woman came out of the house, clutching a wooden spoon. "Delmar, you're right on time for supper."

Delmar smacked his lips. "Thank you, Marie. I am a mite peckish."

She turned her attention to us. "You brought guests. Welcome, I'm Marie Benoit…my husband Chris." She pointed to each of the children in turn. "Luc, Georges, and Liliane."

Before we introduced ourselves, T. Chris galumphed around the corner of the house with a sprightly older woman at his heels. She wore a flowing, multicolored skirt and crisp white blouse. Around her neck was a necklace made of funny pointed beads. She caught sight of Renny and Amelie and gave a delighted cry. They scrambled off the boat and she greeted them with open arms.

"Let me look at you," she exclaimed. "Amelie…such a beautiful young woman. Are you practicing your knife fighting drills?" Amelie assured Odile, her skills were as deadly as ever. "And you, René…I can't believe you're as tall as your father, now."

At the mention of Jean-Baptiste Marchand, Renny's expression darkened. "Father is dead, Odile."

The old woman clutched at her blouse. "I knew something dreadful had happened, but this…"

T. Chris piped up. "*Mamere* read the bones and saw death in the wind."

"Read the bones?" I said.

Odile's head shot toward us and her hawk-like gaze raked over Esther, Mrs. Hart, and me. In that

149

instant, I felt like a sack of flour weighed and measured. I shifted my feet, instinctively aware lying to Odile would never be an option.

Amelie made introductions. "They are friends of ours, Odile. They need your help." She clutched her arm. "We need your help."

"Mrs. Hart's a dog and I have a conjuror on my tail," Esther chirped before I could shush her.

"Do you now?" Odile squatted beside Mrs. Hart. She cocked her head, listening, the way Esther did when Mrs. Hart spoke to her. Every now and then, the old woman nodded as if in agreement, occasionally voicing *oui* or *non.* Finally, she stood. "Tell me the story from the beginning."

"Talking can be done over supper," said Marie. "Everyone come inside. Y'all must be half-starved."

She was right. I wondered happily if Marie Benoit could hold a candle to Ruby in the kitchen. Renny took Odile's arm and escorted her. As they passed, I got a better look at the necklace she wore and almost wished I hadn't. The funny pointed beads were actually long sharp teeth.

Marie bustled around the stove as her husband set extra plates. Something delicious sizzled on the burner in a big black cast iron pan. The children carried dishes to the table, while the one named T. Chris automatically pulled up a chair for Mrs. Hart, as if having an enchanted dog-woman as a guest for dinner was an everyday occurrence. In an instant, a platter of fried meat, a pan of cornbread and large pots of fluffy rice and peppery-spiced greens appeared. We took our seats and dug in. After the first bite, I realized Marie could easily give Ruby a run for her money.

"The chicken is great," I said.

Amelie snickered. "It's not chicken."

Christophe shot me a wicked grin. "Better the gator be in you, son, than you be in the gator."

I found no fault with his logic, so speared another piece. In between mouthfuls, we told our story. Odile listened intently asking no questions. I did most of the talking since Esther had a tendency to ramble and Mrs. Hart's handicap was obvious. Although the few times, she punctuated a comment of mine with a yip, I had the oddest sensation Odile didn't need Esther to translate.

The last morsel disappeared from the plates. Odile leaned back in the chair and pronounced, "He's a powerful conjuror. Pike had training in the black road, for sure."

"What does he want with me?" asked Esther nervously.

"He plainly needs to open an arcane door, but which door and what is behind I cannot say at the moment. I need to consult the bones."

Those bones again. Before I could ask about them, Renny handed her Delphine's recipe book. As the Benoit children cleared the table and washed the dishes, Odile ran a fingertip along each line of print. Every now and then, she stopped and muttered to herself. By the time she finished, her face had twisted in an angry scowl.

"When Jean-Baptiste wrote to tell me he would marry again, I was happy. I knew how much he missed your sainted mother. I was unable to attend the wedding, and for that, I won't forgive myself. Had I met this woman ahead of time, I could have prevented his death." Odile tapped the book. "For surely as I sit here, Jean-Baptiste Marchand was murdered."

Amelie's eyes filled with bloodlust. "I knew it. I knew something was wrong." She half rose from her seat. "I'll kill her."

Odile grabbed her arm and yanked her to the chair. "Delphine is not to be taken lightly. She is dangerous."

Amelie scowled. "As am I."

"She's also well-armed and guarded. You can't fight her alone."

"She's not alone." Renny's voice was cold and hard. "He was my father, too. Amelie and I both deserve revenge."

"Fah. Revenge is for halfwits. Questing for blood will get you both killed. What you want is justice for Jean-Baptiste, and such takes time and planning."

I picked up the book and leafed through the pages. "What are they?"

"Recipes for death and worse," said Odile. "The book has techniques to concoct untraceable poisons, any of which could have killed Jean-Baptiste. Others are used for dark purposes, such as weakening someone's will or causing madness."

Amelie gasped. "Can she do that?"

"I believe she already did." Odile reached over and clasped her hand. "Jean-Baptiste fell in love very quickly, did he not?"

Renny's eyes blazed. "She entrapped my father and then murdered him. You can't deny my revenge, Odile."

Marie placed a comforting hand on his shoulder. "Listen to my mother-in-law. She has faced evil many times before and knows about such things. When the time comes, we'll help you bring Delphine to justice, but such an action cannot be done alone."

Mrs. Hart jumped from her seat. She trotted to Renny and pawed at his wrist. "She says you and Amelie are not alone," said Esther. "She and Peter and me are gonna help, too. She says she knows about revenge and a sound plan takes time. She doesn't want either of you to go to prison." I added my enthusiastic agreement. The storm ebbed from Renny's expression, replaced by gratitude.

"*Bon,*" declared Odile. "Delphine can wait. She won't abandon her comfortable life in New Orleans, but undoubtedly, the hunt will continue for Amelie."

"If she happens to send men this way…" Mr. Purdy gave a nonchalant shrug. "They won't find help in the bayou."

"Our first concern, then, is to prepare for when the conjuror comes for Esther."

"What do you mean, *when*?" I said. "Pike is nowhere near here."

Odile shook a finger at me. "A conjuror never stops. He needs Esther for some task he cannot accomplish alone. He'll search for her, but how fortunate you brought Esther here. She'll be safe while I determine Pike's goal. Meanwhile the hour is late. I'll return to my cabin and think on what to do for Mrs. Hart."

Everyone took the cue to rise. Odile offered room for Esther, Mrs. Hart, and me while Renny and Amelie bunked in the main house. Mr. Purdy, meanwhile, headed to his boat. Traveling at night through the swamp apparently held no concern for him.

Odile's home sat a hundred yards down a well-trod path. The cabin had three rooms; bedroom, kitchen, and living area, neat as a pin. A large screened-in porch overlooked the water. Mrs. Hart and Esther shared Odile's room. She offered the couch to me, but I spied a hammock and requested to sleep on the porch instead.

She raised an eyebrow. "What of the sounds of the bayou? They won't keep you awake?"

Until she spoke, I forgot about the funny chorus of croaks and whistles. "No," I admitted with surprise. "I kinda like them."

Her eyes gleamed. "*Bon*. The bayou accepted you."

I remembered the gator and cast a suspicious glance at the water. "Is that good?"

Odile gasped. "*Ma oui*, of course it is. The bayou doesn't open arms to every newcomer." Odile's eyes narrowed and the intense regard made me squirm. "Lying is a useful skill, otherwise Esther and Mrs. Hart would surely be dead, but don't let lying define you. Life has more in store than that. Instead, allow the bayou help you discover a true reason for being." She patted my arm. "*Bonne nuit*, Peter."

I stripped to my underwear, wrapped myself in an old quilt of Odile's, and climbed into the

154

hammock. Swaying gently, I closed my eyes, and let cares flow down to the murky water.

Odile's words echoed unbidden in my ear. *Allow the bayou help you discover a real reason for being.* I snorted a laugh. Backwater hogwash. I knew Peter Whistler inside and out; orphan boy, ward of the state, no ties to bind him. Though for a loner, I recently collected more people than fleas on a junkyard dog. I heaved a regretful sigh. A few weeks ago, life had been so simple.

Did you really want that old life? Don't you like being part of something bigger?

"Shut it," I grumbled to myself and then pulled the quilt over my head and surrendered to sleep.

* * * *

"Get up." A finger jabbed me in the ribs. Startled, I jerked awake, forgetting where I slept. The hammock pitched wildly and sent me tumbling to the floor. Amused green eyes peered down into mine. "You sleep like the dead."

I glared at Amelie. "Give a guy some warning next time."

"I called you several times. All you did was snore."

Suddenly, I remembered I slept in my underwear. In a huff, I wrapped the quilt around me. "Do you mind?"

"Not a bit." Amelie perched next to a pile of clothes. She wore an old shirt and cut-off jeans with her hair in pigtails. She didn't look much like the proper young society girl of yesterday, especially since I couldn't help but notice the knife sheath now attached to her belt. "Marie sent over outfits more suitable here than one of Renny's old suits. Hurry and get dressed. Odile has breakfast waiting."

"Can I have some privacy?" I snapped.

"*Mon Dieu,* you are fussy." She flounced off the porch.

I threw on the clothing. Amelie and Esther sat at the kitchen table with T. Chris and Renny. Esther wore a shirt and pants that had probably once belonged to the boy. Her sharp ears didn't miss a beat.

"Have some eggs, Peter. I helped T. Chris gather them this morning."

"You two rassle a gator?" I teased, taking a seat.

"They're not gator eggs." Esther corrected me very seriously. "They're chicken. Odile has a coop." She proceeded to give me a description of each and every hen with so much detail I knew the boy allowed her to use his eyes.

"That was nice of you to take her, T. Chris." His response was a shy smile—not that a person got much more than a word in during Esther's chatter. When she finally paused for breath, I asked something bugging me since yesterday. "What's the T. stand for?"

"*Petit.*"

"What?"

"*Petit* is the Cajun word for small," said Odile. "He's named Christophe after his father so instead of junior his nickname is Petit Chris or T. Chris for short."

156

Mrs. Hart nosed open the creaking screen door. She scampered over to join us, toenails clicking against the floorboards. "She went outside to poop," Esther whispered loudly, "but doesn't like people to know." T. Chris hid his mouth in a napkin and tried not to laugh. Mrs. Hart's keen ears must have heard, but she hopped onto a kitchen chair and pretended not to notice.

"What about Mrs. Hart?" I said to Odile. "Can you help her?"

Odile motioned to a bookcase crammed with worn leather volumes. "I searched my references. Placing a human soul into an animal requires very powerful magic. The spell is difficult to reverse, but not impossible." A troubled expression crossed her face. "The problem is she no longer has a body to inhabit."

The truth hit like a bombshell. How could I have been so stupid? The thought never occurred to me. Mrs. Hart's body was destroyed in the fire at the carriage house. We had no way to bring her back. Mrs. Hart eyed me calmly as if to say, *Don't worry about me, Peter.* I knew at that moment she had realized the truth from the beginning, but kept it to herself. It figured. Complaining about misfortune wasn't her way.

Esther buried her face in the little dog's fur and choked back a sob. "Mrs. Hart is stuck forever in Honey Bun? Peter, it isn't fair."

Cold dark anger took hold of me. Mrs. Hart stayed right by our side, putting herself in harm's way to protect us. She fought for Renny and Amelie, too. "Mrs. Hart deserves better," I cried out. "She shouldn't be punished."

Mrs. Hart turned her head away as if embarrassed.

"Do not despair, little one." Renny gently stroked Esther's hair. "Odile won't give up."

"Quite right," said Odile. "Other options exist; however, they require more than a little thought and planning and can't be accomplished yet. I do not intend to forsake her, but she doesn't suffer. For the moment, we must put aside Mrs. Hart's condition and concentrate on Pike." She raised her hand to stifle my protest. "His plan must be uncovered."

Mrs. Hart gave an affirmative yip and Esther translated. "She agrees with Odile. Pike is a threat, and she can wait for a cure." Esther paused. Her brow furrowed as if unsure how to proceed. "You do? I don't know. Are you sure it's polite?" Obviously, she and Mrs. Hart were in deep discussion over a fine point of etiquette. "Okay, I'll tell them…she says we're fighting on the same side and everyone should call her Lucy."

Renny's eyes sparkled. "My pleasure, Lucy."

"Mine, too," said Amelie.

The name felt wrong in my mouth. "I don't know if I can get used to Lucy. She's been Mrs. Hart my entire life."

Esther shook her head. "It just doesn't sound right."

Odile chuckled. "I'm also happy to be on a first name basis with you, Lucy. For now, you'll have to be content with that." Odile retrieved paper and pencil from a desk in the corner. "*Bon*. Since we are now soldiers in the same army, the first thing to determine is the plans of the enemy." She handed the writing implements to me. "Draw the symbol on the door from the night in the carriage house."

I sketched the little flame as best I could and gave the sheet back to Odile. She regarded me with a curious expression. "What?" I said.

"You're left-handed."

"So?"

"I find it interesting."

"Don't know as I'd call it interesting," I grunted. "Being left-handed was one more thing to set me apart from the other kids at school."

"Being set apart is not always bad." Odile traced her fingertip over the lines. Her upper lip curled and she uttered a string of French words that sure didn't sound flattering.

T. Chris peered curiously over her shoulder. "What do the squiggles mean, *Mamere*?"

"I don't know, yet, but, the conjuror uses very dark magic. I must throw the bones to read what lies beyond. T. Chris, fetch my bag."

The boy bounded across the kitchen to a workbench pushed against one wall. Set above were long wooden shelves filled with odds and ends crammed next to Mason jars packed with assorted plant life. T. Chris retrieved a drawstring bag made of gator hide and brought it to Odile. She shook the contents into her hand.

I leaned in to get a better look and gulped. "Are those real bones?"

"*Ma oui*." Her eyebrows raised in disbelief. "What else would I use?" She pointed to each one.

"The knuckle of a gator...the thighbone of an ibis...the rib from a rattlesnake...the spine of a catfish...the femur from a fox...and Cousin Henri's pinky."

My face paled. T. Chris giggled. "You told a good one, *Mamere*."

Odile jabbed me playfully in the ribs. "My mistake...tail bone from a wild boar—not Cousin Henri. His finger is in the other bag." Odile was a real card.

She gathered the bones in two hands and then held them to her forehead, closed her eyes, and murmured in soft lilting French.

"What's she saying?" I whispered to Amelie.

"The chant is a request for guidance," she murmured, "from the spirits of the bayou."

"The who?"

"Odile's people have a deep kinship to the land," Renny explained quietly. "They see the swamp as a living essence, like a relative. The bones are from creatures that live within the boundaries. She uses them to form a connection to the spirits."

"How can swamp spirits in Louisiana know about Pike in New Jersey?"

"The spirit worlds are connected," Odile snapped. "Hush. You make too much noise. Spirits are easily distracted."

She started her chant again while we waited in silence. After five minutes or so, I leaned over and whispered to Amelie, "I guess the spirit line is busy."

Without dropping a phrase, Odile kicked me in the shin. Amelie pursed her lips and snickered as I rubbed my leg. At once, the shaman stiffened and flung the bones. The swamp spirits finally returned her call.

They landed with a clatter in the center of the wooden table. Odile leaned on her knuckles staring with fierce intensity at the jumbled pattern. Her lips twisted in displeasure as if she tasted something unpleasant. I made no sense of the scattered bones. Amelie shrugged. Neither did she. Renny appeared equally confused, but T. Chris, must have inherited some of his grandmother's mojo, because he shivered despite the heat.

Abruptly, Odile leaned forward, catching us in a sweeping glance. Ominous foreboding churned my stomach acid. Something headed this way. Something bad.

"What do you see?" I whispered.

Odile drew a deep breath. "The conjuror plans to open a doorway into the Lower Worlds."

Chapter 8
Feu De L'enfer

"You mean like hell?" I stared at her, dumfounded. "Can Pike do that?"

"Unfortunately, yes. He allied with a powerful demon for such a purpose."

"Who? Why?"

"The demon is Feu De L'enfer. The name means hellfire. Such creatures are not natural to Earth, but confined to their own accursed dimension in the Lower Worlds, a stinking void of eternal nothingness. Demons and monsters are trapped inside, where their powers are useless to harm us. They work the dark magic solely by forging a mystical connection through a human such as Pike. The conjuror made a deal to release the demon into our world in exchange for power. He is a fool." Odile spat out the words. "Pike believes he is immune to the beast's appetite for death, but once released in this plane of existence Feu De L'enfer will be omnipotent. The demon will feed on the flesh of the innocent to forge a kingdom on Earth."

"What does this have to do with Esther?" I demanded. "Why does he need her to open the door?"

"Esther is a see-er."

"A seer?" Amelie wrinkled her brow. "You mean a prophet?"

I gawked at Esther. "How come you never said you can predict the future?"

Esther stuck out her lip. "Because I can't, dodo head. If I could, would I sit here in the dark about Pike's plans?"

I bristled. "I'm not a dodo head and I wasn't the one who said you were a seer."

"Not seer." Odile's voice cut through the argument. "See-er. Esther *sees*. It is a special gift. A see-er who sets foot on a path, always sees the way back. Despite her blindness, Esther can never get lost. She is one of the few who can walk through the door."

I scratched my head. "Why?"

"*Mon Dieu*," she said in an exasperated tone. "Do you think anyone can peer inside the gates of a Lower World and survive? An ordinary human can't bear the sight. The evil within reaches to the soul and drives a person mad, but a blind see-er isn't affected."

Odile gathered the bones and returned them to the bag. "The door is invisible to the demon. The conjuror needs Esther to enter and lead Feu De L'enfer out again. I've seen how quickly the child acclimates to her surroundings. Despite a maelstrom swarming around her, retracing her steps through a Lower World would be a simple enough task."

Esther huddled in her seat, small and vulnerable. "I don't want to go to hell."

Amelie clasped her hand. "You won't. You'll stay here in the bayou far from the conjuror's clutches."

"Yes, child." Odile leaned over and kissed the top of Esther's head. "You're safe with us." Odile's lie hit me like a bolt of lightning. Before I called her out, she shot me a warning glance, and then turned to her grandson. "T. Chris, take Esther to the house. I'm sure she'd enjoy playing with you and the others. You can teach her to fish."

T. Chris gawked at Esther as if she'd grown a second head. "You never been fishing? Even my baby sister knows how to fish."

"Nobody ever let me do stuff," said Esther, "except Peter and Mrs. Hart."

"Well, come on then. Let's go."

Esther beamed, so filled with excitement she left her cane. Not that she needed it. Esther already had the layout memorized. I watched her happily traipsing after T. Chris, thoughts of evil conjurors wiped away by the thrill of playing like a normal kid.

As soon as the sound of their footsteps disappeared, Odile turned to me. "I know, Peter. I lied to Esther, but we have no need at the moment to concern her with the danger. For now, we'll let her simply be a child." Mrs. Hart yipped. I didn't need Esther's translation to know she agreed.

"What danger?" said Renny.

"The conjuror retains his magic as long as the connection with Feu De L'enfer exists. The demon's

164

power also makes Pike immortal, so he can't be destroyed while the creature lives."

I sat back in my seat. "That's how he walked out of the carriage house without a scratch."

"*Oui.* He obviously has no scruples about killing, so innocents will continue to suffer." Odile swept her arm around. "This bayou…this world is in danger."

"There must be something we can do," said Amelie.

"There is." Odile caught us in a piercing stare. "We open a door into the Lower Worlds and kill the demon first."

What the hey? I figured I heard wrong until Renny's astonished cry, "Is such a thing possible?"

"Ways exist. None of them simple. All of them dangerous."

Renny and Amelie exchanged a solemn glance. *Good. They'll say something to Odile. I don't want to be rude to a grandmother, so they need to tell her this is a very, very, very bad idea.*

"We'll help, of course," said Amelie. "What do you need us to do?"

Did I mention folks in the South are crazy? Well, folks in the bayou make the rest of them seem downright levelheaded. I shot to my feet. "Are you nuts? We can't go into the Lower Worlds. Odile said so." I glared at her. "You said no human can survive."

The shaman raised her eyebrows. "That's why the journey is so dangerous." She grabbed my arm with the strength of an eagle carrying off a trout and yanked me hard into the seat. For a grandmother, she

165

had quite a grip. "Shouting is rude," she stated brusquely.

I gritted my teeth. "Sorry. Don't know what I was thinking. Can't imagine why opening the gates of hell isn't a nifty idea."

Odile beamed at me. Obviously, she didn't respond to sarcasm. "*Bon.* Because the spirits told me you are the one who must kill the demon."

I had no words. Oh, I tried to speak, but nothing came except a sputter or two. Mostly, I gawked at her, maybe twitched a little.

"You have the gift," she continued pleasantly.

"What gift?" I demanded. "I'm just a good liar."

Odile clucked. "Don't you realize how special that is—no? I will tell you." She leaned forward on her elbows. Her keen eyes pinned me to my seat. "You feel the truth and can strike at the heart of a lie. More importantly, you can transform what-is to what-should-be. If the conjuror suspected the potential you harbor, he'd have killed you before murdering the Grimaldis."

"What are you talking about?"

"Ah, can you not see your own power?" She shook her head in disbelief. "Esther with her blindness possesses more sight. You can build a lie so strong the lie becomes truth. You will pass through the tortures of the Lower Worlds unscathed and find a way to kill the demon. The power lies within you, Peter. The bones are never wrong." She eyeballed me as if the loony idea was a done deal.

"Odile." Amelie's complexion was pale. "What you're saying…surely we can find another way."

"We can hunt the conjuror," said Renny, "and destroy him before he releases the demon."

Odile gave her head a vehement shake. "I have already explained Pike is bound to Feu De L'enfer. We have no way to kill him. A bullet will pass through his body without leaving a mark. Poison? He can sip a glassful like lemonade. An axe to the neck only dulls the axe. Pike is no longer human. Our one chance is to confront the demon. Only when the creature is dead can the conjuror be vanquished. Even if Pike died, Feu De L'enfer could find another human disciple. The demon built a channel to our world and successfully spread its evil once. It will do so again." She pounded her fist on the table. "Feu De L'enfer must be destroyed. The one vulnerable place is within the creature's own domain."

"Well, I'm not going!" I jumped to my feet so quickly, the chair knocked over. "I'm not waltzing into hell." Amelie grabbed my arm, but I shook her off. "You're crazy."

I stormed through the front door. "March right into the Lower Worlds. Why not? Sounds like fun. How about next Wednesday? My calendar is free."

I stomped along the path leading to the bayou before skidding to a halt with the realization I had no place to go. For one wild moment, I considered stealing Chris' pirogue. The thought passed quickly. Besides not having a clue how to escape the swamp or even pilot a boat, the idea of taking anything from the Benoit family didn't sit well. I never had a twinge of guilt pilfering from Grimaldi's Market, but this was different. Chris, Marie, and their family led a hardscrabble life with little room for luxuries, yet they opened their home without hesitation to us. For all they knew, an evil conjuror would beat down their door any second and the danger didn't mean squat to them. Also, Odile would probably lasso a gator, slap on a saddle, and then she and Mrs. Hart would track me down and administer a royal whooping for thinking such a thing. I kicked at the ground in disgust. Some great adventurer I turned out to be, foiled by a grandmother and an itty-bitty dog.

I rammed my hands into my pockets. Whatever happened to my big plan to roam free, become the world's greatest liar, and never be dependent on a single soul? Now, I was wrapped in these people's lives. Lost and confused, I didn't know who Peter Whistler was anymore.

Squeals of childish laughter cut through my gloom. Esther sat at the edge of the pier, fishing pole in hand, surrounded by Marie, T. Chris, and the rest of the children. They cheered her on. Distracted by the commotion, Chris vaulted from the Sweet Marie where he had been working on the engine.

Esther clenched the pole in a death grip as the line whipsawed through the water. With whoops of encouragement from the youngsters and assistance from T. Chris, she reeled in a shiny, slippery fish. T. Chris unhooked the line and tossed the catch into a bucket.

"You got one! You got one!" Liliane, the youngest Benoit, danced around Esther. "Catch another," she yelled, plunking down next to her father.

Marie hugged Esther. Chris stated she now had to catch them a good lunch. The delight on Esther's face shone across the yard. This was the kind of life she should have had instead of being stuck with the Grimaldis who treated her as nothing but a burden. Here she was merely a little girl who needed help baiting a hook.

I sat on the ground underneath an old cypress tree. Eventually, the squealing laughter faded. Esther and the others went into the house with her catch. Except for the croaking harmonies of the swamp, the world was still again. Shadows cast by the branches lengthened and stretched across the yard. I didn't realize Mrs. Hart found me until a paw patted my leg.

"I'm not brave, you know. I was going to run away just now, except I don't have a boat and don't know where I am. I-I still will. You watch. I'll head out on my own. I'm no hero. You can fend for yourselves." Her teeth closed around my wrist. She didn't bite, merely gave a good shake. Her warm dark eyes filled with understanding.

Mrs. Hart crawled into my lap and placed her head on my chest. I was right. Lying to Mrs. Hart was a waste of time. A lump grew in my throat. I held her tight. Neither one of us was ever much for words.

The foliage rustled behind me, and then Amelie and Renny stepped out. Renny leaned nonchalantly against the cypress and gazed off into the bayou. Amelie sat cross-legged next to me. She absent-mindedly reached over and scratched Mrs. Hart's ear. To my surprise, she didn't object.

"I suppose, you're here to demand I kill the demon."

"No," said Amelie. "I'd never do that. No one should." She motioned to her brother. "Renny and I talked everything over. Despite what Odile thinks, we believe you and Esther are safe here."

"Hiding like scared rabbits," I snapped.

Her face twisted in anger. "Sometimes retreat is the best option—even when one wishes otherwise." The savagery in her tone came as a surprise until I remembered Delphine. Esther, Mrs. Hart, and I weren't the only ones forced to run.

Renny regarded me with undisguised sympathy. "We have no other choice, *mon ami*."

"Yes, we do." Esther walked toward us with T. Chris at her elbow. "I can open the door."

"How did you—Esther," I scolded. "You peeked again."

"So what if I did?"

"You're not supposed to spy."

She stamped her foot. "I don't care. I peeked for an instant to find you and Mrs. Hart and show off the fish. Then Odile came in and I asked her why everyone was upset and she told me. Don't be mad. She said I had a right to know."

Renny put a hand on Esther's shoulder. "Perhaps, Odile is correct. You are a very brave child and deserve the truth. But, *cher*, do you know what opening a door into the Lower Worlds means?"

"Uh-huh. It means the demon is killed before it gets out." Her voice dropped. "It will, you know, someday. Then it will come here and hurt people."

T. Chris squared his shoulders. "Benoits can fend for themselves."

"No one doubts your family's bravery," said Renny, "but against Feu De L'enfer…"

I finished the sentence. "Courage isn't enough." I took in the peaceful setting and imagined the bayou consumed in flames. "Odile's right. The demon must die." As I said the words, suddenly everything was so clear. The doubt and uncertainties I wrestled with in my life faded away. I knew who I was. "And I'm the one to do it."

Mrs. Hart barked. "She says you won't go alone," piped up Esther. "We're coming with you."

"So are Renny and I," said Amelie.

I blurted a protest. "You can't. One lie won't keep everyone safe."

Amelie whipped out her knife and calmly manicured her nails. "Then you'd best learn how to tell a whopper, Peter Whistler, because we are in this together."

"Have I mentioned before you're crazy?"

"Several times." She shrugged indifferently. "It changes nothing."

"Don't fret, my friend," Renny quipped. "Better men than you have tried to penetrate the thick skulls of Marchand women. None ever succeeded. Most of those foolish enough to make the attempt were permanently damaged in the process." He ducked as Amelie took a swing at him. "Truce," he cried with a grin. "One should never fight on an empty stomach, and I smell something good cooking."

"My fishes!" Esther burst in with excitement. "Marie is frying them for lunch."

"Then we must hurry. To be late for a meal is very bad manners."

171

Amelie regard her brother in disbelief. "How would you know? You've never been late for a meal in your life."

"There is always a first time." They continued to banter about the finer points of Renny's lack of etiquette as we headed to the cabin.

Odile waited for us at the table. She didn't speak to me as I took my seat, but merely nodded her approval. Somehow, she knew I came to a decision and had obviously filled in Chris and Marie. Chris clapped me on the shoulder. His eyes shone with respect. To my embarrassment, and Renny's amusement, Marie kissed me on both cheeks. Conversation stuck to fishing as we ate every bit of Esther's catch. Chris declared the meal as the best ever and for the first time I saw Esther blush.

After lunch concluded, we sat around the table discussing the next move. T. Chris parked himself next to Esther while his brothers and sister played a board game on the floor.

"Opening the door won't be simple," said Odile.

"Really?" I muttered. "Do tell."

The sarcasm bounced right off her. "Such a task requires special magic."

"But *Mamere*," said T. Chris, wide-eyed, "I thought you knew everything."

Odile chuckled. "Not everything, *cher*. I never opened a doorway to the Lower Worlds." She stared off into the distance. "But I know someone who has."

Marie gasped. "Odile, you can't possibly consider Clovis Landry."

"Clovis?" I echoed. "Odile, do you really know someone who's been to the Lower Worlds?"

"He says he has and I've no reason to doubt him."

"He's a crazy *couyon*," Chris grunted. "You can't trust a word he says."

"Clovis Landry may be a bit unusual—"

"Unusual?" Chris whispered an aside. "He thinks he's a frog."

"Not exactly," Odile quickly assured me. "He thinks he's King of the Frogs."

I gaped in disbelief. "My vote's with Chris. That's pure jingle-brained."

"A person can't waltz into the Lower Worlds without a few consequences—not for you, though, I'm sure. Clovis was always impatient. He took too many risks and rushed into action without proper preparation. He's learned his lesson." Odile reached over and patted my hand. "The effects of opening a door into an arcane dimension are highly exaggerated."

Marie raised an eyebrow. "Then why does Clovis live in a lily pond?"

"Only during the warm months."

"What does he do in the winter?" I asked, not sure I wanted to know.

She didn't bat an eye. "He hibernates in the mud."

I was right. I didn't want to know.

Odile's expression brightened. "A lucky thing summer is nearly here, no? We'll have no trouble starting a conversation." I couldn't tell if she was kidding.

"How will you find him?" said Marie. "He moves from place to place."

"Don't you mean hops?" Chris muttered under his breath in disgust.

Odile ignored him. "I have an idea where to start. Andre Savoy spotted him running naked through his okra patch two weeks ago. Andre shot at him, but fortunately, can't hit a pirogue tied to a pier, so Clovis may yet be in the vicinity. Peter and I will find him."

"Me?" I sputtered.

"Of course, you." Odile seemed shocked the idea of tracking a lunatic through the swamp held no appeal. "Clovis must be convinced to pass on his knowledge, so has to hear your story first-hand."

"What about me?" said Esther.

"Your presence isn't necessary. Stay here and catch more excellent fish." Esther beamed. Tracking a lunatic through a swamp held no appeal for her, either.

Chris rose from the table. "If you're determined to go through with this insanity, I'll take you to Andre's. I planned to go hunting tomorrow, although not for a *couyon*."

Renny cleared his throat. "I'd be happy to join you. I'm known as a fair shot."

"My brother isn't usually so modest, Chris," Amelie noted with sisterly pride. "He's actually an expert marksman. He and Father hunted often."

"I appreciate the help. We'll take the Sweet Marie. I've shrimped in areas near Andre's place. If hunting is bad, perhaps shrimping will be better."

Mrs. Hart padded over to Odile and barked rapidly. "That's a kind offer, Lucy. I'm thankful for your help and am sure you can track Clovis once you get the scent." She wrinkled her nose. "After six years living as a frog, his odor is rather unique."

"*Bon*, we have an accord," said Chris. "The five of us will leave at first light. Renny and I will drop you off at Andre's and then return the following day."

Chris decided to spend the rest of the afternoon working on the Sweet Marie. We were headed deep into the bayou with a long paddle home if the motor quit. Renny and I volunteered to help. I never spent much time around engines, so was pretty useless. Instead, I scrubbed the deck and stowed supplies. Chris and Renny cleaned the guns. Chris owned several rifles and a pistol. He noted my interest and volunteered to teach me to use the twenty-two.

"Absolutely not."

Odile barked a dissent as she climbed into the boat. Amelie scampered in after her and handed a large sack of supplies to Chris.

Her insistence raised my hackles. "Why can't Chris teach me to shoot? I bet Amelie knows how to use a gun."

Amelie casually examined her fingernails. "I prefer the blade."

"You're missing the point."

"Shooting will interfere with the full development of your powers," Odile stated flatly. "Once you are dependent on a gun for protection, no other action will occur to you."

"Yeah," I sneered, "because shooting stuff works great."

"Not against everything. Not against the things you'll face. A gun can misfire; a shot go wide or

175

wound, but not kill. Bullets run out. The best course for you is not to shoot. Rely on the power within. No, you do not need a gun."

I argued with her, but Odile held firm. Chris was sympathetic, but refused to challenge his mother. "In such affairs, my friend, she is the expert."

Amelie watched the exchange with interest. "Peter will have no protection."

"Don't worry," Chris assured her. "We'll watch over him."

Their comments burned me up. "I'm not a baby. For your information, I've done pretty well all these years taking care of myself."

Odile raised an eyebrow. "And without a gun— *et voila*. You don't need one now." She turned to Amelie. "Come, child, Marie needs help with dinner." Amelie followed obediently, but paused at the end of the dock to peer at me. An undefined look flitted across her face before she jogged after the shaman.

"Don't be angry," Renny said, as I grumbled in annoyance. "People here have their own ways. You must respect their decisions."

"He's right." Chris gave an unapologetic grin. "You can't argue with Cajun crazy."

After another of Marie's excellent suppers, we retired to the living room. Chris, Marie, and Odile discussed the best routes to follow in order to track Clovis. Meanwhile, the Benoit children improvised a game of blind man's bluff against Esther and T. Chris. As Renny, Amelie, and I shouted encouragement, the children tried to avoid capture by Esther. Squeals of delight echoed through the swampland as Esther, using T. Chris' eyes, tagged each one of them every single time.

T. Chris escorted us to Odile's cabin at bedtime. I was amused to see he'd taken on Esther as his personal responsibility. I let Odile know I was still ticked off at her about the gun by clomping around as I prepared for bed, but she cheerfully ignored my snit and wished me *bonne nuit*.

The sky was dark when Odile shook me awake. Esther was already at the table, rubbing the sleep from her eyes. She insisted on seeing me off. Mrs. Hart's head bent toward Odile as if they were deep in conversation. After downing a quick breakfast, we went to the pier. Renny was on the Sweet Marie. Chris kissed his family goodbye and jumped onboard, and I handed Mrs. Hart to him. Amelie ran from the cabin and skirted past me to leap onto the deck. She carried camping gear along with her dagger and a rifle slung on her back.

"Where do you think you're going?" said Renny.

"With you."

"Amelie, be reasonable. The Sweet Marie barely has room for the five of us."

"I am reasonable. I thought the plan over carefully. Peter has no weapons. Odile insists he must develop his powers instead. Until then, he requires protection. I don't wish to brag, but you know I'm an expert with the blade, quite a fair shot, and my hand-to-hand skills are exceptional. The sensible solution is for me to be Peter's bodyguard."

My mouth dropped open. "I don't need a damn bodyguard."

177

Mrs. Hart yipped.

"Sorry," I squawked, "a *danged* bodyguard."

Renny rubbed his chin. "That's a good idea. I can vouch for my sister's abilities."

"Doesn't anybody care what I think?" I hollered.

Odile brushed past me and settled into the boat. "Not if you're going to be pigheaded, and there is no need to shout. My hearing is excellent. Amelie's reasoning is sound. I approve."

I stood on the pier fuming as they ignored me. "I'm not setting one foot on that boat until Amelie gets off. I don't need some crazy girl with a knife hovering over me."

"Yes, you do." Esther's small hands reached around my waist and grasped me in a tight embrace. "I'm afraid something bad will happen to you, Peter." She buried her face in my shirt and snuffled.

My face went red. "Esther, nothing's going to happen…geez."

"It might and I can't help. I want Amelie to go with you."

Marie encircled her arms around both of us. "I think it's an excellent idea, too. We want you to return safe and sound." She kissed the top of my head. My ears burned with embarrassment.

"Me, too! Me, too! Me, too!" A cluster of little Benoits bobbed up and down in a frenzied chorus.

"All right, all right. She can come. Esther, you can let go now. Esther, can't breathe." Marie gently pried apart Esther's hands. I vaulted into the boat before having to deal with another emotional outburst.

"Don't worry," T. Chris called with a wave as the Sweet Marie pulled from the pier. "I'll take good care of Esther."

As we puttered through the bayou, the breeze generated by the boat's movement brought welcome relief from the heat and humidity. No one else seemed to notice the temperature. How did people ever get used to the weather? Even Mrs. Hart adjusted quickly. She immediately took a position in the bow next to Renny, assuming the role of forward scout. Her nose twitched with the array of exotic scents. Renny leaned over and said something to her. Judging by his devilish expression, he must have been teasing. She took the comment good-naturedly, but with a very un-doglike roll of the eyes.

I lost my bearings as soon as the Benoit homestead disappeared from view. Once we hit the main channel, Chris called me inside the wheelhouse. "My mother bars you from shooting, but can certainly have no objections to letting you steer. Want to pilot the boat?"

I jumped at the chance and took the wheel as Chris stood by. Every worry about chasing a nut bar through the swamp quickly evaporated. The heat didn't bother me any longer. The thrum of the engine under my feet created a feeling of freedom like no other. Chris urged me to open the throttle. The engine roared as the Sweet Marie sliced through the water.

Amelie joined us, and Chris gave an impromptu lesson on the flora and fauna of the swamp. Like Mr. Purdy, he had intimate knowledge of every blade of grass, named the animal responsible for each chirp and croak, and read the ripples in the water as easily as I read pages in a book.

After too short a time, Chris took the wheel again. Slight eddies signified shallows and the helm required a more experienced hand, but he promised another lesson soon. We entered a narrow channel and immediately spotted Andre Savoy's homestead. An old man in faded bib overalls and wire rim glasses dangled a fishing line at the end of the pier. He called a friendly greeting.

"Hope we didn't scare away your fish, Andre," responded Chris.

"Naw. They ain't biting. I think that lunatic, Clovis, done scare them already. I need to get me new spectacles so the next time he come steal my okra, I shoot him in the ass, for sure." He spotted Odile in the boat. "What brings you this way, Odile?" She introduced Amelie and me as friends of the family and explained she had business with Clovis. Andre shook his head in doubt. "I hope t'ain't important. He's really far gone this time. Don't make no sense at'all. Done nothing but croak at me when I fired the gun."

Odile insisted the need was urgent, so Andre agreed to show us where he last saw Clovis. Odile, Amelie, and I each carried a bedroll, pack, and canteen. I hoped to find Clovis before we had to camp in the swamp, but we had no way to tell how far he roamed in the two weeks since spotted in the okra.

We waved goodbye as Chris threw the boat's engine into reverse and reentered the channel. Renny and Chris had promised to return tomorrow. Odile agreed to leave a trail, so if we didn't meet at Andre's, the two men would have no trouble tracking us.

Odile, Amelie, Mrs. Hart, and I followed Andre to a large garden behind the cabin. He pointed to a narrow trail behind the okra leading into the brush. "I tracked him a couple hundred yards past a sweet gum tree before he lit out. You sure I can't change your mind, Odile? I tell you, hunting that *couyon* is a waste of time—Clovis got nothing in his brain 'cept swamp water. Why don't y'all come to the house and I'll fry us a mess of beignets. If you ask me—"

"Thank you, Andre. The invitation is very kind, but we've kept you from your fishing long enough." Before he could argue, Odile ushered us ahead. When we were out of earshot, she said, "The last thing I wish to do is try to digest one of Andre's beignets."

Amelie raised an eyebrow. "Bad?"

"Gluey dough balls that sink like a stone into the pit of your stomach. Ruby would knock Andre senseless with her wooden spoon if he tried to bring them into her kitchen. Even a starving dog will refuse them. No offense, Lucy." Mrs. Hart barked reassurance no insult taken.

As Andre described, a few hundred yards along the trail was a sweet gum tree. Odile scrutinized the area and then led us off the path into the woods. We zigzagged through the foliage. I saw no sign a person ever set foot here, but Odile's excitement was obvious. After twenty minutes or so, she stopped to squat on her heels and peer closely at a patch of sandy

181

ground. I peeked over her shoulder and spotted the distinct impression of a bare foot.

"The print is not Andre's, but fresh. No more than a day old." Odile reached into a clump of grass and grabbed a funny green pod. "Fortunately for us, Clovis seems to have developed a taste for okra and returned for more. Lucy, can you track his scent?"

Mrs. Hart placed her muzzle an inch from the footprint and sniffed. Instantly, her upper lip curled and she shook her head vigorously as if to rid her nostrils of something unpleasant. Odile chuckled, "Foul, no? I'm sorry. At least the trail will be easy to follow." With Mrs. Hart in the lead, we headed deeper into the bayou.

The route was slow going. The heavy heat and humidity sapped energy, while the lush undergrowth snagged clothing and whipped around our heels to trip us up. Several times, Mrs. Hart lost the scent and had to backtrack. It seemed to me we headed in circles. When I made the suggestion to Odile, she smacked me upside the head. Amelie snickered and I shot her a dirty look.

"Well," I sniped, "don't you think we're going in circles?"

"Of course," she admitted, smartly, "but I'm not foolish enough to tell Odile."

We stopped once for a bite to eat from our packs, but Odile soon hurried us along. As the day wore on and the shadows lengthened, spending the night outside seemed a sure bet. I reflected longingly on my hiding place in the cellar at Little Angels, musing about a room free of alligators, rattlesnakes, and wild swamp men.

Odile stopped short. "Over there," she whispered, gesturing ahead.

A silvery sheen glinted beyond the trees. We plowed through brush into a small clearing with a lily pond nestled in the middle. On the far side, a piece of canvas strung between two tree limbs created a makeshift lean-to. Scattered about were a few rusty tin cans.

I kicked at a pile of half-rotted okra pods and snorted in disgust. "Do we kneel at the Frog King's throne?"

Odile bent over and examined the ground. "Clovis hasn't been here for some time—"

Mrs. Hart growled softly and darted into the foliage.

Amelie drew her knife. "What is it?"

The shaman's voice dropped to a whisper, "We're being watched."

Chapter 9
The Frog King

My heart hammered against my ribs. "Clovis?"

"Perhaps. Many things have curious eyes in the swamp."

"Swell. I'll have no problem falling asleep tonight."

With a yip, Mrs. Hart bounded from the bushes and held a hurried consultation with Odile. The shaman squinted at the darkening sky. "Lucy found Clovis' cabin. A storm is coming, so we'll shelter there for the night."

We followed Mrs. Hart and came to a patch of singed earth; a perfect circle, a dozen feet in diameter like a weird scar burnt into the snaggly jungle of the bayou. Looking at it formed a cold knot in the pit of my stomach. Mrs. Hart and the others walked right across, but I skirted the edge.

Beyond the circle was a ramshackle cabin nestled in the middle of a clearing nearly reclaimed by dense vegetation. A stiff breeze kicked up and a rumble of thunder echoed overhead. The first raindrops pelted the roof as we fought our way through the weeds to the front porch.

I gawked in surprise. "The door has no lock."

"A shaman has no fear of intruders," said Odile.

"What about wild animals?"

She pushed open the door. "They wouldn't dare."

Amelie scrutinized the interior with a wry look. "Apparently, anything is fair game once the shaman leaves."

The cabin offered shelter, but not much. Abandoned by Clovis once he ascended to the throne of the Frog King, it sorely needed maintenance. As the rain pelted in sheets, a half dozen leaks sprouted from the ceiling. Foraging animals had broken into the cabinets. Smashed crockery littered the floor. A few pieces of furniture remained, most of them with teeth and claw marks. In the corner sat a rumpled pile of old gunnysacks with a depression in the middle as if something recently used them for a nest. Not to mention, the air had a very distinct aroma.

Amelie wrinkled her nose. "It stinks in here."

The odor was a mixture of rotting vegetation and rank musk. I swallowed back a gag. The cabin was less inviting than the thunder and lightning outside.

Odile started a fire in the hearth with some of the debris. The shower stopped and she sent Amelie and me to the pump at the old well, which, fortunately, hadn't run dry. She pulled a cooking pot from her pack and added rice, beans and seasonings. Within a short time, a smoky delicious scent replaced the rancid cabin smell. We sat at the rickety table and dug in.

Amelie swallowed a mouthful. "Can Lucy find Clovis' trail again after this rain?"

Odile gave a noncommittal shrug. "We shall see. He is close. We'll begin the search again at first light."

"How exactly did a shaman like Clovis earn a living?" I said. "You know, before he went nuts."

"People came to him for help. Shamans have different abilities. I throw the bones, fix packets of herbs for aches and pains, or intervene with the spirits on a person's behalf."

Amelie gave the old woman an affectionate smile. "People with Odile's talents are highly sought after. Father often consulted Odile on important business matters to make sure the spirits approved. We were very sorry when she retired. Odile never allowed danger to enter the house."

Odile reached over and patted her hand. "I'm sorry, *cher*. Your father spoke so highly of Delphine in his letters, I didn't suspect her true nature. If only I made time to visit."

"What happened wasn't your fault. She fooled us all."

"I promise, Amelie," said Odile with grim determination. "We'll deal with Delphine."

I almost felt sorry for Delphine. I wouldn't want both Amelie and Odile out for my blood. "What about Clovis?" I said. "I can't see him fussing over packets of herbs for a stomach ache."

"True," said Odile, "but Clovis was the most powerful shaman in the bayou. While I request the spirits' help, Clovis demanded it."

Amelie gasped. "They'd answer him?"

"Yes. The spirits respect power and Clovis is formidable. He can predict a storm's path of destruction, the duration of the rains, and the strength of the winds. He can divine the best hunting and fishing areas, and read the signs of approaching evil, long before anything obvious is amiss. Like you, Peter, Clovis is left-handed. An out of the ordinary trait, but common among those who wield the deeper magic."

"So what went wrong with Clovis?" asked Amelie.

"While Clovis made a connection to the forces in the swamp, I can't say he ever made a connection to the people." Odile clucked her disapproval. "Working with powerful elements made him feel superior to the rest of us. He never married and had children, shunning deep personal commitments, caring more about investigating the supernatural elements. When you have no loved ones to affect your decisions, the consequences of actions don't matter. Power without consequences creates arrogance. Clovis assumed he could defeat any magical danger alone." She sighed. "Poor man paid a very steep price for being wrong."

After dinner, we arranged our bedrolls for the night. I stretched out flat, hands behind my head, staring at the ceiling. Odile's words floated back, although I tried to push them away. They made me uncomfortable. I spent years honing my abilities as a liar to set out on my own; no cares, no responsibilities, and nobody to think about, but myself.

Just like Clovis.

Amelie dropped her bedroll next to mine.

I startled. "Geez, give some warning."

"You should be more alert," she scolded. "I could have been an enemy sneaking up on you."

I yawned. "I thought that's why I have a bodyguard."

"Exactly. You see, I was right. You need someone to watch over you."

I rolled over. "I can't hear you. I'm already asleep."

Odile covered the rest of the rice and beans and put the pot by the hearth. Except for a few glowing embers the cabin was dark. I fished a flashlight from the pack to keep at hand in case I had to use the outhouse in the middle of the night.

The rain began again, this time a gentle patter. My eyelids drooped. Fatigue blanketed my arms and legs. Stumbling around a swamp takes a lot out of a guy. I had a faint recollection of Amelie and Odile wishing each other *bonne nuit* before the rhythmic *plink-plink-plink* on the tin roof lulled me to sleep.

I don't know how long I slept, but when I woke not even flickering embers remained of the fire. I stared into the gloom with the edgy feeling something wasn't right. As my eyes adjusted to the dark, a faint *creak* came from the direction of the door. Nothing to worry about, I assured myself. Old buildings were prone to strange noises.

Creak.

I froze as the door inched open. Outside, moonlight glistened in the puddles. One by one the sparkles disappeared as a hulking beast stepped into the doorframe and blotted out the view. The low light made features hard to distinguish, but the thing was huge and covered with some sort of armor plating. Giant spikes stuck up from where the head should have been. It was the silhouette of a walking nightmare.

About this time, my heart attempted to hammer through my chest.

As noiseless as a cat, it slunk over the old wooden floorboards. I shut my eyes and pretended to sleep. An unbelievable stench hit my nostrils, and I pressed my lips tight to keep from gagging. As I did, my fingers brushed something cold and metallic— the flashlight. I curled my fingers around the grip and felt for the switch. Opening my eyes to slits, I watched as the figure squatted at the hearth, snatched the pot of rice and beans, and then silently retraced the path to the door.

Not being a military strategist, my mind instantly settled on the most direct assault. I shot to my feet and thumbed on the flashlight. For added effect, I yelled, "Aaaaargh," although I'm not sure why.

Needless to say, all hell broke loose. Amelie scrambled to her feet. A swirl of sticks, leaves, and mud with a small snarling dog attached howled in the beam of the flashlight. Brandishing her knife, Amelie plowed into the whirlwind bringing the entire rotating mass to the floor.

"One twitch, hell spawn," she growled, "and I'll cut out your heart."

Mrs. Hart barked. I yelled "Aaaaargh" again for no real reason and played the flashlight over the captured figure. I don't know what I expected.

Certainly not a mud covered man in a loincloth made from oak leaves. He bellowed at the top of his lungs.

"Be quiet, Clovis," ordered Odile in a no-nonsense tone. "What a mess. You spilt the red beans and rice all over the place."

Clovis clamped his lips shut. He squinted in the light, eyeballing Odile with suspicion. "Ribbit."

"Don't give me any of your backtalk. It's me, Odile Benoit. You remember, don't you? We've known each other a long time. I'm no threat."

Mistrust slowly drained from his expression. "Ribbit?"

"Amelie let him up slowly. Clovis, behave yourself, you hear? All we want to do is talk."

Amelie drew her knife from his chest, but kept a firm grip on the haft and a wary eye on Clovis. Mrs. Hart planted her feet in front of the door, daring him to make a break for it. Odile introduced Amelie, Mrs. Hart, and me. Clovis presented his hand to kiss and I snorted in disgust.

"You be nice, Clovis Landry," Odile ordered, "and I'll cook you a breakfast better than cold rice and beans."

Apparently, the promise of a hot meal held more appeal than freedom. "Brrroooorrrkkk?" he croaked.

"Hush puppies," Odile replied. "You always were partial to mine. You said they were the best around." Clovis smacked his lips and got to his feet.

"Oh, geez," I groaned. Apparently, the royal tailor ran out of oak leaves before finishing the loincloth. "His butt is sticking out."

Clovis sniffed. "An underling does not mention the king's posterior. That's a violation of court etiquette."

"Ah," Amelie noted dryly. "Fortunately for us, the king is bilingual."

"And nutty as a fruitcake," I fussed. "Underling? Who's he calling an underling?"

Clovis ignored me and zeroed in on a tangled mass of shrubbery in the corner. "My crown!" He pounced and although we stood inside a cabin, the three of us had a perfect view of a full moon.

"Oh, geez," I groaned again.

Clovis placed the interwoven mess of leaves and sticks proudly on his head. The vegetation cascaded down his neck, giving him the unearthly appearance from before. He squared his shoulders and stood erect. "The king is ready for breakfast."

"*Mon Dieu.*" Amelie clapped a hand over her mouth as the first wave hit. "The smell is back."

We both glared at once at our new houseguest. "He stinks," I snarled.

"I didn't give you permission to speak, varlet," said Clovis. "I shall resume my throne until breakfast is ready. After which, prepare to receive a suitable punishment or you may beg for mercy." He took two bounding hops and planted himself squarely in the center of the pile of gunnysacks. "Ribbit."

"Amelie," I hissed, "give me the dagger. I'm in a stabbing mood."

She patted my arm with sympathy. "Sorry, can't kill him yet." She shot a pleading look to Odile. "Can we?"

Odile chuckled. "I'm afraid not. However, we most certainly can do something about the smell." She dug into her knapsack, retrieved a bar of soap and a washcloth, and handed both to me. "Take him to the pump."

"Me?" I was aghast. "Why me?"

"Because," said Amelie smoothly, "Odile is cooking breakfast and I have both a knife and a gun so you can't make me go."

I glowered at the two of them. Mrs. Hart nudged my ankle. "Lucy says she'll stand guard so Clovis won't escape," said Odile. "Clovis—go with Peter and wash up." The King of the Frogs opened his mouth to protest, but Odile cut him off. "No arguing or no breakfast."

He scrambled off the pile of gunnysacks, but Odile ordered him to wait. She pulled the cleanest one from underneath and used Amelie's blade to cut a slit in the bottom. With the drawstring on top, the new opening made an improvised skirt. Her eyes sparkled in amusement as she tossed the sack to me. "The emperor's new clothes."

"Come on, Your Highness," I groused. "Let's get this over with."

"Lead on, page," Clovis commanded. He hopped across the room until I snapped at him to quit. In a huff, he swung his arms stiffly at his side and paraded out the door bellowing, "Make way for the king. All hail the glorious King of the Frogs." I stormed after Clovis and herded him to the pump. As soon as he discarded his crown and loincloth, Mrs. Hart quickly trotted them both downwind of the cabin to bury.

The sun had risen, the better to note the crusty dirt covering the shaman. Clovis sat contentedly scrubbing under the spigot while I pumped. A steady stream of water gushed out matching his steady stream of nonsensical chatter. Apparently, the King of the Frogs recently declared war on the turtle nation because of some imagined insult.

"They chew right in front of me with their mouths open. Can you believe the affront? No manners at all." Despite my professed disinterest, Clovis outlined his battle plan. "Quite simple, really. I told my generals to flip them over. Brilliant, no? Of course," he confided smugly, "I'm a military genius."

I sneered. "So that's what you do all day—run around the swamp sneaking behind turtles and flipping them on their shells."

"Naturally, boy. This is war."

"Don't the turtles simply flip over again?"

"In time, in time," Clovis huffed, "but it's the principal of the thing." He awarded me a look dripping with pity. "You obviously have no head for military strategy."

With Clovis' vigorous scrubbing, most of the dirt and grime washed away, but hair and beard was another matter. Clovis had braided them into a snarled mass that a steel-toothed comb couldn't plow through. I went inside for Amelie's dagger. She protested, complaining the blade would have to be boiled clean after coming in contact with Clovis. When I told her I couldn't guarantee he didn't already have squirrels nesting in his hair, she grudgingly handed it over.

Fortunately, Amelie kept her blade razor sharp. Clovis hacked off the shaggy mass on his head and trimmed his beard to mere stubble. He slipped on the gunnysack and tied the drawstring around his waist. After running his hands along the rough burlap, he bellowed into the swamp, "The finest raiment from the most skilled tailors of my kingdom—it will never be yours, turtle scum. Do you hear me? Never!"

The swamp was silent. Apparently, the Turtle King didn't care a fig about wearing a skirt fashioned from an old gunnysack. We paraded to the cabin. Actually, Clovis paraded. I stomped behind in disgust.

Odile contemplated the newly scrubbed Clovis with approval. "I must say you look world's better, practically human, again." She sniffed. "Smell better, too."

"Thank you. My new squire has proven suitable."

"I'm not your dang squire," I squawked.

"Although, lacking in decorum. One can't be too picky about the quality of help nowadays. He needs instruction in the niceties of the court. I will see to his education personally." Clovis took a deep whiff of the hushpuppies. "After breakfast."

Without enough chairs to go around, we joined Clovis on the floor. The shaman hadn't eaten a good meal in a while. With the outer coating of dirt scraped off, nothing much remained underneath but skin and bones. The Frog King certainly had no lack of appetite. The pile of hushpuppies in front of him quickly evaporated. Amelie's compassion overcame her disgust and she offered him half of hers. He gratefully accepted and immediately dubbed her Minister of State.

"Odile," I entreated under my breath, "how can he help? He's loony to the bone." Mrs. Hart cocked her head and barked at Clovis.

To my amazement, Clovis stopped eating and addressed Mrs. Hart directly. "Nonsense. Squire Peter obviously has no understanding of court protocol." Mrs. Hart barked again. "Well, if you say so, but…" His voice dropped. "He doesn't appear very bright."

Amelie's eyes widened. "You understand Lucy?"

"Of course, although she talks very quickly. No matter, all are welcome in my kingdom." Clovis shot me a sideways glance. "Including, the slow ones."

"Hey!" I made a move, but Odile held me in place. "Let go. I'm going to pop him one good."

"Sit," she ordered. "As crazy as Clovis appears on the surface, the shaman remains within."

I plunked down with a grunt. "You have to be kidding."

"Not at all. Clovis knows his own name. He can speak to Lucy. He recognized immediately she wasn't a normal dog. That knowledge requires powerful insight. He hasn't run away. Part of him knows me and trusts I want to help. The real shaman is buried somewhere deep inside the Frog King. The question is how to bring the rest of the man to the surface."

I shrugged. "Don't ask me. Liars I can deal with, but Clovis…"

Amelie was thoughtful. "So, he's not a liar? I don't understand, Peter. You haven't challenged Clovis once, but he's lied all along. I mean, he's not really the King of the Frogs."

"No, but I don't sense a lie, either. A lie isn't a lie if you believe it to be true."

"No. It's still a lie, Peter," insisted Odile. "Somewhere deep inside Clovis realizes that. You must find a way to break though and reveal the truth."

I regarded her with disbelief. "Me? How? I don't have a single idea where to begin." Mrs. Hart placed her paw on my knee.

"Lucy says you freed her from a lie."

"That was different. The lie around Mrs. Hart was like a shell keeping her prisoner. I felt it as soon as we touched. I don't sense a lie with Clovis."

"Perhaps," Odile said, "this lie is buried deep and not so obvious."

"Maybe." Was it possible? Could a lie be buried so deep it seemed true?

Odile nudged me. "Freeing Lucy started with a touch."

She had a point. What could I do with a really good grip? Clovis stopped chewing long enough to notice my scrutiny. He circled his arm protectively around the plate. "The hushpuppies are mine. Property of the king."

"I don't want your breakfast." I slid over my plate with two hushpuppies left. "Do you want the rest?"

His eyes glistened in approval. "Putting your king first—very thoughtful, squire. I had doubts, but now believe you are not as mentally deficient as you first appeared and will make an excellent manservant."

"Gee, thanks," I jeered. Clovis reached for the plate. My hand shot out and grabbed his wrist.

Clovis moved to shake me off. "Let go."

I held on tight and took hold of his other hand, too.

Show me the lie.

Fierce hot pain ripped through my arms. Clovis yelped and pulled away.

"Grab him," I yelled.

Amelie pinned the shaman to the floor.

"What are you doing?" he said with a trembling voice. "Your king commands you to stop. You must do as I say."

I crouched beside him.

"Please." Clovis begged with tears in his eyes. "It hurts…don't."

Amelie shot me a questioning look. I shook my head vehemently.

"I'm sorry," she whispered, tightening her grip.

Despite everything, I pitied Clovis. He seemed less and less like a crazy swamp creature and more like a sick man. "I'm sorry, too, Your Majesty." I rubbed the tingling from my hands, took a deep breath, and again seized his wrists.

Although anticipating an electric shock, nothing prepared me for the burning agony rocketing through my arms. The sensation was like submerging both hands in boiling water. I bit my lip hard to keep from crying out and tasted blood. The shock built to a scorching wave. I hazarded a terrified glance,

197

convinced the skin and muscles had been reduced to scorched flesh. To my relief, my hands were still there.

So, the fire was a lie—a good one, but a lie nevertheless. A powerful lie can convince most people of anything but, luckily, I'm not most people. "No fire surrounds us," I murmured to myself. "The pain is nothing but a lie." The pain in my arms disappeared, but the fire fought with a burning intensity as if possessed by a will and mind of its own.

Clovis moaned and thrashed in Amelie's unrelenting grip, still trapped in the lie. This was way stronger than the one that captured Mrs. Hart. Simple recognition wouldn't kill it. This lie built a wall of flames around the shaman's sanity. When his mind tried to break free, the agony drove him back.

How did I fight a lie in the shape of a flame? Fight fire with fire? I dismissed that idea immediately. What a dumb expression. People who did that became piles of smoldering goop. The cries from Clovis weakened.

"Peter." Amelie's worried face told the story.

Clovis arched his back and groaned in pain, slumping into Amelie's arms. The hard years took their toll on the Frog King. He wouldn't be able to tolerate much more.

Fire didn't feel right. I needed another weapon, but what? The answer came in a flash. The best tool to fight fire was water. Enough would douse any flame.

Click.

The other sense locked in. I pushed away the reality of the cabin and built an image of a swirling mass of cool blue water in my mind. I believed in the lie so hard I felt misty droplets spatter my face.

Ignore the pain. Ignore everything. Believe the lie.

Neither Odile, Amelie, nor Mrs. Hart saw anything, but why should they? The lie was my weapon to wield, not theirs.

"Let him go," I ordered Amelie.

She lowered Clovis gently to the floor and strode through the invisible water to Odile's side. Clovis' eyelids fluttered. I knelt over him and murmured.

"Water douses the flame."

My stream connected with the fire guarding Clovis. With a hiss, the water turned to steam and evaporated, but the flaming barricade didn't weaken. The lie wasn't powerful enough.

"No flame can stand against a whirlpool."

The water became a foaming churning eddy with five times the volume, a liquid cylinder to surround Clovis. Tongues of yellow flames lapped at the surface filling the air with hot dense steam.

"The steam turns to rain."

Water gushed in a torrent. The fire reached brilliant intensity, striving to destroy the cylinder. I gathered the rain, pouring the water on the flames. They sputtered and hissed like an angry cat.

"The fire dies."

In a final desperate assault, flames lashed out to break my concentration, but I sent cascades of water to force them back. The raging heat disappeared. The fire withered until at last nothing glowed but a single ember hovering over Clovis. The flickering entity emitted both heat and hate. I mustered every scrap of belief I had to make the lie an unbreakable command.

"I see you now. Your power is gone. Return to the Lower Worlds where you belong."

The ember screamed in rage and disappeared in a puff of smoke.

I dropped Clovis' hands and collapsed, feeling like an old rag forced through the wringer of a washing machine. Something cold and wet poked my arm. Mrs. Hart nosed me with concern.

"Peter?"

I forced open my eyes. Amelie laid a soft hand on my forehead. Her worried face hovered inches from mine. "Are you okay?"

"Mmph," I managed to say.

"Of course, he is," Odile harrumphed. "See to Clovis. The boy doesn't need coddling."

"Hang on a second." I groaned, struggling to sit. "Coddling sounds pretty good."

"Nonsense, too much pampering will make you weak. Battling on the dark road isn't for sissies."

Amelie gave Clovis a quick once over. "He's asleep now. His breathing is regular. What happened, Peter? What did you do?"

Describing the battle with the flames wasn't easy, not being exactly sure about everything myself.

"Did Peter reach him, Odile?" asked Amelie.

She shrugged. "We'll see."

"You don't exactly ooze confidence," I complained. "Can't your shaman powers give a little hint?"

"They don't work that way. On the bright side," she added in a cheerful tone, "you couldn't have possibly made him worse."

Amelie flashed a brilliant smile. "Well, I'm proud of you, Peter." A pleased flush crept up my neck.

"Who said I wasn't proud of him?" sniffed Odile. "Of course, I'm proud of him. He passed the first test for a shaman. He has not been destroyed."

My eyes widened. "The *first* test is don't be destroyed?"

"*Oui.* Good one, too. The bayou is littered with the bodies of those who failed."

"Littered?" I didn't like the way the conversation headed. "How many dead are we talking about?"

Much to my relief, Amelie interrupted. "What do we do with Clovis?"

With a grunt, Odile rose to her feet. "Nothing for the moment, other than make him comfortable. Once he wakes, we'll know how much of his mind is retained."

They lifted Clovis onto one of the bedrolls. I offered to help, but Mrs. Hart put her paw on my chest. She dragged over a blanket, which I tucked gratefully behind my head. I must have dozed off because the next thing I remember was Amelie offering me something to eat. The shadows in the cabin had lengthened considerably as morning progressed to afternoon. A fluttering snore reverberated from the corner.

"Clovis has been like that all day," Amelie said, as a gargling snort ripped through the air. "What a racket. Unfortunately, a personal code of honor forbids me from stabbing him to death."

"Pity."

"I think so."

"Has he spoken?"

"Not a peep…you look worried."

I sat up. "If Clovis doesn't recover enough for us to get answers, then the whole trip was a waste. We're no closer to facing the conjuror than before."

"The impatience of youth," clucked Odile. She handed me a cup of the strong chicory-laced coffee preferred here. "Do not fret. You did what you came to do."

I took a sip. "I'm not so sure."

"I am." She scrutinized me with fierce intensity. "You used natural magic, Peter. The talent is inbred and can't be taught. Why, the very air crackled with mystical energy. True, it was raw and untamed, needing focus and direction. The ability to recognize the lie cast around a victim requires time and training to hone, but I tell you no other shaman could have done better for Clovis. Even I couldn't penetrate the spell."

"Why not?" Amelie asked.

"Although I sensed an enchantment, I can't see it the way Peter can. The deep magic takes many forms. Mine is of the bayou, the healing powers of the plants, and the energy of the spirits. Peter and Clovis share a special ability. They can each see beyond the magic of a lie to the truth underneath."

I blinked. "You mean a spell is nothing more than a lie?"

"*Certainement.* A lie clouds the truth of a person's words while a spell clouds the truth of a person's reality. A spell is much more powerful, but at their essence, they are one and the same—nothing more than lying. Any skilled shaman can recognize the effect, but the difference between you and Clovis and someone like me is you both can destroy the enchantment without having to face the conjuror or know the original spell. The magic isn't easily done. You have the makings of a cracking good shaman."

Amelie elbowed me in the ribs. "Don't worry. I won't let you get a big head, unless you like the idea of hopping around half-naked through the swamp."

"I'll pass."

Odile patted my hand. "You did your best. Once Clovis awakes, we will see if the spell's destruction was enough to penetrate the fog in his brain."

I still wrestled with doubt. "Are you sure Clovis can help against a conjuror as strong as Pike?"

"My dear boy," trumpeted a voice from the corner, "I assure you, whether conjuror, witch doctor, medicine man, or shaman, I possess the necessary skills to subdue mystical threats—and my rates are quite reasonable." Clovis sat up and frowned. "I feel a draft." He peered in confusion at his lap. "Where are my pants?"

Odile toddled over to him. "Well, it's about time you joined us. Do you know who I am?"

"Of course, I know who you are, Odile. Are you playing some kind of joke?" Clovis scanned the interior, eyes narrowing in suspicion. "Where am I? This isn't my cabin. Fair warning, Odile, though you are a colleague in the otherworldly arts, I will show no mercy if you attempt to probe for my secrets."

"Clovis, be quiet and listen. No one, least of all me, wants to probe you for anything."

"You were always jealous."

"Clovis." Odile squatted down and pinned him with an unflinching stare. "Hush. I'm not here to rob you. I'm here to help. This is your cabin. You abandoned it when your mind addled after opening a doorway to the Lower Worlds."

"Nonsense," Clovis sputtered a protest, but uncertainty flashed across his face. "I most assuredly didn't…wouldn't…did I?"

"You did."

"Oh, dear," he said weakly. "I take it the attempt didn't go well?"

"You're wearing a gunnysack. What do you think?"

"How long ago?"

"Nearly six years. You've been hopping around calling yourself King of the Frogs ever since."

"Six years?" Clovis collapsed against the wall, stunned. His voice trailed away. "I was always partial to frogs…."

I prodded Odile. "Ask him how to open the door into the Lower Worlds before he goes nuts again."

Clovis cast a suspicious look at the rest of us. "Who are they?"

Odile made introductions, and Clovis managed a wobbly bow. When Odile got to Mrs. Hart, the shaman grasped a paw to shake heartily. "Madame, a pleasure. I see I'm not the only one who had a run-in with the dark. If it's any consolation, terriers have always been my favorite dog."

I took recognition of Mrs. Hart as a good sign. "You know she's a woman."

"*Ma oui*," he sniffed. "I'm no French Market voodoo shyster catering to the tourist trade."

"You owe Peter thanks," said Odile. "He broke through and cleared your mind."

He eyeballed me with obvious skepticism. "Nonsense. I did it on my own. My powers are exceptional."

"Clovis Landry," Odile snapped, "you did no such thing. Peter brought you back and you know the truth. Doesn't he, Peter?"

"Yep, that statement was a lie." I glared at Clovis. "I can always spot a lie."

Clovis harrumphed. "You said you need help."

"How did you open a door into the Lower Worlds?"

Clovis crossed his arms and gazed at the ceiling. "Anything, but that. I don't want to talk about it." He inhaled deeply. "Do I smell coffee?"

I had enough. "We slogged the whole way through this swamp to find you."

"You're mighty impertinent, Magic Boy. One arcane maneuver doesn't make you a full-fledged member of the League of Professional Shamans."

"I freed you."

"I'd have freed myself eventually."

"Yeah, you were certainly on the road back—hopping around with your butt flapping in the breeze."

Clovis looked at Odile. "As I was saying before I was rudely interrupted…coffee?"

"Fetch him a cup, Amelie. Don't mind Clovis," she whispered to me. "He'll come around once he hears your story."

"I liked him better as a frog," I grumbled.

Clovis sat at the table and Amelie handed him a steaming cup. As we talked, Clovis' sullenness turned to rapt interest. By the time Odile described reading the bones, the coffee cooled, the cup forgotten in his hands.

"Feu De L'enfer," he murmured.

"Is the name familiar?" said Amelie.

"No."

"That's a lie," I said.

Odile shook her finger at him. "Clovis, we've been honest. The least you can do is return the favor."

He shifted in the seat and avoided her eyes. "Perhaps, I heard the name before."

"You more than heard it." Odile said in an accusatory tone. "The demon is tied to the reason you opened the door."

He nonchalantly ran his finger around the rim of the cup. "Maybe."

"Clovis!"

"Oh, all right. I read the signs of a demon probing for an escape route. You know the persistence of these creatures. I thought if I forced a confrontation while it was trapped…"

Odile shook her head. "Clovis Landry, how could you? Feu De L'enfer could have escaped."

"I took every precaution."

"Hardly. You lost your mind as the result."

For an instant, the shaman opened his mouth as if to argue and then his shoulders sagged. His whole demeanor projected defeat. "Yes. I was a fool."

"And arrogant."

Clovis heaved a resigned sigh. "And arrogant."

"Wait a minute," I said, alarmed. "You mean the same demon after Esther is the one who attacked you?"

He cleared his throat. "Yes."

"What else aren't you telling us?" demanded Amelie.

"Go ahead," Odile ordered angrily. "You can't hide the truth. They've earned the right to know. Really, Clovis, your actions were inexcusable."

The last of the shaman's bluff and bluster melted away. "I never met a creature I couldn't subdue and this one taunted me. Demons are weakest in their own dimension. I was confident I could kill it there, but the Lower Worlds are harsh and Feu De L'enfer is powerful." He hung his head. "By the time I escaped, the damage was done."

"You proved to the demon the escape route was viable," said Odile.

"Yes, so Feu De L'enfer went hunting for someone else to create a door."

Chapter 10
Nothing Instills More Confidence than Watching the Blind Lead the Insane

Amelie scratched her head. "I don't understand."

"In certain areas of the Lower Worlds," said Odile, "the fabric separating our two dimensions stretches thin. A door can be made in such a place, but can't be detected by the creatures within. Feu De L'enfer can hunt for an eon and never find the right spot. However, once Clovis arrived, the demon sensed a human approach and realized an escape route was possible."

"That wasn't my intention," said Clovis. "I planned to kill the demon quickly. Feu De L'enfer can't open the door or find the exit alone."

"Which made the creature more determined to locate a person who can," said Odile.

"Like Esther, you mean." I snapped. "The story keeps getting better and better."

Odile leaned toward Clovis, a storm in her eyes. "Feu De L'enfer readily struck a deal with Pike because the demon needed a servant on this side to find someone with Esther's unique gift. Clovis, people have already died because of the conceited belief in your own invincibility. Esther's cousins were murdered. Her life is in danger. Peter was nearly killed, not to mention what happened to Lucy."

Clovis half-rose from his seat. "I never meant to—"

"Your reasons don't matter now." I jumped to my feet. "We have to set things right. Will you help us or not?"

Clovis stood. He towered over us, an undefined expression on his face.

Amelie stood shoulder to shoulder beside me. "I'm with Peter."

"As am I," said Odile, "and the rest of my family." Mrs. Hart barked her two cents worth, too.

For the first time, Clovis' demeanor held a glint of amusement. "Revolt, eh? So much for the power of the throne. A shaman may be in you yet, boy, if you can get three headstrong females to stand by your side with no argument." He rubbed his chin. "We need a plan."

"Which needn't be devised here," said Odile. "Chris will return to Andre's cabin soon with the boat. If we leave now, we'll arrive before dark."

"Andre's not expecting us to stay for dinner, is he?" Clovis shuddered. "I don't suppose his cooking improved over the last six years?"

Odile patted his arm. "Unfortunately, not. It may even be worse. Don't worry, I'll make our excuses. Is there anything you wish to take from the cabin?"

Clovis regarded the remains of his tattered life and heaved a resigned sigh. "No." Then he brightened and tapped the side of his head. "Not to worry. Everything of importance is right up here." Understandably, I didn't take any comfort from his words.

We packed our gear and left the cabin. Clovis took the lead, insisting he knew a shortcut through the bayou to bring us to Andre Savoy's homestead in half the time. I had doubts and kept a wary eye on the Frog King in case he decided to detour into the Turtle Kingdom to launch a final shell-flipping sneak attack.

Clovis' shortcut was no easy amble along Canal Street. We slogged through dense foliage. The clouds gathered again and Odile warned us to expect another afternoon shower. We pressed on to beat the storm and soon arrived at a cut, a shallow channel between two sections of the swamp. Clovis pointed to the opposite bank. "That way. Andre's cabin is no more than a mile ahead."

Clovis, Odile, and Amelie waded across. Mrs. Hart pawed at the water. Although not deep, the steady current held concern for someone her size.

"Want a lift?" I said. She wagged her tail.

I bent to pick her up and froze at the sound of a gravelly hiss. Two beady eyes glinted from the vegetation. A gator raised a massive head from no more than a yard away. A deep rumble issued from the maw. The jaws gaped open to expose wicked rows of teeth. Mrs. Hart growled.

"Don't," I whispered.

Whether spooked by my voice or the sudden realization of an angry dog nearby, the gator tensed, choosing the strike spot. Blood pounded in my ears. The monster would charge. I knew it. At this distance, the gator couldn't miss.

A rifle cocked. Amelie shouted across the water, "Peter, move." I couldn't have picked a worse spot. I stood between Amelie and the gator, blocking her shot.

A tingling energy pricked at my skin. Mystic forces gathered around me.

"A wall…" murmured Clovis to the gator as he waded through the water. "Stone…smooth surface…nothing you can climb…nothing the danger can get over…" The illusion of a sturdy granite barricade three feet high instantly appeared separating the gator from Mrs. Hart and me.

The gator hissed again. "This place is not safe," Clovis said. "You are penned in with no escape. You don't want to be here." He conjured a series of splashes leading to the channel. "Follow the sound. Plenty of good fish are nearby." The gator hugged the wall, slid into the cut, and then submerged underwater. A trail of bubbles broke the surface, leading away from us and into open water.

The wall disappeared. Amelie ran to me. "The illusion was amazing, Peter. Even the gator believed."

"Peter didn't do it," Odile stated with confidence.

"She's right," I said. "The magic was all Clovis." I turned to the shaman and drew a shaky breath. "Thanks. That was something. I never knew a person could tell a lie so powerful others saw it, too."

Clovis' complexion was pale and drawn. "You're welcome, but I'm a bit rusty, I'm afraid. It was merely a simple illusion, but took far too long to set in place and the texture and color were wrong." He shook his head ruefully. "Sloppy, very sloppy—wouldn't have fooled a third-rate conjuror for a moment."

Amelie regarded Clovis with newfound respect, although nothing dulled her brute honesty. "You may not be as useless as you appear."

To his credit, Clovis took no offense. He even seemed amused. "*Merci*. I will endeavor not to disappoint."

Once we reached dry ground again, Clovis led the way through the brush. His once brisk pace now slowed to a shamble. In his weakened state, the small bit of magic obviously wore him out. After pausing a third time to rest, I worried whether we'd make Mr. Savoy's cabin by nightfall. Traveling a mile through the harsh conditions of a bayou was a lot different than strolling paved city streets. The sky had darkened considerably and thunder rumbled in the distance. I had no desire to spend another night in the swamp without the benefit of at least a crude shelter.

With an exhausted sigh, Clovis plopped onto an old stump I swear we passed twice already. "Odile," Amelie whispered under her breath, "Clovis' concentration is failing. He's running us in circles. Do you know where we are?"

"I haven't come this way before, but the path to Andre's should be near."

"If it isn't?"

Odile gave an offhanded shrug. Spending the night in the swamp didn't bother her one whit. Amelie scowled, wiping a sweaty hand across her brow. As the humans in the party clumped together waiting for Clovis to recover his strength, Mrs. Hart pointed her nose in the air and sniffed. Suddenly, she barked an alert and tore into the brush.

Amelie was instantly on guard, dagger in hand. "Where'd Lucy go?" she demanded of me.

Between the heat, humidity, and the encounter with the gator, my temper wore to a raw edge. Amelie's insistence on lickety-split information struck an irritating nerve. "How should I know? I don't speak dog. She didn't sound worried, though."

Amelie swatted impatiently at a persistent mosquito buzzing around her face. "Oh, you can tell from a bark? Aren't you clever?"

The sudden brush with death finally took its toll. I was tired, crabby, hungry, and done with slogging through the bayou. "If you paid more attention, you'd know Mrs. Hart always warns with a growly yelp and that was definitely a…a…yelpy yelp."

"You're ridiculous," she sputtered. "You're making everything up."

I did, but refused to admit the truth. So I attacked with a clever retort. "Am not. You're ridiculous."

"Mine was a perfectly reasonable comment," she hissed, sounding a lot like the gator.

"Reasonable for you."

"What's that supposed to mean?" she said between gritted teeth.

"I don't know," I hollered, not sure who or what I was angry with, "but it means something."

"Enough," ordered Odile. "We're all tired. Clovis, we must keep moving. Not much daylight remains."

He struggled to his feet and took a staggering step forward. "I can make it."

Amelie stuffed the knife in the sheath. "No, you can't. Lean on me." She slipped his arm over her shoulders. "No arguments."

"I make it a point never to argue with a *mademoiselle* prepared for combat." He poked me in the ribs. "Good advice, boy."

I sighed and scooted under his other arm. With Odile leading the way, we stumbled along half-dragging/half-carrying Clovis.

The bayou showed no sign of Mrs. Hart. My worry grew as the sun dipped toward the horizon. Amelie and I were at the end of our strength. Could we help Mrs. Hart if she was in trouble? Just then, a familiar *arf* sounded behind a clump of bushes.

"Mrs. Hart," I called. "Over here."

The leaves rustled and a sandy brown terrier emerged. On her heels were Renny and Chris. They quickly traded places with Amelie and me.

"Am I glad to see you," I said, relieved to be free of Clovis' weight.

"Same here, *mon ami*," said Renny. "I thought we'd have a long walk through the bayou, but Lucy was at the pier when we arrived. She led us to you."

Amelie's expression lit up. "We're not far?"

Chris motioned ahead. Barely visible through the trees was a narrow well-worn path.

Andre Savoy waited at the dock with a grease-stained paper bag. "I see y'all got his royal frogness," he grunted. "I reckon now the rest of my okra be safe." He handed Odile the bag. Although hungry, the rancid oily smell caused my stomach to turn nauseated flip-flops. "Chris said you can't stay for supper, so I fried a mess of beignets. Sure I can't convince y'all to come inside? I made me some rabbit stew two, or was it three days ago? If I throw in more cayenne, the meat will freshen right up."

Odile thanked him, and hustled us to the Sweet Marie. Chris and Renny assisted Clovis onboard. They made a resting place for him in the stern with the bedrolls and a canvas tarp over his head to keep off the coming rain. He collapsed with a grateful sigh and promptly closed his eyes. Chris started the engine. As soon as we were out of sight of Andre's cabin, Odile shook the contents of the greasy paper sack overboard. The beignets plopped like lead sinkers into the water, plunging directly to the bottom.

She wrinkled her nose. "The only thing they're good for is gator bait."

"A gator is pickier than that," called Chris from behind the wheel.

Hunting and fishing had been good. Chris sold his catch and then returned home for provisions before setting out for us. Odile dispensed long crusty loaves of bread packed with ham and a spicy relish. As the first raindrops hit, we crowded into the cramped wheelhouse to eat. She brought Clovis a sandwich, which he accepted with gratitude.

The meal lasted as long as the rain. Once the sky cleared, the others piled outside to enjoy the breeze. Chris volunteered another lesson in piloting. I eagerly gripped the wheel and steered Sweet Marie down the channel. Chris gave subtle corrections and encouraged me to get a feel for the current.

"The bayou is a living thing, Peter, with moods and rhythms. If you learn to read them, the water will carry you as gently as a mother carries her child."

Under Chris' patient guidance the wildness of the swamp grew less threatening. He pointed to landmarks we passed yesterday. When I recognized a gnarled cypress tree, he clapped me on the shoulder. "*Bon.* You learn quickly, Peter. Soon, traveling the bayou will be no different than visiting an old friend."

Food and rest improved everyone's mood. Amelie admitted she no longer feared imminent drowning when I took the wheel, which for her was a compliment. When we arrived at the Benoit homestead, Chris let me pull to the dock. I flushed in embarrassment when the hull scraped against the pilings.

"Sorry."

"One little bump—not bad for a first time," he assured me.

The door of the house whipped opened and a cascade of Benoits tumbled out with Esther and T. Chris in the rear. Chris greeted his family while I got caught in Esther's viselike grip. She clung like a burr, her words colliding into each other.

"I missed you, Peter, and Amelie and Odile and Mrs. Hart, of course. T. Chris and I caught lots of

216

fish. I helped Marie cook them, but there aren't any left. You don't smell very good. You need a bath."

I peeled her off. "Hi, Esther. Good to see you, too." Amelie and Renny each gave her a hug. When Esther bent over to greet Mrs. Hart, the dog licked her nose.

Esther giggled. "That tickles." She then straightened up and demanded, "Where's the crazy man?"

"Esther," I whispered, embarrassed. "Don't be rude."

"Nonsense," Clovis said. "She's simply honest."

He hung back while the rest of us greeted each other, but now clambered off the Sweet Marie onto the dock. Rest and food returned color to his cheeks. He strode up to Esther with a spring in his step. "Fortunately, my dear, although my brain may be a bit scrambled, I have nothing wrong with my hearing." He considered her from head to toe. "So, you are the see-er."

"Uh-huh," she chirped. "You don't sound crazy. Are you?"

"Not as much, thanks to young Mr. Whistler and his lies."

"Yup, they're mighty powerful. They saved my bacon, for sure. Are you going to help us with the conjuror?"

"I'll do my best."

"Okie-dokie." Esther grabbed his hand. "You best come to the house. We have lots to talk about." Bemused, Clovis allowed himself to be dragged away.

217

"Nothing instills more confidence," quipped Renny, "than watching the blind lead the insane."

Marie scrounged more old clothes for Clovis. The worn overalls were too short for his lanky frame, but a definite improvement over the gunnysack. After we sat at the kitchen table, Amelie asked, "What's our first step?"

"We must determine how to open the door," said Odile. "Clovis, do you remember the incantation?"

"Unfortunately," he said wryly, "some magic is impossible to forget."

"Hang on," I said. "I'd like to know how to keep from going nuts once inside. Not to mention, how to kill Feu De L'enfer." I turned to Odile. "I don't suppose a rifle shot—"

She folded her arms. "No guns."

"Guns are useless in the Lower Worlds," said Clovis. "They are earthbound weapons. You need something with a supernatural kick. What are you good at?"

"Pardon?"

"What did they teach you at school? Sword fighting? Axe throwing? Bullwhip?"

"Mostly how to diagram a sentence and the times tables to twelve."

Clovis' mouth dropped open. Renny noted sympathetically, "They have funny ways up north."

"Differences in teaching philosophies are no excuse for an appalling lack of education." Clovis shook his head in disgust. "No wonder so many travelers on the dark road come from New York City."

"Let's get back to the weapon," I urged. "What do I use to kill the demon?"

Clovis blinked in surprise. "Why the choice is entirely yours. The only sure way to destroy a demon is to create a mystical object to attack the weak point."

Finally, something encouraging. "The demon has a weak point?"

"Of course, nothing is indestructible. Feu De L'enfer's vulnerability is the flaming eyes. Annihilate them and the creature is doomed."

"Flaming eyes? Like Pike?" I gaped at him in disbelief. "How the heck do I do that?"

"Well, I don't know. You must magic a weapon into existence after entering the creature's domain. Of course, you should create something familiar, but since you haven't had martial training I'm stumped where to begin."

"What did you use?" asked Amelie.

"An epee." Clovis answered smoothly. "I'm quite competent with the blade."

"So, what happened?" I said. "How come your weapon didn't work?"

His shoulders slumped. "I wasn't strong enough to hold the spell. The flames from the eyes were blistering. The epee melted from my hand. The heat was intense, like being drawn into the sun. I couldn't concentrate long enough to create another."

Clovis shuddered. "Feu De L'enfer isn't the lone horror behind the door. Once you lose your focus in the Lower Worlds, the demon has every advantage. The hellish realm is nothing but a whirling maelstrom shrieking inside your head, ripping thoughts apart, and destroying your sanity. I lost control. Fear overpowered me. My mind slipped away. The single option left was to run."

Odile patted his hand. "It's a wonder you escaped."

"Pure luck. Your sense of direction is twisted about. I created a spell to track my steps, but the energies pummeling me were so great I barely held my thoughts together. I stumbled upon the exit in the nick of time. Feu De L'enfer was right behind me, but I slammed the door in its face." He shrunk from the memory. "The last thing I recall clearly is the unearthly howling from the other side. The spell broke. The door vanished. Everything afterward is a bit foggy."

"He means a bit froggy," Amelie muttered under her breath.

I blew out my cheeks in disgust. "Great. Flaming eyeballs…what kind of weapon fights those? It's hopeless."

Esther tugged impatiently on my sleeve. "You can out-think the demon, Peter. Like you did in the cabin when you freed Clovis."

"How did you know?" I asked, startled, and then realized the obvious answer. "Esther, you were peeking!"

She at least had the decency to put on a show of guilt. "I'm sorry."

"No, you're not. You're just sorry to get caught."

All pretenses disappeared. "I worried about you, so I peeked for a few seconds and, anyway, I'm right."

Clovis studied Esther with intense interest. "My cabin is quite a distance, young lady. Can you see as far with others?"

"I don't know. I'm not exactly supposed to without permission."

"Which doesn't seem to stop you," I griped.

"I said I was sorry."

Odile rubbed her chin in thought. "What Peter needs now is practice. He does not yet have the ability to face the demon on his own. Clovis will teach him. Meanwhile, I'll concoct a potion to protect against the madness, but such a complicated elixir will take time to devise and requires special ingredients. Marie and Amelie can help."

Everyone voiced agreement, but I said nothing. Odile and Clovis huddled together deep in arcane discussion. The younger Benoits grew bored and dragged Esther away to play. I wandered outside and sat on the porch swing. My thoughts drifted as I listened to the sounds of the bayou.

Amelie sat beside me. "You didn't speak out in there about the plan."

"What plan?" I shot back. "Find the demon somehow. Whip up something to kill the demon somehow. Kill the demon somehow. Swell. Terrific. What's not to love?"

Amelie kicked at the floor and set the rocker into a gentle glide. "When I was seven, my father took us on a trip to Atlanta. One night we went to the theater. The huge lobby had walls decorated in gold leaf and red velvet brocade. Suspended from the ceiling were massive crystal chandeliers. Everyone dressed in their finest clothes. The women wore diamond tiaras and strands of pearls, the men in tuxedos. The evening was my first grown-up event. Like entering another world, I didn't know what to expect."

"Going to the Lower Worlds," I grumped, "is a little different than dinner and a show."

Amelie ignored me and continued. "The bill had several acts, but everyone came to see the main headliner." She chuckled. "He was a world famous entertainer whose name completely escapes me. The sole performer I recall was a juggler. The spotlight hit a man on center stage and his lady assistant. The orchestra began to play slowly. She tossed the man three balls. He caught them and juggled. Three balls—nothing special, you see. She threw him another and another. The music went faster and faster. Soon the juggler had ten balls in the air whizzing around so quickly I was certain they flew."

Excitement laced her voice. "Next, he juggled breakable objects; plates, bottles, glassware. The tempo increased. I dug my fingernails into the armrest. Surely, he'd miss, but the juggler didn't drop a single thing. For the finale, the assistant arranged sharp-edged items on a table, everything from a tiny stiletto to a lumberman's axe. She called to the audience to choose. People yelled, 'Hacksaw! Butcher knife!' The woman tossed each one in turn. The music blared. The audience screamed. The noise was so loud I barely heard myself think, but nothing distracted the juggler. He instantly compensated for the difference in weight and balance of each item until everything spun around in the air at the same time."

I yawned and stretched. "I suppose you have a point to the story. Don't tell me, let me guess. There's no business like show business?"

Amelie brushed off the sarcasm. "The juggler didn't know what came next, but the order of the blades didn't matter. His instincts and skill allowed him to adjust his approach each time."

"You can't seriously draw a comparison between a stage act and fighting a demon."

"On the surface—no, but the same abilities serve a purpose in both. No one told you how to free Clovis. You had the gift and instinct guided you in the right direction. Like the juggler, you found the rhythm to keep the balls in the air, so to speak. You'll find the rhythm again when you confront Feu De L'enfer. I know you will."

"Thanks." Warmth rushed through me at the knowledge Amelie had faith in my abilities. I wanted to tell her how much her confidence meant, but the words wouldn't come. Instead, I said, "Have I mentioned today you're nuts?"

Amelie flounced from her seat, eyes twinkling. "Not yet. Goodnight, Peter. Best turn in. Clovis aims to get an early start."

Chapter 11
The New Rules

Amelie didn't exaggerate. The sun barely peeked over the horizon when Clovis shook me awake. "Come along, boy. We've much to do. No time to lie in bed."

"Breakfast?" I mumbled.

He handed me a steaming mug of café au lait. "Work now. Eat later."

I took a sip. "Okay, but that sounds very un-Cajun. Odile would object."

"Odile is busy with Marie gathering the items needed to brew the potion. Amelie went along to help." His eyes twinkled. "The young lady was very concerned for your safety."

"She was?" My pulse skipped a beat.

"Very much. I promised your safe return with most body parts intact."

I grimaced. "Gee, that's swell. What exactly are they collecting anyway?"

"Marie has an extensive garden and they will harvest the herbs and plant life. What she doesn't grow, she'll collect in the swamp. Odile will hunt specialty items."

"Specialty items?"

"Yes, you know, blood from a she-gator, testicle hair from a wild boar—that sort of thing."

"Sorry I asked." I drained the cup, relieved Odile had corralled Amelie into chasing down disgusting animal parts instead of me.

Clovis led us past Marie's garden, insisting we needed a quiet place free of distractions. He wasn't much for conversation, but acted heaps better; alert, focused, and at least a dozen years younger. Nothing in his gait was feeble or shambling. The shaman strode with ginger in his step not there yesterday. I bombarded him with questions about the training, but he wouldn't give.

We stopped in a small clearing out of earshot of the cabin. Clovis perched on an old cypress stump and directed me to stand in the center. "Tell me, Peter, what do you know of lying?"

"I cracked the rules." I couldn't help but feel a tad smug.

"Which are?"

"Practice."

"Naturally."

"Details are important."

"No question."

"The lie has to make sense."

Clovis leaned forward, hands on his knees. "For whom?"

"For the audience, of course. The lie has to sound real in order for them to buy it."

"So you can't threaten someone with being stomped to death by a pink elephant, because everyone knows pink elephants don't exist."

"Exactly." Clovis gazed blankly past my shoulder. His breathing slowed and became shallow. I cleared my throat. "Uh, Clovis, are you okay?"

The shaman didn't answer. With half-closed eyes, he mumbled to himself, swaying to and fro. For a moment, I thought he was going to be sick and debated running to the house for help. Without warning, he sat up straight and his eyes opened. His expression reminded me of a cat that just downed the family canary.

A trumpeting bellow echoed through the bayou and rocketed me a foot in the air.

I whipped around and came face to trunk with a giant pink elephant. My mouth dropped open. "I...I...I..." Nothing much else came out.

"Go ahead, touch him." Clovis beamed at the elephant. "The lie holds together quite nicely."

I prodded the hide lightly with a finger. It was wrinkly and tough and except for the bubble gum color, looked exactly like pictures I'd seen of an elephant. A rumble came from deep in the maw and it swatted me with the trunk. The effect was like being hammered with a two-by-four. I flew nearly halfway across the clearing.

Clovis shook his finger at the elephant. "That will be enough of that. Be nice." The elephant swayed back and forth. It blew a squeak from the trunk in my direction, pulled up a swath of grass, and stuffed the entire wad in its mouth.

I scrambled to my feet and stumbled to Clovis, reeling with stunned disbelief. "How did you...what did you...huh?"

He smiled, obviously pleased with himself. "That, my dear boy, is an example of what happens when a lie becomes a spell."

"But the elephant is real, not an illusion like the wall. It is real, isn't it? I'm not going nuts, am I?"

"You're perfectly sane—one mad Frog King allowed in the bayou at a time." Clovis stood up and the elephant blew a playful gust of air that riffled his hair. Clovis patted the trunk. "The difference between a lie and a spell, Peter, is a lie must be believable for people to accept the words as truth. No matter how well-crafted the lie, you can never convince an audience of the existence of pink elephants. The lie dies immediately after leaving your lips. On the other hand, a spell simply has to be believable to the shaman. Think of it as another rule."

The elephant thrust his trunk into my shirt pocket poking about for treats. Startled, I batted it away. "I don't understand."

"A skillful liar can tell a story, but a skillful shaman can lie one into rock-solid belief. *Et voila*— a pink elephant real enough to touch."

"The wall you made yesterday...?"

"Was step one." He scratched the elephant's ear. "Static illusions like the wall don't require much power. Desperate situations often call for a shaman to act quickly. They function well as a short-term solution, but the magic is easily breached compared with the mystic power circulating through my pink friend here. Necessary to both a magic illusion and a magic spell, however, is the complete and utter faith of the shaman in the fundamental lie itself."

Rule Seven: For magic you can feel, you must believe the lie is real.

I gaped at the elephant, now placidly munching on grass. The ear flapped, batting at a buzzing fly. "The fly thinks the elephant's real, too."

"Of course. The animal will be perceived by anyone, human or not."

"How long will the spell last?"

"Once my concentration wavers, the lie collapses. Before my journey to the Lower Worlds, I could keep one this big going for months, but now, perhaps, a day or two. I'm terribly out of practice." He heaved a disappointed sign. "Already, the color has faded to cotton candy."

"Don't sell yourself short. This is some razzle-dazzle."

"Thank you, and yet when you get down to basics, I only crafted a lie."

"One heck of a whopper. I never made a living breathing lie another person could see and touch." The elephant lifted its tail and something plopped to the ground. I wrinkled my nose. "And smell."

"You will. For someone self-taught, you already made considerable inroads." Clovis settled back on the stump. "For the first challenge, break this spell."

"How?"

"See beyond the visible. Find the lie hidden within, pin it down, and destroy it."

I sucked in a breath. "Okay, I'll try."

How hard could it be to believe what I see, hear, touch, and smell isn't real? I learned a hard lesson that day. It's darn near impossible. The senses fought to keep control of the mind. I stroked the elephant's hide bracing for an electric shock like in the cabin with Clovis. Only the rough feel of animal hide met my fingers. I stood for a long time in the clearing, running my hands across different parts of the elephant. The sun beat down, trickles of sweat pooled in the small of my back.

"Any time now…" Clovis crooned in an irritating singsong.

"How can I find the lie," I groused, "if everything feels perfectly normal?"

"Really?" Clovis casually examined his fingernails. "How interesting. Exactly how should a pink elephant feel?"

His words struck home. How could the elephant feel normal when it wasn't normal and nothing about its existence made any logical sense?

The elephant is a lie. Find the truth.

A tiny spark danced at the tip of my left hand. *Ignore me*, the flicker whispered in my ear. *Move along. Nothing of interest here*. As I focused more attention on the spark, the heat increased. The truth practically slapped me in the head—the spark is the lie.

Catch the spark. Pin it down. Snuff it out.

Click.

The other sense roared in and flexed like an underused muscle. I tried to corral the spell, but the tiny flame fluttered away each time. Again and again, the maddening little spark came within a hair's breadth of capture. Clovis chuckled, and I suddenly realized his tactic.

"Hey, that's cheating. You're moving the spell around to hide the truth."

"Adjusting to the attack," he admonished. "What? Do you think victory comes without effort?"

"Well, yeah. Feu De L'enfer's spell was simple to pin down, compared to this. So was Pike's spell on Mrs. Hart."

"Both the demon and the conjuror never expected anyone to challenge their powers, so neither made an attempt to disguise their spells. In point of fact, any spell, even a small one, can be tricky if hidden well enough." He shifted position on the stump. "Try again."

I played an invisible game of hide and seek, but the little flame successfully dodged every twist and turn. Frustration mounted and then a faint heat trail brushed against my finger. Although barely strong enough to follow, the spark definitely traced a circular pattern. I made careful note of the direction of movement, and then forged the image of a little corral. *Concentrate. See it.* The miniature prison look shape, complete with teeny tiny barbed wire and an added gun turret for flair. Now to herd the flame inside. *Catch the spark. Pin it down.*

"Hah!"

Easy-peasy. Cornered at last, the spell batted futilely against my mystic prison. Capture wasn't so hard. All I needed to do now was close in for the kill and snuff it out...

A blast of water from the elephant's trunk hit me in the face, breaking my concentration. The spark escaped. The elephant trumpeted victory.

"No fair," I sputtered, wiping my face on my shirtsleeve.

Clovis shook his finger at me. "A conjuror won't sit idly by and wait for you to destroy a spell. Try again—and don't be cocky."

I grumbled under my breath and returned to the hunt. The next time I cornered the spark, I didn't stop to gloat. "A big thumb," I muttered. The supernatural finger slammed down and snuffed the spark. With a mournful bellow, the pink elephant disappeared.

"A little theatrical," Clovis grunted, "but not bad."

"Not bad? I think I did pretty good—"

Wham! Something hit me like a roundhouse punch. My knees buckled. I plopped in the dirt at the shaman's feet.

Clovis nudged me with his toe. "Magic has quite an after-kick. If you don't pace yourself, a spell can drain enough strength to give the enemy an upper hand. Now try again."

I swallowed a groan and staggered to my feet. Clovis and I worked all morning on detecting lies. He conjured an assortment of pink elephants, hippogriffs, and fire-breathing dragons. As I finished evaporating a particularly fat cupid in a soiled diaper, I heard a snicker behind me. Amelie arrived with a lunch basket.

"I'm not sure you should be rewarded for snuffing out the God of Love."

"He pooped in his diaper and deserved to die." I snatched at the basket and she slapped my hand away. "Come on," I whined. "I'm starving."

Amelie spread a blanket on the grass. "Sit and wait your turn."

I settled beside her. As she unpacked the food, I noted deep scratches on her arms and legs. "Are you okay?"

She shrugged them off. "Odile gave me ointment for the pain. Trust me nothing is fun about coaxing blood from an angry gator. And you really don't want to know how we harvested the boar's testicle hair. He was a most unwilling donor."

Amelie was right. I preferred not to know. I watched her set out lunch and couldn't help but think even with a bedraggled appearance she was ten times prettier than the girls in New Brunswick. They'd spend hours fussing over hair and makeup and still not be half as beautiful as Amelie in a loose pony tail, wearing ragged cut-offs.

As she scooted over to hand me a plate, her bare leg touched mine. I tugged at my shirt collar. For some reason, the temperature suddenly shot up ten degrees.

"Are you feeling well?" she said. "Your face went funny."

I didn't know what to say, so I stuffed a sandwich in my mouth. For some reason, Clovis found the whole scene amusing.

After lunch, Clovis decided I should try to change a lie into a solid spell that another could see and touch.

Amelie's expression brightened with interest. "May I stay and watch?"

"No," I blurted. "I mean, an audience is too distracting." Even to my own ears, the excuse sounded weak, but the idea of Amelie observing my screw-ups didn't sit well with me one bit.

"Nonsense," Clovis said. "Learning to block distractions is good for you." His eyes twinkled. "Unless you can think of another reason you don't want Amelie around."

For once, I couldn't lie up a credible excuse, so Amelie took a seat on the stump, and I rose to my feet. "Where do I begin?"

"With the lie, of course. See it. Hear it. Smell it. Give it life. Start with something small. How about a frog?" He beamed. "I am partial to them, you know. Hold a picture in your mind. The animal doesn't have to be perfect the first time, simply frog-like. We can work on details later."

Frog-like, eh? "Green, warty skin…"A prickly tingle formed at the base of my skull. "Bug eyes, gangly legs, twitchy tongue…" The tingle spread outward to my fingertips. "See the frog," I commanded, pointing at the ground. "The frog is right there."

A hazy mist formed at the end of my finger, it trembled and wavered. I held the picture of a frog in my mind. "I can see it," I muttered. "We can see it." The cloudlike blob stretched and dropped to the ground. It melded into the rough shape of a frog. Amelie clapped her hands in delight.

I didn't often get a rise from Amelie. Her reaction sparked an equally pleasant thrill inside me and puffed up my pride. *Not bad, not bad at all. Spells are a snap. Now for the details and really leave Amelie in awe of my power.*

The body shape tightened into focus and a row of warts bubbled up the frog's back. *Pop! Pop! Pop! Pop!* Tiny webbed feet sprung out at the bottom. I turned my attention to the head's features, now blank, and hit a wall. Juggling two things at once was well-nigh impossible. As I concentrated on the face of the frog, the body faded.

"Pay attention," Clovis barked.

The outburst startled Amelie, and she gasped. I broke my concentration on the frog and glanced at her. Big mistake. The spell snapped together into the perfect replica of a little green frog wearing Amelie's face.

The mouth opened. A tongue flicked out. "Ribbit?"

Daggers shot from Amelie's icy green eyes. "You think I have bug eyes and gangly legs?"

"No...I didn't mean..." I got defensive. "You distracted me."

Amelie gritted her teeth. "So that monstrosity is my fault?"

"Yes...no...you don't say things like a real girl," I hollered. "You get me confused."

She rose from the stump. "Now I'm not a real girl?"

Clovis stepped in as peacemaker. "Perhaps for now, Peter should practice alone."

"Fine with me. I'm sure I have no interest in more childish behavior." Amelie stormed off, boiling mad. I half expected little piles of lava puddling in her footsteps.

I practiced with Clovis the rest of the afternoon. A good thing Amelie left, since every object I

234

conjured afterward had her face. The more I tried to forget her anger, the more she consumed my thoughts and messed with my concentration. If Amelie wasn't pleased about being a frog, she wouldn't be any happier as a rattlesnake, chicken, and gator. We finally called the lesson quits when Marie rang the dinner bell.

Clovis clapped me on the shoulder. "We'll start again in the morning."

"I'll do better," I vowed. "Amelie gets on my nerves."

"I can see that."

"It's not like I care what she thinks," I added quickly.

"Obviously."

"I'm serious. She appointed herself my bodyguard, not that I wanted her to. Not that I need one. Now, she's always hanging around, looking over my shoulder. Not that she isn't nice." I had the horrible feeling I babbled. Talking about Amelie made me very uncomfortable. "Most of the time she's a little nuts, but then everyone is here. I blame the heat."

Clovis elbowed me in the ribs. "You really like her."

"No, I don't," I protested, turning beet red.

His voice softened. "You forget I can also spot a lie."

"My feelings don't matter," I sputtered. "Amelie is rich and class, and I'm an orphan nobody. I don't have a single thing to offer someone like her."

Clovis gazed off into the distance as if recalling something bittersweet from long ago. "You have friendship, a good enough start for a young man. I had a friendship like that once."

"What happened?"

He roused himself from memory. "The magic became more important. I let her slip away, although not without regret. Don't make the same mistake."

At that moment, Esther and T. Chris appeared on the path and I clammed up. I had no desire to talk about my feelings for Amelie with Esther's big ears and equally big mouth near. She announced Renny and Chris returned from another shrimping expedition and Marie had a large pot of étouffée on the table.

After dinner, Esther dragged me outside to play catch with the younger children. I threw a few lackluster pitches and then begged off and gave the ball to T. Chris. In truth, I was beat to the bone. Working spells drained my energy.

Amelie trailed us outside. She passed on the games and instead sat under the old cypress tree to watch. She hadn't talked much during dinner. Oh, she was polite enough, but the few times I said something she cut the conversation short. Maybe, I thought, she was embarrassed to have flown off the handle at me for nothing. I sidled over nonchalantly to let her see I didn't hold a grudge. I know. I can't believe I was that stupid, either.

"Oh, hi. I didn't see you." I acted surprised to find her sitting underneath the tree.

"I've been in this spot all evening. I realize I'm not as memorable as other girls, but even you should have noticed." Amelie wasn't one to hide her feelings, but I got the distinct impression something other than my bonehead attempt at spellcasting bothered her.

"Heck, you're plenty memorable," I insisted cheerfully, "what with the dagger. I don't know any other girl who can use one."

"Like the girls up north, you mean?"

"Yeah. They're all the time wearing party dresses and afraid of getting dirty, not like you. You're practically a guy." I meant the words as respectful, but they didn't come out right.

Her angry glare confirmed my suspicion I should have kept my mouth shut. "Now I'm not only dirty, but a man, too."

"No, no." I backpedaled frantically. "You're not a man or dirty. I mean, you're sitting in the dirt now, but sandy dirt. You can brush your pants right off." That didn't sound any better.

"Because I am not as pretty and ladylike as the girls you've known is no reason to insult me."

The conversation wasn't going well at all. Quelling a rising tide of panic, I tried to explain. "I didn't mean that."

Amelie would have none of it. "First, you think I resemble a frog, next you say I'm a dirty man."

"I'm sorry, I—"

She rose to her feet, steaming. "The world is full of hidden perils. The women here are taught to take care of themselves. To be of service when danger calls is a matter of family pride. If our beliefs make me manly and unfeminine in your eyes then so be it."

Amelie tried to walk away, but I grabbed her hand. "Let go," she hissed, "or you'll see what my knife can really do."

I held on. Clovis was right. Amelie had given me her friendship, but I was about to ruin everything. The thought of losing her hurt me more than a knife through the heart.

"Listen to me," I pleaded. "I didn't mean you're manly. Being able to handle yourself in a fight is great. The girls I knew would scream and run if they saw as much as a cockroach in their path. No one could drag them into a swamp, and they'd faint dead away for sure at the thought of facing a demon. But you're brave and stuff and…" Without thinking, I jabbered, "Real pretty, prettier than any girl I've ever known. Beautiful even."

The confession stunned me into silence, but stopped Amelie dead in her tracks. "You think so?"

I was hot and flustered. I hadn't meant to admit the truth, but now it was out in the open. *Should I not have said it? Do I take it back? What do I say? What do I do?* While my internal debate raged, my brain grew tired of waiting and babbled the first thought that popped inside. "Well, sure, you know. Even when you're, you know, sweaty and stuff you look, you know, really great."

Oh, geez.

A glint of amusement shone in her eyes. "Peter Whistler, you are the strangest young man."

"Are you gonna kiss her now?"

I jerked my head around at the sound of Esther's taunting voice. She and T. Chris had snuck behind us with the younger Benoits in tow. Amelie and I simultaneously became aware of holding hands and dropped them self-consciously.

"Go on," T. Chris urged. "Give her a big fat juicy one." His brothers and sister let loose with a chorus of hysterical laughter.

An impish grin spread across Amelie's face. She cupped her hand around her ear, pretending to listen. "I hear a hungry gator calling in the swamp. So sad the poor thing has nothing to eat. Isn't that right, Peter?"

I could have shouted for joy. We were friends again. "You're right. Luckily, they're partial to bratty little kids." With a roar, Amelie and I raced forward as Esther and the others squealed and bolted in every direction.

* * * *

Clovis and I trained daily. After the fiasco with Amelie's face on the frog, we returned to fantasy creatures like the pink elephant. Soon, I could cast a darn good spell. Imaginary creations were a lot simpler than realistic animals. I didn't have to be picky about details. I mean, who is to say what an ogre looks like? I was excited about my progress, but observed a distinct lack of enthusiasm in Clovis.

"Good," he noted flatly after I proudly materialized a particularly hideous troll.

"That's it? Just good? He'd scare anybody."

"For a second. Until your subject realized you produced a spell." Without warning, he scooped up a pebble and chucked it at my head.

The sting broke my concentration and the troll disappeared. I yelped and rubbed the sore spot. "What did you do that for?"

"Imaginary creatures are French Market tricks, strictly third-rate abracadabra for the tourists. If you attacked an expert conjuror with a troll, more than likely you'd get a bullet fired at your head instead of a rock. The success of a lie depends on no one recognizing the lie. The success of a spell is the same. As long as the enemy can't pin down the magic, the shaman is safe."

Weeks passed under Clovis' tutelage and I slowly progressed from fantasy creatures to strictly realistic ones. The work was hard and my skill seemed to advance more by inches than feet. By the end of each day I was wrung out, but life still held simple pleasures. Chris continued my piloting lessons in his free time and gave me an open invitation to use the pirogue. When Clovis cut me loose and the weather was good, I took Esther, T. Chris, and Amelie fishing. Esther and T. Chris plied me with question about shaman training. Amelie and I never spoke much, but, strangely enough, having her next to me in the boat made any cares and doubts about my new path drift away as if I cast them upon the murky water of the bayou.

And my qualms were plenty when shaman training hit a dead end. Living, breathing animals proved much more difficult than fantasy creatures. The realism disintegrated with the slightest imperfection. Holding a lie together was darn near impossible when the audience had doubts.

I had to tackle a thousand details at once. Every animal had specific colors, sizes, textures, shapes, along with sounds and smells unique to the breed. The slightest change from reality and the whole illusion collapsed. Odile was the hardest to fool. She had intimate knowledge of not only the appearance of every plant and animal in the bayou, but also, she insisted, how they felt. Every time I was certain the details were flawless, she spotted the spell.

"I don't understand. The butterfly was perfect." Odile had wandered into the clearing and to my dismay noticed the fake immediately.

"Perfect in design, yes," she said, "like a photograph. You have the attributes exactly right, but no matter how clear, a picture nevertheless remains a picture. To be an adept in the mystic arts and create a believable spell, you must capture the animal's essence."

"How can I build something I can't see, feel, taste, smell, or touch?" I complained later to Clovis. "What kind of essence does a butterfly have? It's a bug."

"You continue to rely too much on the outer senses rather than the inner," he chided. "All life has an essence. Odile knows that better than anyone. She doesn't need to see a mushroom to know one grows inside a hollow log. The mushroom speaks to her as clearly as I speak to you."

"What's the point, Clovis? I won't meet Odile in the Lower Worlds. How about we skip to the part where I learn how to kill a demon?"

Clovis stood firm. "Mastering the basics is your one hope of defeating Feu De L'enfer."

"But—"

"No, buts. Search within. Feel the truth of an object and then transfer the truth to the spell. You have the skill, Peter. Until you learn what keeps you from taking the next step, we can't move forward."

Clovis released me for the day. In a funk, I ambled toward the Benoit's cabin, mulling over his words. They made me uncomfortable because I already had a sneaking suspicion why the final step was so hard. Deep down, I was afraid. The closer to mastering the spells, the sooner I squared off against a demon. I'd always been good at laying low and minding my own business. Was I up to the fight?

"Peter!" Amelie waved to me from Marie's garden. She hoisted a basket of produce to balance on her hip.

I waited for her. We made a habit of walking to the cabin together each day after practice. No matter how difficult or frustrating a session, the sight of Amelie with a smile on her face always boosted my spirits.

"Done so soon for today?" she asked, wiping a hand across her sweaty brow. "Clovis must be getting soft."

"I'm having a hard time with the final exam. I can't seem to pin down a butterfly's essence."

She wrinkled her nose. "Don't know what essence you can get from a bug."

"That is exactly what I said."

"Maybe you should focus on something smellier like a gator."

"Clovis didn't mean that kind of essence."

"Then what is he talking about?"

"I'm not exactly sure. I think one of those you-know-it-when-you-feel-it-things."

She nodded with complete understanding. "Like love."

"If that's so, then I'm in deep trouble because I can't ever see myself cuddling with a gator."

Amelie sighed with exasperation. "You are such a male."

When I had no idea what Amelie meant, I found the best approach was to let the conversation drop. As we walked along in silence, her suggestion about the gator stuck in my head. I didn't like gators. They were the one animal in the swamp that scared the pants off me. Forget trolls—gators were a living nightmare, thundering along like pure evil on four scaly, clawed feet. Even the dead ones Chris, Renny, and Mrs. Hart brought back from their hunting trips made me uneasy.

The thought surfaced if I conquered my fear of gators, I'd be one step closer to facing a real demon. The problem was finding one. Any animal wandering close to Chris' homestead ended up skinned on the outbuilding wall. Gators lurking nearby stayed well hidden. Since I was no hunter, tracking was a problem.

"I said, would you like one?"

I raised an eyebrow. "A gator?"

Amelie held out a handful of berries from the basket and stared at me. "What are you talking about? I asked if you wanted some berries. They're very sweet."

"Oh, thanks." As I popped a few in my mouth, the notion suddenly occurred Amelie knew where to find a gator. She helped Odile collect a blood sample not long ago. I decided to cleverly finagle the information from her. "So," I mentioned nonchalantly, "you ran into a gator not too far from here, didn't you?"

"Why do you want to know?"

So much for finagling someone with a naturally suspicious nature. I acted innocent. "I'm making conversation."

"About gators? I don't think so. They scare you."

I sputtered a protest. "No they don't."

"Your stomach gets upset when you see one."

"You're nuts. I make a little rinky dinky comment—"

"I know where to find a gator."

I stopped short. "How did you—?"

"You want to understand the essence, whatever that is, and you need to get close. Am I right?"

"More or less. If you'll be so kind as to point me in the right direction…"

"Nonsense. I'm coming with you. The nasty thing wasn't happy when we collected the blood. I don't reckon she'll be glad to see people again. I better bring a rifle."

I gave up. "I'll borrow the pirogue."

We made plans to meet early the next morning. When I arrived at the dock, both Renny and Mrs. Hart waited with Amelie.

"I invited myself along," said Renny cheerfully. "Chris went to get supplies today."

I hadn't seen a lot of them lately. They helped Chris on the boat except when he went to town, since Renny was still a wanted man. Often, Renny and Mrs. Hart hunted on their own. Between Renny's sharpshooting and Mrs. Hart's keen nose, they always had an addition for Marie's cooking pot. Esther told me Mrs. Hart said hunting made her feel useful. That made sense. She wasn't one to sit idle.

Amelie and Mrs. Hart kept a keen watch in the bow while Renny sat with me in the stern cleaning his gun. "I'm curious, Peter," he asked. "Why a gator? You can pick an animal that doesn't frighten you so much."

I sighed. "Does everyone know?"

"Yes, but pay no mind. We all wrestle with fear."

"Maybe I can wrestle my fear to the ground. At least, that's the plan."

"Face your fear? *Bon.* I approve. And if your plan doesn't work, I'll shoot the gator in the head."

"Sounds good to me." I considered the young man who had grown to be a good friend. "May I ask you a question?"

"Go ahead."

"You said we all wrestle with fear. What scares you?"

An angry flush colored his cheeks. "I'm afraid I'll never regain my honor. I should have been at home and seen the danger from Delphine, but I was ruled by stubborn pride and left. My father paid the price. His death is my fault."

"You're awfully hard on yourself. Seems to me, the fault is Delphine's."

"Not so." His voice dropped. He checked to make sure Amelie and Mrs. Hart weren't listening. "Delphine and I were lovers. A brief infatuation. Delphine soon decided my father's financial assets were more compelling than mine. That's the real reason Father and I fought—not the brooch. I warned him she was merely interested in his money."

"He was under a spell, Renny. Maybe you were, too."

His eyes filled with pain. "I wish I had that excuse. Delphine didn't need to use an enchantment on me. I knew she had a cold unscrupulous heart, incapable of caring for anyone, but herself. The fact made no difference. She was beautiful and passionate. When she threw me over for my father, my pride was hurt. I left when I should have stayed and forced him to see her true nature. Now because of my stupid arrogance, I lost my father and Amelie is in mortal danger." His face twisted in a wan smile. "A gator doesn't sound so bad, *n'est pas*?"

"Guess not."

Amelie pointed to a worn spot on the bank. "The slide is over there, but I don't see the gator."

Mrs. Hart sniffed the air and growled. "Lucy has the scent," said Renny. "Pull over to the bank."

The point of the trip was to observe a gator. Leaving the boat hadn't been part of the plan. I was perfectly content to try again another day, but before I suggested a quick retreat, Amelie stepped off, followed by Renny and Mrs. Hart. Apparently, everyone except me was rarin' to go.

I secured the pirogue. Mrs. Hart sniffed a circle and then with a yip, bounded off into the brush with the rest of us right behind. After thirty feet, she stopped dead in her tracks. Her steady gaze met mine. The gator lay ahead.

"Wait here," I whispered to the others.

Amelie cocked the rifle. "Be careful. She spooks easy."

I parted the bushes and muttered under my breath, "So do I."

The gator lazed in the grass a dozen feet in front of me. Amelie neglected to mention the size. How had Odile taken blood from eight hundred pounds of sheer malevolence? The creature swung the massive head in my direction and hissed.

My stomach dropped to my toes. Primal fear flooded my veins urging a quick cut and run. "E-easy girl," I stammered. "Nice gator."

She hissed again and turned her body fully around to face me. The jaws opened wide exposing jagged teeth. Approaching unarmed felt less and less like a great idea, but the thought of admitting to Amelie I was too afraid to even look one of the nasty things in the eye didn't sit well. I came this far. I wouldn't rabbit now.

How to find the truth about a gator? Green, scaly, and creepy beady eyes were the truth of the physical appearance. According to Clovis and Odile, each animal or object, whether living or not, had essence, too.

I rubbed sweaty hands down the sides of my pants and stretched out my senses. Soon, I held a picture of the gator in my mind. Creating an exact duplicate was a cinch, but a copy won't fool Odile for a second.

See beyond. Find the essence.

I shut out distractions; the sights and smells of the bayou faded away, sounds disappeared. Finally, all that remained was a tiny prickle jabbing at the edge of my consciousness. At first, I took the faint rippling energy as an effect of the glaring summer sun, but then realized the flicker gave off no heat. No cold, either—simply a tingly force dancing at the brink of awareness. I probed deeper and slammed into a flash of savage instinct. A low rumble issued from the beast.

I licked my lips. "Nothing to worry about, girl. I only want a peek at the old essence."

The creature hissed again, sizing me up with sinister eyes. The tail whipped back and forth. I could almost hear her smacking lips in anticipation of snack time.

I squared my shoulders and tore down every mental inhibition. "Come to me. I'm ready for you."

A rush of feral images and wild irrational cravings for blood flooded my mind, and almost knocked me off my feet. Odile was right. The essence of the animal was nothing like the pale imitations I conjured before. The real essence was fierce and untamed, ruled by savage instinct. Man's laws meant nothing. Life was pure freedom, unchained carnage, and living completely secure in wild surroundings.

I embraced the sensations, drawing them inward. Raw power coursed through me. Fear melted away, replaced by awe. For once, I knew exactly what it meant to be a gator in the bayou. Not ugly or evil, good or bad—those were human concerns, trifles. Instead, the gator was in perfect union with nature. With complete understanding came newfound respect.

Rule Eight: Once the essence is right, lock the magic in tight.

I cast the spell, saturating the words with the animal's true essence. "A gator, biggest one around."

Click.

A half-ton beast appeared before me, perfect to the last inch of leathery hide. The smaller gator thought so, too. With a guttural growl, she rose from her sunny lounging spot and crashed deeper into the brush.

"Peter." Amelie pushed through the foliage. "What was that noise?" Her eyes widened at the sight of the gator and she raised her rifle. "Back away," she whispered.

"Don't move," Renny had his finger on the trigger. "I have a clean shot."

"Don't waste your bullet." I swung a leg over the gator's back. The stunned surprise coloring their faces was immensely gratifying.

Amelie gaped. "Y-you made the gator? She isn't real?"

I glowed with pride. "See for yourself."

She jabbed at the leathery hide with the rifle barrel and sucked in a breath. *"Fantastique."*

Renny stroked his fingertips along the spine. "Something is different with this one, Peter. It feels alive, more than any other creature you made."

"You found the essence," Amelie said.

"Yup." I gave a swaggering bow, hard-pressed to contain my elation. "The newest shaman of the bayou at your service." They clustered around offering congratulations. Mrs. Hart sniffed delicately at the torso. "What do you say, Mrs. Hart?" I prodded. "Does it smell right, too?"

"Exactly right," the little dog said. "Odile would be impressed."

Chapter 12
An Alarming Letter

I gasped. "Mrs. Hart, I hear you."

I don't know which one of us was more excited. Despite having Esther, Odile, and Clovis to translate, I missed the sound of her voice. "You're okay? Really?"

"I'm fine, Peter. Better than fine, actually. Honey Bun is a young dog. I have no more aches and pains from middle age. Even the arthritis in my knee is gone." Her voice softened. "I forgot what being young and active was like."

"You won't be a dog forever. We'll find a way to help you."

"I'm not worried. For now, more important events concern us. At least I'm useful. Renny and I manage to keep Marie's cooking pot full."

"Never imagined you as the outdoorsy type."

"Never imagined you as a shaman. Apparently, life had surprises in store for both of us."

I had no argument for that. We returned to the Benoit's homestead, and Odile waited on the dock.

Her eyes shone when I told her I now heard Mrs. Hart.

"Excellent, Peter. Your feet are well along the white road."

Odile was even more pleased when I conjured a gator in the front yard. I flushed with pride when she ran her sensitive hands over the rough hide and declared it indistinguishable from a real one.

The little Benoits crowded around. Georges gawked. "Can I touch it?"

"Better than that," I said. "How about a ride?"

The kids burst out in a combined squeal of delight. Esther, T. Chris, Luc, and Georges scooted up on the gator's back. Little Liliane perched happily on the tail. "Make it go fast," she shrieked. I galumphed the creature around the yard. The kids made so much noise no one noticed the Sweet Marie arrived until Chris pulled to the dock and shouted, "What's going on?"

"Peter made the children a gator," said Marie. "Isn't that nice?"

Chris shrugged, completely unconcerned. "Oh, all right then."

I've said it before, but it bears repeating—the people here are crazy.

* * * *

I worked hard every day recreating real plants and animals for Clovis. In the evening, the shaman now went alone into the swamp, attending to the mystical preparations for opening the door. I offered to help, but he refused saying the magic was beyond my level of comprehension, and had to be done alone. After dinner, the kids always insisted I conjure a gator to ride. I didn't mind. The spell was good practice.

Summer was nearly over, although the high heat and humidity didn't let up. The weather didn't bother me now. Chris declared I had become a real swamper. Never having felt much attached to a place before his words sent a pleasant rush of pride through me.

By late August, the talk at the dinner table turned to school. Classes started soon for the Benoit children except Liliane who was too young. T. Chris expressed vehement opposition to sitting in a classroom and each evening fought a losing battle with his mother to stay home with Esther.

"She needs my help," he insisted.

Marie brushed aside his complaint with the wave of a hand. "Esther is the most self-sufficient girl I know. She memorized the location of everything on the property from the house to each blade of grass. She's already a big help to me in the kitchen. She doesn't need you to lead her around."

"I can help *Mamere*."

"Who is more self-sufficient than Esther."

Esther patted his arm. "It was worth a shot."

Mrs. Hart pricked up her ears and barked a warning. "I hear a boat engine and it's headed this way." Chris went to the water to await the new arrival while the rest of us stayed inside the cabin.

Renny twitched aside the curtain and peered out the window. A boat steered from the channel straight to the Benoits. "That's Delmar Purdy." Sure enough, the portly figure at the tiller was unmistakable. We went outside to greet him.

"What news, Delmar?" called Chris.

Mr. Purdy waved an envelope. "A letter for the Marchands arrived this morning."

"It must be from Ruby," said Amelie with excitement. "She's the only one who knows we're here."

Marie invited Delmar for supper, but he politely declined as his wife expected his return. He turned the boat around and gunned the engine.

We followed Amelie to the porch and got comfortable. She tore open the envelope, skimming over the page. Her face fell. "Pike is in New Orleans."

Renny scowled. "Read it, *cher*."

Amelie began. "Dear Amelie, we have new trouble in the house. Delphine was right steamed after you escaped. As I reckon you know by now, she posted a reward for your return and set the blame on Renny. Word came several days later, you were spotted near the bayou, but the trail went cold. The police now think you snuck out by boat, maybe into Texas.

"The trustees came down hard on Delphine when you disappeared. I hoped they'd see through her phony act as she pretends to be upset-like and worried for your safety, but so far they haven't gone against her. I think they're suspicious, though. I heard word got back some of the guests said you acted eager to leave, so they stay on Delphine to keep up the search. No more fancy dinner parties for her. The trustees also ordered the police to bring you to them first after you're found. Delphine was very unhappy about that. I hoped she'd cut her losses and move on, but no such luck. As I said, we got more troubles and worse than before.

"Five days ago, the trustees were due for the monthly accounting. This time, Delphine had me bring the coffee pot into the study, insisting she'd pour for them herself which isn't like her high-and-mightiness one bit. A few minutes later, I heard her yelling and cussing and wanting to know if someone had been in there. I reckon she opened the safe and found the potion book missing. She must have planned to use a recipe to keep the trustees under her thumb.

"Delphine pitched a royal fit, smashing and throwing things, but nothing was to be done. She managed to get through the meeting and then tore up both your room and Renny's. She didn't find the potion book, of course, but instead came downstairs with an old knapsack."

I slapped my forehead. "I forgot. I stuffed it under Renny's bed. Nothing much is inside—" My face paled with a sudden realization. "Except the Atlanta newspaper with our pictures."

"Keep reading," urged Odile.

Amelie took up the letter again. "Delphine immediate shut herself in the study and made a telephone call. Two days later came a knock at the door and a man in a fedora arrived. Since he appeared, an icy chill crept into the house not even the heat of my kitchen can chase away. I don't know what evil this man brings, but can't stay under the same roof. I'm going home and will remain there until hearing from you. Keep safe, love Ruby."

Renny's jaw tightened. "Delphine allied with the devil himself."

"Wait," said Amelie. "Ruby added a P.S. On her way to the post office she ran into our milkman. He asked if Ruby wanted to adjust her standing order because the house was empty and he assumed Delphine was out of town. Ruby returned to see for herself and he was right. Even the guards were gone."

The same thought crossed our minds at once. Pike was on his way here.

I clenched my fists. "This is my fault. I should have remembered the newspaper. The article talked about the reward and how to contact Pike."

"Don't blame yourself," said Renny. "Pike only knows where we've been, not where we are now."

The stupidity of my actions weighed heavily. "How long will that last?"

"Not long," answered Odile. She rubbed her chin. "I'd sorely like to know their plan."

"I can sneak back into New Orleans," said Renny, "and pick up their trail."

Odile shook her head. "Too dangerous. We need you here, and they have too great a head start. We must think of another way."

The discussion continued through dinner and into the evening. Plans were devised and discarded until Marie spotted Georges stifling a yawn. "We won't decide tonight and the children must go to bed." She glared at her son. "No argument." He clapped his mouth shut. None of the Benoit children ever won against Marie.

Esther and I said goodnight and went with Odile to her cabin. The shaman busied in her work area, while Esther went right to bed. I wandered to the porch and sat in a rocker. For once, the sky was free of summer haze and a comfortable breeze blew through the bayou.

I had a clear view of the stars. Funny how the exact same sky appeared over kids in New Brunswick and yet New Jersey seemed a million miles away. Their minds were on buying supplies for the new school year while mine was on the best way to kill an immortal demon. A sudden movement near the house drew my attention. Clearly visible in the moonlight, Amelie strolled to the cabin.

"You're up late," I said.

She sat next to me. "Can't sleep."

"Thinking of Delphine?"

"No. Thinking of Delphine with a knife through her heart. My knife, actually. Usually such a pleasant vision is enough to lull me to dreamland, but not tonight. Did Esther go to bed?"

"She must be sawing logs; otherwise, she'd be out here bugging us."

Amelie giggled. "Sounds like Esther. She's better, don't you think?"

"Esther?"

"Yes. She was so thin and pale when she arrived, but now can keep pace with the Benoit kids, and that's saying something. Esther is happy here. I think the bayou agrees with her." She regarded me sharply. "I think the bayou agrees with you, too."

257

I shrugged. "I guess so. The heat doesn't bother me."

"What about the gators?" she teased.

"We're practically best friends."

"In some aspects," Amelie scolded, "you remain a terrible liar." She was silent for a moment and then asked, "Does this mean you'll stay after everything is over?"

"I don't know. I hadn't planned that far. Be kind of hard to hunt like Chris," I groused, "when no one lets me near a gun."

"Guns aren't everything." Amelie sounded suspiciously like Odile. "You don't have to be a swamper. Plenty of opportunities for a budding shaman exist in New Orleans."

I considered her words. A shaman in New Orleans was a long way from an orphan boy in New Brunswick. My intention had always been to live a life of free abandon with no ties, but a long time had passed since I toyed with the idea of moving on. Despite the heat and humidity and the lurking danger, life was…well…comfortable here. I had friends who treated me like family. I had Amelie.

The color rose in my cheeks and I was grateful for the darkness on the porch. Where did that idea come from? Despite Esther's teasing, Amelie was absolutely just another friend. I never tried to kiss her. The thought hadn't crossed my mind.

Okay, the thought occasionally crossed my mind.

Maybe more than occasionally.

As much as I enjoyed my sessions with Clovis, my heart always skipped a beat at the sight of Amelie waiting for me in Marie's garden at the end of the day. I never had a friend to talk to before and the girls I knew in New Brunswick were giddy and silly—a bunch of dizzy dames who circled rich boys like Chauncey Edwards as if they were orbiting moons. I never carried a torch for any of them, but Amelie was special; half cultured Southern belle, half fearless warrior. She possessed grace and charm, but wasn't afraid to get her hands dirty. With Amelie by my side, I felt different, not a kid anymore. More like a man.

Kissing her, however, was out of the question. The opportunity never presented itself. At least, I didn't think so. Not that I'd mind kissing her. I mean if she wanted to and stuff, I'd certainly try. Just to be polite. On the other hand, she still considered herself my bodyguard, so was always armed. A razor-sharp dagger was more than a little intimidating.

As Amelie gazed across the yard, I stole a glance at her from the corner of my eye. I wondered idly if she kissed other boys. She must have. She was rich and beautiful and had been to lots of fancy parties in New Orleans. I bet all they did was dance and then kiss each other. Kissing was probably another social requirement for well-bred young ladies. Schools offered classes along with hand-to-hand combat.

If Amelie wanted to kiss me, how would I know? Were there signs? An anxious knot formed in my stomach. People with Amelie's social status knew the subtle clues to mark a girl's interest, but not a poor slob like me.

Should I ask Renny for advice? He had an active social life in New Orleans, but Renny was also a bit of a rake. He probably got his face slapped more than once, which didn't bode well.

Should I ask his permission to kiss her first? She was his sister, after all. What would I say? I could tell him Amelie seemed to like me and I liked her, for sure a lot. What if Renny didn't approve?

I swallowed hard. What if he did?

I tugged at my shirt collar. Despite the cooling breeze, the porch was now uncomfortably warm. I stifled a groan. Why was life so complicated?

As Amelie continued to peer across the yard, her shoulders stiffened. With a subtle movement, she reached over and gently squeezed my hand. Panic shot through me. Was this the sign? What do I do? Should I say something? Yes, I should say something. I cleared my throat.

"Shhh," she said.

Okay, no talking. Was silence part of the routine? Maybe words spoiled the moment. *You're spoiling it now you dope, because you don't know what to do. If you miss this chance, you may not get another.* I took a deep breath, puckered up, and learned toward her. Suddenly, she turned her face in my direction and we clunked noses.

"What are you doing?" she said.

I jerked my head back. "What? Me? Nothing. What are you doing?"

Amelie motioned across the yard. "Giving you a signal. Something's moving over there."

"I knew that. Um, where exactly did you mean?"

Amelie drew her dagger. "By the big cypress. Wait here."

"I'll go with you…"

260

She was fast. By the time, I got to my feet, Amelie melted into the dark. I stifled a curse and peered fixedly into the shadows, but didn't see a thing.

Skritch, skritch, skritch.

"Amelie?" I whispered. "Is that you?"

Skritch, skritch, skritch.

The strange rustling noise moved closer. I followed the sound around the corner of the cabin. For a moment, nothing stirred and then a rat bounded from the bushes and skittered along the wall. Tiny claws pawed frantically at the wooden siding until securing a foothold. The rat made a beeline for Esther's window. Because of the heat, the glass pane was open. The single barrier separating the rat from entry into the room was a flimsy metal screen.

I grabbed a handful of pebbles and flung hard. "Scat!"

The stones clattered against the cabin, and the rat stopped short. The head turned toward me. Two yellow glowing embers burned deep within each eye socket. The muzzle curled back to bare glistening teeth. With a maniacal screech, the rat jumped onto the sill and attacked the screen.

"Get away from there," I yelled.

In a flash, the rat ripped a quarter-size hole and forced its head into the room. Jagged metal edges from the torn screen sliced through the hide leaving a sticky trail of blood. The wounds had no effect on the rat's deadly determination. With frenzied thrashing, it wiggled through one front leg up to the shoulder. I snatched the tail and the rat let out a horrific shriek.

Esther's frightened voice called from inside the cabin, "Peter, what's going on?"

"Run," I shouted, struggling to hold the whipping tail. "Get Odile!"

Esther bounded from the bed. At the loss of the quarry, the rat exploded in rage, writhing and squirming in my grip. I slammed the body against the side of the cabin. Bones cracked, but instead of stopping the attack, the rat went berserk. It twisted until the spine bent nearly in half and sunk needle-like teeth into my wrist. I yelled and let go. The rat pounced at my leg, biting and scratching. Mrs. Hart hurtled around the corner and with a snarling growl, her jaws snapped on the rat and yanked it off me.

Amelie dashed across the yard, dagger in hand. "Peter, throw it against the wall."

Dodging the rat's gnashing teeth, I snatched the tail. Mrs. Hart let go and I flung it hard against the cabin. At the same time, Amelie let fly with the blade, pinning the creature helplessly to the wood siding. The rat flailed mindlessly, yellow eyes burning. Blood gushed down the wall, as the jerky movements caused the dagger to slice through internal organs.

"Mon Dieu," whispered Amelie in horror. "Why isn't it dead?"

Odile ran from the house and tossed Amelie a cleaver. "Cut off the head."

In one smooth move, Amelie caught the cleaver and let fly. The skull severed neatly from the neck and bounced to the ground, eyes aflame. The mouth sagged open. The rat expelled a final demented hiss and then the light in the eyes died.

I ran a shaky hand through my hair. "What was that thing?"

Odile spit on the body. "Foul, hell spawn creature of the dark—a conjuror's work, to be sure."

"Pike did this?"

"Peter!" Esther scooted around the corner.

"I told you to wait inside," clucked Odile.

"I had to see if Peter was hurt."

"He is." Amelie pointed to blood dripping down my leg and glared at me. "Why didn't you say something?"

I forced on my best face. "It doesn't hurt." Actually, it hurt like crazy.

"Ridiculous. You're lying again."

"Enough," ordered Odile. "The wound needs tending and we must tell the others. Can you walk to Chris' house?" I assured her I could. She directed Amelie to bring the rat's body.

We sat on the porch. The pain faded as Odile dabbed a cooling ointment on the wound. Esther insisted on holding the bandages as the shaman wrapped my leg. Everyone crowded around to peer at the carcass. Most of the low muttering was in Cajun patois. I heard Pike's name a time or two. I couldn't translate the rest of the words, but no dictionary was necessary to know they were unflattering.

"The rat isn't much like a city dweller," said Marie, "nor from the swamp. It's thin and scrawny, as if it hadn't stopped to eat in a long time. What has Pike done?"

"We can merely guess," Odile muttered.

"Perhaps not."

Clovis had been silent throughout the discussion. After Amelie placed the rat on the floor, he merely gave the corpse a quick once-over. The rest of the time he sat in a chair, placed his fingertips together, and appeared to fall asleep.

Now he peered sharply at Esther. Something about the expression on the shaman's face made me uneasy. Clovis moved from his seat and knelt down beside her. He clasped Esther's little hands between both of his.

"When Peter was in my cabin, you were able to see through his eyes. Miles into the bayou posed no problem. You are a very powerful see-er, my dear. More so than you realize."

My suspicions rose. "What are you getting at?"

"Esther was alone with Pike long enough to get a good sense of him. The distance is considerable, but I believe she can find his eyes."

Esther's lip trembled. She drew back her hands. "I-I don't want to."

Odile crooned encouragement. "*Cher,* I know Clovis asks much, but he's right. You are a powerful see-er. You can do this."

"Peter?" Esther appealed to me with her blind eyes. "I'm afraid."

The jokes and teasing evaporated. All that remained was a scared little kid. I glowered at Clovis. "She doesn't have to. You can't make her."

"No, I can't," he said gently, "and wouldn't ask if another method was at hand. I have no desire to frighten the child, but we need information. Pike and Delphine joined forces, and this rat is part of their plan."

264

Marie appealed to her mother-in-law. "Surely, you can think of something else."

Odile shook her head. "Clovis is right. If Pike and Delphine act together, the danger is greater than before." Her eyes dared anyone to contradict her. No one spoke, including me. I tried to think of a good argument or a satisfactory lie, but had nothing. The gift of the see-er was the only way.

Esther sunk into the seat, so small and helpless. "I'm not brave enough." Her voice barely topped a whisper.

"That's dumb," I announced stoutly. "You're brave enough to ride a gator. This'll be a cinch."

She shivered. "The gator wasn't real, but Pike is. He's dark inside, not like you."

"You're plenty brave." T. Chris jumped from the doorway. "As brave as any of us."

Marie raised an eyebrow. "I thought you were asleep. How long have you been listening?"

"A bit." His face turned red. "I'm not tired. I want to help."

Chris nudged his wife. "Let the boy stay." A smile twitched at Marie's lips and she nodded. T. Chris happily settled between his parents.

Mrs. Hart trotted to Esther. She patted her gently with a paw. "You've proven your courage time and again, my dear. I'm certain you can find Pike. Don't worry. Peter and I will keep watch so no harm comes to you."

"All right," she said in a small voice. "I'll try."

Odile squeezed her hand. "*Bon.*"

Unconsciously, I reached for Esther's other fist, balled tight. I covered her trembling fingers with mine. Esther's fingers unclenched. Her unblinking stare focused somewhere in the distance. I wondered how long she would take to plug into a mind so far removed. I soon had my answer. Esther sucked in her breath. Her hand stopped trembling. She keyed into something.

"I feel the path," she said.

Odile leaned forward. "Tell us what you see."

"Nothing yet. It's dark."

We waited patiently as Esther forced herself deeper. For a long time, she was silent. I suspected she summoned the courage to take the final step. I knew exactly how she felt. It's one thing to state intentions. It's another to stand at the edge of the cliff and jump.

No one spoke. The tense atmosphere didn't help Esther's concentration so I whispered in her ear, "Tell Pike he's a poophead."

Esther relaxed and snickered. "I sure wish I could, but seeing doesn't work that way." She stiffened. "I'm inside Pike now. He's on the grass. It's dark. I can't see much. Someone is standing next to him. Come on, poophead," she muttered. "Turn around the other way...Hah! I see Delphine right over there." Esther pointed, forgetting in this instance that we were blinder than she. "Delphine is with a bunch of men." She swallowed. "They got guns."

"The guards from the house," murmured Renny.

Esther leaned forward, peering into the darkness. Seeing a blind girl squint was an odd experience. "Pike's watching something in the grass.

I can't see—wait, it's moving. It's a rat's butt. I see the skinny tail."

Mrs. Hart emitted a low growl. Amelie and I exchanged uneasy glances.

Clovis laid a gentle hand on her shoulder. "Esther, concentrate. What is Pike doing?"

Esther's breathing quickened. "I'm not sure. He's bent over the rat. It's getting dark again."

"Try harder, Esther. You must see."

Her face showed the strain of holding the vision. "I can't—hang on a sec. The rat turned around." She gasped. "Clovis, the eyes are yellow. Pike's holding something crumply like cloth." She wrinkled her brow. "I've seen it before. It's my old black dress, the one I left in the house. The rat is sniffing it. Now the nose is in the air. It's running. Everyone's following. There's something else moving in the grass, something around them." Her head snapped back as if whatever tie bound her to Pike had broken. "I'm sorry. I can't hold on. He's gone."

Odile squeezed her hand. "*Cher*, you were wonderful. I'm very proud of you." Esther gave a weary smile.

"We've got big trouble, haven't we?" I said.

"I'm afraid so," said Clovis. "The dead rat was definitely under Pike's spell. He's using the animals to track Esther. Although a rodent's sense of smell is extremely acute, it can't follow a trail that long. However, a conjuror with Pike's power can heighten sensitivity a hundredfold, enough to sniff an old scent through the air. Pike must have then planted an imperative."

"What's that?" asked Esther.

"A command in the animal's mind to force obedience."

Amelie paled. "Pike knows where we are now?"

"Not yet, *cher*," announced Renny with certainty, "or he'd already pound at the door."

"I agree," said Clovis. "Pike is not like Esther. He can't see through the rat's eyes." He prodded the corpse with his toe. "This one was probably ordered to return to Pike as soon as Esther's location was verified. Fortunately, you killed it first."

I gazed at the peaceful bayou. "But others will come."

His jaw set in a hard line. "Oh, most assuredly, others will come."

Odile drummed her fingers on the arm of the chair. "Time isn't on our side. I must finish the potion as soon as possible. With Marie's help—"

"Whatever you need," she said.

Chris got to his feet. "Meanwhile, I'll set traps around the house." Renny immediately volunteered his assistance, which Chris gratefully accepted.

T. Chris piped up. "Papa, I want to help, too."

He tousled his son's hair. "*Bon.* We'll make them regret ever setting foot in our bayou."

Clovis turned to Esther. "I have another idea. My dear, I need a lock of your hair."

Concern flitted across her face. "What for?"

"A rat may be susceptible to a trap other than steel, if one uses the right bait."

She stuck out her chin. "Take all you want."

"That's very generous, but one small snip will do." He borrowed Amelie's knife and cut off one of Esther's curls. He wrapped the hair in his handkerchief. "Peter, you and I will take the pirogue. Rats can swim. Chris and the others can set traps on land. We'll cover the waterways."

My excitement grew. Finally, a weapon—maybe something explosive, like a depth charge. I smiled envisioning a rat body launched into the sky, making a tracer trail with glowing eyes. Perhaps, I could add a flammable after burn, detonating the rat in midair like fireworks. A trifle bloodthirsty, but heck, it wasn't a cute little puppy.

As I pushed the pirogue from the dock, Clovis pointed to the land on the other side of the channel. "We need to direct unwelcome guests on the waterway over there away from the house."

I fidgeted with excitement. "How do we kill the rat?"

"Kill? There's no point. The best we can do is misdirection."

My hopes for a fiery rodent death plummeted. "Why?"

"Have you not paid attention these weeks, Peter?" he scolded. "A conjuror is behind the magic, one who made an accord with a demon. We cannot stop the magic. We cannot stop him. One rat dies. He sends another. The way to end the danger is to kill the demon. Only then is Pike vulnerable. We need to buy time."

"Sheesh, I'm sorry," I said, taken aback by the outburst. "Why didn't he save himself the trouble and control Esther from the beginning?"

"He can't. Pike's power is through his eyes, which Esther can't see. At any rate, once Esther stepped over the threshold to the Lower Worlds, she'd be free of Pike's commands. His spells are earthbound and can't extend beyond the door." Clovis punched me in the shoulder. "Cheer up, boy. The conjuror's magic can still be affected by a good solid lie."

My interest piqued. Granted, losing the exploding rat was a huge disappointment, but I was sorely interested to see what lie Clovis devised. He directed me to the opposite shore. I anchored the pirogue and joined him at an old sweet bay tree. He stuffed the handkerchief containing the hair into a knothole.

"Every rat under Pike's control will be drawn to Esther's scent," said Clovis. "Their attention must be diverted." He muttered softly. My skin tingled as magic permeated the air. "The prey is here. Esther's scent surrounds the area." The lie clicked into place. Clovis sighed and rubbed the nape of his neck. "The spell is done. Pike's rats will be fooled into thinking Esther is near the tree."

I motioned across the water. "What about Pike and Delphine? What will keep them from heading straight for the Benoit's house?"

"Nothing. All we're trying to do is confuse the rats long enough to give Esther and the others a chance to escape."

"A few minutes head start doesn't seem like much."

"I know, my boy, but unfortunately, a distraction is the best we can do."

We returned to the Benoit's property and Clovis went to the house. I sat on the pier to think. My gaze strayed across the channel and easily spotted the tree in the moonlight. Esther's hair was close. Confusing the rats long enough for everyone to escape was a long shot at best, especially if Pike wasn't far behind them. Amelie and Esther sauntered from the house.

"Are the others home?" I asked.

Amelie sat next to me. "Marie is. Odile doesn't need more help. Renny is still setting traps with Chris, T. Chris, and Lucy." She wrinkled her nose. "Odile's potion looks like sludge and smells worse. We came outside for fresh air. What's the matter? You seem worried. Didn't the magic go well?"

I described Clovis' spell. "The magic worked, but the house is too vulnerable. I wonder…" No—I brushed the nutty idea aside.

Amelie pounced on my words. "What are you thinking?"

"Tell us, Peter," demanded Esther.

Amelie chuckled. "May as well. Esther won't stop nagging, now."

"Danged right, I won't."

"Something Clovis said," I told them. "Pike can't be stopped, but he's vulnerable to a good, solid lie."

"Lie up a guillotine," Esther said, "and chop his head off." For an angelic-faced kid, she had a surprisingly bloodthirsty side.

"How would you get him to stick his head under the blade?" asked Amelie.

Her face fell. "Oh. I didn't think about that."

"In any case," I said, "the demon's magic keeps him immortal. I can't even explode Pike's rat. He'd just send another."

Amelie's sympathy showed plain. "That's a pity, but you have an idea. Tell us."

"I might be able to hide the house."

Her eyes widened. "You can do that?"

"Maybe. I don't know."

"The dock, too?" said Esther. "Odile's cabin?"

My heart sank. The Benoit's property encompassed acres. Hiding the main house without dealing with the other structures was pointless. I wished I hadn't mentioned anything.

Too late. Esther was revved up. She bounced with excitement. "Do it. Do it. Do it now, Peter."

"Wait a second, Esther. I don't know if the idea will work."

"Yes, it will. You can do it. You're the best liar ever."

"Go on, Peter," Amelie urged. "I believe in you, too."

Their confidence heartened me. "I'll try, but only if Esther is quiet." She mimed zipping her lips.

I scanned the surroundings, not sure where to begin, but very conscious of Amelie's gaze on me. My first inclination was to build a wall like Clovis did with the gator. By now, I could conjure a good one, brick and mortar with a dollop of barbed wire on top. I discarded the idea. Men can scale a wall, even one with barbed wire. If I made it too high to climb, Pike would recognize a spell. A solid tangle of vegetation, perhaps? I shook my head. Same problem as the wall—too phony. What's left, I thought in despair. *How do I make a cluster of buildings along with a dock invisible to Pike and his gang?*

Invisible?

I stopped short. Was that possible? So far, I made imaginary objects solid and real to the touch. How did one go about making nothing, or rather unmaking something that already existed? I scratched my head. The spell would take some mighty creative lying, but, then again, creative lying was my forte.

Amelie nudged me. "Peter?" Her voice held a note of eager expectation.

"Keep your eyes on the house."

Amelie and Esther tagged behind as I walked to the center of the yard. In my mind, I traced a circuit around the Benoit's property, holding a picture of the house and garden all the way to the water. Having often used the mental map technique to find my way around New Brunswick, I plotted a course in no time.

I extended the vision to include the sheds and storage buildings and then increased the range to Odile's acre of land. I concentrated hard until every nail, every board, and every tomato plant in the garden locked into my mind. The family owned a large parcel. A convincing spell needed a heap of lying.

"A barrier surrounds the property. Nothing can be seen within the boundary."

Instead of the answering prickle in the atmosphere, the air was flat and heavy. I dug down deep, throwing every bit of force into the words. "I see no house, no garden, and no dock. Everything is invisible to the eye." A shimmer developed, a swirl of undefined energy. The magic gathered ready to be plucked.

Believe. Believe with all your heart. "I see no house."

Click.

Everything from the bright blue door to the tin roof vanished.

Amelie sucked in her breath. "Where did it go?"

"Nowhere," I assured her. "It's just hidden from sight." I inhaled deeply. "I see no dock." Where an instant ago the Sweet Marie and pirogue bobbed placidly on the water, now no evidence existed. "The garden, the sheds, Odile's cabin..." One by one, they vanished, until the only objects remaining in the empty clearing were the three of us.

Amelie gaped in awe. "*C'est incroyable.*"

Not bad at all. I was getting pretty good at this magic stuff.

Esther tugged impatiently on Amelie's shirt sleeve. "What's he doing? Can I see? Can I see?"

"Yes, yes, go ahead."

I waited for the same thunderstruck reaction, but instead Esther said, "Where are Marie and the others?"

"Oops."

Chapter 13
Pike's Army

My ego shattered like a jelly jar hitting the kitchen floor.

"Peter," said Amelie, "you made Marie and the children invisible, too."

"Not merely them." Odile's words drifted out of thin air. "I thought for a moment the potion backfired."

Aw, geez. My cheeks burned hot. "I'll break the spell."

"Wait," demanded the disembodied voice of Clovis. "You have an excellent idea, but the lie needs fine-tuning."

"What's going on, Mama?" Luc's voice floated across the yard from the direction of the house.

"Hold tight to your brother and sister and don't let go," Invisible Marie ordered briskly. "Peter—a solution sooner than later, *s'il vous plaît.*"

I sighed. "Clovis, do you have a suggestion?"

"Make the surroundings invisible only to outsiders."

A sharp yelp came from the porch. "Luc stepped on my foot," Georges yelled.

"That's 'cause your feet are so big."

"Are not."

"Are too."

"Enough," said Marie. "Both of you stand still. Hurry, Peter. The children are restless."

I summoned the energy stream and strained to hold tight as it danced around my fingers. One lie was draining. Throwing in off-the-cuff changes was ten times harder. My head pounded with the effort to build the spell. "Everything is invisible only to our enemies."

Click. The magic locked in place.

The house and grounds flickered into view along with Marie and the children. Amelie let out a startled squeak as Clovis materialized in front of her. "Everything is back," she said. "Did the spell collapse?"

"No, my dear," Clovis stated with assurance. "The lie is altered, but remains in place. Within the barrier, we are invisible to our enemies." He clapped my shoulder. "Well done, Peter. The illusion should confuse inquisitive eyes at least for a time. Why not go a step farther? Esther's scent is already across the channel. Add the rest."

"You mean a vision of the cabin?"

"Exactly. Hold the picture in your head. Build the lie. Lock it down."

I peered across the water, doubts rising. I never cast a spell that far. "I don't know…"

"You can do it, Peter," said Amelie.

Her words spiked my confidence. *Hold the picture in your head.* I concentrated on an image of the cabin.

Build the lie. Beyond the bank was the sweet bay tree with Esther's hair. "Every board, every pane," I muttered. Energy crackled against my skin. A hazy outline of the Benoit's cabin formed around the tree, but even in the bright moonlight transparency wavered in and out.

I gritted my teeth, fighting to hold the lie together. "Lock it down."

The magic dragged like a heavy weight. I never climbed a ladder with sandbags tied to my ankles, but now knew exactly how it felt. I dug down deep, forcing my power into one final command. "Now."

The lie snapped shut with a click. The house took solid shape.

Clovis clapped me on the back. "Bravo, Peter."

"Thanks." I blinked. Now Clovis was out of focus. I tried to rub my eyes, but my arms refused to move.

"Peter," said Amelie. "Are you all right?" Her voice sounded very far away.

I forced a smile. "Never better—" My legs gave out. I sank to the ground and into oblivion.

* * * *

I woke stretched out on the couch in the Benoit's cabin. Amelie hovered over me with an anxious expression. "Feeling better?"

My head throbbed. Every muscle on my body screamed, *Don't move, stupid.* Then I remembered passing out in front of Amelie and struggled to sit. "Everything's Jake. I had to rest my eyes a bit."

Esther pushed her head past Amelie. "You fainted dead away, for sure."

"Pipe down, Esther." Even blinking hurt. I wanted to cradle my head in my hands and moan. Instead, I turned to Amelie and forced a jaunty grin. "I didn't faint."

"Keeled over like a pile of wet noodles," said Esther.

"Hush, child," scolded Odile. "Let the poor boy be." She shoved a mug of steaming hot liquid into my hands. "Drink."

I sniffed. "What is it?"

"A potion to cure the headache. Don't try to convince me you don't have one."

I took a sip. It went down easy; hot and spicy with a brisk herbal taste I couldn't place. As I drained the last drop, my headache disappeared. I handed her the mug with thanks.

"You should eat something," said Odile. "Magic is very draining, especially to those new to the white road."

Esther pulled at my sleeve with an impatient tug. "Marie has breakfast ready and I'm starving." She smacked her lips and sighed happily. "Biscuits and gravy."

Breakfast already? I slept through the night. I got to my feet, brushing aside offers to help, and managed to stumble into the kitchen with what I'm sure was a cocky saunter rather than an invalid's shuffle. As I sat at the table, Renny, Mrs. Hart, T. Chris, and his father arrived.

"Glad to see you're finally conscious," said Renny.

"I took a nap." To my relief, Amelie showed no inclination to disagree, and by happy chance, Esther's mouth was full. I quickly changed the subject before she swallowed. "Are the traps set?"

Chris assured me everything was finished. "We saw no signs of rats in the area. The one Amelie killed must have been the first to arrive. From now on, at least one of us must walk the grounds to check the traps and make certain nothing gets through."

Odile announced the potion was nearly finished. Suddenly, nervous butterflies competed for space around the biscuits and gravy in my stomach. I learned so much since arriving in the bayou, but the lessons seemed pitifully inadequate for facing a demon.

"We must decide where to conjure the portal," she said.

"Someplace far removed from here," quipped Marie. "I don't need an entrance into the Lower Worlds in the middle of the parlor."

"Once I open the door," said Esther, "Peter's gonna whup Feu De L'enfer good. There's gonna be demon parts flying every which way."

Their eyes turned to me. "Absolutely." I excused myself as soon as breakfast was over and wandered outside to plunk down on the porch step.

Mrs. Hart followed and sat beside me. "Worried?"

"No."

"Do you have a plan?"

"Sure. I'm, um, working out the bugs."

She nipped my ankle. "Don't lie to me, Peter Whistler. You haven't the slightest idea what to do."

"I know the basics. Destroy Feu De L'enfer's glowing eyes. Easy, right? Clovis believes I'll think of something. Everyone does."

"I have no doubt. Once you come face to face with the creature, you'll find a way."

"If I get that far. Feu De L'enfer will know the instant we step through the door. It'll hunt both us and the exit."

"Therefore, we must keep one step ahead of the demon and its minions."

"Minions?" I goggled at her. "There are minions?"

"According to Odile."

"Well, that might have been handy to know," I sputtered testily.

"Don't be concerned. I'm certain Renny and I will keep them at bay. The last few months, we perfected our hunting technique. Despite the fact, he can't hear me, we work surprisingly well together."

"Mighty sure of yourself," I teased. "You and Renny spend an awful lot of time together. Admit it, you like him."

Mrs. Hart hesitated as if searching for the right words. "He's not as bad as he would have one believe. He bears a lot of guilt."

"Renny told me. I said his father's death wasn't his fault—hey, how did you know?"

"He talks to me when we're hunting. He doesn't understand my thoughts, of course, but I believe his mind is eased to have a sympathetic ear. Renny knows I made plenty of mistakes in my time and won't judge."

"Did you really—" I clapped my lips shut.

"Kill Mr. Hart? I suppose I can thank Esther for blabbing gossip." She cocked her head. "What do you think?"

"You didn't."

"You are certain?"

"Yes. You're cleverer than that." I shot her a sly look. "That's not to say he'll ever trouble anyone again."

"You're right. He won't." She gave me a doggie smile. "Renny told me the same thing, and said whatever punishment I had devised, Mr. Hart surely deserved. If he ever dared to show his face in New Orleans, he'd face ten times worse from him." Her voice softened. "Renny is quite kind."

"Aha," I chortled. "You don't just like him, you *like* like him."

She made the equivalent of a dog snort. "Now you sound like Esther."

"What's the problem with liking Renny? You won't be a dog forever, you know. Odile promised."

"Perhaps. I don't count on returning to human form soon. In any case…" For an instant, I got a flash of something sounding like regret. "Those years are far behind me. I'm too old for emotional entanglements—old enough to be his mother, in fact."

"That's perfect," I insisted. "He's immature. You two were made for each other."

She growled. "Why don't we talk about you and Amelie now?"

I shifted on the step. "Why don't we change the subject?"

"Agreed."

Renny opened the door. "I'm off to check the traps. Care to join me, Lucy?" She jumped to her feet, tail wagging.

I whispered an aside, "You two make a lovely couple." Mrs. Hart nipped my ankle—not playfully, either.

"What did you say, Peter?" asked Renny.

"Nothing. Don't keep her out late, you young whippersnapper."

He grinned. "Lucy, remind me to tell Clovis he's working our young friend too hard. Peter is beginning to sound like him. Next thing you know, he'll be running half-naked through the bayou flipping poor turtles on their backs." With a jaunty wave, he jogged off with Mrs. Hart at his heels.

I spent the rest of the morning walking the boundary of the property, testing to make sure the invisibility barrier held. After lunch, I borrowed the pirogue to check on the duplicate Benoit house. Everything was perfect from the outside. Not until I went to a window and spotted the sweet bay tree growing in a completely empty shell, did I realize the spell hadn't been specific enough in the interior details. One glance inside showed the house wasn't real.

Esther hailed me from across the water. "Odile says come to her cabin, now. The potion is ready." She held her nose. "It sure does stink."

I had no time for a complicated fix, so I darkened every window and hoped for the best.

Stink was right. A putrid odor smacked me in the face from a dozen yards away. Clovis and Amelie were in the kitchen with Odile, watching the contents of a small black pot bubbling on the cast iron stove. The musty rancid vapor wafted through the room.

Neither shaman appeared to notice, but Amelie vigorously fanned the air. "It smells like sour wine and armpit."

I made a face. "You're too kind. I think this is the weapon I've been looking for—wave a bottle of that stuff under Feu De L'enfer's nose and it'll keel over dead."

"Pity, it doesn't have a nose," remarked Clovis dryly.

Before I asked if he was serious, Odile harrumphed. "Nonsense, the potion is simply a trifle zesty." She hefted the pot from the burner to the table and poured the contents into a small Mason jar. After screwing the lid tight, she plucked a tablespoon from the cutlery drawer and placed everything in a sack. "One dose for each should do the trick."

"I don't have to drink the stinky stuff," Esther sang in a singsong voice. "I'm specialer than you."

I ignored her and asked, "How long will the potion last?"

"Hard to say, a few hours, perhaps. These things aren't exact."

"That's not very comforting. I don't suppose you bothered to run tests?"

"What's the point?" Odile said cheerfully. "Either the potion works or everyone is dead. Clovis, do you need long to prepare?"

"No. I completed the mystic groundwork required for the summoning. All that remains is to locate an adequate clearing. The materialization of the entrance kills the vegetation in the area."

"We have plenty of appropriate spots on the property, but don't call the door near Marie's garden or Feu De L'enfer will be the least of our problems."

The door would open tonight. I drew a steadying breath. By this time tomorrow, I'd have killed a demon, died, or ended up nuttier than one of Marie's pecan pies.

The screen door opened with a squeak, and Chris poked in his head. "Has anyone seen Renny or Lucy?"

"Not since this morning," I said.

Chris rubbed his chin. "The sun is setting. They should have returned an hour ago."

An uneasy feeling crept up my spine. "I don't like this."

"Don't fret," said Odile. "If they ran into trouble, we would have heard gunfire."

"I'm sure you're right." Chris shot a troubled glance toward the bayou.

"Maybe we should go after them," I said.

"If they're not here in ten minutes—"

"I hear Mrs. Hart," said Esther.

We rushed outside. Mrs. Hart bounded along the path. Renny trotted behind carrying something wrapped in an old handkerchief.

"What did you find?" said Chris.

"Trouble." Renny unrolled the cloth. The body and severed head of a rat tumbled to the ground.

I sucked in my breath. "Did it have—?"

"Flaming eyes? Yes. Lucy and I spotted fresh rat tracks, but the creature ran into a hungry fox before reaching the barrier. We backtracked and followed the trail for a mile or so." He nudged the carcass with the rifle barrel. "We discovered his little friend nose down along the same path."

"Where was this one?" said Chris.

"At the water's edge, near the big bend. It must have followed the channel."

I mentally charted the map of the waterways in my head. The big bend wasn't far from here.

"By the way, Peter," Renny continued, "the barrier works. Coming back, we spotted a third rat making a beeline for the Benoit's property. It hit the invisible wall, and then stopped short as if the scent disappeared. Before we killed the foul thing, it sniffed the air and peered across the water to the false cabin."

"Did you find signs of Pike?" I asked. Beside me, Esther shuddered.

"No, but I fear he isn't far behind."

Odile turned to me. "We're out of time. Esther must go immediately."

"We can't leave you alone."

"We'll be fine. The barrier is holding."

"Why not open the door before Pike arrives?" said Amelie.

"The conjuror is too close. He'll sense an opened portal to the Lower Worlds and try to stop us. The false scent trail will fool rats, but not Pike for long, and once he breaks the spell, Esther can be tracked. You need to be far enough ahead to give Clovis time to summon the door."

As much as I hated to admit the truth, Odile was right. "Where should we go?"

"My cabin is far from neighbors," said Clovis. "If we fail, at least Odile and the others will have time to warn the rest of the bayou."

A shiver ran through me. How did one warn people the end of the world was at hand?

Chris ran ahead to tell Marie of the change in plans. The entire family escorted us to the dock.

Amelie pointed down the channel. "Over there!"

At first, I thought the sun's fading rays reflected in the water, but then I saw the churning froth and realized the horrifying truth. The light came from glowing rats' eyes. Hundreds of them swam toward the opposite shore. They moved silently, mindlessly, united in a single purpose.

My blood ran cold. "Chris, we can't desert your family."

"We'll be fine," he declared stoutly. "The barrier will hold."

Mrs. Hart nudged my feet. "Peter, I hear a boat engine headed this way."

I turned to the others. "Pike is near."

"Take the Sweet Marie," said Chris. "Clovis' cabin can't be reached by water so you'll have to anchor downstream and then travel the rest of the way on foot."

"Come with us—"

"No. Speed is essential. Too many people weigh down the boat." Chris peered at the sky. "Not much daylight remains. Clovis, can you find the way to the cabin in the dark?"

The shaman squared his shoulders. "I will. Have no doubt."

"Good. Peter, man the helm. Keep to the water as long as you can." Chris clapped me on the shoulder. "Remember your lessons and you'll do fine."

Mrs. Hart hopped aboard. Marie kissed the rest of us goodbye. Amelie took Esther and sat with her in the wheelhouse. Renny untied the boat while I started the engine.

"*Bonne chance,*" shouted Odile.

I steered the Sweet Marie as close to the shoreline as I dared to keep the boat under the protective cover of the barrier. As we edged into the channel, more and more rats piled onto the opposite shore. Their blazing eyes cut through the twilight and cast eerie yellow beams across the trees. When a new wave of rodents arrived, they scrambled on top of ones already there, so the earth appeared to writhe and heave. For the first time, I was thankful Esther was blind.

Mrs. Hart scampered to the stern and placed her paws on the edge. Her ears pricked up. "Peter, the other vessel is almost here. The engines are very powerful."

"Amelie," I shouted, "can you spot a boat?"

"I see it now," she cried.

A sleek craft sliced through the water around the bend, and I pushed the Sweet Marie's engines to the max. We roared down the channel and after a sharp turn, out of sight.

Renny loaded the rifle and took position next to Mrs. Hart. "Their boat is much faster," he yelled over the straining engine. "If the conjuror chooses to follow, we won't have much time."

"I wish I knew what Pike was doing," fretted Amelie.

Esther huddled at my feet, eyes staring blankly into the distance. "Hush. I'm concentrating." Frown lines marked her brow as she hunted frantically for a connection to Pike. "I got'm now. He's in the boat. Delphine is with him, so are her goons."

"How many?" called Renny.

She dabbed her finger in the air counting off men visible only to her. "Six, seven, eight…Peter, they reached the shore across from the Benoits."

So soon? My heart sank. "Did they find the real house?"

"No. Pike looked around, but I can't see the house through his eyes, so he didn't either. Now, the boat stopped. Delphine is saying something to her men. Everyone is getting off, including Pike…yuck, rats are everywhere, hundreds of them." She leaned forward. "The rats are backing away, making a path to the fake cabin. The men…they've got guns. They're breaking down the door. Pike sees the tree growing in the middle."

Esther giggled. "Delphine is real mad. Good thing I can't hear what she's saying 'cause I don't think it's very ladylike."

"What are they doing now?" I said.

"Not sure…Pike is walking around like he's hunting for something. I—wait a minute. He stopped at the tree…he pulled out the handkerchief with my hair…." Esther gasped. "He's looking across the water."

My stomach knotted up. "Does he see the Benoit's cabin now?"

"No. It's still hidden from him, but something's happening…" She squinted her eyes. "The path is fading."

"Keep trying," Clovis urged.

"The people are on the boat, but rats are jumping in the water. Wait—one rat is in the bow sniffing the air. The others rats are swimming. Their eyes are on fire." Her face paled. "The rats are headed right to the Benoits."

Esther blinked rapidly. "I lost the path." She jumped to her feet and grabbed my arm with ice-cold fingers. "Peter, we have to do something. The rats will get T. Chris and the others. They'll die."

"Have no fear, child," said Clovis. "Peter's lie will hold. The rats won't find the cabin."

"Are you sure?" I said. "Pike saw through the spell around Esther's hair soon enough."

"Pike knows magic is afoot, but won't stop to investigate. His focus now is the rat in the bow tracking Esther's scent. The spell will hold and the Benoits protected until you cross the door's threshold into the Lower Worlds."

I stared at him open-mouthed. "Are you saying the lie will collapse?"

"Your mind keeps the spell in place. Crossing the threshold severs the link."

"You might have mentioned that before," I snapped.

Clovis raised his eyebrows. "The knowledge makes no difference. The spell was only meant to buy time."

Esther's eyes filled with tears. "They'll be eaten."

Clovis placed a comforting arm around her shoulders. "The Benoits are very resourceful people. Odile is aware of the danger. Believe me, she has a trick or two up her sleeve."

"How long can they hold out, Clovis?" said Amelie.

A shadow passed over his face. "Let us hope, long enough."

In my mind appeared the gruesome image of a tidal wave of savage rats, flaming eyes aglow, boiling up from the channel. They surged over the Benoit's property directly to the cabin. Gnawing at the siding in mindless fury, they chewed out an opening. The family huddled together as the rats poured inside…

I gripped the wheel so hard my knuckles turned white. The Benoit's graves wouldn't be on my conscience. Tonight, I either destroyed Feu De L'enfer or died trying.

Clovis motioned to the bank. "Pull in here, Peter. We can't go any farther by boat."

I veered toward the shore and slowed the engine to a crawl. The hull gently scraped the sandy bottom. We were still several feet from dry land so Renny carried Esther. The rest of us jumped off and splashed behind him while I kept a tight grip on Odile's potion.

Clovis led us with confident strides into the brush. The terrain was rough. Thick vegetation snagged legs and tore clothing. Esther had a hard time. Being blind was a hindrance moving through unfamiliar territory. None of us thought to bring her cane as she hadn't used it in weeks. Now Esther clung to Renny's arm, but every vine and tangle of undergrowth seemed determined to trip her.

Our only rest came when Clovis stopped to get his bearings. After the sixth time, Amelie muttered, "Are you sure we can trust his sense of direction? Floundering around here won't help."

"He seems to know where he's going," I assured her as Clovis took off once again at an unfaltering pace. Truth is, I had doubts as well, but we had no choice except to follow the shaman deeper into the bayou.

Renny glanced behind with an uneasy expression, and pulled me aside. "Peter, take Esther with you. We left a clear trail for the rat to follow and Pike wasn't far. At this rate, he'll catch us long before we reach the cabin. Clovis needs time to open the door, so I'll slow our pursuers. Lucy, care to go hunting?" Mrs. Hart growled an accord.

Amelie grabbed his arm. "Renny, the plan is crazy, even for you. Pike has at least eight armed men with him, not to mention Delphine. She'd gladly put a bullet through your head. Those aren't good odds."

Renny kissed his sister. "Don't worry. I excel at self-preservation and Lucy will watch my back." Mrs. Hart yipped an affirmative.

I held out my hand to Renny, but he grabbed Esther and me and pulled us into a bear hug instead. "Be careful, *mes amis*."

"We will," I said with tightness in my throat. "You, too, Mrs. Hart."

Esther added in a trembling voice, "Please come back safe."

Renny winked and jogged off.

"Take care of each other," said Mrs. Hart. She took a step to follow Renny and then suddenly turned her head toward us. "I love you all." Then, she too melted into the brush.

"What's the delay?" shouted Clovis. "We have a lot of ground to cover yet."

I gripped Esther's hand. Amelie took her other one and shot a frightened look over her shoulder.

"They'll be fine," I said. "I know they will." She flashed a grateful smile.

We pushed harder than before, racing shadows that stretched wispy fingers across the tangled mass of vegetation. Soon, Clovis had to switch on a flashlight. If Pike was close behind, the beam betrayed our exact location. Esther's foot caught in a vine. She fell to her knees with a cry, and I helped her up.

"I-I'm okay," Esther insisted stoutly. Blood dripped down a leg.

"You're hurt."

"A little." She took a limping step.

"Climb on my back."

Amelie gave her a boost and Esther wrapped her arms tight around my neck. We trudged through the swamp following the beam from the flashlight clutched in the shaman's hand. Darkness brought some relief from the heat, but not enough. Esther's extra weight sat heavily on me. Sweat ran in runnels down my arms and legs. Within a short time, my calf muscles screamed for mercy.

Ignore the pain...keep going...one foot in front of the other.

Sweat pouring off me attracted hordes of stinging insects. They buzzed around my face adding to the misery. How long did we travel? Minutes? Hours? I can't say. All that mattered was follow the light. Finally, Clovis pushed past a clump of trees and stopped short. I staggered to a halt beside him and gasped, "How...much...farther?"

He played the flashlight into a clearing, and I spotted the silhouette of a ramshackle cabin. "We're here."

"Great," I heaved. "Swell. Esther, please, I'm dying, get off." She slid down my back. I let out a groan and sunk to my knees.

Amelie pushed a canteen into my hand, and I gulped the cool water. Gradually, my jackhammer heartbeat slowed to a respectable throb.

The moon had risen, painting the clearing with a silvery sheen. Clovis switched off the flashlight. I retrieved the jar and spoon from my pocket.

"We'll wait to swallow until the last minute," said Clovis. With a somber expression, he gazed at the circle burned into the ground. "I opened the door right here and after six years the earth remains black with char. Will it ever be green again? I almost wish it remains as a constant reminder to others of my arrogance and pride."

"You're being too hard on yourself," I said.

"Others shouldn't have to correct my mistake. I should enter the Lower Worlds alone."

"Entering alone," Esther piped up, "is what started this mess to begin with."

He smiled at her. "Point taken, young lady, yet I—" He broke off at the crack of a rifle shot.

Amelie flinched. "Renny."

"Clovis," I said, "we're past the point of arguing fault. Open the door now."

"Agreed. Stand in the center."

Amelie and I led Esther inside. Clovis spread his arms. "The border is complete, the magic concentrated within and under my control. The door will stay open if the circle remains unbroken." Flames burst along the circumference to make a wall of fire. The little hairs on the back of my neck rose in unison at the gathering energies.

Clovis raised his left hand and made a circle in the air. *"Le Premier*—I summon the first section of the door." A fiery orb appeared at his fingertips, the symbol of the little flame etched on the blazing surface.

"La Seconde—the second section of the door is ordered into being." Another globe flashed to life and hovered next to the first.

"Le Troisiéme..." A third brilliant shape added to the mix. The little objects vibrated and then spun in a wild rotation like a tiny frantic solar system. Beads of sweat popped out on the shaman's forehead.

A rifle shot rang through the dark followed by four more in rapid succession.

"They're getting closer," Esther cried. "Mrs. Hart, Renny—they may be hurt. Peter, I-I want to know what's happening. Can I look?"

"No. They're fine, Esther. Don't worry." No way would I give permission now. If either Mrs. Hart

294

or Renny was in trouble, I didn't want Esther to see them breathing their last. Another flurry of gunshots ripped through the air, this time followed by the shouts of several men. They were close.

Amelie clutched my arm. "They'll be here in minutes."

"*Le Quatriéme*," shouted Clovis. The last globe joined its companions whirling in the circle.

Magic crackled around me; I smelled it, tasted it. The very air came alive.

"The four parts are now complete." Clovis' breath came in a wheezy gasp, his face deathly pale. The little globes of fire darted about him. "The four parts are now one." His voice rolled like thunder across the bayou. The globes flared brilliant yellow-gold fire and smashed together. He staggered and I extended a steadying hand.

Clovis waved me away. "Stand firm. Don't break the circle." He drew a deep breath and roared. "I summon the door!"

The single fiery orb warped and twisted into the shape of a door with four rectangular panels; a perfect duplicate to the one in the carriage house—right down to the glowing handle and the flaming symbol embedded in each section.

Barbs of magical force stabbed at my skin like an electric charge. "You did it." I cheered.

His lips twitched in a weary smile. "So it seems. Quick, Peter, take the potion."

I offered the jar. "You first."

"I'm not going. If the conjuror gets past Lucy and Renny, someone must be here to prevent him from breaking the circle. This way, you and Amelie will have more potion for yourselves."

"Those men have guns," said Amelie. "You have no way to defend yourself."

Despite obvious exhaustion, his eyes twinkled. "I have a few tricks up my sleeve, too. No more arguments. The conjuror senses the door by now."

The blazing light shown like a beacon through the swamp. Whether Pike sensed it or not, the portal was no longer a secret. I unscrewed the jar and the foul earthy odor immediately enveloped me. I forced down a gag. The spoon stuck straight up in the gooey black tar.

"The woods," Amelie shouted.

A flashlight beam played through the trees past the cabin, but no more gunshots. Renny and Mrs. Hart must have failed. My heart wrenched at the sight of Amelie's stricken face.

"Stay with Clovis," I said. "Help Renny. It might not be too late."

"No." Her face set in iron determination. "I can't do anything for Renny now. The demon must be stopped. I'm going with you."

Clovis towered over us. A fierce light shone in his eyes. "Kill Feu De L'enfer. Vengeance will wait."

I nodded tersely and made a silent vow. If I survived, Pike and Delphine would pay dearly for their crimes. I scooped half the contents from the jar and swallowed. The potion smelled foul, but the taste was infinitely worse. The sludge oozed like slimy bilge water down the back of my throat. I was vaguely aware of Amelie snatching the jar from my hands before I doubled over fighting a convulsive heave. Digestive acid rose from my stomach and for several agonizing seconds tried to push the stuff back to my mouth. The acid should have known better. Any potion made by Odile wasn't so easily defeated. The goo dropped down my gullet with a nearly audible thud. An eerie tingling sensation rocketed to the tips of my fingers and toes. My eyes watered, and I blinked hard to clear my vision.

"Good stuff, eh?" said Clovis. "Odile knows how to brew 'em right."

I straighten up and managed to say "Gak." My vision cleared and the tingling disappeared, leaving only a mild itch on my skin.

Amelie's complexion was ashy pale. She wiped a shaky hand across her brow. "Gluck."

Clovis crouched beside Esther. "They are ready, my dear."

Esther squared her little shoulders. "Take me to the door."

I gripped Esther's hand tight. "I won't let go." I slipped my other hand into Amelie's.

A rough voice shouted near the cabin, "I see them!"

Esther touched the doorknob. The symbols on the panels glowed like the sun, and then the entrance to the Lower Worlds swung silently open.

Chapter 14
The Lower Worlds

We stepped over the threshold.

Click.

My spell around the Benoit's homestead released. The entire family was now at the mercy of the rat army.

The entrance to the Lower Worlds howled with a maelstrom of light and sound. I felt like a ping-pong ball tossed around inside a hurricane. No up or down, no right or left, merely a hellish wind slashing through my mind with demonic claws.

Foolish mortal, the roaring chaos screamed. *I will tear apart your soul.*

Lights…sounds…colors…everything swirled together. I fought cold panic and the urge to run blindly into the distance. Esther…Amelie…One clear thought remained. My friends still gripped my hands tight.

Hold fast. Think of them. Don't let go.

Odile's potion kicked in. Electrical current danced across my body. A transparent shell settled on my skin as if I had been dipped in flexible armor plating. The maelstrom died and the demonic voice in my head faded away.

Amelie dropped my hand and wiped her brow. "I can't believe Clovis tried to walk through this without Odile's potion. No wonder he went insane."

My vision cleared. The misty nothingness around us lifted. The door was gone. We were in a wasteland of scorched earth crisscrossed by arid winds, baking under an eternal sun. My pulse raced. "Esther, can you find the way back?"

She pointed with absolute confidence. "Sure. We came in right over there."

I squinted at a hazy outline, barely visible through the blowing sand, and shot a glance at Amelie. "One more step and the door will disappear."

"I know. If Esther's sense of direction doesn't hold true, we're surely trapped for eternity." She squared her shoulders. "No time to worry about that now. The potion won't last forever, so where do we go from here?"

The one break in the flat, monotonous vista was a massive outcropping directly ahead. "That way." I took Esther's elbow and guided her forward. We entered a narrow canyon and reached a cave flanked by giant columns. Carved into each surface was a different battle scene. Each warrior was a hideous creature direct from a madman's darkest nightmare—most in various states of disembowelment. Piles of bleached white rubble littered the ground. I kicked the nearest one. Not rubble…bones. None were human. I didn't know whether to be relieved or worried.

Amelie peered into the cave. "I guess Feu De L'enfer is inside."

"Uh-huh. Guess so." Neither one of us made a move forward.

Esther stamped her foot. "What are you gawking at? Are we going to stand here forever?"

I started to say standing there actually sounded like a pretty good idea when an unearthly howl echoed from deep inside the cave and then bounced along the canyon walls. The howl came again. Whatever made the bloodcurdling noise moved swiftly toward us. I herded Esther and Amelie behind the nearest boulder.

Two creatures exited the cave with snuffling growls. Although wolf-like in shape, they sported several rows of teeth like a shark and had a scorpion's stinger instead of a tail. The biggest one sniffed the air. "Huuuuman." A slobber of drool splat onto the ground. "Near." The massive head whipped around to its companion. "I find. I do. I bring to Feu De L'enfer. Not you. Me. My reward. All mine."

"Yessss," hissed the second monster. "All yours."

Satisfied, the bigger one turned away. Without warning, its sidekick bared the double row of teeth and lunged. Bear trap jaws opened wide, clamped around the neck, and bit down with a sickening crunch. The creature struggled futilely as the spinal column snapped clean in half. The back legs hung limp, while the front ones pawed uselessly at the ground.

The champion spit out the body and howled in victory. "I find human. I bring to Master. Me. My reward. Not yours. Mine." It tore into the gullet with undisguised relish.

The feast was a trifle premature. In one final spasm, the scorpion tail of the defeated monster quivered and then in a blink stabbed the smaller one in the shoulder. The wolf-scorpion roared in agony. The body slammed repeatedly against the rocks, twisting in convulsive jerks. The full-on seizure slowed to mere fitful twitches, and then with a final heaving breath, the wolf-scorpion collapsed on top of its companion.

I stared at the two inert bodies for a good thirty seconds before I nudged Amelie. "Do you think they're dead?"

"One way to be sure."

She stepped from behind the boulder, and I yanked her arm. "Are you crazy?"

"I'm certain they're dead." As if to prove her point, she walked to the nearest creature, and to my disgust, prodded it with her toe.

"What is it?" Esther demanded. "Can I touch it?"

"No," we both chorused at once.

"They're…they're…" I couldn't think of a word nasty enough to describe the hideous duo drenched in blood and gore.

"Unsanitary?" suggested a familiar voice.

Esther's expression lit up. "Mrs. Hart!" The sandy terrier sprinted over the cracked earth and into Esther's waiting arms. She buried her face in the fur. "Are you okay? We were so worried."

Mrs. Hart sported a deep gash on one leg along with a painful-looking burn. She nuzzled Esther's cheek. "Don't fret, Esther. I'm fine."

Relief flooded over me at the sight of the little dog. "How did you find us? We heard gunshots. When they stopped, I was afraid...well, we were afraid..." I swallowed. Emotional outbursts came hard.

Fortunately, Esther had no such problem. She hugged the little dog's neck. "We thought you were dead meat, for sure."

Amelie crouched beside her. "Lucy...my brother...is he?"

Mrs. Hart's voice betrayed a slight tremble. "I don't know, my dear. Renny insisted I go ahead. He and Clovis are defending the door."

Amelie paled. "Against so many?"

I gawked at Amelie. "You understand her?"

Amelie blinked. "Perfectly. It must be this place...Lucy, how did you find your way to us without the potion?"

"Clovis hypothesized since I was under a spell and not human I would probably be fine."

I raised an eyebrow. "Probably?"

"He estimated a thirty percent chance of retaining my sanity, perfectly acceptable odds. So far, entering the Lower Worlds appears to have been the right choice as I'm no less clear-headed. Once through the door, I tracked your scent."

Amelie gazed across the wasteland. Her hands clenched. "How many guards remain?"

"Four. Plus Pike and Delphine. The others are *indisposed*." She tilted her head meaningfully at Esther as if not wishing to divulge distressing details.

She needn't have bothered. "Hah. Plugged 'em full of lead," declared Esther with ruthless glee.

"Be that as it may," Mrs. Hart continued, "they won't bother us again."

"But the rest…" Amelie's voice trailed off to a whisper. "Renny is the last family I have."

"The rest," I said, "have to deal with both a Marchand and the King of the Frogs. They haven't got a chance."

She turned from the wasteland and gave me a grateful smile. "Time to go."

"We can't simply march into the cave," I said. "You heard those monsters—Feu De L'enfer sent them. The demon knows a door opened and a human came through."

Mrs. Hart cocked her head. "You have a plan?"

A sliver of an idea took shape. I gestured to the two dead wolf-scorpions. "Mrs. Hart, can you track their scent?"

She wrinkled her nose. "Unfortunately, yes. They're quite pungent."

"Good. The trail will lead us straight to Feu De L'enfer."

"The demon will see us coming," protested Amelie.

"Not if I make an invisible border around us, like at the Benoit's, but…" I hesitated.

"But what?"

"The magic is tricky. I have to keep the border in place while we're moving. I'm not sure I can. Maybe, if we stayed close together…"

"Fine by me," spouted Esther, "I don't plan to wander off."

"Me, neither," said Amelie wholeheartedly.

"Give it a go, Peter," urged Mrs. Hart. "I have every confidence in you."

"Okay, then. Stand together and don't move while I figure this out." The three of them clustered close around.

Amelie removed her ever-present dagger from the leg sheath and tucked the weapon in her belt. The blade was obviously newly sharpened.

I raised an eyebrow. "A knife won't work against Feu De L'enfer."

"I know, but it makes me feel better." Amelie flashed a smile and punched me playfully in the arm. "Anyway, it'll be a good distraction while you think of something that does." She took Esther's hand. "Ready when you are, shaman."

Her faith bolstered my spirits. I quickly discarded the idea of four separate barriers, one for each of us. As I had learned, magic was draining. I wasn't certain I could draw on my limited power to create multiple spells before Odile's potion wore off. I needed one good lie to travel with us. We also had to see whatever I created in order not to stray from the protective boundary.

What to use, though? A roof was protective. No—a roof stayed in place and didn't feel aggressive enough. A person hides under a roof and prays trouble went away. Another image flashed into mind. Something deep inside latched on. *Yes. That's exactly right.*

"A shield overhead," I murmured.

Internal energies stirred. The power was sluggish, though, and difficult to capture—perhaps, a residual effect of this hellish domain. A spell would be tricky to maintain, but I brushed aside any doubts. Worry was pointless. I'd hold the magic together as long as possible.

"The shield is visible only to us." A shimmery haze floated in the air a foot over my head. "The shield is strong and powerful." The haze solidified into a shiny metal object, circular in shape, with vicious metal barbs studding the rim. The entire surface glistened like polished gunmetal steel.

"The shield prevents discovery. No vision, no sound, no odor will escape to warn enemies of our advance." Light danced across the metal, imbuing the surface with mystical force. A pale gray shadow spread downward to encompass the four of us. The essence of the shield was complete: stable, unbreakable, and impenetrable.

The last and most important step. *Believe the lie, Peter Whistler. Believe with all your heart.* "The shield is real. The magic will protect us."

The lie snapped into place.

Amelie studied the hovering armor. "Very nice."

I rubbed my neck. The spell drew almost as much from me as the border around the Benoit's property. Maintaining the magic would continue to drain my energy reserve. "Better check the shield. Mrs. Hart, you have the best senses. Go outside the shadow and see if you detect us."

The little dog took a few steps beyond the barrier. Her ears pricked up, nose quivered. "Excellent, Peter," she called, trotting inside. "I didn't see, hear, or scent a thing."

"Let's hope Feu De L'enfer and its minions can't either. I don't know what kind of power of perception they have. I can't shield from something I don't understand."

She nudged my leg. "Then my suggestion is not to worry. Let's go."

We shuffled together to the cave entrance. The shield floated obediently over our heads, dogging every move. Once inside, I paused to let our eyes adjust to the dark. The cave wasn't pitch black. The walls held a faint trace of luminescence, enough for us to navigate safely.

Mrs. Hart took the lead, following the scent of the dead monsters. Nose to the ground, she guided us effortlessly through a series of twisty turns and branching offshoots.

"Remind me to have a word with Clovis when we get out of here," I squawked to Amelie. "It would have been nice to know ahead of time the demon hid inside a labyrinth. We could have wandered around for days."

Mrs. Hart froze. "Something's coming."

We scrambled into a shallow alcove. A snuffling growl echoed down the stone walls, and another wolf-scorpion loped into view. Padding along, the jaw hung open exposing the murderous double-row of teeth.

I held my breath. The creature would pass within an arm's breadth. Pressed against the wall, we had nowhere to run or hide if the shield didn't hold. It bounded by without as much as a flick of the gruesome head in our direction.

Amelie flashed a smile and squeezed my hand. "Good work."

I shuffled in embarrassment. "Thanks."

"You can play kissy-face later," griped Esther. "We have work to do."

"Shut up, Esther." Amelie and I barked simultaneously.

I don't know how long we walked. Time had little meaning on the meandering route. Finally, Mrs. Hart announced, "The scent of those creatures is stronger, and I hear noises ahead. What we seek is near."

Soon, the silence of the tunnel filled with a rising din. Definitely more than one "something" made the racket. We reached an opening in the rock. Bright light spilled out while flickering shadows against the cave wall suggested movement inside of many bodies.

Despite the constant protection of the shield, instinct was hard to fight and instinct cautioned me now to move slowly. The entrance led into a huge cavern lit by torches. Dozens of agitated wolf-scorpions milled about in a clamorous snuffling pack.

"What has them riled?" whispered Amelie. "Did they catch our scent?"

"If so," I murmured, "we wouldn't have this conversation since we'd already be dead. Maybe, they always act that way."

So distracting was the noise, none of us noticed a wolf-scorpion exit the tunnel holding something in its jaws. I spotted it out of the corner of my eye and shoved Esther aside a split second before the monster crashed into her. My hand was outside the protection of the shield for an instant before I yanked it back. The wolf-scorpion stopped and tilted the massive head in our direction. The nostrils flared, as if casting for an elusive scent.

My heart pounded against my ribcage as I poured my will into the shield. After several tense seconds, the creature turned away and continued toward the pack. Next to me, Amelie exhaled a sigh of relief.

It loped to the center of the cavern and spit the mouthful on the floor. The head of another wolf-scorpion rolled across the rocky surface. The pack let loose a concerted howl and closed in. One large brute butted several smaller ones out of the way, and then the muzzle pulled back in a savage snarl, daring the rest to approach.

"Mine," it roared. Whimpering, the others cast down their gazes and backed away acknowledging defeat. The victor crunched into the skull with relish.

"No!" A raspy shriek rang along the cavern walls. "No one eats until the human is found and brought to me." A fireball slammed into the feasting wolf-scorpion. The walls blazed with reflected yellow light as the creature incinerated.

Howling and cringing, the wolf-scorpions skulked away, making room for a figure striding arrogantly through the pack. The newcomer walked upright like a man, but the resemblance ended there. It was ten feet tall, spindly legs bent backward at the knee, and a familiar fiery symbol blazed on the chest. Instead of fingers, a cluster of long thin talons sprouted from the wrists, making a metallic clicking as the thing moved. A single narrow slit ran vertically down what I optimistically considered a face. On either side of the slit was a deep pit. Inside each burned a brilliant flame—as if I could peer right into the malignant force that powered the demon.

Not that I wanted to.

Esther tugged at my sleeve. "Is it…is it…?"

"Yes. It's Feu De L'enfer and, trust me, you don't want to look."

The demon grabbed the wolf-scorpion who brought the head and lifted the bulky creature with ease by the scruff of the neck. "Where are the others I sent to retrieve the human?"

"Dead," yowled the cowering wolf-scorpion. "Both dead. No human. I bring head." It whimpered like a frightened pup. "To you. To show. All dead. Fighting, always fighting them were, but not me. I bring. To show."

"The human!" Feu De L'enfer tightened its grip. The piercing shriek scraped against my eardrum like a rusty nail.

The wolf-scorpion choked out, "No human." Flames shot from Feu De L'enfer's eyes. The wolf-scorpion instantly vaporized into dust.

"Does another care to fail me?" The beam raked across the pack, blasting two more of the creatures into smoldering ashes. "Anyone?" The rest of the wolf-scorpions groveled at the demon's feet, carefully avoiding a direct gaze into the fiery eyes.

"Scour the wasteland. Find the human. Now!"

In unison, the pack released a nightmarish howl. Bolting for the exit, they snarled and snapped at each other in an effort to be the first to flee the cavern. The demon sent a few more fire bolts racing down the passageway to encourage them along.

Once the pack disappeared, Feu De L'enfer strode from sight. Noise from the clicking talons faded behind a rock formation. Without a sound, we crept into the open.

"What are you going to do?" whispered Amelie.

"I'm working on the plan."

She gaped at me, horrified. "You don't know, yet?"

"Of course I know. I'm hammering out the last few details."

Amelie snorted in disbelief. "You have nothing."

"My intention," I blustered, "was for an idea to have occurred to me by now."

"And?"

"Nothing has."

Amelie muttered several words in French under her breath. We rounded the formation and stopped short. Thirty feet in front of us perched Feu De L'enfer, on a throne carved from solid rock. The creature stared straight ahead, motionless and silent. The flames in the eyeballs had dimmed.

Amelie nudged me. "Do you think it's asleep?"

"Dunno." I responded, half-afraid Amelie would suggest kicking its shins to find out.

"The demon is alone," she noted, "unaware of its surroundings."

She was right. The situation was in our favor for now. None of us knew when the wolf-scorpions would return. Invisible or not, I had no desire to stroll through the murderous pack. I'd never have a better chance to kill Feu De L'enfer, but I needed a mystical weapon. The empty cavern held nothing—at least, not yet. A desperate plan of attack formed. "Amelie, give me your knife."

Perplexed, she extended the hilt. "The blade won't kill a demon."

I ran my fingers along the gleaming steel. "Maybe it will, with the right lie attached."

For a moment, her hand rested lightly on mine. "Make the lie a good one, Peter."

The finely honed blade easily slit tough, unforgiving alligator hide, but was completely useless against Feu De L'enfer. Now, I had to believe the knife would work, more than any lie I ever told. Failure meant bloody death.

I gripped the haft. "I no longer hold a normal blade. The metal is transformed and filled with power to kill Feu De L'enfer." An answering tingle of mystic energy coursed to my fingertips. A tiny spark exploded from my left hand and danced along the razor sharp edge. The pain was hot and biting and totally unexpected. I nearly dropped the knife before recovering. Lying never hurt like this before.

What did you expect? You never went after a demon, either. Forget the pain, and get on with the magic. You didn't lock the spell in place.

I ignored the searing burn. "The knife can destroy the demon's eyes." The spark skittered across the surface, etching the symbol of the little flame into the hardened steel. "The knife and demon are bound together. No other weapon will do."

"Peter, something's wrong with the shield." Mrs. Hart's urgent warning broke my concentration. A dull haze now covered the shiny protective surface suspended over our heads. No—the shield had turned into a dull haze, slowly becoming transparent.

"The shield is strong, covering us completely." It became dense and solid once more.

"Peter," Amelie motioned to her knife. "The symbol is gone."

What was happening? "The knife and demon are bound together."

"Peter," Mrs. Hart cried, "the shield is disappearing again."

"The shield is strong…"

"What's wrong?" demanded Esther, anxiously.

I rubbed my neck. "I have a problem with the magic. Either the shield or the knife—I can't hold both spells. One of them has to give."

"If the shield goes," said Esther with a shaky voice, "Feu De L'enfer will spot us."

"Human." The harsh grating words rumbled ominously across the cavern. "I know you are here. You cannot hide from my power." Feu De L'enfer's eyes were wide open, and my heart sank. The momentary loosening of the spell on the shield had been enough for the demon to sense our approach. Brilliant beams raked across the rocky surface in search of his prey. We froze as the uncanny light passed right over us and then as quickly moved on.

Amelie blew out a relieved breath. "The demon can't see us."

"We're Jake for now," I warned, "but as soon as the shield drops we'll be visible."

"Human." Flaming eyes scoured the darkest recesses. "You cannot harm me here. My rule is eternal. My power unstoppable. Behold." The fire concentrated into a tight beam, turning a two-ton boulder instantly into a pile of slag. "Thus will enemies fall before me."

"Full of himself, isn't he?" remarked Mrs. Hart. "He rather reminds me of Chauncey Edwards."

My mouth gaped open. I stared at her in disbelief. "Chauncey wasn't ten feet tall with fireballs shooting from his eyes."

"He might well have been, the shameful way he treated others. He was callous and indifferent and thought he was invincible. He was, too. No one stood up to him."

"Peter did." Esther tugged at my sleeve. "You beaned him with a pie. He sure didn't see that coming." The fear had drained from her voice. "I haven't been picked on by a single bully since I got to Bayou St. Gerard. I don't ever want to be again."

"Join me human." Feu De L'enfer leaped nimbly from the throne, and skulked through the cavern, peering into each shadowy crevice. "The journey to the Lower Worlds proved your worth. I will anoint you my seneschal on Earth in place of Pike. Millions of slaves will grovel at your feet. Rewards beyond comprehension will be yours."

Amelie hadn't taken her gaze off the creature. I once saw a photograph in *National Geographic* of a mongoose with the same intense expression studying a cobra. "The demon keeps saying human," she murmured, "singular not plural. It doesn't know four of us entered the Lower Worlds. Despite the boast, Feu De L'enfer isn't all powerful. We have our advantage. I can create a distraction long enough for you to get close."

"Me, too," said Esther. "I want to go home. T. Chris is waiting for me. We're going to go fishing."

T. Chris…right now the boy and his family fought for their lives against an army of possessed rats because of Pike and Feu De L'enfer. My blood boiled at the thought.

Mrs. Hart gently nudged my leg. "Complete the spell on the knife, Peter. We'll keep the demon occupied."

"Feu De L'enfer wants Esther," I cautioned. "There's no telling what the thing will do when laying eyes on the rest of you."

Amelie shot me a sly look. "You think you're the only one who ever told a lie? I can talk a good line myself." At that moment, the demon disappeared behind a rock pillar. "Drop the shield and run. We'll do the rest."

"The shield is gone." With a slight shimmer, the shield collapsed. I bolted from my friends and scurried behind a boulder.

Feu De L'enfer must have instantly sensed the shield's disappearance. It strode triumphantly across the cavern. "Wise choice, human—" The steps came to a sudden halt. I peeked around the boulder. Emotion was impossible to read on the monstrous face, but the creature was obviously thrown off by finding two humans and a dog where only one person was expected.

Not so omnipotent now, are you?

"We hear you've been hunting for Esther," Amelie announced in a cheerful voice.

Despite the initial surprise, the demon recovered quickly. "Who are you? How did you come to this place?" The eyes narrowed in suspicion. "You are not conjurors."

"The reason is not important," she answered tartly.

The creature sized them up. "Only the child is significant."

The eye sockets blazed flame. Hidden behind the rock, I felt sick and helpless. Any second now, it would blast them to ashes.

Amelie held fast. "If you harm either one of us, Esther won't help you."

"You best believe it," yelled Esther. "You need me to escape. If you touch my friends, I'm not leading you out of here."

Light from the eyes cast a sickly glow on their faces. "Humans...so fragile." Contempt dripped from the words. "Shall we see how much pain is needed for you to talk? I think..." It spoke more to itself than to them. "Not much."

"You want to take that chance?" countered Amelie. "Especially after you waited so long, and are so close to getting what you want?"

The demon rose to its full height. Her words must have hit a nerve. "Speak, human."

Amelie nudged Esther. "Go ahead. Tell the demon what you want."

Esther obviously hadn't thought that far ahead. "Um...a new fishing pole." Feu De L'enfer seemed perplexed.

"And dominion over the inhabitants of New Orleans," added Amelie with an exuberant shout, "and into the far reaches of Bayou St. Gerard."

The demon nodded. A thirst for power was perfectly understandable. "Such can be granted."

A shade of relief passed over Amelie's face. "We have other requests."

"Go on." The voice boomed across the rocks.

Having no interest in the rest of Esther's Christmas list, I sidled around to the far side of the boulder and held up the knife. The shiny metallic surface reflected my face, dead set with determination. "I no longer wield a normal blade. Magic courses through the metal." The steel glowed softly as the lie built.

"The magical forces are harnessed to kill Feu De L'enfer. The knife will destroy the demon's eyes." The spark blazed from my fingertips. I shook off the pain as it skated across the surface and once again etched the arcane symbol of a little flame.

"The demon has no defense for my magic. I will stand against Feu De L'enfer. I will destroy the lights in its eyes. The knife will kill the demon." I imbued the weapon with the essence of death. I felt the energy. I believed the lie.

The magic locked in place.

The blade tingled in my hand. Barbs filled with arcane power jabbed my skin. They wanted out. I rubbed my thumb against the haft. Not yet, but soon.

I eased my way around the boulder. Feu De L'enfer was a good ten feet tall. I had to get to eye level. Most of the cavern had little in the way of hand and footholds. Then I lit upon the perfect platform—the throne. Fortunately, the demon continued to be distracted by Esther's negotiations.

"...and then a flying pony."

I dashed from behind the boulder. Whether alerted by the sound of footsteps or simply the sense of someone approaching, Feu De L'enfer's body tensed, suddenly on guard. The creature swung its head in my direction.

"Hey!" A rock thrown by Amelie plinked harmlessly off the massive chest. The demon turned toward her. "We're not done, yet," she said tartly. "Esther's talking."

Heart beating wildly, I ducked behind another boulder, a dozen yards from my goal. If the distraction held a little longer…

Both eyes blazed hellfire. Feu De L'enfer threw back its head and bellowed, "Enough! Join me now. Swear your allegiance and lead me to the door."

A fire bolt launched from its eyes and blasted into the rock knocking Amelie, Esther, and Mrs. Hart off their feet. I had no more time to reach the throne. I had to make a stand now.

"Okay, okay." Amelie and the others scrambled up. "Go ahead, Esther. Tell it where to find the exit."

Esther curled her lip. "The door is…" The creature leaned toward her. "Up your fanny, poophead. Surprised you didn't find it already."

Feu De L'enfer roared. Stalactites jarred loose from the ceiling, plummeting downward. Mrs. Hart dodged aside. Amelie yanked Esther out of the way as deadly missiles crashed to the floor. I bolted, dodging the falling debris, and skidded to a halt behind Feu De L'enfer. I grasped the hilt in both hands and thrust the blade into the creature's leg.

The effect was like trying to hammer a stick of butter into a steel wall. The jarring shock tore through my shoulders. The knife imbedded in Feu De L'enfer's calf. The demon, howling more in rage than pain, spun sharply around. The jerky motion freed the blade, and it clattered across the cavern floor.

"Who dares?" Feu De L'enfer screamed. Blazing eyes caught sight of me scrambling over the ground. "So small," the demon sneered.

I touched the throne.

"So weak."

I grasped a handhold.

Feu De L'enfer moved with surprising agility. It vaulted the space between us in an instant. Amelie, Esther, and Mrs. Hart scrambled to their feet, but I was trapped, wedged between hellfire and the throne.

"You are working together," said the demon. "You came to kill me." It screeched a jeering laugh. "Did you really believe a little toy had a chance against a denizen of the Lower Worlds?" Feu De L'enfer crouched down. Two fiery orbs scrutinized me with malicious intent. "I am God. You are nothing."

Scorching heat raked across my skin. Being close to the demon's eyes felt like standing next to the open door of a blast furnace.

"Don't like the fire, do you?" the creature noted slyly. "Not at once. No, I'll burn you piece by piece. Keep you alive long enough to watch the others fed to my pets."

Amelie crept across the floor and retrieved the knife. With Mrs. Hart at her heels, she snuck toward me.

"You can't kill us," I taunted. "You need our help to find the door."

"Only one of you is needed," Feu De L'enfer jeered. "The smallest one. The weakest one. When I am finished with her, she will take me through the door, and then watch as I burn the Earth to ashes."

Mrs. Hart tore ahead. She attacked the creature's foot, biting and snapping. Feu De L'enfer turned toward her and Amelie slid the knife, skittering between its legs. I pounced on the blade, stuck the haft between my teeth, and scaled the rocky surface of the throne. As I reached the top, Feu De L'enfer swatted viciously at Mrs. Hart. The monster's talons hit a glancing blow. She yelped in pain, sailing into a pile of rocks.

Rage boiled inside me. The symbols in the metal burned white hot. "No defense," I shouted. The dagger and I were one.

The demon faced me. Bubbling pools of fire churned within the sockets as it prepared a lethal blast. I leaped off the throne and struck. The knife pierced the right eye up to the hilt.

Feu De L'enfer shattered the air with an agonized wail. Taloned fingers slashed through clothing and ripped down my back. I yanked the knife free, dropped to the ground and rolled, landing hard against one of the throne's legs.

Light poured like blood from the eye socket, hitting the ground with a spattering hiss. The creature staggered about the floor. Both arms flailed in front, seeking contact with any of us. I held my breath as Amelie dodged a razor-sharp talon by inches.

Scrambling to my feet, I tucked the knife in my belt and once more scaled the throne.

The demon heaved a panting breath. The slit down the center of the face quivered. "I smell you, human. You can't hide forever."

"Who's hiding?" I taunted, waving the knife. The light from the tiny flame etched into the blade and lit the cavern like a small sun.

Feu De L'enfer sprung. I dodged far right into the blind side. Confused by my sudden disappearance, the demon froze looming over the throne. I slid underneath the head, lunged upward and thrust the knife into the left eye.

The piercing scream went on and on. I plugged my ears, but the sound drilled into my head. Rocky chunks dislodged from the ceiling. They rained in a deadly shower, raising clouds of choking dust. I jumped off the throne, squeezing against a shallow overhang for protection. My friends disappeared from view.

Feu De L'enfer lurched across the ground, oblivious to the cascading boulders. Talons snagged the knife protruding from the left eye. The flesh turned white hot and dissolved with a crackling sizzle. The fire licked across its arms. Bellowing, Feu De L'enfer collapsed in jerking spasms. Flames engulfed the remainder of the body, and then billowing clouds of acrid smoke hid the demon from sight. I doubled over, gagging at the awful stench.

The cavern was silent once more.

The smell of blood hung heavy in the air while something hot and sticky dripped down my injured back. The rock wall brushed against me and racking pain exploded through my body. I forced myself from my knees to my feet, waving both hands in a futile attempt to waft away the smoke. I couldn't see two feet in front.

Where were my friends? I inched forward and my foot hit a solid object. Amelie's dagger, black with soot, lay on a bed of ashes—the remains of Feu De L'enfer. I spit right on top of the pile. "Not so tough now, are you?"

I rubbed the dirty surface of the knife against my shirt, exposing shiny metal. The mystical symbol had vanished. I tucked the blade into my belt and peered through the thinning haze.

"Amelie? Esther? Mrs. Hart, where are you?" I shoved aside an awful vision of the three of them trapped under tons of rubble.

"Here!" Amelie's anxious cry came from straight ahead. "Hurry, Peter."

I followed the sound of her voice. She and Esther hunched over the ground, frantically digging at a mound of rocks. "Lucy is buried underneath."

Tears streaked Esther's cheeks. "The rocks fell, and she pushed me out of the way and now I can't see her eyes. I've called and called." Esther choked back a sob. "Mrs. Hart doesn't answer."

In a frenzy, I pitched dirt and rocks until my fingers touched a soft furry body. I gently eased Mrs. Hart into my arms. She lay limp and unmoving. Amelie placed a shaking hand on the ribcage. Her face creased with anguish. "Lucy has a faint heartbeat, but she's hurt badly. We have to get her to Odile." At that instant, a mournful howl broke through the silence of the cavern. Amelie paled. Her voice dropped to a whisper. "The wolf-things are coming."

My resolve hardened. Mrs. Hart had come so far and suffered so much. I refused to let her die in this awful place. "Let's go."

We rose to our feet. I ripped off the remains of my tattered shirt to wrap around Mrs. Hart and then cradled her against my chest. "The shield is overhead, hiding us from our enemies." The spell snapped instantly into place, no doubt or hesitation in my voice. Cold stone anger forged purpose now.

Amelie took Esther's hand. The four of us entered the winding tunnel as the first of the wolf-scorpions bounded into the cavern. Sensing death, they made a beeline for the pile of ashes. Upon realizing their master was gone, they immediately tore into each other, jockeying for leadership of the pack.

"So much for loyalty," Amelie noted, wryly. "At least, fighting will keep them busy for a while."

"Let's go before they suspect a human loose in the cave. Esther, it's up to you, now."

Without hesitation, Esther pointed down the long corridor. "That way."

We moved quickly, hugging the wall to keep from crashing into pack stragglers headed for the cavern. The agony in my back increased with each labored step. I clung to Mrs. Hart and tried to push the pain away, but it's well-nigh impossible to ignore a raging forest fire burning with abandon along your shoulder blades while at the same time keeping a mystical shield in place. My steps soon faltered.

Amelie held out her arms. "Give Lucy to me and drop the shield."

"Are you crazy?"

"You're exhausted, Peter." Her voice projected a no-argument tone recalling Mrs. Hart at her best. "We haven't passed a wolf-thing for a while. They must have returned to the cavern by now."

"We don't know for sure."

"You're hurt and can barely walk. The shield takes too much energy. We'll make better time without it."

"If the pack follows…" I left the awful thought hanging.

"We run like hell," said Esther.

"Exactly," said Amelie and in the next breath added, "and don't curse, Esther."

I dropped the shield and took Esther's hand. With her unfailing sense of direction, she led the way through the tunnels for what seemed like hours. The air grew hot, stale, and difficult to breathe. Drawing a deep breath left caustic pain in my lungs.

Amelie shot me an uneasy look. She felt it, too. Odile's potion was fading.

We rounded a corner and I stifled a cheer. Dead ahead loomed the opening to the wasteland. Another storm moved in since we arrived. Scorching winds laden with stinging sand whipped across the open range.

"Not much farther," Amelie panted. "I—" Frenzied howling spewed from the depths of the cave.

"They're coming," I said. "Stay together. I'll call the shield."

"No. We're out of time." Amelie pulled the tattered remains of my shirt over Mrs. Hart's muzzle to protect the dog from the blowing sand and then she pushed me into the storm. "Like Esther said—run like hell."

"And don't curse," Esther shouted.

Chapter 15
The Last Lie

We fought through howling wind threatening to tear us apart. I held Esther with one hand and looped the other around Amelie's shoulders to pull her close. Fierce gusts blasted granules of rock and dirt into our faces. Amelie and I were as sightless as Esther now. The three of us staggered forward, once again relying solely on a little blind girl's sense of direction.

The wind behaved like a living thing, tormenting us with an unwavering screech. The sound reached deep inside my head, ripping at my thoughts. *You're doomed. You'll never escape.* The air was impossible to breathe. Rational thought slipped away. *Run,* screamed the wind. *Don't think. Just run.*

Is this how madness feels?

An ear-piercing bay cut through the roar of the unearthly storm. Barely visible in the chaos, dark shapes loped across the wasteland. Wolf-scorpions had the scent and closed in fast. The shot of adrenaline cleared my scattered thoughts. "Move it," I yelled. We stumbled forward, unmerciful death snapping at our heels.

Esther pulled up short, waving her arms frantically in front. "Can you see it? The door is near."

"I don't see anything," cried Amelie.

I reached forward and a tingling prickle plucked at my skin. "Here!"

A snarling black form lunged out of the storm. I pushed Esther and Amelie ahead of me. Esther touched the door, a brilliant light flashed, and they disappeared. I suffered a glancing blow by the wolf-scorpion and scrambled to my feet clutching Amelie's knife, a pitiful defense against the creature. The wolf-scorpion circled in, the venomous tail arched high overhead ready to strike. The howling of the pack grew louder. They were just beyond the edge of sight.

"I kill human." Saliva dripped from its gaping jaws. "I be leader. Me."

As the stinger whipped downward, Amelie's hand appeared out of nothingness and yanked me through the mystical portal. In a bright flash of light, I fell over backward, landing hard in the dirt. Instead of the blazing arid heat, the air was humid and cool. Gray dawn light filtered through leafy trees.

"Clovis, destroy the door," she shouted.

"Le Quatriéme est mort." The glowing symbol on the fourth panel died.

"Le Troisiéme est mort." The third symbol winked out. Something heavy hit, jarring the door open a crack.

"Hurry," Amelie yelled.

"La Seconde est mort." One symbol remained.

"Le Premier—" A snarling muzzle forced its way through the opening. *"Est mort."* The symbol vanished. The door disappeared, instantly severing the wolf-scorpion's head. I scooted gingerly aside as the skull rolled toward my feet and burst into flames. Within seconds, nothing remained but wisps of gray smoke rising from a handful of ashes. All evidence of the door was gone. The circle of fire disappeared. We were safe.

Clovis toed the smoldering pile. "Ugly little spud, wasn't it?"

I got to my feet and handed Amelie the dagger. "Thanks for the loaner." Her face covered with scratches and her clothing torn and bloody, but no girl ever looked so pretty.

Amelie flashed a brilliant smile. "My pleasure."

"Esther?" I called.

"Here." She huddled off to the side, cradling Mrs. Hart tenderly in her lap. "Clovis," she sobbed, "can you help her?"

The shaman laid his hand gently on Mrs. Hart's head. "I'll do what I can, but healing is Odile's gift."

My heart sank as the truth set in. Mrs. Hart was dying. "We have to get to the Benoit's. The rats may have gotten through."

Clovis raised a hand. "No need. I already sent Renny."

Relief flooded Amelie's expression. "He's alive?"

"Yes, yes, of course, my dear, although I can't say the same for the rest of Delphine's guards. One of them lived long enough to admit they had orders to shoot to kill. Delphine planned to blame your death on Renny and take over the estate. I sent your brother to fetch Odile in case her services were required once you returned through the portal. As to the rats—Pike's power was broken. His hold over the filthy creatures disappeared once Feu De L'enfer was killed. I'm sure Chris and Marie easily disposed of them." He raised an eyebrow. "You did kill Feu De L'enfer, didn't you?"

"Dead as a doornail," I said.

"Excellent, Peter. I'm very proud of you." He draped an arm tenderly over Esther's shoulders. "We'll wait in my cabin and make Lucy as comfortable as possible."

As we made our way across the clearing, I noticed the singed holes in the shaman's clothing. A smoky scent lingered in the air while huge swaths of newly burnt vegetation crisscrossed the ground. "Clovis, what happened here?"

"A little run-in with Pike." He snorted in disgust. "The conjuror had fireballs and arrogance working for him and precious little else, especially once the demon was vanquished. He felt his powers fading and took off into the swamp just when I began to enjoy myself."

"What of Delphine?" Amelie demanded.

"She ran after Pike. Renny wanted to follow, but I insisted he go for Odile. Your brother said he would have no trouble tracking them once he returned. Neither Delphine nor Pike know the swamp," he assured her. "They won't get far."

The interior of the cabin was as we left it weeks ago, if not a trifle shoddier. I held Mrs. Hart as Esther settled on the pile of gunnysacks. The little dog lay cold in my arms. Sudden fear that we were already too late gripped me, until her chest slowly rose and fell and she took a shuddering breath.

"Lucy's so weak," Amelie whispered. Her voice held a slight tremble.

I laid Mrs. Hart gently in Esther's lap. She buried her face in the soft fur with a muffled sob. "Mrs. Hart will be okay won't she, Peter?"

I swallowed the tightness in my throat. Esther didn't need to hear me blubbering. Esther needed a hopeful lie. So did I. "Of course, she will. She's tougher than any of us."

Believe the lie.

The magic had drained from me. I had nothing left but my own heartfelt words. "You hear me, Mrs. Hart?" I whispered in her ear. "You'll be fine. You, me, and Esther are a family now, something I never figured to need. But I do. So does Esther, and that's no lie. Don't leave us now." I drew a shuddering breath. "Please."

I stood up gazing at the little dog's broken body. Blistering anger rose within me. "As soon as Renny returns," I said to Amelie, "we're going after Pike and Delphine." She didn't need words. Her savage expression said it all. Neither one of our enemies would leave the swamp alive.

Clovis patted my shoulder. "Your back needs tending, boy." Amelie offered to collect wood and start a fire. I filled a bucket of water from the pump. While the water warmed, Amelie and I took turns filling Clovis in on the battle with Feu De L'enfer. "An invisibility shield," he chuckled. "That's a good one. Should have thought of it, myself. Of course, I was too busy going insane at the time."

"I couldn't hold both lies together."

"Tosh, no one could at your level of magic. Endurance requires more training."

Esther held up her empty cup. "Peter, I'm still thirsty."

Grimacing, I rose to my feet. Every nerve ending in my body uttered a fierce protest at the slightest movement. "The rest of the water is heating. I'll get more from the pump."

Amelie snatched the bucket from me. "I'll go. You can barely move."

She was right, but her comment ticked me off. The pain, exhaustion, and fear for Mrs. Hart wore my nerves to a frazzle. I thought I did a darn good job showing Amelie and the others (well, mostly Amelie) how stoic and manly I was. Physical and emotional suffering meant nothing to me.

"I can carry a bucket," I snapped, more harshly than intended.

Amelie arched an eyebrow and brushed past me out the door. "No, you can't."

I followed in a huff. At every step, each wound called out for me to stop being such a jackass and sit. Of course, I didn't listen. "Give me the bucket."

"Why are you so angry? I want to help. You won't admit you're hurt."

"I'm okay."

"No, you're not. You're being completely unreasonable." Her voice softened. "I'm scared for Lucy, too."

Don't be kind to me, I wanted to cry out. If you're kind, I can't keep the feelings locked in. The last person beautiful, wealthy Amelie Marchand would be attracted to was a poor orphan boy hunched in a useless blubbering pile at her feet.

"Stop being so nice. I-I don't need—"

"I do." Amelie dropped the bucket and leaned against my bare chest with her head on my shoulder. "When you pushed us through the door, I thought I lost you Peter. I-I can't lose anyone else."

I held Amelie in my arms, closed my eyes, and rested my cheek against her hair. My heart beat so loudly, people must have heard the pounding halfway to New Orleans and wondered at the sound. Suddenly, the world wasn't bleak. I'd happily stand in the middle of the bayou forever with her at my side. "Amelie, I—"

Without warning, she knocked me flat. Excruciating pain rocketed up my back. I couldn't tell if she was angry or in the middle of a strange southern courtship ritual. An instant later, a gunshot from the bushes posed a third possibility.

"Delphine," Amelie snarled. In a flash, she was on her feet, bolting into the underbrush with dagger in hand.

"Amelie, don't kill Delphine. We need her alive." Odile trotted briskly down the path. "Peter," she panted, "go after her."

"Odile? Where's Renny?"

"No time—get Delphine."

"Mrs. Hart is hurt."

"I'll tend to her. Hurry!"

331

I darted into the swamp. Odile had discovered something, perhaps about Amelie's inheritance. Maybe Delphine hid the assets before she left New Orleans. If she didn't talk, Amelie would be broke. Whatever happened bought Delphine a little more time, if only I could get to her before Amelie slit her throat.

Gunfire exploded off to my right, too far for the shooter to aim at me. Immediately, I veered in that direction. More shots echoed through the swamp. They grew farther and farther away until I lost the sound entirely. The air was still, except for the whisper of a breeze rustling through the leaves overhead. My gaze darted about, frantic for a sign of Amelie.

"Amelie," I shouted, "where are you?"

I forced my way through a tangle of vines and glimpsed running water from another cut, and a subtle movement on the opposite bank. "So you're here, too," I muttered, eyeing the gator whose essence I divined weeks ago. She sunned in a pile of vegetation at the top of the slide. "I don't suppose you saw a dark-haired girl with blood in her eye headed this way?" The gator lifted her head and noted me warily before hunkering down. The mottled hide blended perfectly with the surroundings.

Frustration gnawed at me with the thought of returning to Odile to admit defeat. Amelie might end up penniless because I wasn't quick enough to stop her from killing Delphine.

The shot exploded out of nowhere. Excruciating pain slammed into my head, bringing me to my knees. I reached for my scalp. My hand came away smeared with blood. I struggled to stand, but instead fell back sick and dizzy.

Pike strode from the brush, smoking pistol in hand. "I wouldn't be so quick to move if I were you." Icy cold arrogance marked his words as he leveled the weapon at my head. "Did you honestly think the death of Feu De L'enfer would stop me? I know the path to the other world. I'll make an accord with another demon. The next bargain I strike will be for even more power."

No fire distorted his eyes any longer. They were merely two dark brown orbs filled with hate. He kicked me hard in the ribs and I collapsed in agony. Pike dropped to his knees and grabbed my hair, yanking hard to regard me square in the face. "I'll take the child. I know where she is now and the people hiding her. Mrs. Marchand and her men were extremely helpful in that regard."

Death was at hand, of that I was certain. Why didn't Odile let me have a gun? I could have ended the conjuror for good. Instead, I stared down death empty-handed. My brain cast about for any reason to delay the inevitable. *Keep him talking. Maybe Amelie heard the shot.*

I spit out a mouthful of blood. "Delphine?"

He let go of me. "Dead by now, attacked by the little spitfire with the dagger. While they were busy, I made my escape." An air of contemptuous self-confidence wove around him like a mantle. "I have no further need of Mrs. Marchand and once you answer a few questions, I'll have no further need of you."

Behind Pike's brazen arrogance, I caught a glimmer of something else. The conjuror's tone held a shade of desperation. He wanted information and he wanted it badly. I pushed myself to a sitting position. The simple movement brought an excruciating wave of pain.

"How did the shaman do it?" he demanded.

The torment in my ribs made drawing a breath difficult. "Do what?"

"How did he kill the demon?"

If I hadn't been in so much pain, I would have laughed. "What makes you think Clovis killed Feu De L'enfer?"

Pike backhanded me across the face. "Don't play games. I saw the open door. Everything I learned taught me such a journey to the other side was impossible and yet..." He shook his head as if unable to believe the obvious. "The shaman made no bargain, but he crossed over and killed a demon. The only way he could have stopped me was to return with stolen power. A mere boy," he jeered, "is incapable of understanding the intricacies of arcane forces, but you have been in the swamp for a time. Tell me everything you saw of his magic. I won't be defeated again."

I glared at him in defiance. "If I don't?"

Pike jammed the gun barrel against my forehead. His voice dropped to a rasping whisper. "Nothing in this useless wasteland is worth salvaging, except the child, but I think you feel otherwise." His icy tone chilled my heart. "This place and these people mean something to you. I'll lay waste to the swamp. I'll kill every inhabitant, but death can come in many forms, merciful and quick or slow and agonizing. Tell me what I want to know and they won't suffer."

My vision blurred, blood loss from the head wound sapped more of my dwindling strength by the second. The pain dulled. My time was over. No rescue was coming, but I didn't fear death. Victory was complete. The demon was dead and Bayou St. Gerard safe. Pike would meet an unmerciful end before he took Esther or found another demon. My friends would see to that.

Amelie was my sole regret. I'd never get the chance to tell her how much the summer together meant to me. Perhaps not knowing was for the best. She'd have no reason to mourn. No more sadness should ever reflect in those warm green eyes.

I glared at him. "I'd tell you to go to hell, but the Lower Worlds are too good for you."

Pike straightened up and sneered. "You're nothing, orphan boy, but a little fish playing in a big pond who is about to get eaten." He raised the pistol and sighted along the barrel right between my eyes.

Fish?

A crazy idea sprung to mind. Cajun crazy. The world stood still, tranquil and calm. "I'm not a fish. You are." I called upon every remaining scrap of my power. One last lie—and it would be a whopper.

The conjuror narrowed his eyes. "What are you talking about?"

"A tasty fish, best one ever," I murmured. "So rich in fat, it'll slide down easy. The kind of fish you dream about forever." The prickle of energy sparked. My will poured into the lie, forging its purpose.

Blood pounded in my ears with the strain as the lie exploded into life. "Come one, come all," I cried. "Plenty to eat for everyone." I cast the spell across the cut and into the bayou.

"What are you doing?" Pike snapped. "What are you talking about? What fish? Is it something that shaman said?"

Breaths came with wrenching pangs. "I am the shaman. The same one who walked through the Lower Worlds and killed a demon."

"You?" he jeered. "You expect me to believe a useless orphan killed a god of the dark road? The same orphan who fled from me like a scared rabbit that night in the carriage house? You can tell a better lie than that."

The water in the cut filled with bubbles as dark shapes glided under the surface. The gator on the other side eased silently down the slide.

"Yes, I can." I held a vision of the conjuror on the shore, slick and scaly—an easy meal for a gator. "This time the lie is about you, fish."

The conjuror stiffened in disbelief as the magic wrapped around him, blurring his true shape. "Impossible...it's a trick." The bayou boiled and frothed as a cluster of reptilian heads led by the behemoth from across the cut broke the surface.

"No, it's a lie." With my last scrap of strength, I locked the spell in tight. "Dinner's ready!"

Hungry gators exploded from the water.

Funny thing about a gator, a single pistol shot will kill the largest animal if hit in the right spot. Otherwise, bullets bounce off the leathery hide. Of course, a dozen sets of teeth and claws tearing at flesh makes the perfect shot darn near impossible.

With a bloodcurdling scream, Pike was dragged into the water and pulled underneath. The murky bayou churned bright red, splashing crimson rivulets against the shore. In a moment, no evidence remained of his descent except for scattered bubbles breaking the glassy surface. One by one, they popped, and then only the peaceful silence of the swamp endured.

I collapsed on the grass. I couldn't move or speak. As the world faded away and darkness closed in, I had a vision of Amelie holding me her arms, calling my name.

Dying wasn't so bad. With a smile, I plunged headfirst into nothingness.

Chapter 16
The Afterlife

Who knew the afterlife was so cozy? Heaven felt distinctly like a downy mattress, encased in silk sheets. I attempted a feeble movement and then sucked in a breath as every body part screamed a protest. The afterlife was also awfully painful. I groaned and forced open one eye. Very bad idea. The light in the room instantly produced a roaring headache.

Something stirred near my feet. A small furry body wiggled against me. Startled, I opened both eyes this time and came face to muzzle with a familiar little black nose.

"Mrs. Hart," I cried joyfully. "I didn't know dogs were allowed in the afterlife. I'm glad I'm not alone."

She sported a new pink collar. Her little tongue darted frantically about showering me with kisses. "Y-you can stop now," I sputtered as slobber plastered my face. "Mrs. Hart?" Instead of her intimate voice in my head, the terrier responded with more frenzied licking inside my ear.

"Blech...please...I don't...blech...not on the lips." Maintaining her silence, she ignored me completely and continued to lap with relentless zeal. Her actions were very...well...un-Mrs. Hart-like. Death obviously affected her reserved nature.

Raising my hands to shield my face from Mrs. Hart's enthusiasm, I touched a heavily bandaged head. Doubts crept into my fogged brain about my present location. Why did the dead need bandages? Then I noticed Mrs. Hart also sported fresh scars and a bandaged foot.

I pushed the enthusiastic terrier away. She responded with a surprisingly doggish whine of protest before settling beside me. I shifted my head and peered at my surroundings. I lay in the middle of a large mahogany bed in a strange room I'd never seen before. Light filtered through gauzy curtains at the windows. With a *whoosh,* soft breezes parted the drapes. Outside, leaves rustled through the top of a magnolia tree. I was on a second floor.

"I thought I heard someone. You're finally awake."

I froze in horror as Delphine Marchand waltzed through the open door. She was alive with not a mark on her. Her untouched appearance meant Amelie failed. The awful consequence tore at my heart.

Delphine shook her finger at Mrs. Hart. "Some watchdog, you turned out to be. You were supposed to signal me immediately once he woke." The little terrier raised her head off the comforter and yipped an apology. Delphine patted her affectionately on the head. "I know, you were excited." Mrs. Hart responded with an enthusiastic wag of her tail.

My mind disregarded the odd tableau of Mrs. Hart cuddling up to a she-witch. Fury raged through me as I struggled to sit. "Amelie…where is she? If you hurt her—" Not for the first time I wished Odile allowed me a gun.

"Amelie is fine."

Delphine's voice held a gentle lilt I never heard from the woman who mercilessly killed her husband and casually plotted the death of her stepdaughter. Her eyes twinkled in merriment. Those eyes—they reflected none of the cold arrogance of Delphine Marchand.

"No…" I sank into the pillow, gaping in disbelief. "You can't be…Mrs. Hart?"

She uttered a deep rich laugh. "Took you long enough to discover the truth. Some shaman you are."

"How?" I finally managed to say. "Where? When?" I gaped at the little terrier next to me sporting the happy doggy grin. "Who?"

"Delphine is gone for good. Honey Bun returned to normal, too. Thanks to Odile."

"What?" I croaked, too stunned to say much else.

Mrs. Hart chuckled. "That about covers the pertinent questions, but complete answers will take a while. Much has happened since the fight in the bayou." She placed a cool hand to my forehead. "You've been unconscious over a week. Odile worked her healing magic, insisting you were too stubborn to die, but we were worried, especially Amelie."

My ears pricked up. "She was?"

"Peter!" An excited squeal came from the doorway. Esther took a bounding leap and hopped onto the bed. The aftershock echoed through my aching body. "Peter! Peter! Peter! You're awake." Honey Bun yelped as Esther squashed her tail. "Sorry, Honey Bun," she chirped.

Mrs. Hart lifted Esther from the bed, planting her firmly on the floor. "That will be enough of that, young lady. Peter is not well enough for your gymnastics."

"I have so much to tell him," she whined.

Whatever Esther meant to say had to wait as the sound of running footsteps interrupted her plea. Renny and Clovis each tried to shoulder their way first through the door, before Renny graciously stepped aside.

Clovis beamed. "Quite some feat, my boy, quite some feat. Turning the conjuror into gator bait—very clever. Oh, yes, I know about the spell. The residual magic lingered in the air. Not to mention a morsel or two of Pike floating on the water."

"You found me?"

"Not exactly. Renny turned back after hearing Delphine's gunshots. He arrived right after Odile. As she tended to Mrs. Hart, he and I left to offer assistance. Amelie discovered you after subduing Delphine and was already by your side. You were unconscious, so Renny carried you to the cabin."

"Thanks," I said with heartfelt gratitude. "By the way, where am I?"

Renny perched on the foot of the bed, casually ruffling Honey Bun's fur. "You're in my father's old room at our house. Once at the Benoit's, Odile determined you were in for a long convalescence. Since Amelie and I needed to clear matters, we returned to New Orleans."

He made the events sound routine, but my head pounded with unanswered questions. "What happened? Are you still wanted for kidnapping? How did Mrs. Hart end up in Delphine? Are the Benoits safe? What about the rats?" I nearly burst with the one question I really wanted to ask. Where was Amelie?

"See," Esther noted with a know-it-all tone, "I told you I had lots to tell him."

"Aha!" Odile stormed in carrying a glass vial. Everyone around the bed exchanged guilty looks except Esther, who never felt guilty—period. "You disregarded my orders as soon as Peter awakened. He is not to be bothered and needs rest. Leave this instant." She cast a fierce glare, daring anyone to argue. No one uttered a peep, not even Esther. Such was the power of Odile Benoit. Mrs. Hart was last to leave and shut the door.

Odile sized me up in a glance. "*Eh bien,* you decided not to die."

"Guess so." I attempted a nonchalant shrug, but even that brought a wince.

"You are in much pain."

"No."

"*Bon.* You spoke very manly and merely turned slightly green. Amelie will be impressed."

I cleared my throat. "Um, is she here? I mean, I didn't see her. Is she okay?"

"Of course. I simply sent her to the apothecary for more herbs for my healing. She spent entirely too

342

much time brooding in this room, a very unhealthy activity for a young woman her age. She became almost as pale as you."

"She is…I mean she was…I mean…" I cleared my throat again. "When will she return?"

"Soon." She held out the vial. "Drink. The potion will put you to sleep so I can change the bandages."

"I just woke up," I squawked, not wanting to miss Amelie. "Go ahead and change them. I'll be fine."

"Very, very manly." Odile sniffed. "The young ladies of New Orleans will be so very impressed."

She slipped an arm around my shoulders and forced me to a sitting position. The simple movement of my muscles felt like hot coals streaking across my back. My ribs and head joined in a chorus of pain. I opened my mouth and howled. Odile quickly poured the contents of the vial down my throat.

"Hey," I sputtered, "that's not necessa….you didn't hafta…" The liquid had an instant cooling effect. The pain vanished and enjoyable delirium took its place. My head lolled from side to side. My thoughts blended to mush. "I think…I'll take…a little…nappy."

"Really?" Odile feigned surprise. "Well, if you insist."

Everything went black. The next thing I noticed was the delicious smell wafting through the room. "Yum."

"Ruby made soup for you."

My eyes shot open. Amelie sat in a chair next to the bed. "I'm glad you're awake." Her brilliant smile did funny things to my insides.

I should have said something clever and debonair, but instead blurted, "You look like you were thrown under a streetcar." Dark circles ringed her eyes. One wrist was bandaged. Scratch marks and deep purple bruises healed on her neck and arms.

"You look worse," she responded tartly.

"I reckon I do." Heat filled my cheeks. "You're okay though, right?"

"I'm fine."

"Good. I'm glad." Despite the whirling ceiling fan, the air felt twenty degrees warmer. "I worried about you."

"Peter and Amelie up in a tree…" Esther sang from the doorway. She had Honey Bun, sporting a jaunty pink bow, tucked under an arm. "K-I-S-S—"

I glowered. "Pipe down, Esther."

Amelie motioned to a tray on the end table. "Can you manage something to eat?"

At the mention of food, my stomach rumbled with enthusiasm. "If you promise to fill me in on everything I missed."

"Me, too! Me, too! I got lots to say." Esther jumped up and down. "Can Honey Bun and me sit on the bed with Peter?"

"You may sit at the foot," Amelie said, "if you both promise absolutely no bouncing."

With her hand, Esther raised Honey Bun's paw. "We promise."

They crawled on top of the comforter. I forced myself to sit, bracing against a wave of pain. To my surprise, Odile's potion continued to work and I suffered nothing more than a minor twinge. Amelie placed the tray on my lap. I took a tentative sip of Ruby's soup and sighed with pleasure as the velvety smooth liquid slid down my throat. Immediately, I felt better.

Amelie filled me in as I ate, assisted by Esther's colorful commentary. The Benoit family was safe. Odile concocted a potion to confound the rat's senses. She had enough for Chris, Marie, and T. Chris, so Odile barricaded herself in the house with the younger children while the trio fought a desperate battle outside against the rats.

"Hah," crowed Esther. "I'm almost sorry for the rats. They didn't have a chance. T. Chris and his folks killed bunches. The rest croaked once Feu De L'enfer died and Pike's spell went poof. Odile figured out the demon's power broke once the rats began to keel over. She took the pirogue and came straight-away."

"I heard Pike's pistol." Amelie's voice betrayed a slight tremble. "I-I thought you might need help."

"Your dagger would have come in handy." I joshed, touched by her concern. "A gun would have been nicer."

Esther snorted. "Good thing you didn't have one. You'd have shot your foot off, for sure."

I ignored her. "What about Delphine?"

"I tracked her." Amelie's hand touched the black eye. "She fought. She lost. I wanted to kill her. I almost did, but Odile said she needed her alive." She chuckled. "Poor Lucy. If I'd known what Odile had in store, I wouldn't have treated Delphine's body so roughly."

"She looked okay to me."

"Two stab wounds and a cracked rib. Lucy's very stoic."

I was all ears, now. "How did Odile make the switch?"

"Odile had another potion simmering on the fire when we arrived with you. She poured a cup and told Delphine to drink or she'd let me and my knife have at her. Delphine swallowed and then collapsed on the floor. When she woke, Lucy was inside."

I chuckled. "Must have been a shock for everyone."

"You've no idea. Funny thing, Renny recognized her first, even before Odile knew for sure the potion worked."

"Where did Delphine, uh, go?"

Amelie shrugged. "Odile said since the law couldn't touch Delphine, she made certain the she-devil paid for her crimes."

"Wherever she is," announced Esther with glee, "you best believe she's miserable."

"Speaking of crimes," I said, "has Renny been cleared of kidnapping?"

Amelie responded with a sly grin. "Completely. Thanks to a statement from my dear stepmother, Delphine. The kidnapping was a horrible misunderstanding, you see. Why, we're one big happy family now. You're in the clear too, by the way."

I raised an eyebrow. "For what?"

Esther giggled. "For me, silly. Don't you remember? You kidnapped me and killed the Grimaldis and burnt down Little Angels. You were very naughty."

"Once we arrived in New Orleans," Amelie continued, "Lucy told the police Esther was a distant relative of the Marchand family. You brought the child here to escape the clutches of evil Dr. Pike. He had discovered the connection to the Marchands and killed her guardians in order to hold Esther for ransom. Renny and I went with you as protection. We left in a hurry and didn't have time to explain, hence the misunderstanding."

I raised a skeptical eyebrow. "The police bought the story?"

Amelie stiffened. "Of course. The word of a Marchand holds much weight in New Orleans. We also had a deathbed statement signed by Pike confessing to the murders in New Jersey and a birth certificate proving Esther was definitely a second cousin once removed on my mother's side." She beamed with pride. "Dear Renny really is an accomplished forger."

"You're wanted for dognapping, though," needled Esther.

"No, he isn't," Amelie chided. "You're quite aware Lucy sent Mrs. Murphy a generous check. Honey Bun is here to stay."

"Yup," Esther announced happily, "Lucy is her guardian. She's mine now, too."

"Lucy?" Her free and easy use of Mrs. Hart's first name was a jolt.

Esther wrinkled her brow. "Well, she doesn't look like Mrs. Hart now or sound like her, either. I don't want to call her Delphine, so I guess Lucy fits."

I was about to ask another question when Odile arrived and chased everyone out of the room, insisting I needed rest. I disagreed, but no one ever wins an argument with Odile. Maybe the shaman slipped a mickey in the soup, too, because once settled under the covers, I fell asleep.

While I recuperated, the others kept busy. Confident of my recovery, Clovis left for the bayou to see to the repair of his cabin, professing to return soon. Renny, Amelie, Odile, and Mrs. Hart dug into the late Jean-Baptiste's business affairs. Mrs. Hart also enrolled Esther in Amelie's school in New Orleans. The fall term began soon, and the principal gladly assured her she would make accommodations for a blind student. Esther would never be sent away again. Esther protested the whole idea of school at first, wanting to return to the bayou, but Mrs. Hart prevailed. She was like Odile in that regard, no point arguing with her. She assured Esther visits to the Benoits would be plentiful.

After another day of rest, I managed a staggering walk across the bedroom, supported by Renny. A few days more and we got as far as the end of the hall. The morning after that, I woke clear-headed, the pain from my wounds reduced to minor aches.

The house was unnaturally quiet. Usually by this time, Esther, with Honey Bun in tow, made a racket outside my door, both whining to come in. Bored with being an invalid, I determined to walk downstairs by myself. I carefully eased along the grand center staircase, clinging to the banister to support my unsteady legs. I reached the bottom, pleased I merely had to pause once for breath.

Ruby spotted me in the foyer and accused me of doing permanent damage to my health for moving on an empty stomach. Mrs. Hart popped out of the study to see about the commotion. She eased Ruby's concerns by asking her to bring refreshments to the front porch, promising to sit on me if I tried an activity more athletic than blinking.

I shuffled into one of the overstuffed wicker chairs and sighed. The little trek wore me out more than I cared to admit. Ruby brought a tray packed with enough food to feed a small army. She threatened dire punishment if I didn't eat at least half.

After Ruby left, I whispered to Mrs. Hart, "Does she know you're not Delphine?"

"Oh yes," she assured me. "Amelie told her. Ruby was delighted. She congratulated Odile on such a natural solution to a thorny problem."

I snorted in disbelief. "Yup, sticking the spirit of one person into the body of another. Perfectly natural."

Her eyes held a smile as she poured a glass of sweet iced tea for me. "It is here. So, how are you feeling?"

I took a sip. "Good as new."

She tsked. "Has anyone ever mentioned you're a terrible liar? I place the fault on your shameful upbringing."

I grinned. "My upbringing wasn't so bad, and I think I'm a pretty good liar." I bit into a sandwich. "Where is everybody?"

"Odile went to mail a letter to Chris and Marie. Renny drove Amelie and Esther to the seamstress. Esther needed a fitting for her new clothes."

I swallowed and took another bite. "Why do girls need so much stuff?"

"The school term begins soon and she requires uniforms. Also, as the ward of Delphine Marchand, Esther will enter New Orleans society. She must dress the part." The idea of Esther entering high society caused me to whoop with laughter. My ribs instantly regretted the action. "At least she'll be prepared to fit in," said Mrs. Hart. "What about you?"

"Me?"

"Yes, you. I had planned to wait until you fully recovered, but now is as good a time as any for a discussion. You have a choice to make, Peter. I know I was appointed legal guardian, but I'll never force an unwanted life on you. You can return to New Jersey, free and clear, or a different place altogether. I have the money to send you anywhere your heart desires; New York, San Francisco, Paris, or travel the world. I've ordered everyone not to voice an opinion. They agreed the decision is yours. Everyone wants you to stay, but what is Peter Whistler's desire?"

The question took me aback. At Little Angels, I never thought much beyond the next day. Somewhere down the road loomed a hazy future, carefree, footloose, searching for adventure. Adventure enough existed in New Orleans, but was I willing to put down roots here? Among these people?

"It won't be an easy life here," she warned. "Much is expected of a shaman."

"I'm not a real one," I protested, "not yet. I have a lot to learn."

"Yes, but while you learn, life will certainly be interesting."

The tone of her voice told me she made her decision already. "You're definitely staying," I said.

She sipped her iced tea with a thoughtful expression. "Mrs. Hart is dead. I can't return to that life. Not that I want to." Her face darkened as if with unpleasant memories. "Mr. Hart was unkind. I'm happy to lose the name, grateful to start over. Although," she added with a wicked grin, "Delphine Marchand sounds unnatural, too."

"How about Lucy? How does that sound?"

Delphine Marchand's expression filled with delight. "Between family and friends, the name sounds perfect."

A convertible coupe pulled into the long driveway. Renny tooted the horn in greeting. Esther sat in the backseat with Honey Bun on her lap and Amelie beside her. Brightly-colored packages surrounded both girls.

I leaned over and whispered in her ear, "You realize they're bug nuts here, Lucy?"

Lucy's gaze lingered on Renny. "Which can also prove interesting."

Amelie caught my eye and flashed a brilliant smile, filling me with warmth. I settled happily in my wicker chair to await her arrival. "That's no lie."

THE END

Peter Whistler's adventures continue in *The Book of the Practically Undead*. Zombie nuns, voodoo magic, and asking Amelie for a date. Which will strike the most fear in the heart of our intrepid young shaman?

A Note from the Author

I live in the South and write fantasy and science fiction adventure stories. The South is a good place for speculative fiction since most people speculate the heat and humidity here have driven us slightly mad. In my spare time I enjoy calling in Bigfoot sightings to the Department of Fish and Wildlife. They are heartily sick of hearing from me.

Thank you for reading *The Rules for Lying*. I hope you enjoyed it. If so, please leave a short review on Amazon. No essay needed, a few words or simple rating are fine. Marketing is the hardest part of being an indy author. A few kind words make my day and generate interest in my books. Thanks a ton.

Lurking Spots
Want to connect? I love to meet readers. My lurking spots are below. If you have a blog, I'd be happy to do a guest post or interview. Just want to say hi or have a recipe to share? I'm up for that, too.

Email: l.a.kelley.author@gmail.com
Website: https://lakelley.com

Check out my other series: Rimrider, Rimrider Adventures Book 1
Orphan, pirate, spy.

Awakened by her father, teenager Jane Benedict is ordered to memorize a mysterious code. Hours later, Mathias Benedict is dead and Jane and her brother, Will, are wards of United Earth Corporation. To evade the company's murderous clutches and uncover the meaning of her father's last message, Jane leads Will on a desperate escape across the galaxy aboard the Freetrader smuggler ship, Solar Vortex. Tangled in the crew's fight for freedom, Jane saves the life of a young smuggler, Mac Sawyer, and learns her father's code identifies a secret cargo shipment. The trail leads to the planet Rimrock and the massive prison complex of Golgotha. Undercover as a spy, Jane stumbles into a conspiracy that can spell doom for the entire Freetrader cause and the extinction of an alien race. Can she escape the prison confines and deliver a warning before it's too late?

Piracy, intrigue, romance, space battles, and a daring rebellion from Earth wait on the galactic rim. Will Jane answer the call to adventure and find new purpose, or is death for high treason her fate?

Lagniappe

What's lagniappe? It's a common word in New Orleans and means a little something extra. It often appears on menus, an extra treat from the chef free of charge. New Orleans cuisine is a glorious mixture of Cajun and Creole. Cajuns are descendants of French Canadians (Acadians) who fled religious persecution and settled in rural southern Louisiana. I tweaked history in *The Rules for Lying* and made shamans escapees from political oppression who left Europe in order to freely practice magic. Creole people are the more sophisticated city folk; the term was once used to describe those native to New Orleans to set them apart from the riffraff in the rest of the country. Clovis and the Marchands are Creole while the Benoits and the good folk of Bayou St. Gerard in Terrebonne Parish are Cajun. Creoles can have an interesting ethic background since many different cultures settled in the Big Easy including French, Spanish, African, Italian, Native American, and English among others. Each one added their own touch to New Orleans' cuisine.

A favorite local dessert is pecan pie. This recipe has a different type of piecrust and makes 24 individual tarts. You'll need 1-3/4 inch muffin pans.

Pecan Bites
Preheat oven to 325

Crust

1/2 cup (one stick) butter
One 3 ounce package cream cheese
1 cup sifted flour

Filling
2 eggs
1 cup light brown sugar
2 tablespoons softened butter
1 teaspoon vanilla
1/8 teaspoon salt
1 cup chopped pecans

To make the crust cream butter and cream cheese. Blend in flour. Form dough into a ball. Wrap in plastic wrap and refrigerate one hour. Divide the dough into 24 balls. Place one ball in each 1-3/4 inch cup of an ungreased tart pan. Press so that the dough comes up the sides to form a tart shell. In a bowl beat eggs, sugar, butter, vanilla, and salt until smooth. Place two teaspoons pecans in each tartlet. Spoon filling over pecans. Bake in a 325 degree oven for 25 minutes or until set. Cool; remove from pans.